Creation Node

Creation Node

STEPHEN BAXTER

This edition first published in Great Britain in 2024
First published in Great Britain in 2023 by Gollancz
an imprint of The Orion Publishing Group Ltd
Carmelite House, 50 Victoria Embankment
London EC4Y 0DZ

An Hachette UK Company

1 3 5 7 9 10 8 6 4 2

A CIP catalogue record for this book is
available from the British Library.

ISBN (Mass Market Paperback) 978 1 473 22897 9
ISBN (eBook) 978 1 473 22898 6

Typeset by Input Data Services Ltd, Bridgwater, Somerset

Printed in Great Britain by Clays Ltd, Elcograf S.p.A.

www.gollancz.co.uk

To the memory of my father Eric Augustine Baxter (1929–1983), my grandfather William Henry Baxter (1882–1946), and my great-grandfather William Charles Baxter (1844–1919).

Year 0

AD 2255

1

In the year 2255, of all the sentient beings in her universe, it was a woman named Salma, twenty years old, who was the first fully to see the object called Planet Nine. See with her own eyes, albeit moderated by her ship's instruments. If not to recognise what it was, not yet.

And not that the object had turned out to be a planet, or the 'ninth' of anything.

But when she inspected the startling results of her first analysis of the radiation leaking out of Nine, and although she wouldn't know it for some time, Salma's universe had changed for ever.

In essence, she was the first person Nine spoke to.

As these observations were made, as the first analyses ran, the first conclusions tentatively formulated, Salma took her time before even telling her crewmates.

Even before calling Hild Kanigel, captain of this small crew since the *Shadow*'s launch thirty-five years ago. Or Meriel Breen, hydroponic farmer and doctor, who Salma had come to think of as an honorary aunt since the death of her own mother. The two closest human beings in Salma's world, two of just six crew aboard the *Shadow*. She needed to be sure this wasn't some careless glitch. Pride mandated that.

Her detection had been a chance sighting. Anybody else could have made it. But, to be fair, the odds were relatively good that it would have been Salma who would make that key observation, given that she so often volunteered for the longest stretches up on the science deck.

Salma was the product of the *Shadow*'s only onboard birth. All her life she had been the only growing child on the huge, slow ship. And for that reason, maybe, she had grown to love the hours she spent here alone. Work filled her days.

You were in a big bubble of toughened glass, sparingly fashioned from Oort-cloud materials — comet stuff, like most of the fabric of the *Shadow* — and held away from the ship's main hull by a transit tube. The glass itself was nearly perfectly transparent, the view spoiled only by your own ghostly reflection, illuminated as you were by the dimmest of emergency lighting, and by banks of analysis screens beneath the bubble's attachment to the base structure.

You sat surrounded by a sphere of deep space. If you wanted to be alone, this was quite some place to be alone *in*.

And what a view. You, and the edge of the Solar System, and the distant stars.

The edge of the Solar System . . . She knew she was about seven hundred astronomical units from the Sun. Seven hundred times Earth's distance from the central star — Earth, a place she had only ever glimpsed in the ship's records.

Over twenty times as far out as the furthest major planet, Neptune. Around fifteen times further out than the outer edge of the ragged cloud of primordial debris beyond the planets that was the Kuiper belt. She was five or six times further out even than the limit of the heliosphere, where the wind from the Sun, a breeze of fast-racing charged particles, finally dissipated into the cooler interstellar medium.

4

And if she looked back that way she saw the inner Solar System only as a puddle of misty light, the light of an inner space cluttered with planets, moons and asteroids, the debris of planet formation. It would be a strain to find the Sun itself, still the brightest star in the sky — just — its light having taken nearly four days to reach across the gulf of space to the *Shadow*. But that much-scattered sunlight was still intense enough to push at the *Shadow*'s enormous solar sail.

And all the people that existed, the teeming billions, even those far away from Earth itself — even those aboard the busy space-bound industrial hubs of the Consortium, even those in other Conserver colonies and craft scattered around the inner edge of the Oort cloud — all of them were down in that puddle of light.

All save the six aboard the *Shadow*.

But as she had grown, the only ship-born child without senti-mental attachment to the birth planets and their teeming crowds, Salma had come to relish the view in the opposite direction. Amid the sprawling light of star clouds, she knew where to seek the Galaxy's very centre, with its supermassive black hole — a centre readily found behind the curtain of relatively close stars that was the spectacular Sagittarius constellation.

In fact that giant black hole was a big sibling of what some theorists had long guessed 'Planet Nine' to be, long before a crewed ship ever got here. Not a planet at all, to the chagrin of some other theorists.

A black hole, at the edge of the Solar System itself.

Now, at last, beyond all the theorising and the arguments and the heroic engineering, the *Shadow* had made it out here, and there was Nine itself: revealed, yes, as a black hole, unmistakable from its gravity profile if nothing else — even if it had not been visible to human eyes before, thanks to the storm of glowing gases that surrounded it.

But now it was visible. Glimpsed through brief gaps in the light storm, the glowing nebula, that it itself created. As mediated by her instruments, Salma saw it at last.

A perfect black sphere.

Salma pored over the data once again.

The black hole – as Nine did seem to be – was both very small and very large. As expected from the theory.

Small in human dimensions, in one way, in its physical size – no larger than a human head. But larger than most planets in terms of its mass – and, crucially, its gravity field – for it massed some ten times the mass of Earth.

And as Nine had followed its own twenty-thousand-year orbit around the Sun, that hungry planetary-scale gravity well had drawn in whatever nature could provide. Not that there was much per cubic metre out this far – scattered dust and ice, the remnants of ancient comets from within the Solar System, and debris from destructive events far, far away. But in time Nine had passed through an awful lot of cubic metres, and Nine had a deep, wide gravity well, and it had had a lot of time to gather an irregular cloud around itself.

A cloud that the electromagnetic fields of the spinning hole worked on assiduously, ionising material drawn in by gravity, then grabbing it magnetically and hurling it around – 'like a matador's cape,' Hild had once said, a reference that baffled Salma. The result was changeable, asymmetric, startlingly messy, given the pure geometry of the object at its centre. A 'damn fireworks show,' as grumpy old Boyd contemptuously had put it, another baffling reference.

But if you wanted to see Planet Nine for yourself, you had to penetrate this cloud, this light show. And that was what the *Shadow* had been doing for more than a year already, ever more cautiously, since it had slowed to a near halt relative to Nine. Edging into the inner cloud, trying to avoid the more angry-looking masses of this rootless storm – not an easy trick when you were propelled only by a solar sail nearly forty kilometres wide.

Closer and closer to the demon in its cage of light.

And at the key first moment of clarity, it happened to be Salma's place in the duty roster on this science deck, maintaining 'eyeball lock' on Nine, as instructed by Hild. Salma who finally got to *see* the object hidden within. Salma who was there when, briefly, miraculously, the storm cleared along the ship's line of sight. A chance adjustment of the ship's trajectory, an unexpected break in the glowing debris cloud—

It was as if a corridor of light had opened up. And there, at last . . .

Salma worked feverishly, observing, recording, studying the data as it poured in.

Especially the visuals.

It was a perfect sphere, just as the theory said it must be – a sphere you could wrap your arms around, and yet with a gravitational influence that extended across the whole of the Sun's outer domain, and the chill bodies that inhabited it. This was the most exotic object she was ever likely to see in her life, Salma thought, and yet the most mundane of forms to the naked eye: in profile, a dark circle. And as she considered that, something tugged at her, a kind of – recognition.

She touched the medallion she wore on a thread around her neck.

A heavy pendant, a disc, shadow-black – it had been a gift from a mother she had never known – she wore it habitually, had worn it as long as she could remember.

7

A muddle of memes, of feelings.

She tried to be analytical. Her mother's pendant. A black hole. Perfect circles, featureless . . .

She was dreaming. On her consoles, more flags lit up.

Something had changed.

With the veil of hot gas temporarily parting, she was picking up a paler signal, a more tenuous radiation, coming not from the glowing gases, but from deep within the hole's gravity well itself.

She had studied black holes, theoretically. She knew what that deep signal must be: *Hawking radiation*, random noise created at the event horizon itself, called after the long-dead sage who had predicted its existence. She recorded it all.

But on her consoles, still more attention flags lit up. Now, she saw, scanning the data quickly, there were anomalies in the data-gathering. The event-horizon radiation was *not* quite featureless, not quite random, it turned out. There were *patterns* in that trickle of radiation.

Patterns that must be coming from *the hole itself*. From the event horizon, that spherical knot of distorted spacetime.

Radiation from a black hole, with a complex structure.

Almost like . . . a signal.

Startled, she considered the results.

They checked out. She was baffled. Overwhelmed.

Overjoyed.

A *signal*?

Enough wallowing in triumph, she told herself. Nobody else knows what you have found, not yet. Time to make your report.

With a murmur into the air, she sent Hild, the captain, a private page – a quick summary, a quicker headline, a simple verbal tag: 'About Nine. There are anomalies, Captain. You'd better get up here.'

Hild called straight back. 'Anomalies? Not just a miniature black hole? Well, I guess we didn't come all the way out here to be bored. On my way. Be ready to show me what you have.'

'I'll be ready.'

But what *did* she have? Only a hunch.

A hunch that the black hole was trying to talk to them.

2

When she arrived, Hild wasted no time on pleasantries. 'Let me look.' Hild leaned forward to see the data, the images.

Then she spent a good quarter of an hour studying the readouts Salma selected for her.

Salma drifted back in the gravity-free air of the deck, as she knew the captain preferred, as she perused the data for herself, in silence. Hild was seventy years old, whip-thin — kept that way by regular use of the ship's exercise facilities — and with thick white hair shaved efficiently close to her scalp. And as she worked, Salma noticed, Hild kept one eye on a small ship-wide notification and alarm screen. Hild was captain of a ship parked in a hazardous place, and was never off duty.

At last she looked up at Salma. 'So, your report on this?'

Salma took a breath. 'It's clearly a black hole,' she said. 'As has long been suggested, even from Earth. This is the final confirmation. Ten times the mass of Earth, hence our cautious orbit. But small in size, only a quarter of a metre across—'

'Amazing we found it at all. And its size pins down its origin, correct?'

Salma had grown up with this kind of provocative questioning, as Hild, or some other meddler, had tried to get her to think for herself. She had been born the only child, the only *pupil*, on a ship crammed with easy-access information outlets, and a crew of clever, bored adults. But given her mother's illness and death, an orphan, effectively – with unknown donor father presumably back in the main Solar System.

Anyhow her answer was inadequate, she knew before saying it.

'Sort of.'

'*Sort of*? We may as well have stayed at home if that's the only observation you can give me—'

'This is apparently a primordial black hole,' Salma said hastily.

'Apparently?'

Salma treated it like a test and trotted out the facts. 'We know of three types of black hole in nature. There are massive black holes at the hearts of galaxies – including our own . . .'

And Hild absently looked out through the wide windows at the glowing heart of the Galaxy, away in Sagittarius – or at least at the veil of dust and gas and stars that concealed that object.

Salma said cautiously, 'These are black holes with the masses of millions of suns, presumably formed in the early days of the universe where huge gas clouds were gathered in by turbulent dark matter fields. Naked objects that then settled into the hearts of the new galaxies . . .'

'And?'

'And then you have stellar-size holes, relics of later generations of star-making. Formed when a large star runs out of fusion fuel, cools, and leaves remains massive enough to implode through the white dwarf stage – past even the neutron star stage, where the pressure of gravity overcomes quantum effects that resist collapse – you are left with a remnant many times the mass of our Sun.'

'But this thing has multiples of *Earth's* mass, not Sol's mass. Even further down the scale from all that. So now you are going to tell me that, if Nine *is* a black hole, it must be primordial. Right?'

'Right,' Salma said. 'Meaning, not a relic of star formation, but a by-product of the high-energy quantum-gravity field that created the universe itself. When spacetime itself was unfolding, expanding, in places falling back, perhaps creating black holes of a whole range of masses and sizes. Even as small as an atomic nucleus.' She frowned. 'But I thought the smallest ones should have quickly evaporated—'

'So the theorists have been speculating, for a couple of centuries, I think,' Hild said. 'And at the same time they were wondering about Planet Nine. Evidently a massive object, with a planet-sized mass and so exerting Solar System-wide effects – just as if you threw planet Uranus itself out here, its gravity dragging comets and planets out of their orbits – but *never seen*. Makes you think. If this *is* a primordial black hole, it's as old as our universe. Billions of years older than Sun and Earth. Older than any of the stars in the sky. Older than the galaxies.' She eyed Salma. 'You aren't old yet. You haven't *seen* anybody really old, not yet. Even I'm only seventy. You get more interested in the ages of things, and their survival, the older you get, I think. And if this is a relic of the birth of the universe, a direct relic – well, even the raw science data might sell well. And there are even more exotic possibilities. Some cosmologists have argued for centuries that maybe these ancient black holes were formed in another universe . . . An earlier cosmos, which collapsed into the Big Bang which created *our* cosmos, a vast cataclysm which these older black holes survived . . . I think the main candidates for survival are the big galaxy-centre holes, but . . .'

Salma listened absently. She knew that the Conservers were not above selling such data to academies on Earth – even to the miners on the Moon, the so-called Consortium, who generally concentrated on such practical priorities as how to squeeze a little more helium-3 fusion fuel out of a given kilogram of dry lunar soil.

But she knew this wasn't the point, just now. When Hild slowed down a little, she said so.

Hild frowned. 'Then what *is* the point?'

Now Salma hesitated, and not for the first time in her life she wished she had someone her own age to back her up.

'This black hole seems to have some – unusual – features.'

'Unusual? Not that we handle primordial black holes every day of the week.'

Salma had never been entirely sure what a 'week' was, or what the point of it was.

'No. Maybe unusual is not the right word. Puzzling, then. For one thing it's spinning,' she said firmly. 'Rotating very rapidly.'

Hild frowned again. 'All right. And you can tell that by—'

'Drag effects. Even light suffers drag effects near a black hole. I'll show you.'

Trying not to look too eager, she produced images of Nine taken against a background of distant stars. And these images, carefully magnified, showed distorted halos around the hole, as, Salma knew, starlight itself was deflected as it passed the horizon of the hole.

The event horizon was a place where the escape velocity itself was the speed of light. Nothing material could escape, because nothing material could reach lightspeed.

Hild nodded. 'I've seen such images of the Galaxy-centre hole. On a much larger scale. You have a zone called the ergosphere where light itself is dragged aside and pummelled. Beautiful imagery . . . And these must be the first images taken of such effects around a *primordial* black hole.' She smiled. 'Good work, Salma.'

13

Salma didn't smile back. 'Thanks. But there's something else.'

Hild studied her. 'You're building up to something, aren't you? I know you. All this is preamble, to something you're not sure about. Just tell me what you have.'

Salma took a breath. What she was building up to was indeed outrageous, she knew. But it also seemed to be true. And Hild was still smiling, for now.

'You know that black holes aren't truly black,' she began.

'OK,' Hild said slowly. 'Hawking radiation, right?'

'Yes. I suppose you know the basic mechanism.'

Hild didn't reply, forcing Salma to plough on.

'Nothing material can escape a black hole's event horizon — but there is a catch. In the extreme conditions *near* the event horizon, the gravity is so intense that some packets of energy can be folded down into short-lived particles—'

'Energy to mass. Virtual particles, correct?'

'Correct. A particle and its antimatter opposite. And it can happen that *one* of that pair will fall into the black hole, while the other escapes. And *that* is Hawking radiation, stuff escaping from the black hole, as if the gravity field is bleeding energy through its own strength.'

'OK. And you looked for this radiation, and detected it—'

'There's a *lot* of it, coming out of this hole. The Hawking radiation. More than the theory would suggest — as far as I can check it, understand it.' She hesitated.

Hild was smart enough to wait for what might follow.

Salma said carefully, 'And it isn't just a, a quantum hiss. The Hawking radiation.'

That made Hild stare. 'What? So if it's *not* just a hiss—'

'Captain, this is why I called you. There's structure in there. I think. *I think there's a message in the Hawking radiation.*'

*

14

There. It was out.

She looked at Hild nervously. 'Does it sound as dumb to you as it does to me?'

Hild opened her mouth, closed it. 'I – no, it doesn't sound dumb. Outlandish, but—' She glared at the viewscreen. 'You can't get much more outlandish than where we are already, right?' She looked again at Salma. '*Message*. You mean structure in the radiation?'

'Bullshit,' Boyd broke in, over the comms, without warning. 'Listening in, here. Can you blame me? Yes, information can be stored *in* a black hole. When a body collapses down into a hole, the data that characterised that body can be retained, down to a quantum level. In a sense. And the area of the black hole is proportionate to the information it holds. As if it's covered by tiny quantum-scale tiles, each black or white or . . . But you can't get information out of there. Didn't your buddy Hawking prove that?'

Hild said, 'But aren't there theorems that show that information, quantum information, can never be lost, just – moved around?' She winked at Salma. 'Anyhow, since when were you a cosmology fan, Boyd?'

'Since I woke up one day on a mission to nowhere with nothing to read, except textbooks on the black hole I might have been heading for. It was that or the days-late sports results from Earth . . .

'Hawking radiation, though. That's a real phenomenon. You're right about that, Salma. OK. As you said, at the event horizon you'll get a bit of energy, of *information*, that gets stretched by that boundary and transmutes into two particles, one of matter, one of antimatter, one of which falls back into the hole, the other goes flying off. And having lost a bit of energy the black has evaporated, just a little more . . . But it's all just random. Any information encoded into that surface, such as the black hole's history of formation, is lost as the stay-behind particle falls back to the event horizon. You can't get information out of a black hole. Which has always been a paradox, I grant you, because quantum information isn't supposed to be destroyed, ever.'

Hild nodded to Salma. *Put him right.*

Salma plucked up a bit of courage. 'That's not quite right, Boyd. There are theorems that show—'

'Proved in later life by your buddy Hawking, by the way,' Hild said.

'That *show* that the particle pair created at the horizon stay *entangled* – still linked by quantum mechanics – as one stays behind and the other flies off. And if you can capture that escaped – partner – then, through that entanglement, you can reconstruct the data that had been trapped at the event horizon.'

Boyd hesitated. Then he said, 'OK. Prove it.'

Hild smiled at Salma. *Do it.*

Salma tapped a screen. 'Boyd, look at this plot. This is the leakage radiation coming out of the hole. And you can *see* there's structure – there are clearly defined pulses of different but repeated lengths. Sets of those pulses, evenly spaced, with uniform, repeated contents. All incredibly rapid, very compressed, but it's there. Structure. I haven't got too far with any analysis of it. Once I thought I saw the Fibonacci sequence—'

Hild laughed out loud. 'The one where you add up the previous two terms? One. One. Two. Three. Five. Eight . . . A simple signal. My God. And if this black hole really is a survivor from some older universe, it's a signal from – someplace else.' She shook her head. 'Those old SETI guys must be turning in their graves. They were looking in the wrong place the whole time. Instead of looking for alien signals from out of the stars, they should have been looking at the edge of our own Solar System. Or across the boundaries between universes . . .'

There was a term in there Salma didn't know. 'Sss . . . eighty?'

'Never mind.' Hild drifted out of her chair. 'Salma, you have already paid off the value of the food you eat – and you eat like a hero. You were right to call me in.'

'And me,' Boyd said.

Salma thought she could hear his grin. Boyd pushed you, but he appreciated good work.

Hild went on, 'We'll get the whole team on this as soon as. And if you're right we can start to download all this to the Outpost, and *they* can start negotiating with the Earthside universities and think tanks, for support with an extended analysis—'

The Outpost, orbiting just inside the heliopause, the physical boundary of the Solar System, was the nearest thing the Conservers had to a fixed base.

Hild chewed her lip, 'Although I imagine the Outpost will have to negotiate politically. There's going to be pressure for a wider scrutiny. More ships, proper scholars. Something like this might go as high as President Mason's office—'

But Salma shook her head. 'I don't want to wait for all that.'

Hild frowned. 'Then what?'

'Hild—'

'*Captain* Hild.'

'I . . . I got carried away. Look, I prepared an experiment. I haven't run it yet, not without your say-so.'

'What experiment?'

'I recorded the Hawking stuff. The information. I couldn't make sense of it, but I thought it was a message, you see. And *I thought we could play some of it back*. At Nine. You know, bathe it with a laser spot. We can't produce gravity waves, and we don't know the meaning of the message, but we could send back the same pattern. Just to see — just to show we understood.'

'My God,' Hild said softly.

That was a strange archaism to Salma.

She ploughed on, 'We can't — translate — whatever's coming out of it. But if we echo it back, at least that would show intelligence is *out here*, wouldn't it? And we could do more than just reflect the signal back. Make it obvious we are intelligent. We could speed up the signal, chop it around to show it's not just random reflections. And maybe if there is intelligence *in there*, it could recognise what we're doing, and — well, respond?'

'Respond? How?'

But Salma had thought no further.

After a few more seconds, Hild snapped, 'Do it.'

'What?'

Hild grinned. 'The reply. Of course we should try this. You're right. We seem to have received an information-rich signal from some . . . intelligence. Maybe it's signalling precisely because it can sense the artifice of our ship, our technology. Somehow. Or . . . I don't know. Of course we should reply. And you're right about the timing. A signal exchange with the Outpost would take a lot of hours right now, given our relative positions. And besides, what could the Outpost tell us that we don't already know? What the hell is there to wait for? Have you got it set up now?'

'Well, yeah. Are you sure?'

'Do it. I take full responsibility . . . No. Wait.'

She took over the comms and gave the rest of the crew a hasty heads-up.

When she was done, she grinned. '*That* is one of the more unusual ship-wide announcements I've ever had to make. Probably since you were born yourself, Salma. Nice to keep them on their toes. OK. Set it up.'

Heart pounding, Salma murmured instructions to the ship's systems.

It took only an hour to set up the reflected signal.

The sending itself was silent, of course, high-frequency radiation bathing the ancient black hole with its faint heat. But Salma could see from her instruments that the transmission was working, in that the laser-delivered signal was indeed a faithful copy of the data delivered by the original Hawking radiation. She made sure the continuing feed *from* the black hole was being monitored too.

And then—

She took a breath. Two. Waiting to check first that the changes in the readings she saw were more than noise.

'I think I'm detecting a change . . . Hardly a signal . . . I think it's working!'

Hild made notes. But she seemed distracted, staring out of the window, at the Galaxy-centre light show.

And as Salma watched her displays, she saw an anomaly in the corner of her eye. An odd reading. 'Something's happening. The external hull temperature seems to be rising slightly. The ship's hull . . .'

Hild pointed at the main screen. '*Something's happening*? You think?'

She pushed her way out of her chair, floated in the air, grabbed Salma by the collar, and pulled her physically over to the window, to face the star fields.

Not an easy manoeuvre in zero gravity, Salma knew.

'*Look* at that.'

'At what?'

'Sagittarius. The star clouds. The centre of the Galaxy, damn it! Can't you see?'

'I don't—'

'Since when did the Galaxy centre have a bright red spot glaring out of it?'

And now Salma did see.

Hild tapped at readouts. 'It lit up, according to the monitor here, to within a second of you sending that damn signal. We'll have to tie down the sequence of events . . . It has the same spectrum as the background Galaxy, just more intense. I'm trying to get a perspective lock. If the red spot *is* actually somewhere close, light-seconds away, just happening to line up with the Galaxy centre, I should find it quickly—'

She was distracted by more displays.

'Oh. And we're detecting a *heat rise*. Minuscule, but . . . On the outer hull, I mean. Can that be connected to the red feature? . . . No, this makes no sense. The Galaxy centre is twenty-five thousand light-years away. If that's real, if it's not some artefact of the system—' More unhappily tapped keys. 'There *can't* be any kind of causal link; the feature would have to be enormously energetic to be detectable from here. And whatever the mechanism, its – ignition – must have happened twenty-five thousand years ago. Given that the light-up we saw coincided with your feedback experiment.' She checked a screen. 'Umm, to within a second . . .'

She ran down.

Boyd called. 'I hesitate to bring this up. If you're looking for a connection . . . If Nine is a primordial black hole, and so maybe a survivor from another universe, *so may the Galaxy centre be*. It's another primordial hole, and so maybe another survivor from – someplace else?'

They shared one silent, horrified moment. Wordless.

In a ghastly, speculative way, Salma realised, it all fitted together.

What does this mean? What have we done?

Hild shook her head. 'No sense. This makes no sense. Keep monitoring. I'll gather the rest of the crew. And I do need to talk to the Outpost at some point. And the Outpost needs to talk to Earth . . . I wonder how long it will be before President Mason herself hears about this.'

Salma stared at her displays. 'Hild. Look at this. I think we're getting *another* Hawking signal . . .'

So it began.

And elsewhere, elsewhen—

Far away across the quantum-froth multiverse – 'far' by a definition that would have meant little to most humans – it was as if the softest, most hesitant knock on a door had been made. And that knock was heard.

Later, humans would call him Terminus.

Much of his duty was simply to sit and wait. Wait by a door.

Scattered across every universe, in every bubble in the reality foam, there were what might have been called doors, or lesions, or portals – each a breach of a boundary. Humans might have labelled some black holes, but most were far more sophisticated than those crude ruptures in spacetime. But in a sense, they all worked the same way.

They connected universes.

Terminus did not know how the portals had been created, distributed. That had been done in an unimaginable *before*. But, he knew, they all had a single purpose. And his job was to wait and watch . . .

Wait for somebody, on the other side, in one target universe, to find one such portal. To reach out to that portal. To *touch* it – whatever that meant in terms of their own embodiment.

And after that, for that somebody, everything would change.

21

Now one such portal had loomed in his awareness. One such touch.

That was all Terminus needed.

To smile was a human reflex. Yet now, it could be said, Terminus smiled.

Meanwhile, elsewhere, the news of the discoveries in the Oort cloud spread across the human worlds.

3

High above Earth, Bheki Molewa, holding his husband's hand – and waiting for the Presidential Science Adviser to show up – said, 'Are you *crying*? Are you kidding me? It's only Earth out there . . . You've been to much stranger places than this.'

For a moment Jeorg North, peering out of this grand old space elevator's viewing window – staring out at the brilliance of Earth below – couldn't reply.

Bheki was right, Jeorg thought. You didn't need to be a psychiatrist, specialising in the psychological impact of long-duration spaceflight, to understand. Bheki himself was a pilot, and surely sympathised.

Jeorg had been out in deep space many times. Too many? His most famous mission, catching the eye of an introverted terrestrial public, had been piloting a prospecting trip to Ceres, the largest main-belt asteroid – a quasi-legal trip that had been watched carefully by the Lunar Consortium, who wanted to get their hands on the asteroid's resources themselves. Possibly when and if Earth decided to license the mining of the body, or when the Consortium decided to go ahead anyway.

But as for Jeorg, he had gone out so often, and on such immense journeys, that in the end he had stayed too long in space, had risked his health, his chance of longevity – even his chance of a long marriage to Bhekiokwakhe Molewa, at his side now.

He had done this knowingly. For what exactly? Not the glory alone. Not the science data-collection that had been the object of most of his missions, and he had done well enough with that – evidently enough for the Science Adviser herself to come meet him in person up here, today, bringing, perhaps, a chance to go out once again – though he had no idea where. And she was late, Jeorg reminded himself . . .

He had done it all for no reason but to fly. To be the first, to Ceres, wherever. That was the reason he couldn't sit still. Even if Earth drew him back at the same time . . .

Only Earth. He pressed his hand against the glass, and now Bheki covered Jeorg's hand with his own, the backs of their two hands dark, the paler palms facing the glowing Earth.

He knew he wasn't alone in this odd disturbance when he was in the proximity of Earth. Jeorg was only one pilot among many currently flying, but a lot had confessed to similar feelings when gazing at the home planet from space.

From here, suspended at geostationary orbit high over the Pacific Ocean, they saw Earth as a dish of water and cloud, a world ocean broken only by the elevator's anchoring island far below – the mid-Pacific island itself artificial. But Jeorg had seen for himself how the works of twenty-third-century humankind had spread far out from the old shorelines, with raft cities floating over the drowned wrecks of coastal communities. Beauty and tragedy in a glance. Having given up so much of his life to space – and as many others had found – Jeorg thought it was cruelly paradoxical that returning to Earth always made him want to cry like a baby.

For long moments the two of them were silent, as if they were alone, orbiting the Earth in this enormous structure. You could never shake off the pull of the mother world, no matter how far you travelled.

. . . It's only Earth . . .
A subtle tap on the door.

Science Adviser Elizabeth Vasta was immediately recognisable from her media appearances, though neither Jeorg nor Bheki had met her before. She was a small, compact woman, perhaps in her fifties. Strong-looking.

Jeorg felt relieved at the distraction.

They made brief introductions. Vasta wore a long, dark robe, a sombre black. As far as Jeorg could see, she'd added only one adornment: a simple pendant, a silver cage containing what looked like a pearl – a perfect sphere, also deep black. It seemed an odd choice, given the darkness of her robe. Black on black. A sentimental token, perhaps.

Her look was almost monastic, Jeorg thought. But then the business of government was a sombre matter these days.

And as Vasta made her way into the room, the fact that she was unused to space told immediately in the way she handled her smart zero-gravity navigation frame. There was a white-knuckled clinging to the rail at chest height, and feet rammed deep into the slipper-like footpads, as the frame guided her through the viewing lounge, with the soft hum of electromagnetic fields emanating from the walls and the occasional hiss of reaction jets.

Jeorg and Bheki waited patiently. Everybody not born in space faced these fundamental challenges of adaptation. And even though the space elevator was as firmly rooted to the Earth as a great sequoia, up here you were in net zero gravity, and definitely in space.

But Vasta was making determined progress.

Elizabeth Vasta was the Senior Science Adviser to Melanie Mason, President of a united Earth (somewhat united anyhow).

A figure deep-buried in the heart of government. But in fact, Jeorg thought now, given the modern centrality of science, technology and related threats and opportunities, arguably Vasta was a more significant figure even than the President in the world's affairs. And today, here she was, having sought out Jeorg North, peripatetic pilot, engineer and explorer. For what purpose, though?

Jeorg had never been so glad to have Bheki at his side.

When the guide frame finally brought her to a halt, a couple of paces from Jeorg and Bheki, Vasta reflexively glanced at a smart-looking bangle on her wrist. Perhaps checking for urgent messages, even though it was probably only minutes since she had left whatever staff she had up here with her.

Then, resting at last, she looked up and smiled.

'Captain North. Pilot Molewa. Thank you for agreeing to see me in person. Captain North, I'm told it had to be this way – you can't safely be brought down to the surface of the Earth—'

Bheki put in, 'And so thank you too for coming up to see him. Yes, my husband has spent too long in low or zero gravity to be able to adapt back, despite his having replaced much of his skeletal structure, internal organs – his *eyes* – with bio-cyber replacements—'

'As have you, some of it,' Jeorg retorted.

Bheki shrugged. 'That's what comes from following you around most of my adult life. Though it is ironic to see you weep over an Earth you can never land on again . . .' But he softened this by reaching out and touching his husband's shoulder.

'You're both charming,' Elizabeth Vasta said, voice a little strained, her fingers white where she was clinging to the assist frame. 'But, paradoxical as it seems, I think I would feel happier sitting down rather than floating around in the air. Also this frame reminds me of my mother's walker support in her final days. Down on Earth, I mean. I'm not *there* yet. How do I, umm . . .'

They suggested heading for a small café, which Jeorg and Bheki knew well. Bheki showed Vasta that all she needed to do was tell the frame what she wanted, and it swivelled gently, nudging the clinging Vasta, until it was able to lead her down the curving corridor with all-but silent hisses of reaction gas.

This orbital hub had been created as the core of the elevator's construction, suspended more than five Earth radii above that artificial island on the Pacific equator. At this height a satellite would orbit Earth in twenty-four hours, matching Earth's rotation, so that the hub, itself built in space, had seemed to hover over that oceanic location.

From here a tether cable had been dropped down to the island, and fixed there, so that the hub was like an enormous kite on a string, but held far above the planet's kilometres-deep layer of air. At the same time a counterweight, another complex space-borne machine in itself, had been slowly lifted further outwards from the position of this main hub, on another tether itself fully eighteen thousand kilometres long. This arrangement kept the cable as a whole under tension.

The elevator had, since its opening a century ago, become the key space-transportation node for the newly united planet. All achieved with a minimum of energy expended, a minimum of waste heat: no more vapour-spewing rocket launches from Earth's surface, no more atmosphere-burning high-speed re-entries. People nowadays took care of their planet – 'what's left of it' being the qualifying slogan of a group of planetary protection organisations.

But even the space elevator, ten decades old, was embedded

in modern-day politics, Jeorg knew. What little energy it did require to keep running – like much of the rest of human civilisation – was now supplied by super-efficient, super-clean helium-3 fusion reactors on Earth and in space.

Ah, but where was the vital helium-3 fuel to be found?

It was at such low concentrations on Earth that it may as well have not existed on the planet at all. So low that an occurrence as low as four parts per *billion* in the soil of the Moon made it more economic to recover it from there, and bring it down to Earth.

And that brute set of facts, to Jeorg's understanding, was the driver behind the strained politics of the entire Earth-Moon system – and, perhaps, soon, the politics of a more widely exploited Solar System. In space there was helium-3 in abundance, relatively speaking, in the icy asteroids – like Ceres, which Jeorg had prospected himself – and, too, in great quantities in the atmospheres of the huge gaseous outer worlds such as Jupiter and Saturn.

All that for the future. Earth needed the helium *now*, but for the present could only buy it from the ragged mining colonies on the Moon. The economic set-up was brutal – and favoured Earth.

For example, Jeorg knew, the Moon was rich in uranium, and once Earth had bought as much of that as could be delivered, in preference to mining the home planet. But now Earth preferred helium-3. You would think that would drive up the prices – but Earth had monopolies of its own, for now. Especially in nitrogen, a foundation for any human-habitable ecosphere – a gas that was the unnoticed bulk of Earth's atmosphere, but vanishingly scarce on the Moon.

It was a kind of mutual stranglehold, each faction using its own monopolies to seek to limit the growth of the other. But all the strongest cards were held by Earth.

And presumably as a result of all *that*, through a long chain of logic, here was the World President's Science Adviser, far above the world, come to meet with one beat-up deep-space pilot and his stay-at-home husband.

That, and, possibly, the discovery of something very strange outside the inner Solar System altogether, Jeorg wondered now. But something which, he suspected, as probably did many others, could have profound implications for the economic and political balance of the human Solar System.

Which was pretty much all Jeorg had known, when Vasta's staff had asked for this meeting. But he dared to hope all this spelled opportunity for him and his husband.

In the café, each table was set over a kind of portal, showing magnified images of the Earth, permanently stationary beneath their feet – but the smart system would show more than just the customary Pacific-hemisphere outlook below. Networks of cameras in lower altitudes around the planet delivered more variegated views, live, of ocean, of land – as if they were sailing through low orbit in some primitive spacecraft.

Vasta seemed pleased by the view as they sat. 'Very tourist-trade, I suppose. But very effective.'

Jeorg smiled. 'When the viewpoint pans quickly, it can make you feel like a god.'

'Not necessarily a good thing, in this humbler day and age . . .'

They were served by discreet dome-shaped robots, fat and low, the domes unfolding to reveal trays of food or drink retrieved by articulated arms.

The spacers ordered water; Vasta asked for coffee.

'Which is a little cold,' Vasta murmured when her flask was delivered. 'Low air pressure?'

Bheki shrugged. 'Lower than Earth sea level. As much as you need to keep breathing, without excessively loading the structure. If it bothers you there are self-heating flasks which—'

'No, no.' She sipped her coffee. 'This is my second spaceflight. I'm becoming known as a curmudgeon about it among my staff, I think. This is the dream of ages! I should immerse myself in the experience, blithely disregarding discomfort, such as complaining about the coffee.' Then she glanced over at Jeorg's withered frame, and shook her head. 'Oh, I'm sorry. I mean no offence about your condition—'

'None taken.' He clenched a fist, flexed his fingers. 'The bits you use in space, like your hands, tend to get stronger. The bits that can afford to be lazy – well, they lose some of their function if you aren't careful.'

'As you never were,' Bheki said, with a slight edge. 'Minister Vasta, did you know I'm a pilot myself? Though he's been flying longer than I have – flying long before we met. So I've had a ringside seat as the brave Captain North ignores all advice and makes it a personal mission to collect *all* the direst physical symptoms of extended spaceflight. Low bone density, imbalance of blood pressure, a weakened heart, visual problems—'

'OK, OK.'

'If you dislike space, he *loves* it to the detriment of his health. Eventually I married the bits that still worked—'

'I can see how much you love each other.' Vasta smiled as she spoke. 'You're lucky, both of you. And I can appreciate your – sacrifice – Captain North. The sacrifice of your health, to be the first to Ceres among other accomplishments . . .'

Since that mission, which had been of great interest to both terrestrial and lunar concerns, Jeorg had carefully kept up his contacts, within and outside Earth's gravity well. You never knew. Now it looked like that strategy might be paying off . . .

He found he was eager to know what precisely Vasta wanted of him.

But Vasta was distracted again, North saw. Even as she spoke she dipped her head, evidently to see better the edge of the viewing field.

Bheki smiled. 'You really don't get up here often, do you?'

'My work rarely offers useful excuses. Even if this is one of mankind's most significant engineering achievements. And finest views.'

Jeorg grunted. 'I would agree with you. But a lot of the Moon miners would disagree. This is – old-fashioned. Yesterday's tech.'

'Of course, in your line of work you must mix with a lot of them.'

'The Lunar Consortium? Some. Over the years.' The decades, actually, he reminded himself; he was fifty-two years old. 'And, ironically, I hear more about Earth's plans from gossip on the Moon than on the ground.'

Vasta nodded. 'Then the news about the expansion of the use of helium-3 will be familiar to you,' she said dryly.

Jeorg's heart beat a little faster. *Keep calm, old man.* For the pilot community, this was a hot topic. Propulsion powered by the energy densities afforded by helium-3 fusion promised journeys to the outer planets of *weeks*, not years. Even the Oort cloud would be in reach. Some day, the stars . . .

Bheki leaned forward. 'I did hear something about that. The government is itself already trialling a helium-3 extraction operation – but *at Saturn*, isn't it?'

Vasta shrugged. 'Hmm. I should have expected you to know about *that*. Your husband's fame brings connections, I imagine. Yes, the Earth government is considering a major expansion of the use of helium-3 fusion. Yes, the plan, for now at least, is to mine helium-3 from the clouds of Saturn. Where it is abundant, relatively. The gas giants are much richer lodes, obviously, than the asteroids. We skipped Jupiter, though it's closer, because of its deeper gravity well, the radiation belts . . . That's for the future.

'But we estimate there is enough helium-3 in the clouds of Jupiter and Saturn alone to sustain a Kardashev Type I culture at Earth for tens of thousands of years . . . Do you know what I mean by that? I mean an industrial culture providing the energy equivalent of *all* the sunlight the planet gathers. You must imagine an orbital installation – perhaps this elevator hub will be a key node – managing the industrial energy provision, without tapping sunlight or the planet's own resources – so you would have a way to preserve the planet *and* allow human civilisation to fulfil a new potential . . .

'We've had debates about the moral validity of it all. We aren't Conservers, who wouldn't touch anything non-renewable whatever – though they serve as a valuable moral touchstone. Yes, we'd be plundering other planets, the gas giants. But we have no evidence of life, let alone mind, there. We plunder *there* to preserve life and mind *here*.'

Jeorg nodded. 'I can see how all these developments would snowball.' He glanced at Bheki, took a breath. He couldn't contain it. 'But in the immediate future – *you're developing a helium-3 drive, aren't you? A fast, powerful helium-based trans*port capability—.'

She smiled. 'I knew you would be informed. And of course that would interest you. Yes, such a fast ship would be key to opening up Saturn, for example, to large-scale helium-mining – the returns from which would support more and wider explorations and exploitations, as well as feeding Earth's own industries. The latter being, in the end, our main preoccupation.'

Bheki thought that over. 'But is that still true? Forgive me. Haven't the priorities changed now – all the current excitement is about Planet Nine, isn't it? Even more exotic physics to exploit, maybe? Who knows how *that* might upset our interplanetary economy? And it's in the hands of the Conservers—' He shook his head. 'Who are harmless at least, though they seem to me to be becoming ever more mystical.'

Vasta nodded, grudgingly. 'You're right, of course. We don't know what potential for destabilisation that wild card might prove to have. And destabilisation, given the present state of our civilisation, could be catastrophic. In fact that's what I want to talk to you about.'

Jeorg and Bekhi exchanged a glance.

As if by unspoken consent, they fell silent, and watched the Earth through the window.

As he watched from this eyrie, high over the face of Earth, Jeorg saw a low-orbit spaceborne factory complex drift by, an angular artificial moon sailing *beneath* his current altitude. The old industries of Earth were being slowly peeled off the planet, piece by piece, as a goal of returning Earth into a simulacrum of its old pre-industrial, if not pre-farming, self was pursued.

But among those factories, Jeorg knew, weapons complexes lurked – their weapons pointing, not down any more, but out to space. Weapons not yet fired in anger, but ready. And more weapons further out: small, fast assault craft that protected solar farms in Earth orbit, and the supply chain of helium-3 scraped painfully from the thin Sun-deposited traces in the lunar soil. Even further out, a network of deep-space monitors sought traces of incoming asteroids, or asteroid chunks, threatening impacts. Asteroids coming this way at random, or purposefully directed.

A recovering planet, a planet turning green – a Solar System being slowly, tentatively colonised – and becoming a potential field of war at the same time.

And now, Saturn . . .

Bekhi said, 'Advisor Vasta, I think you should tell us what you want of us.'

4

'Very well,' Vasta said. 'It's a question of – high-level strategy.'

Bheki said, 'And given who you report to, that's pretty high level.'

'True. And President Mason takes a keen interest in this, believe me. But what you can see through this window tells the story.'

'Look – a century or so back, we, we *humans*, were united in the effort to save the Earth. But now we're expanding again, and that spirit of unity is fading, and we see the emergence, or re-emergence, of broad factions of mankind, philosophically speaking.

'Of whom the most significant, or disruptive, may be the industrialists, the free-market thinkers who would plunder the resources of near-Earth space for economic growth. Which growth would fuel even more economic growth, and on it would go.'

'Yes. Such as the Lunar Consortium,' Bheki said.

Vasta nodded. 'They are the largest such grouping, yes. Working within world government law, we've managed to hold them back from Ceres, so far, for example.' She nodded at Jeorg. 'Despite your own prospecting trip. But meanwhile we are looking further ahead. As they are too. The industrialists.'

'To the gas giants,' Bheki said. 'And if you can tap the gas giants—'

'We've trial sites working already.'

Jeorg gaped at that. 'Already. Well, in the immediate future that will cut the Moon's economy off at the knees. And their own hopes from long-term growth, exploitation.'

'Maybe. We hope for some peaceful, cooperative transition. But even if the Lunar Consortium does collapse, there will be similar pressures from elsewhere.

'You see, in historical terms the Consortium isn't an anomaly. This pressing for profit, for consumption, for technological advancement and growth as fast as possible – once that was what everybody was doing, what everybody aspired towards, ever since the Industrial Revolution – until it all crashed. Now the lunar miners think they have taken that dream out into space. Maybe it will lead to another crash – not yet, not for a long time – millennia perhaps. *But they don't care.*

'Whereas on Earth, post the climate-rebuild decades, we now have a different vision. A second philosophical faction, if you like, which – for now – has a stronger influence on government. They call us the Kardashev faction.' She looked at them, one then the other. 'As I described to you.'

Jeorg said, 'A city-sphere girdling the planet.'

'That's the dream.' She smiled. 'On the other hand, a Conserver wouldn't approve of our plans. *They* believe in using only resources that would otherwise be lost, or are truly renewable. So, tapping sunlight energy is allowed. Harvesting comets that come from outside the Solar System altogether. The result: a static, starved economy. We hope we have found a middle way.'

Bheki nodded. 'OK. But the key to all of this is to get hold of extraterrestrial helium-3 . . . ? And you've already started at Saturn?'

'Correct.'

And connections were being made in Jeorg's head. 'Ah. I think I know something about this. And why you've come to speak to me. The *Cronus*, correct?'

Bheki frowned. 'The *Cronus*? That's the big Saturn freighter, right? Uranium-fission drive—'

'About the most majestic ship to sail since the heyday of the ocean liners. After she got back from her first mission to Saturn I thought about applying to join the crew for the next mission. Even if not in command. What an adventure!'

'And you never told me?'

Jeorg shrugged. 'Well, I dropped it. Come on. It takes six years to get to Saturn, using minimum-energy trajectories. Six years there, six years back. I knew you would be unhappy about my going. I know you think I've spent enough time in space, done enough to my body. Anyhow I thought there was no point in an argument if I had no chance of making the crew.' He glanced at Vasta. 'OK, truthfully – I did put out feelers. I got polite rebuffs. I wondered if the whole project had been abandoned. I gave up. Now I guess I'm learning why I heard nothing. But still it's only a fission-drive ship.'

'True enough. For now.'

For now. Jeorg and Bheki exchanged a glance at that.

'Even so,' Vasta said, 'through its first missions the ship has already carried the seeds of a major industrial development out there to Saturn. And as I told you the atmospheric mining operation there has already started, successfully. Mining the clouds of Saturn – for helium-3. It's already happening. It won't be long before the first shipments of helium will be returned to Earth, aboard *Cronus* or a sister ship, even a dumb freighter . . .

'*But*, given the news of Planet Nine, we changed the strategy. Now there's somewhere else we need to get to, much further out.

'And so we are modifying *Cronus*, our best ship. She's at Earth now, being turned around, will be on her way back to Saturn soon.' Vasta smiled. '*Where we were already developing a proto-type helium-3 drive*. Much more powerful than uranium-fission propulsion, as you know – much more *fast*. And out there, there's plenty of fuel from the atmosphere-extraction project, and other assets – building materials from the moons. And then—'

Jeorg guessed wildly, 'Then you're going to take *Cronus* to Planet Nine! Using helium-3 from Saturn, the drive you're de-veloping – why, with that you could make it out to Nine in – a handful of years? As opposed to the decades it took the *Shadow*. Have I got that right?'

Vasta smiled. 'That's the plan.'

Bheki frowned. 'But what about the politics? It's some Conserver faction who have hold of Planet Nine right now – whatever it is. And they took decades to get there. Why should they welcome you? Mustn't they despise you as much as they do the miners? From their point of view, if the Solar System gets plundered, will it matter who by in the end?'

'The Conservers' vision is radical,' Vasta said. 'And admira-ble. Even if it's a goal that could surely never be fully achieved. *But* – isn't that what this government is trying to do with the Earth? Isn't this government already implementing the greenest of policies, in the jargon – with the vision of our green-again world wrapped in a bubble of high-tech civilisation? Aren't we the intellectual heirs of those early conservation movements on old Earth, just as much as the Conservers are?'

Bheki wasn't convinced by that. 'You'll have to explain all that to them.'

'Not just that. I want to try to make sure you understand the significance of all this – of getting it right. Because otherwise, some think, if we do fall into some interplanetary war – whether it's triggered by the Oort-cloud anomaly situation or not – we may be looking at an extinction event.'

That stopped the conversation.

Vasta sipped her coffee, fingered her pearl pendant nervously, Jeorg saw. Waiting for their reaction.

Jeorg nodded. 'Well, I get it. It's clear enough to an old space hand like me that war in space would be calamitous. Suicidal and genocidal at the same time, like the old one-planet nuclear wars could have been. It's so *easy*. Throw a little rock at a space habitat and it pops like a glass bowl, spilling people like stranded fish. Throw a big rock at Earth, and you wipe out the dinosaurs' heirs in an afternoon—'

Bheki said, 'So what's the strategy? Better Earth takes over Planet Nine than to let this mystery fall into the hands of the Moon miners?'

Vasta shrugged. '*Wouldn't* that be better? Whatever that thing is, wouldn't you prefer to have it in the hands of a government you can vote down? In principle.'

Bheki had to laugh. 'Nicely qualified. OK. Practical matters – and the reason you've come here. *What do you want from us,* Adviser Vasta?'

Jeorg smiled ruefully. 'I think I know.'

Bheki's frown deepened.

But Jeorg already had his head full of a new mission. Everything had changed. 'You've got to get that ship out there,' he murmured. 'The *Cronus*. You just have to. Out to Nine. Before all this leaks out and somebody else beats you to it. And this is why you came to see me. You want *me* to take it out there, right?'

Vasta smiled at him. 'You were first to Ceres. Who is better qualified? Your very presence on the mission will serve to promote the cause. And you're right. We've got to get that ship out there. Out to Planet Nine with all its threat and potential. We haven't discussed it, but the President is especially concerned about the new galactic-warming event that seems to be linked to the events at Nine . . .'

But Jeorg wasn't listening. He grinned wildly. He looked up at his husband, an impulse to share this extraordinary, sudden gift.

But Bheki was scowling. Furiously.

5

The rumours of the existence of a ship fast enough to reach Planet Nine in a mere few years – compared to the decades taken by the Conservers' spindly sail ship – leaked out of Earth, were picked up by the Conservers' own sparse information-gathering networks – and were passed on, ultimately, to *Shadow*, at its station orbiting Nine.

And that prompted Salma to take, belatedly, another look at her own craft, the craft that had brought her and her companions out here.

She had always taken it for granted, she supposed. She had been born aboard the *Shadow*; it was her home, all she had ever known. Somehow the prospect of new ships arriving, of probably quite different designs, and *new people*, made her want to understand her own ship better – and her own life, and how she had got here.

It had been a long journey for sure. Hild Kanigel, Salma knew, was the ship's oldest crew member, as well as serving as captain since the launch of the *Shadow*. Thanks to an assiduous exercise regime Hild was compact, confident, her build stocky. Only her near-white hair gave away her age, around seventy standard years – even a Conserver living at the edge of the Solar System still counted her age by Earth years. But Hild had been a mere thirty-something years old when the *Shadow* had been launched, an event itself some thirty-five years ago.

The ship had been fabricated by the culture that had already been labelled 'Conservers' by the commentators on Earth, and even by the venture-capitalist miners of the Lunar Consortium. The Conservers — consciously seeking a way for humans to expand and live across the Solar System *without* depleting its resources in the process — were despised by both sides. They had accepted a label meant as contempt. *Conservers*. That would do.

And in that spirit they had constructed *Shadow* using mainly the discarded, mined-out remains of an asteroid, a near-Earth object from which all supposedly valuable materials had already been extracted. It wasn't easy, but the Conservers were making tangible their basic policy: tap as many plentiful or renewing resources as possible, use the waste of others.

So Salma had learned as she grew up. All this was history, a culture war Salma had never thought she would see close up. She had been born on this ship, a Conserver vessel, and she had always believed, at the back of her mind, that she would die on the ship — if not on the mysterious Planet Nine. Now everything seemed likely to change, and she tried to find out more.

And, she learned, it had been necessary for this ship, this one austere Conserver initiative, at least, to dip deep into the inner Solar System, and 'steal' a little of the Sun's energy, its radiation output, even its gravitational energy, to achieve its tremendous journey.

Salma had been born twenty years ago, in the mission's fifteenth year.

And she had been born, or *allowed* to be born, because of the death of her mother.

It had been a form of bone cancer that, it seemed, was rare but not unknown in denizens of deep-space zero-gravity habitats, and not eradicated even after more than two centuries of human spaceflight. A deep weakness yet to be scrubbed from a genome of ever-improving resilience. So she had been earnestly told.

And so here was Salma, having once been a harvested and frozen embryo, created from the union of her mother and a man still alive in the outer Kuiper belt – a father she never expected to see. Here was Salma, allowed to live only because her mother had died, and had made room for her on this small ship – and the older she got the more complicated her feelings about that became.

She had only ever seen images of her mother, a few other records – and nothing at all of her father. All the images, save for excursions outside the ship, showed her mother wearing the onyx pendant that had been her only legacy for Salma – and her mother had given Meriel Breen, ship's medic, an identical gift, as if to acknowledge Meriel's necessary role as an honorary aunt to Salma in the future.

As Salma had grown, she was starting to look like her mother – so her crewmates said – with her dark hair, pale skin, rather empty blue eyes. The onyx pendant somehow reinforced that impression. For a time Salma had put aside her mother's images – and, too, had become averse to looking at her own face in mirrors and monitors.

She never gave up her pendant, though. Nor Meriel hers.

And meanwhile she got on with living.

With their whole lives confined to a few habitat modules, and with, frankly, not much change to the view outside, most of the crew spent the journey time – thirty-five years of it now – in virtual environments. Most of these were essentially play, augmented with downloads from the inner System, and Salma had slowly learned to explore the suite with help from her crew-mates.

That had been her childhood, pretty much.

In recent years she had, with subtle guidance, even been encouraged to find virtual worlds rich in romance and sexuality, for it had been made plain to her all her life that, on the ship, she would find no partners among a set of adults who regarded her as an honorary niece, if not a daughter. Even the second youngest of the crew, Zaimu, propulsion specialist, was sixteen years older. And Salma came to perceive a shifting network of romantic and sexual relationships among the rest of the crew – a network of which she had no part.

But as her own adolescent frenzy had faded a little she had been gradually drawn to other stuff, more sober material. Mostly on the culture that had produced this ship, the mission of the *Shadow* itself, and its target in Planet Nine.

So here was Salma the adult, at twenty years old, having been gently trained all her life to take her mother's place in the crew. And here was Salma doing just that, learning to fulfil her mission at its climax.

The only difference being, she supposed, she hadn't been given the privilege of being able to *choose* to take part in this mission. She liked to think she would have been swept up by the heroics, even if she had had the choice to opt out. Anyhow she would never know; she had never been given the opportunity to find out.

But now she had her reward.

Now she had been the first to see *it*. The real Planet Nine.

Planet Nine: an old label for a hypothetical planet-size mass beyond the eighth true planet, Neptune – an inadequate, parochial, probably incorrect label for a phenomenon discovered

more than two centuries ago, in an antique time when astronomers were still mostly confined to Earth.

Salma learned the theory.

The Solar System in large was a thing of layers, like an onion,
if a flattened onion. You had the Sun at the centre of it all, with
the eight major planets in roughly the same orbital plane, some
with moons the size of planets themselves. Between Mars and
Jupiter were the main-belt asteroids, the debris of the System's
origin – including the largest and richest, Ceres, full of precious
water, settled in its orbit.

Beyond Neptune, outermost major planet, lay the Kuiper belt,
full of trans-Neptunian objects – TNOs – some resembling planets or moons, such as chill Pluto.

And beyond even that, stretching into interstellar space, was
the Oort cloud, a realm still poorly mapped but inhabited by objects massive enough, if they chanced to wander into the inner
System, to blossom into comets, bringing beauty and occasional
doom.

And it was to the Oort cloud that the *Shadow* had come
searching for the elusive Planet Nine. Supposedly seven *hundred*
times as far from the Sun as Earth was, and at least the mass of
Neptune.

The point was, from Earth you couldn't see Planet Nine itself,
for whatever reason – but you could see the marks of its passage
among the wider cloud of Oort objects.

Salma had grown up trying to understand this mystery – how
you could see the unseen. When she was still quite small one
older man, a non-specialist engineer called Boyd – or 'Uncle
Boyd', at that point – had tried to explain.

He dropped a cup of rice grains into a transparent flask of
water. When he shook the flask, without gravity or acceleration
the rice grains would not settle. But then Boyd opened the flask,

popped in an ice cube, and pushed it with one finger so it sailed, gravity-free, through the water, perturbing the cloud of grains as it went. *Can you see the ice in the water? Just barely? Imagine you can't see it at all, so that it's invisible . . .*

He had had to explain that word, *invisible*, and she had to practise for two days before she could say it herself.

Even if you couldn't see the ice, you could see where it has been and where it is going, from the way it stirs up the rice grains . . .

And that is how we know Planet Nine is out there, even though we can't see it, yet. We think it is on a long, slow, looping orbit around the Sun – travelling all the way out into the far Oort cloud when it's at its extreme. We can't see it, for whatever reason, but we can see how it scatters the other TNOs – the trans-Neptunian objects, the comet cores and other stuff out there. And if we put all that in the computer it can work out where Planet Nine is – or where it must have been before, and where it is going now.

So we know that right now it is about seven hundred times as far out as Earth is from the Sun, although it probably loops around in a big ellipse: it comes further in, it goes further out, and it takes about twenty thousand years to complete one orbit around the Sun. And as it passes it tweaks and twangs the orbits of small objects that we can see.

And that's also how we know how big it is, by the way – ten times the mass of Earth, we think. And when I say 'big' I just mean how massive, not how wide. If it's a rocky planet like Earth, it will have about twice Earth's diameter. If it's not a rocky planet – and it may well not be, given we haven't seen it after centuries of searching – well, all bets are off . . .

A lot of that made not much sense to Salma, as she grew up, never having seen Earth, or walked on it.

For another thing, for a long time she didn't know what a 'bet' was.

But she got the essence. That this thing was *big*, and they were steadily sailing out to find it — or at least going to where they thought it must be, as most of the adults said to her more cautiously.

Although she was never sure *why* they had come so far to find Nine. When Salma asked Meriel about that, she suggested Salma read a book called *Moby-Dick*.

With time, and with the precisely scheduled mission unrolling through its slow stages — and as she grew herself — Salma's attention started to veer away from the unfathomable mysteries of the universe beyond the curved walls of the enclosures that confined her, and away from the bunch of adults who all treated her with faultless kindness — and towards the mechanics of the craft in which she lived.

After all, Planet Nine was a dry abstraction; you could *touch* the stuff of the ship, and (under suitable supervision) you could even tinker with it. The others encouraged this. As Boyd said, 'Somebody's going to have to fix the plumbing when the rest of us are in our basket chairs.'

So she had started to learn about engineering, or at least about the engineering of the faithful *Shadow*.

And it soon struck her how apt that name was.

She saw images of the more brutal, heavy craft of Earth, and the Moon miners' freighters. They were mostly huge, mostly ungainly collections of cylinders and spheres, mostly pushed here and there by the power of nuclear fission: ferocious energies released by the consumption of irreplaceable resources, on Earth and in space.

By contrast the *Shadow* complied with the Conservers' basic philosophy that you should consume the absolute minimum possible of the resources of Earth, the wider Solar System — even the Sun – while achieving your goals. The ultimate dream was to use nothing that was useful for other purposes at all – to live off sunlight, and the slow rain of comets wandering into the Solar System from beyond even the Oort cloud, from deep interstellar space.

So, four decades after the fact, Salma had studied the unique commissioning, design, building and launch of a ship with a touch as light as a shadow's.

Constructed mostly of that waste asteroid material, the ship's main hull was a block with, Salma had been oddly pleased to learn, about the same mass as the old ISS – the International Space Station, the first purpose-built multinational station to orbit the Earth, although *Shadow*'s expansive, thin-walled, inflated modules offered a lot more leg room.

And, like the ISS, the *Shadow* gained much of its power from sunlight – and, in the case of the *Shadow*, its motive force too.

Even now, seven hundred times as far from the Sun as Earth, the collecting area required to supply sufficient solar energy for the ship's systems was only a few kilometres in diameter. From the beginning that solar energy sustained the ship's bubble of life – the raw, focused sunlight to grow onboard crops, a conversion through light-collecting panels to make electricity for heating, cooling, air cleansing, water purification.

And, more spectacularly, that solar capture area was embedded in a much wider sail, for it was solar propulsion too that had driven the whole craft out into deep space.

A relatively friendly Earth government had allowed the craft to complete its assembly in a high orbit of Earth, with the 'loan' of some resources purchased from the Moon: a few hundred tonnes of aluminium and other products from Moon rock and dust, even some of the Moon's precious water, to assemble and provision it.

47

Relatively friendly: Salma learned that the Earth authorities had no great love for the Conservers, but the simple fact that they weren't Moon miners made them worth cultivating. Hild would say that Earth's support for the *Shadow* project was, in fact, a cynical ploy to manipulate possible long-term allies. But the Conservers took those gifts just as cynically, it seemed to Salma, looking back at those times. She wondered if she would have made the same choices, had she been around then.

The six crew members of the *Shadow*, carefully selected from a wider pool of volunteers, had been smart, educated, well informed and healthy – or they had been at launch. Later they liked to debate the ethical compromises made by Earth and Conservers that had led to the creation of their ship, and as she grew older they had used such debates as a learning exercise for Salma, their only child. In life, she was taught in those sessions, you for ever had to make compromises with your values to achieve greater goals.

Well, however it was funded and resourced, however morally compromised, the *Shadow* was built.

Then, in the year 2220, a punch from a small nuclear stage had knocked the completed *Shadow* out of Earth orbit and into the first leg of its long, complicated journey.

The nuke was quickly discarded (and retrieved for use elsewhere). From now on, renewables only. In particular, the ship would sail into deep space on the light from the Sun – but, at first, it would sail *towards* the Sun, and not away.

After the launch, Salma learned, at first the craft had spiralled inwards, reaching a minimum distance from the Sun of about a third Earth's orbital radius after the first year's travel, holding up its solar-energy capture sail like a shield. And *then* the great propulsive sail was opened – this one with a radius nearly six times that of the energy capture sail, some forty kilometres across. Light exerted a measurable force, even on the palm of a hand held up to Earth's sunlight. Now this immense sail trapped enough light from the close-in Sun to push the ship at an acceleration of about three per cent of Earth's gravity.

The final dive into the Sun's gravity well was conducted as an 'Oberth manoeuvre', a tactic evidently used from the earliest days of spaceflight. At closest approach, the craft 'stole' some kinetic energy from the Sun in those brief moments when ship and star were coupled through the Sun's gravity. And after a day of this the ship shot out of the Sun's deep gravity well at a speed of more than a hundred kilometres per second – more than three times Earth's own orbital velocity.

All of this was a classic Conserver tactic, Salma had learned. Thanks to Oberth, the *Shadow* had needed only a little sunlight, a little of the Sun's enormous fund of radiative and orbital energy.

Salma was never sure she fully understood any of this. Anyhow it had evidently worked.

After that, as the ship sped away from the Sun and inner System with its new, enormous velocity, as Hild and her crew had grown steadily older – as Salma waited to be born – the milestones were reeled off: three months to pass Jupiter's orbit around the Sun, Saturn's in six months, Neptune's in two years – three years to the outer edge of the Kuiper belt. And at last, after a full thirty-five years, to reach the computed position of Planet Nine.

On arrival they had managed to slow into orbit around Nine with an Oberth manoeuvre in reverse, effectively giving Nine a little of the ship's kinetic energy. (To get away, Salma knew – if they chose to return to the inner Solar System at all – this crew of Conservers could cheat a little, sacrificing some of the mass of the sail to create a small fission rocket.)

And now here they were.

Salma knew that some of the adults were surprised that there had been no further effort from Earth (or Moon) to send a faster, if more wasteful craft to overtake the *Shadow* and claim the prize. She got the sense that in an inner System full of political turmoil and fast interplanetary industrialisation, such abstractions as distant Planet Nine were irrelevant. Which wasn't to imply, cynical old Boyd would say, that if Nine turned out to be made of diamonds, or better yet helium-3, the inner civilisations would not come chasing out to seize it.

In the end, though, Salma had always been more interested in where this ship onto which she had been born was going, rather than how it had got there – or where it had come from. Earth's federal government, the Lunar Consortium and the factional politics of mankind: these were all just words to Salma, without emotional content. Even the cautious creed of the Conservers themselves, into which she had been born, left her unmoved. She knew this was a kind of personal flaw; but at twenty years of age she was growing up to suspect that it was probably a necessary outcome of her peculiarly isolated upbringing.

For better or worse she was more interested in what was out there in the universe than in what was in people's heads. Just because she didn't know many people.

So she had deliberately studied what she could of Planet Nine long before the slow, final, agonising crawl to this position, a high orbit about the object.

Which was turning out not to be what they had expected.

'What a mystery,' Hild had said, going through the first observations. 'We were right to come, though. As we said all those years ago, *We've got to get a ship out there . . .*'

6

'We've got to get a ship out there,' Doria Bohm said. 'A ship from here, from the Moon, out to Planet Nine before Earth gets there. We just have to. Or at least to Saturn so we have cards in the game *there*. All that helium-3. And meanwhile those Conservers found a planet-mass black hole! Why, we could build a whole technological civilisation around that one thing. Just throw stuff in and pow! Catch the white-hot debris . . .'

Which was a sentiment Matt Kord shared, more or less. But the aspiration wasn't realistic, even if a capable ship had been available on the Moon, which it wasn't.

And Kord, who as 'Resource Coordinator' was the nearest thing to a head of this semi-independent colony under the Moon's Sea of Tranquility, had a zillion better things to do than argue about Planet Nine – mostly tangling with Earth's endless multinational and interplanetary politicking and commercial manoeuvring. And he might have demurred altogether if he'd known this conversation was going to be about more madcap missions to the edge of the Solar System.

But then, Moon-born Doria Bohm, twenty-three years old, was a nascent rebel who had a voice among the young here, and he was a sixty-nine-year-old Earthborn who probably didn't look like a rebel to anyone, even himself. So Doria had to be indulged.

'We just *have* to find a way to get a piece of the action,' she said now, and reeled off reasons why, in a highly articulate, high-speed peroration.

Kord just waited. He had become good at listening with half of his aged brain while analysing, assessing with the other. Let her get it off her chest, he told himself. Only react to something substantial.

When she ran down, briefly, he butted in, not harshly.

'What can we do about it? I understand the dream, Doria. I really do. But you have to see the bigger picture.'

With an angry gesture, Doria grabbed a bag of water from a dispenser, held it up, and squirted the water into the air, a transient low-gravity stream that she caught neatly in her mouth without spilling a drop.

Kord suppressed a sigh. Still essentially a creature of Earth, he would never be able to pull stunts like that.

She was looking back at him. 'What "bigger picture"? I just spent the afternoon arguing with some go-between flunky about why our shipments of nitrogen from Earth are being cut, *again* . . .'

'That *is* the bigger picture. And nitrogen is the key to the interplanetary politics of the Solar System. For now, anyhow.' *Until helium-3 becomes the issue*. He waved a hand. 'Because you need nitrogen to buffer the air that you breathe, and sustain the plants you grow in your life support cycles . . . And the Moon has none.

'Look at it from Earth's point of view. Historically, you know, at first Earth did allow some limited exports of nitrogen and its compounds from its own atmosphere, to supply the Moon and the other colonies, the free-flying space habitats. But for a long while now there has been a ban on such exports.'

She snorted. 'Because of "environmental impacts on Earth".'

'Yes. That's valid enough. The rationale was to protect the environment of Earth itself from the effects of multiple space launches, atmosphere scoop-mining, high-speed re-entries and so on. A lot of heat *was* being dumped into the environment. Earth's air can literally burn under a fast craft's heatshield – *nitrogen* will burn, ironically, leaving you with various toxic compounds. All that is history.

'But there was a political background to the ban as well. Or an ideological one. Even by 2100 or so there had been threats to Earth from space – criminal gangs or rogue nations would threaten just to dump massive objects onto the planet, artificial meteorites that could cause a lot of damage if they hit the ground. Later there was one ambitious plan to divert a near-Earth object, a whole small asteroid, onto a collision course. It came to nothing, but people learned.

'People on Earth, that is.

'The mood shifted, with space being seen not as a resource, not as some wonderful arena of adventure, but as a source of threat. Or at best a dangerous place to retrieve valuable goods from. Like an unstable gold mine.'

'Gold is cheap—'

'Just a metaphor,' he ploughed on. 'Short term, space defences were beefed up. Longer term, the mood towards supporting the establishment of new off-world colonies turned hostile. And an easy way to impose control of such colonies, and to contain the growth of existing colonies, was to keep a tight control on nitrogen, among other essentials. Which meant, in particular, putting the squeeze on *us*.'

'And now we're threatening Earth again, are we? Us, a new generation of miners. With our sharper teeth.'

'Well, maybe,' he said dubiously, not wishing to provoke her any further. 'It might look like that, to *them*. All we can do is react to Earth's latest moves.'

'Moves such as blocking us from Ceres, and the gas giants and their moons . . . Never mind nitrogen. As far as the helium-3 trade is concerned, it's their turn to try a home run to Saturn . . . Did I use that idiom correctly?'

He nodded grudgingly. 'Not quite.'

'Economically that would shut us out completely. And now there is this complication of Planet Nine too. Whatever the Conservers have found out there, whatever opportunities and risks it poses for our future. Earth means to take it all, that's clear . . .'

'What can we do about it? This is the Moon. We're a mining colony. We don't have huge interplanetary liners like the *Cronus*. We don't even have a slow deep-space craft like the Conservers' *Shadow*. All we have are our rock-hopper surface craft, and a few Moon-Earth freighters . . . much loved as that battered old fleet may be . . .'

But with scarcely a breath she launched back into her case.

While Kord distracted himself by thinking about spaceships.

Of which the most modern and impressive on the Moon, to his own ageing eyes, was the *Aquila*, a graceful hundred metres long, spinning end over end in flight to create artificial gravity, carrying its loads of lunar aluminium, uranium – and, especially, precious helium-3 – to Earth orbit.

But even *Aquila* had been designed, to his understanding, to reach no further than the asteroid belt – and, given Earth's embargoes, it would probably never even get that far. Certainly not out to the giant planets and their resource-laden moons and their own heavy, resource-rich atmospheres.

But here was Doria Bohm, who seemed to be making a case for some kind of dash out to Saturn, chasing the *Cronus* – a mission which itself, by the way, was linked to the Conservers' discovery of Planet Nine, whatever the hell *that* was. Making her case by shoving her way into his subterranean office without an appointment. Well, what case? He had yet to grasp it, but no doubt he soon would.

Bohm, Moon-born, young as she was, was forceful, relentless. Whereas Kord had been born long ago on Earth, and so had his stomach, and, increasingly, neither of them relished being reminded of how far they were from the home world's comforting ground, its enfolding one-gravity field.

By profession Kord was a mineralogist, and had found a perfect fit on the Moon, in some ways, a world of little *but* minerals. Such was the churn of staff, though, through low-gravity medical issues, confinement and a general sense of demoralisation, that he had eventually found himself the last one left on the Moon of his own generation of lunar scientists and prospectors – and had been given the job of Consortium director, since, it seemed, nobody else would take it.

He had never had aspirations to lead, in this organisation or any other. In a job he never wanted, he liked to feel he'd been conscientious, if not always as competent as he'd have hoped for.

But now he had to listen to Doria, because Doria was the future, he told himself. Doria, and the generations who had mostly been born on the Moon, unlike their parents, grandparents. Young as she was, she was impressively forceful, he thought. And just as he often felt pulled back to Earth, so she seemed to be pulled outwards . . .

Quite possibly she was right that the anomaly that was Planet Nine, let alone helium-3 caches in the outer Solar System such as at Saturn, were all part of that outward future too. If only such things could be reached. And legally mined.

But, whatever the validity of her argument, to Kord, Doria was utterly intimidating. Aside from the force of her personality

– apart from the striking face, the sharp jaw, the intent blue eyes, the neat stubble of black, shaven hair – she had a whip-thin frame, muscular yet tall, typical of those born on the Moon with its one-sixth of Earth's gravity. After nearly three centuries of human spaceflight hard lessons had finally been learned in how to cultivate the human body in such conditions. And Doria Bohm had been brought up as expertly as anyone he had ever met on the Moon.

She was the future, he reflected glumly. Probably no human being existed, or had yet existed, better adapted to off-Earth conditions than Doria and her generation. He supposed he envied her, in a dull, cloddish way, even as he attempted to deal with her, and the shadowy factions in lunar society that she represented. While Matt Kord – pale and bloated, born on Earth, at sixty-nine more or less exactly three times Doria's age – represented the past.

Maybe it would be different if he had been that bit older still, one of the true pioneers of the exploitation of the Moon: one of the first 'miners', as they had been called even back then, who were now the subjects of dramas of heroic pioneering days, of battles with an unforgiving nature. *That* was the quasi-legend that had drawn him out here himself as an idealistic youngster.

He supposed he had been atypical in staying around as things slowly soured, as the global Earth government's relations with its lunar pioneers became harsher, with excessive control and punitive taxation. An exploitative relationship in all but name. But legally justifiable because, in Earth's eyes, the Moon's riches, like all the resources of space, *belonged* to nobody.

Such resources were to be regarded as a common benefit – evidently a philosophy and legal principle descended from early space law, in turn derived from the centuries-old law of the sea. Which meant in practice that the resources of deep space, including essentials for living such as water, even that most precious of fusion fuels helium-3, even before they were extracted, *belonged by right to Earth* – or at least to mankind as a whole – and ought to be dedicated to supporting the sedentary culture of Earth and all its billions. You could be paid for the labour of digging it up, but Earth didn't *buy* helium-3 and the rest, as it owned it already. Legally.

While all the time the descendants of the first miners bred and swarmed and explored their way across the face of the Moon, and chafed against the political and commercial constraints that resulted in resources needed for growth up *here* being sent back to prop up a bloated society down *there*.

More recently all this had come into a sharper focus. Doria was a leading figure in a newly rebellious faction of lunar folk, mostly younger citizens. Younger miners who pushed even against older miners, who had once seen themselves as rebels. Even now he half-listened to her continuing and quite eloquent monologue on the inequities of the modern social set-up.

But in the longer term the real problem, as Kord was in a position to know better than anybody, was the sheer *smallness* of the Moon, at least in economic terms. Its poverty. No matter how you bought or sold it. The Moon itself had been created in the aftermath of a tremendous primordial collision between Earth and another protoplanet during the formation of the Solar System. An accident like that tended to drive out any volatiles before the remnants even cooled down. So there was hardly any lunar water. What little there was, a residue of later comet impacts, was scattered thin through the regolith and gathered in Shackleton and other permanently shadowed craters at the lunar poles.

There were treasures to be had here: uranium to be mined in Copernicus Crater, for example, at a density of a relatively rich hundred parts per billion of the regolith, the Moon's impact-gardened soil. The greatest treasure of all was helium-3, the optimal fusion fuel. The richest lunar deposits of that were found, alongside Apollo footsteps, in the Sea of Tranquility — but even these offered only *four* parts per billion of helium-3 in that dust — a tiny fraction even of the already low uranium density. To get a useful cargo load you had to strip-mine the regolith down to three metres and across square kilometres, creating scars you could see from space, or even from Earth with binoculars.

But despite the wailing about that ugliness, Earth hypocritically welcomed the helium-3, a vital isotope for its power plants, and imported all it could, paying a pittance for the labour of the lunar colonists. For now.

Meanwhile leaving the lunar colonists themselves with nothing but low-power fission engines to sustain their habitats and drive their ships, most of them slow freighters shipping aluminium and other products to Earth orbit.

Miners and their families living in hovels constructed largely of lunar rocks and dirt, because they couldn't spare the water to make decent bricks, even.

Thus the romance of space.

At the back of his head Kord always remembered that the Moon would offer such meagre treasures for only a few more centuries before even marginally accessible useful resources would be depleted — leaving much of the regolith ploughed up in great trenches and fields that would be visible from Earth for a million years.

And quite possibly the Moon had less of an economic future even than that, since Earth had already set up a trial plant at Saturn, so the rumours went, that could sift out helium-3 from that huge world's atmosphere. When that treasure could be returned safely, and in huge quantities, from Saturn direct to Earth, when that supply chain started operating, what then for the Moon?

Still Doria spoke, reiterating now over-familiar arguments.

And he found himself staring, distracted, at a pendant she wore at her neck: a disc of what looked like lunar glass, a kind of obsidian perhaps, volcanic, smoothed, polished. Her one adornment; he'd noticed it before. Was this some kind of statement of identity? He didn't remember such a thing being worn by anybody else . . .

He tried to focus.

The problem was, when it came to views about this situation, of the two of them in this box of an office it was Doria Bohm who was by far more representative of the population of the human Moon as a whole. Unfortunately that also meant that Doria's impatience and aggression – her lack of judgement, as he saw it, despite her sharp intelligence – was typical of an increasing percentage of the electorate. Whereas Matt Kord – fat, old, his body Earth-bred but much abused by too much space travel – still, like it or not, represented much of what wisdom there was to be had among the Moon's inhabitants.

He didn't feel his authority was threatened. Not quite yet. Give her a few more years, a little more of the power she seemed to have accrued among her peers already – the mail-bombing he had received about meeting with her to discuss this project was testament to that. *Some day you will have to stand against me in an election*, he thought, studying her as she spoke. *Even our primitive, this-isn't-Earth lunar constitution puts limits on the terms of people like me, and my powers. And yours in the future. Then we'll see whose judgement wins out, generation rivalry or not. We aren't there yet*, he told himself. *But for now . . .*

Now she faced him.

Here it comes. The proposition. What all this has led up to.

'Look,' she said. 'I think we agree on the situation. The real reason for me coming here to see you is to tell you we've decided to do something about it.'

He'd known this was coming – or at least, that something was. *Brace yourself, Matt.*

'Who is "we" . . . ? Never mind. So what is it *specifically* you wanted this meeting for?'

She looked irritated, but shrugged. 'Specifically, to let you know we've been refitting the *Aquila*. Refitting for a new mission.'

That gave him pause.

The colony's most up-to-date and useful freighter, mostly dedicated to transferring cargoes to and from low Earth orbit . . .

He suppressed a frown. Suppressed a snap back: *You did this without my permission, even my knowledge?* He let that go, for now. He needed facts.

'What mission?' He made a stab in the dark. 'Ceres. You're here to talk about Ceres, right? Any such mission would break Earth's embargo – you know that.'

She shook her head, and sounded almost diplomatic. 'Not Ceres. Bigger than that. We always intended to show you it all first – hell, to give you the final decision as to its deployment, or otherwise.'

'Kind of you. The deployment of *what*?'

She shrugged. 'It's simple enough. Earth is trying to keep the Solar System bottled up. Yes? But *now we know about Planet Nine.* Nobody knows for sure what it is yet, but it appears to be a massive, energetic object. Who knows what we could make of that? A game-changer—'

He nodded. 'Maybe. Yes, the potential could be huge. But the Conservers found the thing, they're on top of it now . . .'

'Sure,' she said. 'But the Conservers won't *do* anything with it, will they?'

'Perhaps not. I admit I never really understood their programme . . . But right now it's not the Conservers you're worried about, is it?'

'No, it's not. We're worried about the *Cronus*. Earth.'

Again he had heard hints about this. '*Cronus*. Earth's super-freighter, on the way to Saturn—'

'And launched since the Planet Nine news broke. Limping along on its fission drive, but it will get there in a few years.'

'And then?'

'And then . . . You've heard the rumours, you know as well as I do. They already have a pilot helium-3 extraction plant at Saturn, right?'

He hadn't heard anything beyond that. But he now put it together quickly. 'Oh. I get what you're thinking. And then, *what if they already have a helium-3 fusion drive*? Much more capable, much faster . . .'

'Such drives have been on the drawing boards for decades. Centuries? But nobody had the helium-3 to spare. Saturn offers that. And there are rumours that Earth is close to such a drive.'

'I hadn't heard that.'

She shrugged. *I had.*

A small triumph for her, he saw.

'So, you see the strategy. The news breaks of the existence of Planet Nine. The *Cronus* dashes out to Saturn, refuels there with helium-3 – *and then on to Planet Nine*,' Doria said. 'Taking years, I guess, rather than the decades of that Conserver sail-ship. And the decades our own best fission-powered ships, like the *Aquila*, would take.'

He was stunned; suddenly he understood what she and her allies had perceived. What he should have perceived. And they were right. Thus Earth would requisition the greatest mystery in the Solar System, and whatever wonders flowed from it.

On to Planet Nine . . .

He nodded, grudgingly. 'You have a point. Talk about a hegemony. Whoever owns all *that* could end up with the control of an emperor – you could shut out others from alternate sources, even the other gas giants. What a play to make.'

'That's the long view. But even from the start, when Earth starts shipping home Saturn's helium-3 on a large scale, with *Cronus*-sized freighters—'

'It's the end of us.'

'An economic assassination. I can show you the scene of the crime from this window . . .' She turned to a control panel.

And a wide stretch of grey wall turned transparent. Doria, impatient, messed with the smart window's settings until the star fields came clear. At first he could see little, a scattering of stars, shining above the dusty horizon of the Moon.

She pointed. 'This is the constellation of Sagittarius.'

He shrugged. 'Is it? I was never an astronomy buff as a kid, ironically. Even though my parents chided me about how much clearer Earth's air was than when *they* were kids, after the climate restoration programmes—'

Doria brushed that away. 'See those star clouds? You're looking towards the centre of the Galaxy, as it happens.'

He squinted. 'And there's that odd red spot at the centre. Has anybody got a handle on that yet? I heard something about an anomalous heat flow coming out of there . . .'

She ignored that question too. 'And the bright star over here—'

'Not a star. A planet, I'm guessing. Saturn?'

'Right. Where *Cronus* will be on its way soon. And beyond, much deeper into space, not visible to us, is Planet Nine. Happens to be neatly lined up just now – Earth, Saturn, Nine, Galaxy. 'She laughed, bitterly. 'So the *Cronus* crew will actually have a head start. A start on sewing up the whole damn future of mankind, as they have done the past.'

Kord tried to focus. 'And you're the genius who's going to fix all that, are you? You and your covert cohort.'

She seemed irritated at that. 'You want to hear our proposal, or not?'

'I need to, I'm guessing.' He asked more gently, 'What do you intend to do, Doria?'

'We're already doing it.'

She tapped the smart window again.

The star-field picture dissolved to reveal what Kord recognised as a loose construction jig, a frame of girders and lines, floating in space.

This was a now venerable space construction technique: you used the jig to line up a large assembly quickly and accurately in the microgravity of space. The detail of the craft or structure being assembled within this particular jig, constructed first, was hard to make out: a rough cylinder, with two massive sections connected by a spine, reinforced with a framework of triangular struts . . .

Suddenly he recognised the basic layout. 'Of course. That's *Aquila*! Why am I seeing this? What's that in the hold? Oh . . . Propellant tanks, right? She won't be able to carry much like that, but she can go a long, long way . . .'

She grinned. 'The fact is, although we only have a fission drive here – uranium fuel, hydrogen propellant – right now we can match the performance of the *Cronus*, to Saturn at least. Because *Cronus* hasn't got its helium-3 drive up and running yet. All it can do is follow a minimum-energy trajectory out that far. Six years. We can match that. And we will. In *Aquila*, we are going to match *Cronus*, and Earth.'

He nodded cautiously, trying to pry out the logic. 'So you track *Cronus* to Saturn. And then?'

'And then – well, we'll see what's what. At least we'll be a player in the game, as the whole of humanity's future pivots. What do you think of that?'

I think I'm as scared as hell.

Looking at her, his eye was distracted by that lens of lunar obsidian at her neck, like a third, wide-open pupil.

And he thought back to the Sagittarius image, that strange red light at the heart of the Galaxy, another inhuman eye that seemed to peer back at him.

He was bewildered. And Doria's faction already had *Aquila* set to go.

He, it seemed, had no control over what was to follow.

'So,' he said. 'What next?'

She seemed taken aback. 'I guess we find us a pilot.'

7

About a month after the arrival of the *Shadow* at Planet Nine, after several ship's days of observation and analysis – and one final sleep period – nominal captain Hild Kanigel called two of her six-strong crew to the habitable core's science deck.

Once more facing the anomaly, displayed on screens and other readouts, that they still called, simply, Nine: Salma, Boyd Hart, and herself. She knew the rest of the crew would most likely be listening in.

She quickly summarised her strategy since receipt of the two Hawking signals from Nine: the original Hawking radiation, and the modified output they'd started to receive after Salma had echoed back the first.

And, Hild said, she had already backed off *Shadow* to a safe distance. And she had ensured that the ship's escape pod stroke planetary lander was readied, tested, fuelled. This was a wasteful throwaway rocket with the ability to get the crew away from any imminent ship-wide disaster. Wasteful, yes, breaking Conserver minimum-energy protocols, but to save lives a pragmatic fallback, and thus acceptable. So she had options to escape – or explore.

Depending on what she decided to do next.

Whether to continue to probe this strange situation, to explore it.

Whether to go further, to reply to the second. Hawking set — whether to bathe the black hole with their carefully prepared, if bland, message of welcome, prepared by Salma, based on an elaborate echo of Nine's second, more complex emission, encoded with the help of comms guy Joe into the spectral characteristics of fake Hawking radiation.

Whether or not to act at all, for the present.

Whether to leave it until whatever ships from Earth or elsewhere came crowding out. Nobody favoured that.

At such moments of decision, Hild had a habit of picking out one or two crew for a focused session of input, opinion, advice, as relevant. The crew knew this. This time she had chosen Salma and Boyd for this moment.

Salma herself, who had done so much to observe the object and to divine its nature — well, to guess at it anyhow.

And Boyd, the oldest of the crew and most experienced, a sort of mirror image of Salma.

Though right now, Hild saw, Salma was barely paying attention. She was looking at the display screens arrayed under the bubble-window of this cramped chamber, screens which showed images of Nine in various wavelengths, along with analyses ranging from the latest estimates of the object's mass, size, spin rate, to very fine recordings of the complex, evidently information-rich signals still leaking out of that rotation-distorted event horizon.

Absently, Salma fingered the black pendant at her neck.

She looked so immature, Hild thought, not yet grown, and surely too inexperienced to even guess at the consequences of what they were meddling with out here. But then, none of them could guess that. And for now at least, Salma was staying calm enough.

Hild spoke to her directly. 'Let me sum up where we are, and why we're here. Salma, I've brought you in because you are the youngest of us all, with the freshest perspective, maybe – and the longest life to live ahead of you in a world that's about to change for all of us. Change for good, I hope, but change anyhow, like it or not. Also you have done more than the rest of us to divine the nature of this thing – a black hole leaking information in its Hawking radiation—'

'Or anyhow that's what it looks like,' Salma said, distracted.

'Fair enough. And Joe and Salma have worked up a package of reply signals, correct? Beyond simple echoes, like our first reply.'

Joe's voice and image were relayed by the comms system. 'Listening in.'

Joe Normand – head and shoulders showed a stocky frame, a shaven head – was their comms specialist, as well as a generalist on most of the ship's systems save life support and propulsion.

Hild said, 'About those signals—'

'Ready to go. Not simple echoes, of course. We can't produce Hawking radiation, not without a black hole of our own, but we have prepared a package of electromagnetic signals from X-ray down to far infra-red. Patterns to match the Hawking radiation structure, where the wavelengths make it practical. And our strongest signal is in our own radio wavelengths, hopefully a clue as to how we prefer to communicate ourselves. As to content, for now we are simply reflecting back much of whatever information content Nine's own signal contains, along with additional material – number sequences, attempts at pictorial representations. Of us, the Solar System, with Nine at the periphery . . . I'm imagining this will be just the start, if it wants a dialogue. Other than that—'

'Yes, I know, I've been following your reports, and you've evidently done a good job.'

Boyd said gruffly, 'Well, that's yet to be proved—'

'Goes without saying,' Hild broke in. 'But I said it anyhow. As for you, Boyd . . .'

'I'm here to supply grumbles and put-downs?'

Over seventy, Boyd was the oldest member of the crew — older indeed than the Conserver movement itself, of which he had been a founder member, Salma knew. He had been born and bred in the culture of old Earth, and while he had never been a prominent media voice, he was a pioneer Conserver, a key contributor of ideas and structural proposals as the nascent movement had slowly self-assembled, in reaction to the rapid expansion of industry and trade into the Solar System. For all his bluff old-guy exterior, he was a thinker, one of the deepest in the crew.

And on this mission, he was senior enough to have acted as a kind of surrogate wise old senior officer, or maybe grandfather, to the younger crew. Especially to Salma herself, born and raised during the long journey of the *Shadow*.

Which was why Hild valued him so much, Salma knew. That and the fact that he knew so much more than she did, about so many subjects.

But it didn't pay to flatter him.

Hild said to him now, 'Experience can't hurt. Also you're a generalist.'

Boyd just shrugged. 'Don't make me blush. Do what I can. Glad to be here. You do know the rest of the crew want to be in here, whatever the outcome? I'd be banging on the door myself.'

Hild frowned, and glanced over tell-tale displays. 'Well, happily, the other three are staying where I ordered them to stay. The backup hydroponic banks still need de-sludging, by the way, Meriel, when you've time.'

Salma saw in a monitor how Meriel reflexively touched the

pendant on a choker at her throat: white cloth, a disc of polished black stone, just like Salma's.

And now Meriel snapped back, 'Shouldn't I be in that conference with you? I am the nearest you have to a doctor, or a biologist, or even an exobiologist. *What if there is life out there?* On Nine? What then?'

Hild couldn't have helped but entertain the idea, Salma thought.

Hild replied calmly. 'Maybe so . . . But it seems a long shot. Nine is a black hole, or something like it, complete with Hawking radiation, and that's pretty much all we know at this point. How can there be anything *living* connected to such a thing? And especially life as we might understand it—'

Boyd grunted. 'You mean life close enough to terrestrial life for Doc Breen to be useful with her potions and sticking-plaster?'

'I'm right here, you know,' Meriel Breen called in.

Hild went on, *'Life*. Maybe − but on the other hand I can't imagine what we're going to find in there anyhow. Doc, I can't visualise just yet how we're going to need you in that regard. Stick to the plumbing for now.' She glanced at Salma, with a grin. 'Salma, you're here for the insight you've already shown. Boyd for his experience and judgement − but why myself? Because the buck stops with me.'

'Wow,' Boyd said. 'What soap opera did you get that line from?'

'All this is my responsibility, below the authority of the Conserver council at the Outpost. Most of whom will be listening in to the log, most likely, in a few hours when the signal reaches them.'

'So no cussing,' Boyd said.

'So,' Hild ploughed on, 'given their oversight, ultimately it's my strategy, my decisions − my judgement about how we handle,

well, whatever we face here. You follow my orders. Especially if
what we encounter is something totally unexpected—'

'Hope so,' Salma said eagerly.

'*Especially* if we have to pull back out of whatever we encounter. All understood? All agreed?'

Murmured yeses from Boyd and Salma, more over the comms
system from Meriel Breen and the others, Joe Normand, even
Zaimu Oshima, propulsion guy.

'Then let's do this.'

And at a snap of her fingers the wall screens filled with images
and data.

8

Hild settled back in her chair, suspended at the centre of the science desk's big glass bubble, and spun slowly around, glancing over the various feeds.

Boyd, slower and stiffer, and Salma, young and eager but just a mite clumsy, turned too.

Before Salma now one large screen carried a real-time image of Planet Nine, relayed by close-in camera drones, heavily processed and enlarged – but nothing to see, nothing but a perfect sphere, perfectly black – to the naked eye anyhow. Only centimetres across. She knew that the black hole was in fact subtly flattened at the poles, an oblate spheroid, the event horizon distorted by the hole's spin. And then there were the mysterious patterns in the Hawking radiation, invisible to a naked human eye.

In addition there were images returned from free-flying drones, further out. Just in case something dramatic happened on a larger scale. All you could see of what those returned was star fields.

Ten Earth masses, crammed into an object, as Boyd had once observed, no larger than a human head. And now we dare to approach it, Salma thought. To challenge it. To roar back at the lion. Not that she'd ever seen a lion outside of downloads from Earth.

Hild snapped, 'Enough staring. Enough wonder. Enough awe. Time for science. Joe, can you confirm a comms lock back to the Outpost?'

'As well as the laws of physics allow,' Joe Normand called in, with his usual deep drawl.

And Salma knew what he meant, that the various systems were aligned, and signal pulses already sent would reach the Outpost three days later, limping out at lightspeed, pulses focused using panels of their vast solar sail as an antenna – all would reach home unless their status changed drastically.

'Propulsion?'

Zaimu Oshima called in briskly from the engine control deck. 'Ready to get us out of here if you say so, Hild . . . The landing pod is ready to go too.'

'Good. Stand ready. And, navigation . . .

Salma quickly consulted screens, systems, backup systems. 'All looks good.'

This was one of Salma's own specialities, and not a demanding one in the normal course of things, given the slowness of the craft, and the emptiness of the outer Solar System through which they had travelled. Even now it was a straightforward task, with the relative position of the ship and the target – Nine – observed, measured, triangulated against the Sun, distant stars and other landmarks routinely selected by the systems. Salma wondered vaguely if the smart automatics were learning to lock onto that red spot in Sagittarius – unmoving, as it turned out, over a number of days, so presumably a very distinct beacon . . .

She was wool-gathering. *Focus, Salma.*

'We are exactly where we should be,' Hild said now. 'Around a hundred and thirty thousand kilometres out from Planet Nine, for the sake of anybody who hears this when the signal arrives, wherever you are. Twenty Earth radii out . . . OK, Salma. It's time. Send your signal.'

Salma checked her monitors. 'Beam aligning. Ship's position steady, locking onto Nine . . .'

Salma herself was to be given the privilege of giving the final send command. She held her hand over the relevant console, trying not to tremble visibly.

'All right,' Hild said. 'Hold steady. Clock counting down from thirty seconds.'

Twenty Earth radii. Always they referred back to Earth for such comparisons, Salma had observed.

Salma wondered if this message, and recordings of the incident as a whole, would actually be passed on from the Conservers' Outpost to Earth itself – and maybe the Moon too, that other knot of a nascent extraterrestrial civilisation. Only after some kind of security deal, she imagined. She hoped so, she imagined so. Surely a situation like this, which might impact all of mankind – and for all time, if it did turn out to be some kind of exotic first contact – demanded openness from the start. For the consequences would surely be unending.

That was the way a Conserver thought, she knew – but perhaps not the way Earth or the Lunar Consortium would react, given their deepening rivalry over the future of the Solar System and its treasures of metals and water and nitrogen and fusion fuel. Was it best, then, that it was a Conserver ship that had found this anomaly? Perhaps it could *only* have been a Conserver ship, in this epoch anyway; the thinly scattered resources of the Oort cloud were not yet the focus of those growing, rival, materialistic cultures.

Nothing here for them, Salma thought. *Or so they believed. So only we came here, to the dark. And, lurking in that generous dark—*

On a screen, a digit turned to five, four, three . . .

'Two, one, lock,' Salma said briskly. She was still holding her hand over the contact pad. A deliberate gesture was required for such a grave moment, she knew. No chance of a misfire because of a poorly pronounced word, or a hesitant button-push . . . 'Permission to send the message?'

Boyd sighed. 'And with one touch of the finger of a twenty-year-old, the future will change irrevocably.'

Salma asked again. 'Commander?'

'Permission—'

Salma laid her hand flat on the terminal.

And even as she completed that motion the contact must have been made.

At lightspeed, Salma knew, it would have taken just two-fifths of a second for the signal, rich in emulation of the Hawking-radiation patterns, to cross the twenty-Earth-radii gap to Nine. Two-fifths of a second back, the minimum time for any response to be visible. Fragmentary intervals, over before Salma was even aware of them.

But. Nothing.

She was aware of everybody holding their breaths, Hild at her station, Boyd expertly scanning the various readouts and displays around the cabin. Watching, watching.

And when the change came, it was sudden.

'Shit,' Boyd Hart said.

Hild was out of her chair and at his station in a heartbeat. 'Tell me what you're seeing . . . Oh.'

Boyd stabbed at a screen, shared, enhanced and expanded his display with a stroke of stiff fingers. 'You know that before now we've been sending down radar pulses, just routine pings.

You get some echoes back from the ergosphere – you don't get reflections from the event horizon, but you get some of the ping energy being thrown back out at you, the photons coming back after a half-orbit around, or one and a half—'

'I understand. Not a reflection, but it works that way.'

'Yeah. Well, suddenly that echo interval is dropping. As if the hole, the event horizon and all the mess outside, is *expanding*. And uniformly.'

Hild stared. Then she snapped out, 'Go to one of the cloud drones. Further out.'

Boyd hit another screen.

And Salma saw what looked like an immense bubble, pitch black, spreading across the star fields. Briskly scattering the residual hot, ionised gases that had gathered in the black hole's gravity well. Spreading, growing rapidly; within seconds the drone's field of view was utterly obscured.

Hild snapped out orders. The free-flying drones pulled back fast, to enable them to see, to avoid being hit by that bubble – whatever it was.

'And this started . . .'

Boyd checked. 'Yeah, just as our message ping reached the event horizon. Umm. And the echoes are different too. It's reflecting more like a solid surface now, rather than a gravity well. Simpler echoes, less distortion, not the multiple orbits of light we saw before.' He glanced up at Hild. 'And it's still expanding. I guess we woke up the tiger.'

'Well, I've never seen a tiger. Zaimu, stand ready to get us out of here if you have to.'

Zaimu Oshima called back from his station at propulsion. 'Just say the word, Hild, checked and ready.'

Salma put in, 'Boyd's right that we've evoked a response, though.' She felt excited, even thrilled.

But Hild was worrying about her ship. 'Maybe. But since when did black holes *expand*? What's next? Let's just keep working, folks, monitoring, measuring, thinking . . . Expanding, you say. How fast?'

'Umm . . . around thirty kilometres a second now,' Boyd said. 'And pretty uniformly. A neat sphere.'

'And we are, what, a hundred and twenty thousand kilometres out? So that will take—'

'About an hour for the event horizon to reach us. If that surface still is an event horizon. At that rate. But I think it's already slowing.' Boyd's hands flew across his screens with remarkable precision, Salma thought. 'Modelling it . . . That horizon is a pretty sharp surface, and the speed curves are smooth. It looks like it will slow up at about three Earth radii, perhaps a little more. Slow to a halt . . .'

Hild glanced at his modelling. 'If you're right, it's going to settle down to that radius in, what, ten minutes?'

'About that. Fitting data points as we have them. Look, the prediction tracks are converging already . . .'

'He's right,' Salma called, excited, nervous. 'It's behaving itself. Whatever *it* is. And I'm studying the surface as it approaches. I seem to be seeing some kind of leakage radiation too. Less exotic. The Hawking signals and traces are still there, but the surface around the traces, and patches nearby, seems to be *glowing*. In the infra-red. Invisible to the eye, but—'

'Glowing like what?' Hild snapped. 'You need to give me more than that, Salma.'

Salma said, feeling baffled, 'I don't know what to report first. It's as if the effective surface temperature of the black hole – well, whatever this is, it's no black hole, not any more, not physically; the temperature of *Nine* – is climbing fast. I mean, it was close to absolute zero a few minutes ago, and now . . .'

Boyd was staring back at Salma. 'You say it's climbing fast. Bet you ten to one your curves are already levelling off.'

'I hadn't projected them that far. The data is patchy—'

'So's mine. Use what you have.'

'I . . . OK. Yes. The models haven't quite converged, but it looks like it's flattening at around—'

'Two eighty-eight Kelvin?'

'I was going to say three hundred. Around thirty Celsius . . . No, it's dipping below that . . .'

Boyd laughed, rubbed his face with one huge hand. 'Of course it is. Three Earth radii. It all fits. Let me know when it reaches two eighty-eight or so.'

Hild murmured, 'That number's familiar . . .'

'Space-dwellers ought to have it by heart.'

Hild scowled. 'This situation is spiralling out of control. Just tell us, Boyd, enough with the riddles. Have you figured out what's going on here?'

'I think so. This thing is *smart*. From the beginning, this black hole, whatever it is, has been *communicating* with us. The Hawking radiation patterns. We echoed them back, right? We don't know what it was saying, but that's our most basic way to say, *Here we are! We're listening!* We swapped signals. We announced our presence.

'So since then it – whatever this thing is, no simple black hole – has been tracking other signals, from the Conservers, the traders on the Moon. It's probably been monitoring us since it arrived here. And *Earth itself*, the loudest, brightest, hottest, noisiest of all. To an alien visitor, it's a fair bet that that would look like our origin world, don't you think?'

'I don't know what to think—'

'And now here we are, and it's – making us welcome.'

'Welcome?'

'Oh,' Salma said. 'I get it. Two eighty-eight Kelvin. Fifteen Celsius. *That's Earth's average surface temperature.*'

Hild frowned. 'Earth. Oh, wow. So it knows about Earth, and about us. I feel – I feel a deep conceptual shock unfolding, deep inside. Earth's temperature. OK. And this sudden expansion to three Earth radii—'

Boyd said, 'This black hole – no, this *Nine*, this artefact – masses ten times Earth. And a planet, or a planet-shaped body, with ten Earth masses and three Earth radii gives you—'

'One standard gravity at the surface, just about,' Hild said. 'Wow.'

'Newton could have worked that out,' Boyd growled. 'But the significance—'

'It's making us welcome,' Salma said slowly. 'We showed it where we come from – or gave it enough data to figure it out – and now it's inviting us in. The right gravity, the right surface temperature.'

'Not that welcome,' Meriel the doctor called in. 'No air down there. No sunlight, or anyhow not strong enough for photosynthesis – you couldn't sustain a biosphere. But, gravity and heat – it will be the second most comfortable place in the Solar System for humans, after Earth itself. You could land, safely. And it only just got here. Quite a stunt. And doesn't that tell us more?'

Hild frowned. 'Such as what?'

'Such as, *it wants us to land.*' That was Zaimu, calling in from propulsion. 'In case you haven't thought of it yet: the escape pod's well capable of landing down there, Hild. Since it's capable of landing on Earth. The gravity well is deeper but . . . Using a fission engine is a sinful lapse for us Conservers, but in the circumstances – the lander could go down there and bring me home. It's well capable of that, even without aerobraking.'

'"Me"?'

'Let *me* go,' Salma said immediately. She looked at Hild wildly. 'I'm the youngest. The most adaptable.'

Boyd snorted. '"Most expendable" would be a better argument.'

'Come with me, then, Salma,' Zaimu called in immediately. 'You may be expendable but you can't fly the pod.'

'Have you ever heard of automatics? All I'd need do is set a course—'

'And when the landscape on this chimera of a world changes again?'

'I just mean—'

Hild held up a hand. 'Shut up, both of you, and let me think.'

Boyd looked over at her. 'You have to send someone in. They're right about that. Come on, you can't refuse this invitation. It's first contact with extraterrestrial life, after all. The first contact with extraterrestrial *intelligence*. Evidently. And it's an obvious invitation.'

'Let him go down,' Salma said. 'And – let me go with him.'

Hild buried her face in her hands.

And elsewhere, elsewhen—

To smile was a human reflex.

Yet now, it could be said, Terminus smiled.

9

The debate was long and unproductive.

'You have to let us go,' Salma insisted.

'You *can't* let them go,' Meriel Breen, the doctor said.

'Nine is going to finish growing soon,' said wise old Boyd flatly. 'Need a decision soon, Hild.'

Hild looked to Salma as if she was starting to wish she'd stayed in her sleeping bag today. 'Tell me once more why you two must go down,' she said to Salma. 'If you can leave aside your youthful lust for adventure.'

Boyd snorted. 'Is that such a bad thing? From what I remember. And the youngest, most inexperienced *are* also the most expendable, if you want to be rational about it. Salma especially.

'Look, we have to do it for the science. This is a first contact with another intelligence. *Humanity's* first contact. What could ever top that? We could learn so much. An entirely different culture – maybe with an entirely different perspective on reality. A different biology. A different *science*. And we need to do it now, while we have the chance. This window could close any time—'

'A different biology. But that's why we *can't* go meet them,' Meriel called in. 'Not without strict controls. Maybe even at the most basic level of life, there may be conflict. I know biology, remember. I've read all about the mass extinctions of the past on

80

Earth – such as when the photosynthesisers started filling the air with oxygen, thus poisoning the billion-year-old anaerobic kingdoms that went before. Or when humans went sailing around the planet, unleashing rats and other pests that trashed more complex ecospheres – carrying plague vectors that wiped out whole nations without anybody even understanding what the hell they were doing. Look – if these people, using the word loosely, have gone to all the effort to access our universe, there must be something they badly want. And suppose that something is – *not us?*'

Hild nodded. 'Good points. So what would you have us do?'

'Seal up this place. The whole planet – whatever. Put a guard on it, until we know what, or who, we are dealing with. And what they want. Come back when we're ready, maybe decades from now, with a properly equipped expedition—'

'Come back with what?' Boyd said, sounding tired, Salma thought. He went on, 'Properly equipped when and how? Put a guard on this place – how? You know as well as I do how much effort it took us to get out here, in this paper-and-spit spaceship of ours. Are you going to wait for a battleship?'

But Salma had heard mutterings among the others that they had heard, via Conserver Outpost monitors, that Earth might in fact be assembling just such a battleship.

'And besides, we don't know what we're dealing with here; how could we know what to send that's better equipped than us?' Boyd shrugged. 'I think we need information above everything else. Caution be damned.' He added ruefully, 'If I were a few decades younger I would go down myself.'

Hild folded her arms, one of her ways of signalling that the discussion was done. She got a moment of silent consent. 'All right. Boyd – Meriel – do you think conditions down there are stable now, at least?'

Boyd checked. 'Stabilising anyhow. A neat one gravity, more

81

or less, a toasty fifteen Celsius. No air. Our first impressions seem to have been correct. *It is making us welcome*, I think. Based, presumably, on guesses from what it saw of Earth. You'll need pressure suits, but—'

'I see nothing immediately lethal,' Meriel said cautiously – perhaps reluctantly, Salma thought.

'Agreed,' Boyd said.

Hild called, 'Zaimu, how soon can the pod be prepped for the journey?'

'Already done, Commander.' Hild could hear the smile in his voice. 'Had it ready, just in case we needed to move fast.'

Salma could see Boyd grinning at that. Hild scowling.

And Boyd said, 'I've been a little forward too. I've continued to scan the surface. Most of it *is* featureless – save the stretched-out relic of the Hawking signal, but that's nothing more than a bump in the surface temperature, with no visible component. You won't even feel it.'

'Damn it,' Hild said. 'Doesn't anybody on this tub wait for my orders before doing what they feel like?'

'You have an efficient crew,' said Meriel, 'with enthusiasm and initiative. I want to put on record my objection to this jaunt. But I wish you two luck.'

Salma stared at Hild.

Hild crumbled. 'Oh, hell, go suit up. But I want Doctor Breen to check you over first, and your suits, before you set foot in that pod.'

When Salma had gone, Hild floated over to Boyd and put a hand on his shoulder. He felt frail, his muscles oddly soft.

'Just so you know. I know you'd have gone if I'd ordered it. Even though you're out of condition. Meriel tells me you skip your zero-g calisthenics—'

He shrugged. 'So what? It's a young person's game now, down *there*. I wish I was down there. But I accept your decision.'

She didn't believe a word. But she hoped he felt better at being left behind.

'Oh, this old man has found a landing site for them, by the way.'

She bent to see his displays. 'We can patch that into the pod's navigation systems . . . What site, though? I thought you said it was featureless, save for the—'

'Hawking relic radiation, yes. Until a few minutes back. Then one of our drones picked up this.'

He dragged an image across his screen, expanding it with stiff swipes. And he pointed. Hild had to bend down again to see.

It was a small blemish on an otherwise featureless plain. At first it looked like a rogue pixel, but as he expanded further – she imagined a drone buzzing ever lower towards the site – more pixels coalesced out of the smoothness, gathering into a symmetrical form – a *cylinder*, lying on the surface.

'Maybe two metres long,' Boyd said. 'One wide. Seems to be regular. But it also seems to be the only significant inhomogeneity on the whole damn planet.'

'Which isn't a planet,' Meriel called in from her station deep in the bowels of the craft. 'I'm looking over your shoulder. What do you think that is? Any guesses?'

Boyd shrugged. 'Some kind of container. Cargo?'

'And, Meriel? Your guess?'

'That's a cocoon. Or an egg.'

10

It took them a cautious six hours to set up the descent.

Then they left.

For Salma, sitting side by side with Zaimu Oshima in the cramped cabin of the pod, both sealed up in heavy-duty environment suits – there could be radiation threats, Meriel had warned them bleakly – the journey to the surface of the new expanded Nine was surreal.

'It's so smooth it's like a training sim,' Zaimu reported at one point during the descent. 'And a stripped-down sim at that. Flat plain below, nothing but stars outside . . . We do see your lights, *Shadow*.'

Looking back as they sailed away, Salma saw that the mother ship, with its gauzy sail and dim hull lights, was barely visible as a distortion of the stellar background. Its presence was a comfort even so.

And in fact the ship wouldn't stray far. Hild had ordered it placed in an orbit about a hundred thousand kilometres out from the planet's centre, around five radii of the new planet. Here, the ship was in a synchronous orbit above the landing site – where the 'cocoon' on the surface was – so as to track the site as the planet turned through its thirty-hour day. There ready in case the explorers needed a fast escape.

Meanwhile, Zaimu was guiding the little craft through its descent. 'That smooth, geometric surface down below. Like a sim. You almost expect it to light up with marker lines to tell you your target landing vector . . .'

Salma said, 'A smooth surface, and *that*.' Leaning forward so her face visor almost touched the pod's window, she pointed down to the one blemish on that abstract surface: the pod, the 'cocoon' that Boyd had seen from the ship. The smart window, helpfully following her gaze, picked out the blemish, lit it up with guide lines. To rendezvous with the blemish, all Zaimu had to do was hold his course as specified – and Salma knew he could switch over to fully automatic with a word.

About a hundred metres short of the blemish, Zaimu monitored the pod as the automatics took them down to a smooth landing. The thrusters, spewing out hydrogen propellant heated by the vehicle's compact fission reactor, kicked up no dust, Salma saw, no debris – this anomaly was surely the smoothest large body in the Solar System, if such a strange object, so far out from the Sun, counted as being in the System at all.

And as the lander descended further, Nine's size, or its current size, became evident, with the curved horizon flattening out, featureless, an exercise in perspective, on a sphere far larger than the Earth.

Salma barely felt the landing itself. Only a smooth, descending tone that told her the propulsion system was closing down.

They sat still, shared a look, took a few breaths.

And looked out at a flat, featureless landscape – featureless save for that one low mound-like form, the only bit of geography on this strange world. Beyond that, a sharp horizon. Was it visibly *flatter* than a similar scene on Earth itself? As if seen over an ocean, perhaps . . . But Salma, born aboard the *Shadow*, knew nothing of Earth save through simulations – and even Zaimu, an orphan, had been taken aboard the ship as a five-year-old child.

Zaimu gently elbow-bumped her. 'It's your show, kid.'

They didn't debate the order. Salma was first to seal her pressure suit, first to the airlock, first to exit, first to climb down the short ladder.

It was another experience evocative of endless training exercises, Salma thought, where you suited up, climbed in and out of mock-up airlocks, trying to ignore the pull of gravity. But here the gravity felt Earth-normal, as predicted, expected – even though Salma herself could only compare it to the simulated Earth-normal gravity of the tiny centrifuges aboard the *Shadow*.

But this was real. Salma, first ever to set foot on Planet Nine.

She stepped away from the lander, cautiously. The texture of the flat surface wasn't quite smooth, it seemed; she felt a grip under her booted feet.

Zaimu murmured, 'Focus, Salma. Report.'

'Right. I'm down. The gravity feels normal, Earth-normal. Or as normal as the centrifuges on the *Shadow*, I'm no expert . . . The surface feels – gritty. Rough. I can walk easily.'

'And I'm recording this thrilling moment of history,' Joe Normand, the comms guy, spoke dryly in her ear.

Zaimu was brisker. 'Let's get this done.'

Once Salma was out of the way, he jumped down the last few steps and onto the ground without ceremony. Then he made for the cargo pallet attached to the lander's base. He pulled on a tab to release the pallet, which folded itself down to the ground, small wheels touching the flat surface of this odd not-world. The most significant piece of gear aboard the pallet was an airtight shelter, of fabric and cord. The rest was survival gear: emergency oxygen, medical stuff, radio packs, a little food, water.

Once the pallet was down and assembled and had got its own

orientation, it rolled smoothly and silently across the surface of Nine towards the blemish – as Salma kept calling the anomaly on the surface, in her head.

As Salma and Zaimu followed, another small drone rolled across the surface behind them, capturing every movement – a wheeled, rocket-equipped drone prepared to go into emergency mode at any moment, on the ground or above, laden with cameras and first aid.

'Speak to us,' whispered Hild, in their ears.

'Huh? Saying what?' Salma snapped back as she walked.

'It's what explorers do when they achieve their goals. Be – historic.'

Salma and Zaimu exchanged a look. Shrugged. *Old-folk stuff.*

Salma said, 'OK. Hello, *Shadow*. We're fine, as you can see. The gravity feels Earth-normal – as our suit instruments tell us too. The suits are fine too, flexible, comfortable.'

'We commend the manufacturer,' Zaimu said.

'Skip the gags,' Hild murmured. 'Keep your focus.'

Salma said, 'It's just like a virtual training exercise, though not with this gravity.'

Meriel said, 'The suits have exoskeletal support if you need it—'

'We know,' Zaimu said. 'The ground – actually, as Salma said, it feels slightly rough, useful for walking over. The temperature—'

Salma glanced at a display inside her helmet. 'The ground is a balmy fifteen degrees or so, as predicted. Doesn't make much difference to us hikers, but I imagine it would if we pitched camp in some way.'

Meriel said now, 'It really is like Earth without the atmosphere.'

'So where does the heat come from?' Zaimu asked.

'I'm not sure,' Boyd put in. 'Obviously not sunlight. Not from ordinary planetary sources. Earth has left over heat from its formation, and heat from the decay of radioisotopes in its interior – this has a far higher intensity. Here, the ground heat is basically emulating the influx of energy from sunlight on the Earth. As if this is a night hemisphere, giving up the heat of the day.'

Zaimu laughed, perhaps a little hysterically. 'So they heated up the whole planet just for us!'

'Whoever *they* are,' Hild muttered.

'So it seems,' Boyd said calmly. 'As with the gravity. But it's not magic. With the right technology, it isn't so much. Just playing with the numbers here. I figure that with matter-antimatter technology, for example, you could heat this whole planet's surface to the same intensity with a cost of about twenty kilograms a second . . .'

'We are approaching the surface object,' said Zaimu.

So they were. But as they approached they could see it wasn't a simple cylinder.

Something else, then.

Salma and Zaimu stood side by side looking down at what, for all the world, close up, looked like a *coffin* to Salma, roughly shaped to fit the profile of a human body.

She felt oddly reluctant to move, to approach closer, let alone touch this thing.

'Like the pharaohs,' Boyd said in their ears. 'They had coffins like this, body-shaped, though they had their features painted on . . . Has to be more than that, though. Who would ship a corpse between universes?'

Hild murmured, 'And why a coffin that could fit a human?'

A brief silence.

'Come on,' Salma said. 'Let's do this thing, before we lose our nerve.'

'Pallet,' Zaimu said with an air of command. 'Shelter. Contain us and this – feature.' He pointed at the coffin.

Now the pallet rolled a little closer, and broke open, like some tremendous pale beetle opening its carapace, Salma thought.

Salma and Zaimu stepped back.

Out billowed a cloth-like material, pure white.

The cloth, like an unfurling sail, stiffened by internal ribs, swept up and over the two of them, over the coffin, descended to the ground on the far side.

Once the perimeter was settled, internal lights in the ribbing lit up, and Salma found herself enclosed in abstract whiteness. Just her, Zaimu – and a coffin from another reality. She shivered, and forgave herself for doing so.

There was a hiss of air.

'OK,' came Hild's voice. 'Can you see in there?'

'Like being in a white-out,' Zaimu said. 'But we see fine.'

'And – ah, we see you.'

There were button cameras everywhere: on their suits, in the shelter's inner surfaces, on the pallet.

Zaimu said, 'We can hear the nitrogen pumping in.'

'Good. Nice inert buffer, and expensive. Don't waste it. But you need to check your oxygen supplies before opening your suits. In fact, don't open your suits unless you need to.'

'We know the drill,' Zaimu said. He raised an eyebrow at Salma. *That was Hild all over.* 'Needless to say we are relying on the automatics to do their stuff—'

A sharp crack.

Zaimu, startled, shut up.

'Look.' Salma grabbed his arm, pointed. *'Look.'*

The featureless coffin was featureless no more. Now a dark

seam ran around the edge of the container, separating upper half from lower.

Nobody spoke, on the ship, on the ground. Salma and Zaimu just stood and stared.

After maybe a minute, Boyd Hart came on the line. 'I think the next step is obvious, guys. I think you need to open that damn thing. But try to get a sample of whatever's inside that box first. I mean the environment, any atmosphere—'

They exchanged glances.

Then they went to work, hastily improvising.

They wrapped the coffin in a lightweight plastic sheet that Salma shook out of one suit pocket, and added a backup air-quality sensor from a pocket of Zaimu's. Soon they had the coffin entirely sealed by the sheeting, with button-sized sensors carefully placed inside the wrap.

Another exchange of glances.

Zaimu said, 'Opening it is going to be tricky, through the wrap. But we ought to be able to push our gloved fingers into that crack in the coffin, under the lid, without breaking our seal.'

'Right.' Salma said. 'We open the coffin, but we don't break the wrap until the air sensor has given its report. Then when we're sure it's safe, we open it all the way.'

'Safe for who?' Boyd snapped.

Zaimu grinned. 'Good point. But I don't see any completely safe options here. Here goes nothing.'

'Together,' said Salma.

'Together.'

They bent easily in their suits. Salma's hands were clumsy in their gloves, but she managed to get the tips of her fingers under the lid on her side. When she saw that Zaimu too had got that far, she nodded. 'One, two, three—'

The lid lifted silently, effortlessly.

And through the plastic wrap she caught a glimpse of what looked like flesh – *a body*, curled up like a foetus. Smeared with a transparent, faintly purple, viscous fluid. The skin hairy, perhaps – she couldn't quite make out the texture.

'I – there's a body,' she struggled to say.

'Confirmed,' Zaimu said in a small voice. 'As far as I can see.'

A short silence. Then Meriel snapped, 'The image capture is poor. What kind of body? Human?'

Zaimu seemed stunned, and didn't reply.

Salma spoke up. 'Human-like. Humanoid. Not human.' 'Zaimu, help me shift this lid.'

Working together, they managed to get the lid out of the way without breaking their improvised seal.

Boyd reported quickly, 'Testing the air that was in there. Nitrogen, oxygen, some trace gases. Water vapour. Carbon dioxide. Nothing that will kill you immediately, or damage your suits. And the buffer supply in the lander is pure nitrogen. *That* surely won't kill any occupant immediately. OK. We need to maintain a secure, continuous environment. I'll have the equipment pump in trace gases into the shelter, to match what was in the coffin. You two keep your suits sealed. The – occupant – may be able to breathe that stuff; you won't, and there's a danger of contamination, one way or the other.'

'Noted.'

'Meanwhile I'll get to synthesising coffin air back here on the ship, in case we need it.'

'Good,' Salma said. She found she was breathing hard, even though she wasn't exerting herself particularly.

But Zaimu said, 'You're thinking a few steps ahead. A

continuous environment. I take it that means we have to bring the – occupant – back.'

'So long as it's safe, at every step of the way,' Hild said sternly.

They exchanged glances.

'Of course we ought to bring it back,' Salma said. 'Whatever it is.'

'Short of a bomb. In that case,' Zaimu said, 'before we move it, we ought to take a proper look at our visitor. Come on, Salma . . .'

They both braced beside the coffin. A small camera drone hovered over them. At a nod from Zaimu, they ripped aside the thin plastic sheeting.

To reveal the body.

'Speak to us,' Hild ordered.

'I . . . it's human-ish,' Salma said. 'Soaked in some kind of purple gel. I'll get a sample of that.'

She reached in to do that. She tried to avoid touching the – occupant.

She saw arms folded across the chest, legs tucked up against the torso. Limbs very thin, Salma noticed. The 'arms' were spindly, leading to odd 'hands', three long bony fingers – or perhaps one was opposable, like a thumb. She repeated those observations aloud, for the record.

Meriel came on the line. 'Human or not? Can you confirm that?'

They shared a glance.

'Human-ish.' Zaimu shrugged. 'Still hard to tell under all this purple crap. Humanoid, maybe.'

Salma heard Boyd grunt. 'A human, or even a humanoid alien? What are the chances we'd find *that*? How did it get here? What's going on here?'

'Not now,' snapped Meriel. 'Analysis later. Just keep observing, working, you two. Is the . . . occupant . . . breathing?'

'I don't think so,' Salma said. 'As I said, the body is covered in some kind of – gunge. Purple. A nutrient? There seem to be clothes of some kind underneath that layer . . . or maybe not clothes. It's hard to see—'

Abruptly the body jerked, thrashed, the legs straightening so the narrow feet kicked the bottom of the container, the arms tightening clumsily around the torso.

And the head turned, to disclose a little more of the face. The eyes opened, revealing wide pupils; a gaping mouth – no teeth, a bone-like carapace for lips. No hair on the head—

Salma discovered she was gabbling out observations.

Meriel broke in sternly. 'Salma. Zaimu. Calm down. Damn it, I knew I should have gone down there myself. Is it breathing? Is it alive?'

Salma replied, 'She's thrashing, but – I think she's choking. There's some of that purple stuff blocking her mouth.' She hesitated for one heartbeat. 'I'm going to clear her mouth and throat.' She reached down.

'What's with the "she"?' Meriel asked.

'Don't know,' Zaimu called. 'But that feels right.'

'Salma, for pity's sake – OK, clear the airway, but use a spatula from the med kit, not your damn finger. That's basic training.'

That made Salma pause. 'She isn't human. We trained on humans—'

'I know she's not. Never mind. Emergency medicine, Salma. All you can do is what you've been trained to do. Adapt to the circumstances. But do it properly, damn it.'

Salma did as ordered. She found a spatula, and pushed it carefully into what felt like a small, hard mouth – no, a *beak* – and down the narrow throat. She could feel nothing solid, but dug out a mass of viscous, purple gloop.

When it was done, Salma snatched the spatula out of the mouth.

A high-pitched cough shook the frail body.

Meriel called down, 'Oxygen, damn it!'

'Zaimu, help me. Sit her up.' Salma scrambled for an oxygen pack, while Zaimu put a beefy suited arm around the frail body, helping it — her? — to sit up. More of the containing gloop ran away, revealing some of the garment beneath. If it was a garment; there were panels of white, brown, black.

Salma opened the oxygen pack, and pulled out a mask that was going to be too large for that face, she saw immediately. 'Meriel! How do we know pure oxygen is the right thing to give her?'

'As before! Because it's all we've got! Just do it—'

Salma slammed the mask over the visitor's mouth, trying to fix straps behind the head. The visitor thrashed, as if trying to reject the mask, but Salma held it in place, tried to stroke the visitor's back with her free hand.

Slowly, the visitor seemed to settle.

'I think it's working,' she reported. 'She's growing calmer.'

And she found she was staring into wide open eyes, huge pupils. *Eye contact.* Salma shivered. What *was* this?

Hild called down, 'We'll bring her back. Wrap her up again, seal her in as best you can. Get her to the lander.'

Zaimu broke in, 'Think about quarantine. Once she's calm, and in the lander, you'll have to rig up some kind of isolation bubble. And when you return to *Shadow* we'll need a chain of safe environments to get her from the airlock to some kind of reception bay—'

'Leave that to us. Just get her up here. *Now*,' Hild said.

94

'But take a sample first,' Meriel said hastily. 'A blood sample, a bit of tissue, spittle – even one of those panels on her skin . . . Anything to let me get started on the biochemistry. Send up the results.'

Take a sample in case we lose her. Salma knew that was what she meant.

Bewildered, nervous, unwilling to harm the visitor, she took a tissue, wiped a little of what seemed like spittle from the rim of the beak, stuffed it into an assay unit. 'Sample taken.'

And Zaimu whispered, 'Hey, Salma. Take a look at this. Under the purple stuff.'

'Her clothes? Oh. *Not* clothes?'

He picked at those brown and black panels.

Not panels, Salma saw now.

Feathers.

11

Even before they got back into the escape pod – crowded with the three of them now – Salma and Zaimu were told that Meriel had already rigged up a kind of isolation area to receive them aboard the *Shadow*.

It hadn't been difficult, since most of the cabins and other compartments were capable, in an emergency, of vacuum-tight self-sealing. So Meriel had simply co-opted a small med suite meant for recuperation stays, set up a clean route from the airlock they would use, and had begun bundling equipment in there – working by guesswork as to what would be needed, as far as Salma could advise.

Meanwhile, even as Salma and Zaimu struggled to use plastic sheeting to rig up isolation cells within their own little craft, Hild had tried to order them to bring up the coffin itself as well. If Feathers was a representative of some alien culture, then the coffin looked like the only piece of that culture's technology to hand. 'Even a mineralogical sampling would be interesting, let alone manufacturing techniques, even any evidence of aesthetics—'

But, having already dragged an alien wrapped in a plastic sheet across the surface of a planet that shouldn't exist, and now pulling more plastic sheets across their sole minuscule cabin to improvise quarantine, Salma had kept her mouth shut about the aesthetics of coffins. Feathers alone would have to do, for now.

Feathers, though . . . She began to realise she was starting to think of that as a name for this impossible refugee.

After they had done customising the lander, with Feathers isolated and secure, the flight home to the *Shadow*, at least, was an interval of calm.

But once the lander had docked the chaos started again.

Aside from a couple of fresh isolation suits thrown into the airlock, nobody was to be allowed to help the two of them – or three. Meriel wouldn't take any more risks of exposure than Salma and Zaimu had already suffered, and Salma couldn't argue with that.

In the same spirit, from the moment of opening the hatch after docking, it was up to Salma and Zaimu, in the new suits, to get their passenger cum cargo, still clumsily wrapped in plastic sheeting, out through the airlock tunnel, and through the ship itself to Meriel's isolation chamber.

The body, the size of a small adult human, was clumsy to carry through the corridors of the *Shadow*'s main hull, the more so given their isolation suits and face masks. Zaimu held the legs, and Salma the upper body. There was no gravity here, and it was a case of pushing or pulling the inert load, rather than carrying. But the body itself was floppy, limp, and awkward to shift, especially as they were trying to do it no harm.

It.

The body.

Her. For all you know it, she, is still alive, Salma . . . She found herself longing for that to be true.

And even as they struggled along Meriel kept talking, observing, speculating.

'The problem is that it's so *like* us, superficially at any rate,' she said urgently over the comms link.

'Which surely isn't a coincidence,' Hild, the captain, put in. 'I've been thinking about that. If they somehow knew we were coming – *they*, whoever set this up – maybe it's some kind of bait. This body, this creature. Human enough to attract our attention. To motivate us to save it. I mean, why only one . . . entity? Why not a crew? Why not some kind of literal message? Instead, a body, a single creature, close enough for us to recognise as being *like us*. Something to lure us in. It's like a worm on a hook – or something that looks like a worm – and *we* are the fish . . .'

Salma had literally no idea what Hild was talking about.

'Angling metaphors now,' Boyd whispered through the comms in her ear. 'She's just being paranoid.'

'Heard that,' Hild said. 'Just being cautious, more like. Look at the evidence, what we know so far. It's not just that her appearance is so human-like. The air in her coffin was Earthlike, a nitrogen buffer with water, oxygen and cee-oh-two among other components. That suggests to me that, not only does she look humanoid, but her biochemistry must be – well, at least similar to ours.'

'Very likely, from what I've already seen so far from Salma's emergency sample,' Meriel said. 'I'll be very surprised if she doesn't have some kind of proteins-in-water life system like our own – if she doesn't come from such a biosphere. Oh, and she *is* a she, I think now. One scan I took revealed the presence of what has to be an ovary . . .'

'Unless she's been *made* to look that way,' Hild said. 'As I said. A plastic worm on a hook.'

'Some hook,' Zaimu said, grunting as he hauled the inert body. 'Some worm.'

'We're nearly there,' Salma announced.

*

They had come to an open door at last.

It led them into an empty med suite, with a second door leading off to a room evidently rigged out as a decontamination chamber. There was a single bed in the middle of the floor. Med robots waited, squat cylinders hovering in the air with manipulator arms, and, Salma knew, veritable medicine chests in their interiors. And with the knowledge, if not the authority without explicit human permission and oversight, to perform independently even major procedures.

Robot nurses for this exotic patient, rather than human crew. For now, at least.

Once Salma and Zaimu had staggered in, the door slammed sharply behind them, sealing them in with the robots, and Feathers. Salma thought she could hear the snap of locks, mechanical and otherwise. And she could hear voices outside, muffled commands: others of the crew, evidently having followed the rescue party through the ship, no doubt decontaminating the route they had taken.

Salma and Zaimu just drifted in the air for a while, bits of vaguely medical junk floating around them.

Feathers, floating. Salma felt overheated, exhausted.

But they weren't given long to recuperate.

'On the bed with our feathered friend,' Meriel's voice snapped. 'Then, you two, into the decontamination chamber yourselves.'

Which was a wardrobe-sized room, reached through that inner door. Salma knew that decon facilities were only here at all because of contingency planning. Those designing the mission had never expected an encounter with an extraterrestrial life form – save for perhaps some bug lodged in an icy comet – but you never knew.

Zaimu grinned through his face mask at Salma. 'Let's get her onto the bed.'

Salma and Zaimu got hold of Feathers, still sealed up in her floppy plastic bubble, Zaimu at the head, Salma with the legs.

'One big heave. One – two—'

Together they pulled the body through the air, then gently guided it down to the bed. Everything was weightless, but inertia made the body awkward to handle.

Once Feathers was on the bed, Salma reflexively reached for straps and harnesses to hold the body in place.

There was no resistance from the creature, any more than there had been since the retrieval from the 'coffin' on the surface. No apparent expression on the sketch of a face. Visibly in repose, even as seen through the plastic layers, with large, closed eyes, a sketch of a nose, what looked like a long, hardened upper lip, no jaw to speak of – a beak-like mouth—

'Less of the eyeballing, Salma,' Meriel snapped, her voice again hanging in the air. 'You're only getting in the way of the bots. You'll have plenty of time to get to know each other later, believe me. For now, decon tank. Both of you. *Now.*'

Zaimu shrugged and led the way, stripping off his decon suit and the sweat-stained under-suit he had worn during the EVA.

Salma followed him, pulling off her own gear. Once she was out of the way of the bed with its sole occupant, she saw the bots close in on the supine Feathers, with more emerging from behind wall panels, even from beneath the bed.

Zaimu called, 'Plenty of time, Meriel? What do you mean by that?'

'You don't think I'm going to let you two lab rats out until we prove there's nothing in there to die of? But don't fret if it all goes south. Your sacrifice will be memorialised in a hundred historic technical articles.'

Zaimu dumped his coverall, vest and pants into a hopper, pulled med sensors away from his exposed skin with ripping sounds. 'You really aren't as funny as you think you are, you know, Meriel.'

'Which is why I went into life support by choice, rather than the genuine medicine that I've had to learn to earn a place on this ship. I prefer to deal with people only as unhygienic components of my recycling systems . . .'

Salma dumped her own clothing in a bin. Stripped down, naked save for the black onyx pendant at her neck, it occurred to her that she had not the slightest interest in Zaimu's bare flesh, any more than he seemed to have in hers. It had always been that way. The mantra had always been that she was an honorary niece for the rest of the crew, and there relationships ended – for better or worse.

But right now Salma felt oddly self-conscious – as if the alien presence aboard the ship emphasised her closeness, relatively speaking, to the human crew.

So Salma turned away from Zaimu, and stood there while she was sluiced down by the chamber's systems, with water – a couple of times hot enough to sting, a couple of times cold enough to make her shiver – then a spray of liquids that smelled like disinfectants, but probably weren't. All-over body scans came next – X-ray, MRI and other technologies. Then retinal scans, hearing probes, and a series of questions fired at her – her name, date of birth, who was the President of Earth right now? 'Melanie Mason'. Other stuff she paid even less attention to. And finally a couple of simple blood samples.

Zaimu just stood and endured it, as she did.

At last Meriel told them they could have a final shower, a dry-off, and then dress again.

That was when Salma heard a scream. Thin, high-pitched, apparently wordless – but a scream.

She glanced at Zaimu, stark naked and dripping as she was.

'Feathers,' he said.

'Let's get out of here.' She tried pushing at the door out of the chamber, but it wouldn't shift. She called into the air: 'Meriel? Open the damn door. We have to help her.'

She could hear Meriel sigh.

'OK. My instinct is still to keep her isolated. Evidently we can't rely on the bots – but you two are the only crew I'm about to let get close to the specimen for now.'

'Meriel, her name is Feathers. Not *the specimen*. Let us out of here!'

'OK, OK.' A door folded out of the wall, revealing a compartment with towels, fresh coveralls, slip-on shipboard shoes.

The two of them rubbed down hastily with a last towel each, and pulled on coveralls and shoes.

'Underwear's for losers,' Zaimu said, breathing hard.

Once dressed, or as dressed as she was going to be, Salma tried the exit door again. This time it opened easily, and she pulled herself back into the main room.

And faced a mess. There were plastic shreds all over the floor, all around the bed, evidently the remains of the wrap in which they had carried Feathers out of her coffin to the lander, and all the way up here. Bots swarmed all over the bed, each about the size of a human head, and equipped with a variety of tools, mostly medical instruments and probes. One bot was still clearing away more torn remnants of their improvised isolation tent.

Salma could barely see the occupant of the bed, save for a blur of brown and white, twitching, trapped movements beneath the machines. She had a sense of utter fragility.

And then another scream – no, it was weaker than that, more a crying out, and not a featureless noise – 'Ch-kah! Ch-kah!'

Salma and Zaimu exchanged wild glances.

'Words,' Salma said. 'Those sound like words to me.'

'Yeah. Me too. And I'll wager my salary for this trip that those "words" mean something like "Get these floating garbage pails the hell off me". Or, "Where the hell did the gravity go?"'

A wordless glance at each other.

'Let's fix this,' Salma said. 'Bots. Move back.'

The bots ignored her, even when she repeated the command.

So they both pushed forward, into the cloud of bots. Salma just grabbed one and pulled it aside. Zaimu actually punched another.

Salma knew that the bots were heavily programmed not to harm a human, not even by passively resisting – only if they were stopping you coming to obvious harm would they disobey verbal orders, or resist this kind of physical control. As Salma and Zaimu worked, soon they started to move to a wider distance.

And then, as the bots cleared out of the way, the alien was exposed.

Feathers had been strapped, loosely, to the bed. Loosely, but her four spindly limbs were held, at wrist and ankle.

Cuffed.

Salma exchanged a glance with Zaimu. 'Let's get her out of all this.'

'Agreed.'

They got to work breaking the bonds that held Feathers down on the bed. The bots just stood by, and Meriel stayed silent, evidently outvoted. *Wrist, ankle*. Salma had no trouble assigning these labels to the joints of the limbs of this alien, as she worked at the bonds.

This was the first time Salma had had a chance to see the creature she had saved (*abducted*?) down on Nine – to see her properly, and not in the middle of wrapping her up in plastic sheets and bundling her into a spacecraft.

And she looked more human than not. *Feathers*. A person, with a name, human or not.

If she had stood straight Feathers might have topped out at a metre and a half in height – a short human adult. She was as naked as when they had found her, but now, with the wrapping gone, her skin, covered with those feathers, was easily visible. The feathers were flat, plate-like growths in brown, black, white, which Salma would have had no trouble calling feathers on a terrestrial bird. (Not that she had ever seen a terrestrial bird live.) The feathers were ragged, though, as if disordered. Some missing altogether. No doubt a result of the handling she had received en route from her casket to here, for all the care they had tried to take.

Feathers seemed to have no breasts – no nipples.

Her face was distorted, if you took the human as a norm. Soft, short feathers brushed back from a low brow. The beak-mouth seemed drastically different to the human arrangement, with a hard plate where nose and upper lip might have been—

Suddenly Feathers' eyes were open.

She was staring at Salma. Large, dark eyes (did they have pupils?).

Salma forced a smile . . . No, she found. It wasn't forced.

Feathers stared back. Those eyes were huge, unblinking.

Zaimu said, 'She does have a *beak*. She really does. But – look, with small teeth . . .'

Meriel spoke out of the air. 'I can confirm it's female, from more evidence. It, she . . .'

104

The disembodied voice seemed to alarm Feathers; she looked round uneasily, as if seeking the source.

'The scans show it,' Meriel said. 'There's an ovary, I'm sure. But – I'm drawing on loose terrestrial parallels here, parallels to the structures I see – she doesn't have the facility to deliver live births. Salma, I think she *lays eggs*.'

Feathers seemed to be growing still more alarmed. She cowered back, staring at Salma, Zaimu. She was shuddering, or shivering.

Salma reached forward, hesitantly, stroked her head. 'Hey. It's OK.'

Feathers just stared back with those huge eyes. But she seemed to calm.

Salma pulled back her hand.

Captain Hild's voice boomed in the air. 'Feathers and eggs and a beak? Watching in here. Well, we all are. You know what, Meriel? If you made a human out of a bird, that's pretty much what it would look like, isn't it?'

That second voice coming out of the air seemed to be the final straw for Feathers. After a few seconds of it, she threw back her head and screamed.

Not a human scream, Salma thought immediately. All she had seen or heard of birds had been in virtual dioramas recorded in the renewed wilderness areas of Earth. But that call had sounded like the call of a bird, a *caw*, a cry of alarm.

Meriel's voice was louder than Hild's. 'That's it. I'm closing this down. You two, out; I'm leaving it to the bots.'

Salma glanced at Zaimu.

He shook his head, a small gesture, but firm. 'We stay,' he said.

'Damn right,' Salma said. 'But we shut everybody *else* out. And shut *up*. The voices in the air are spooking her.'

A bot descended right in front of her, hovering between

Feathers and herself. She peremptorily shoved it out of the way. 'That's not negotiable.'

'Crew Salma.' That was the captain's voice.

Feathers cringed even more at the new sound, yet another new voice. She curled up on the bed.

'*Crew Salma*. Do as Meriel orders. You and Crew Zaimu, out of there, now.'

'Like hell. Zaimu—'

'I'm on it.'

Zaimu was useful in zero gravity, Salma knew. And he knew the ship's systems intimately. Now, quickly, nimbly, he cleared away the cloud of hovering bots. When he grabbed one, it would not resist, not risk injuring him, even as he threw it aside. Salma saw how he didn't shove hard enough to do any damage, or not significantly, though one bot did catch on the frame of the bed and went spinning out of control.

Once the bots were cleared away Zaimu hovered by the bed, waiting to fend off any more intrusions.

As soon as she got the chance, as soon as the bots were out of the way, Salma leaned forward – slowly, gently, but deliberately – and put her arms around Feathers. Lifted her to a sitting posture. The feathers at arms, legs and waist had been damaged by the cuffs, she saw. And immediately she could feel how Feathers was trembling – or shivering, she thought.

At first Feathers resisted. She twisted her head in panic, as if looking for a way to escape.

But Salma held her, not tightly, in a loose embrace. 'It's all right. They won't hurt you. They're only trying to help . . . Damn it, she's still shivering. She's *cold*. What if this room is too cold for her? And she's wet – did you sluice her down as you did us?'

'Crew Salma—'

'She's cold, and she's alone, and she's terrified. Zaimu, help me—'

'On it.' He sailed through the room, grabbed a towel from a holder on the wall en route, passed it to Salma who caught it neatly.

Gently she drew Feathers towards her again, wrapped the towel around to enclose her but not so tightly that Feathers might feel trapped, and started to rub her back through the towel. Still Feathers shivered, and twisted, as if restless, though her moans were dying down.

'Smooth downward,' Zaimu said. 'The way the feathers lie. That will be easier for her – more comfortable.'

'Yeah. Good thinking.'

Stroking Feathers' back softly, smoothly, Salma felt her relax – although she could sense what felt like a heartbeat, oddly rapid. Now Salma was able to look into the creature's face once more. Her eyes were pools of darkness that showed her own reflection.

Gradually the shivering slowed.

'Shit,' said Meriel, quietly, as if whispering. 'If I really were a doctor I'd probably say you were doing exactly the right thing, Salma. Do you want my job?'

'She was scared, and alone, and *wet*,' Salma said. 'All she needed was a hug.'

'OK. But listen, try to do a little science while you're there. We need to understand her to be able to help her. Don't put any stress on her. But do you get any sense of – of weight, robustness?'

'I . . . maybe. I'm holding her, not lifting her. I get the sense she'd be lighter than a human, though.'

'That's what I'd expect from the scans we've already done. Her bones look built for strength with lightness – not as solid as human bones, but with hollow cavities, struts for strength. And a big breastbone, an anchor for powerful muscles—'

Zaimu said, 'Like a bird. A bird has such features, a skeleton built for flight. The big breastbone to ground the flight muscles.'

'Correct . . .'

Feathers still seemed relaxed, but a little more restless; she turned her face this way and that, her beak-mouth opening and closing.

There really were *teeth* in that beak. Did any birds have teeth? Salma knew that some dinosaurs, relatives of the birds, once had teeth . . .

'I think she's thirsty,' Zaimu said now. 'Look. The way she's opening her mouth. Not surprising. We've given her nothing since we picked her up on the surface. Can she have water?' Anticipating the answer, he went to a spigot, filled a covered cup.

'I'm pretty sure she can,' Meriel said. 'We've already analysed some body-fluid samples, including the spittle you collected and what the bots have managed to retrieve. As non-invasively as possible, from scrapes and scraps, before you launch into me . . . We have blood, tissue. Her biochemistry is like ours, but not identical. Proteins in water, as I thought. What looks like a genetic system based on amino acids – but not our DNA. More like our RNA, in fact. So – water, yes.'

Zaimu came over. Salma gently rested Feathers' head back a little, pushing back the towel, so that the creature could see Zaimu's offer. The lidded container seemed to baffle her. So Salma took a sip herself, to show how it was done, and then let Feathers take the cup herself.

Feathers reached, a wing-arm unfolding with a rustle of feathers, and fragile, bony fingers extended from the wingtip.

Meriel said softly, 'Look at that limb. It's more like a wing with a claw, than an arm. But if it's meant for flight it's evidently devolved. Her ancestors may have taken to the skies, but this bird never flew . . .'

It took a couple of tries, but soon Feathers was holding the cup for herself and sucking water into her beak-mouth with ease.

Salma, feeling protective, took back the cup after a few

mouthfuls. 'Maybe we ought to take it easy for now . . . Meriel, what about food?'

'Well, I have her genetics. And we know she's a meat-eater, or I think so—'

'The teeth in the beak.'

'Yeah. I'm thinking of synthesising some kind of meat-substitute based on her own flesh's composition. It feels a little queasy to feed her back her own kind's flesh, but it will keep her alive until we can do better.'

'Or until she can tell us what she wants,' Hild said. 'That sounds like good work, Meriel. And you, Salma.'

For once, no smart come-back from anybody. All Salma cared about now was Feathers.

But Hild said, 'So we made a start on *what* she is. Now we also need to know *why* she's here. What the hell this is all about.'

Zaimu murmured, 'All in good time. And it's going to take a good *long* time, I think. A lot of patience.'

Hild said quietly, 'Patience we've got, it seems. And – empathy.'

Feathers, resting now, wrapped in the towel and Salma's arms, looked up at Salma with those big, watchful, unblinking eyes.

'Well,' Salma said, 'I don't know where you came from, or how you got here, or *why* you are here. But I guess we're stuck with each other.' She pointed to herself. 'Salma. *Sal-ma*.' And at Feathers. 'Feathers. *Feathers*.'

The creature reached up one wing, feathers rustling. One of those fingers at the end of the wing touched the black amulet at Salma's neck. Those big eyes fixed on Salma, and the beak-mouth opened and closed.

'Shh – aa – maa . . .'

And, her eyes closing, Feathers slid into sleep.

12

And elsewhere, elsewhen—

The contact was going well, he saw. Far away across the quantum-froth multiverse – 'far' by a definition that would have meant little to most humans – it was as if the softest, hesitant knock on a door had been made.

That was all he needed.

Later, humans would call him Terminus.

Him. They would assign a gender.

And a god's name.

But even that 'him' was nothing but a *human* label associated with the *human* name they had applied. It had nothing, intrinsically, to do with *him*.

His own awareness of himself was quite different, of course.

To him, the universe that humans inhabited – so large to them! – was just one transient bubble in a high-energy foam, a foam barely even describable within the limits of human physical theories. To Terminus, this foam of realities, all of it, was home. Indeed, he had once learned about his own origin, had looked back and watched his own creation.

That is, as if he had watched such foam until, purely by

chance, those swirling bubbles self-assembled to form a pattern. An image.

His own image. His mind, his self.

This was how he had been 'born', he came to understand. Not conceived as a procreation of other life forms, not as a member of any species, not a product of any chain of life – not even an automaton, created as the result of a decision of other minds.

He had been 'born' in a place – a universe among an infinitude of others – that was so vast and so long-lived that there was time for minds like his own to come about through the random collisions of stray matter particles, the pushing of stray wisps of energy. Not through the slow working of any kind of natural selection or evolution – but *by sheer chance*, all a mind's complexity could be created. Given enough time that scenario could play out, over and over.

Even before their first encounter, humans had guessed at the existence of such creatures as Terminus. In theory, purely through logic. It was all a matter of time, and chance. Given enough time, the wildest, most improbable act of creation could appear literally out of nowhere. The shards of the broken vase would leap up to the shelf, reassemble, all spontaneously. All you had to do was wait.

But, however born, once born Terminus had been given a purpose.

Scattered across every universe, in every bubble in the reality foam, there were lesions, or doors, or portals – each a breach of a boundary. The portals came in a variety of forms and designs, lodged in the hearts of giant stars, or on the surfaces of rocky planets, or drifting in the thinnest of intergalactic dust clouds. Humans might have labelled them black holes – but most were far more sophisticated than those crude ruptures in spacetime . . . But, in a sense, they all worked the same way.

Terminus did not know how the portals had been created, distributed. That belonged to an unimaginable *before*. But he knew they all had a single purpose.

His role, as he understood it, was to spread complexity – life and mind of a wide definition – spread it out from the intricacy of his own origin, his own unimaginably ancient cosmos, across reality, across a wider multiverse. And, since not all universes could endure as long as his own, he would reach out to other universes and *rebuild* them – or at least start that process – share with them the gift of infinity. Of eternity. Eternity and infinity.

What else was there to do, in a multiverse of eternities and infinities, but to share? As to what came after that – what became of the universes he touched – Terminus had no interest.

But for now the game was unfolding, once more, as it had so often before.

It was simple. Wait for somebody, on the other side, in a target universe, to find one of his portals.

To reach out to that portal.

To *touch* it – whatever that meant in terms of their own embodiment. Sometimes, a mere wisp of deflected relic radiation was enough. A mere glance.

After that, for that somebody, everything would change.

And now one such portal loomed in his awareness.

One glance. One small touch.

Terminus would eventually learn all things about humanity. Humans would eventually call him 'Terminus' after a Roman liminal deity. A god of boundaries. Indeed, the very name meant 'boundary stone'. In their early days the Romans had made sacrifices to such stones, in the belief that the god Terminus, if pleased, preserved such boundaries, and so ensured a little piece of civilisation stayed peaceful and intact a little longer.

Of course *that* didn't quite fit his own role.

But a later generation of Romans, under the Emperor Diocletian, had invoked their god of the boundaries to push back, actively, at the cult of Christianity, which at that time was rapidly infecting and destabilising the pagan core of their ancient culture.

A terminus could be an active, expansive entity, then. A weapon. Even in human culture.

Perhaps the name was apt . . .

To smile was a human reflex. Yet now, it could be said, Terminus smiled.

13

Elizabeth Vasta, Special Scientific Adviser to the President of Earth, still hated being in space.

'I hate this,' she said, as the ferry from the space elevator hub slowly made its way around this synchronous-orbit altitude to the Conservers' embassy, yet another satellite in a twenty-four-hour orbit about the Earth.

'Patience, my friend,' said Jeorg North. 'We are nearly there . . .'

She tried to take some consolation from that. North had been sent essentially to hold Vasta's hand on this hours-long orbital hop, in a ship perfectly capable of piloting itself. A top pilot she already knew – that had been the recruitment pitch. He wasn't a lot of comfort, frankly, but at least he shamed her into keeping up an illusion of calm.

And now, at last, through the window of this passenger lounge, she saw the grey sphere that was the Conservers' embassy to Earth and Moon. She leaned forward in her harnessed chair. There wasn't much to see: a dull globe adorned with sheets of solar-energy panels, and heat-dump radiators. A glimpse of sunlit green through what looked like an extensive picture window. Wispy sails spreading wide behind the main structures.

'Conservers prefer to maintain their position in space using solar sails,' North said, pointing. 'No consumables, you see. But the planetary government does insist on their having rocket packs fitted for emergencies, if they're going to hang around in such a crowded orbit.'

'Everybody has to make compromises,' she said. 'Even the Conservers.'

'That's about the size of it.'

'Well, let's hope they're in the mood for compromise over Planet Nine, today . . .'

It was already some six months after the first landing on Planet Nine, and the discovery of the creature the crew had called Feathers – and months too since the eruption of the anomaly at the heart of the Galaxy. And there had been no significant advance in understanding any of it.

Which was why the President's science adviser was coming to talk to the Conservers' embassy to Earth.

'I'm sure you'll charm them,' Jeorg North had said dryly.

The Conserver habitat loomed closer now. Vasta leaned back – and her black pearl pendant floated up at her face. She tucked it into the neck of her shirt, slow-motion fiddly. *I hate zero gravity.*

Closer yet. Looking out now Vasta caught more glimpses of green, through windows in the structure. She thought she made out a door, or a hatch: just a frame etched into the dull grey wall.

'You sound cynical,' she said to North.

He grinned back. 'Cynical like a politician?'

'I'm no politician. I'm a scientist, just an adviser to politicians – but I've learned how to figure people out. And these Conserver characters, for all their fine principles, are still people, their ambassadors still politicians working in a political human world. All this ostentatious austerity is as much a display of nation and culture as a World Flag Day parade in Beijing or Bangkok, Berlin or Boston. Paradoxical as it may seem.'

'*Paradoxical, yes,*' murmured a voice in their ears.

Jeorg glanced at Elizabeth. 'Oops.'

'*Ariel Uwins speaking, Adviser Vasta. Manager of this facility. And, political, yes, as you say. No matter what our goals – how divergent from your own – we are humans in a human society, and we have to operate as such. Especially as we now all seem to be facing an inhuman situation. Or superhuman, possibly.*'

And possibly more than one situation, maybe, Elizabeth thought, if you counted the weird quasar-like object that had simultaneously popped up in the centre of the Galaxy – mysteriously simultaneous if you factored in twenty-five thousand years of lightspeed delay. Months on, the 'quasar' was *brighter*, by around one part in four thousand of the Sun's insolation, it seemed, compared to its first appearance. Already that amounted to the equivalent of two extra hours per year of sunlight for the Earth. That didn't sound much, but the heating seemed to be increasing faster than the linear, possibly even compounding exponentially – there were traces of that in the data . . .

After a decade, forty extra hours of sunlight – two days' worth per year, so said the models. After a century, twenty days' . . . Quasi-linear at first, truly exponential later, rising ever faster . . .

This wasn't just an esoteric scientific mystery. If this went on, all the worlds of mankind could be imperilled.

It still seemed unlikely to Vasta, but there were some who speculated that the two extraordinary events unfolding – Planet Nine, the disruption at the heart of the Galaxy – could be linked, somehow. If not, the argument went, the timing was a hell of a coincidence. But, she wondered, how could that be, given lightspeed and the remoteness of the quasar?

And the centre of the mystery, Planet Nine with its sole

indigenous inhabitant, was in Conserver hands. Which was why Vasta, representing the global government she advised, was here at this Conserver station.

There was a soft shudder. Displays told her that the shuttle had achieved its docking with the station. As gently as you pleased.

Jeorg leaned forward so his smiling face could be seen in the smart screen, and thus in the habitat. 'North here. We have a contact light. May we proceed?'

A different voice replied. *'You are welcome. Please come aboard.'*

Jeorg grunted. 'I'm only the pilot. Follow me.'

They passed easily out of the cabin and through a lock into the Conserver habitat, then followed a short connecting corridor through to an open doorway.

The light inside the chamber beyond was bright, evidently sunlight, filtered through some kind of green-tinged glass. Jeorg pushed through the door frame, guiding Elizabeth with a gentle hand in the small of her back.

She tried not to show her discomfort in this situation. She was no veteran of spaceflight, but she knew to keep her motions simple and contained in zero gravity. *Never* get turned upside down compared to your companions, or the room . . .

The door folded back behind them. Elizabeth heard fresh air hiss into the sealed chamber. No doubt the air and the visitors were being subtly scrubbed clean of bugs and toxins. They moved forward, towards a shaft of sunlight admitted by a wall window. Here they waited patiently. Good a place as any.

Once various hidden sensors had evidently declared the all-clear, a second door folded back, revealing the wider interior of the Conservers' habitat.

Vasta's immediate impression was of openness, of space. People were scattered throughout the volume in three dimensions, in small groups, some holding hands or belts so they didn't drift apart. Sunlight splashed through transparent panels in a domed roof. Slim pillars, apparently not structural, spanned from floor to ceiling. Windows gave views of the full Earth, several planetary radii away.

The floor was *grass*, a lawn. There were inner structures, floor to ceiling, that looked as if they were made of *wood*. Trellises, panels, poles, some wrapped in some kind of fabric.

And, Vasta saw now, off in the distance of this big, roomy volume, there were what looked like trees, growing naturally – or almost. Some had evidently been trimmed to fit under the low roof.

She wondered how the trick was managed. Trees and grass would grow towards the light, but what about the circulation of fluids, of tree sap, without gravity? The trees must surely be trained in some kind of centrifuge to grow healthily, and wheeled out here for display . . . the lawn too?

Nobody paid any attention to the visitors, not immediately. They were allowed to just float there for a few moments, perhaps for orientation, Elizabeth thought.

At last they were approached by two people, a woman and a man, both dressed in well-fitting but drab outfits: jacket and shirt, trousers, sandals without socks. The jackets especially were much patched – ostentatiously so, Elizabeth thought cynically, presumably to show Conserver thrift. She felt vaguely irritated.

The woman might have been sixty, with tied-back grey hair. The man, maybe a little older, was shorter, stocky – perhaps overweight – with an unruly grey-streaked beard. To Elizabeth they both looked like farmers, or gardeners. The woman even seemed to have dirt, soil, under her fingernails.

Elizabeth introduced herself and Jeorg, briskly. 'Though you know who we are.'

The woman smiled back. 'Ancient courtesies. And we have spoken before, though only over a short-delay link to Earth. My name is Ariel Uwins. This is John Smith.' The man with the grey beard. 'Our legal counsel.'

'I'm pleased to meet you . . . Mister Smith?'

Smith smiled. 'We Conservers are frugal in all things. When I was born there was a fad for naming babies with the most common names, from various cultures. That fell out of favour; as we grew, we John Smiths found we needed a more practical way of distinguishing ourselves. But when I first travelled to Earth I learned that "John Smith" is a venerable label . . . So, here I am.'

'You weren't always the greybeard, though,' Uwins said. 'And he won't tell *me* a thing about himself when he was younger. I'll dig it out of him some day.' She glanced at the visitors. 'If we all have time.'

And the feel of the little gathering immediately turned slightly sombre, Elizabeth felt.

'We have offices we can use – or we can just find somewhere to sit here.'

Elizabeth and Jeorg exchanged glances, shrugged. 'Why not here?' Elizabeth said. 'There's no need for formality.'

'And we enjoy being hospitable. Then, please – this way.'

Ariel and John led the way, drifting over that floor of short grass. Those slim pillars served as handholds to aid zero-gravity passage, it turned out.

'Of course,' John Smith said as they moved, 'here in low Earth orbit, we are always aware that while you are the guests in this facility, we are *your* guests on a larger scale.'

Elizabeth smiled. 'Well, and we are pleased that you see the necessity of having this embassy here, actually in orbit around

Earth. I know that many of your own compatriots and colleagues are light-hours away, off beyond Neptune, and the object called Nine was discovered four light-*days* from the Sun, wasn't it? The information lag is always going to impair decision-making across the Solar System – authorised avatars do help – but at least here we representatives of our different communities can speak face to face.'

Uwins said, 'True enough. And in return we ask only for your help in case of emergency – and to share a little of the sunlight that falls on this satellite.'

'Don't worry. I'm familiar with the protocol under which this little base is governed. You're very welcome here.'

They reached a bank of seats, with lap straps to hold you down in the lack of gravity – all set fronting a huge picture window giving a view of Earth, diminished by distance. It looked as if they were positioned over equatorial Africa. Given this was a stationary orbit, Elizabeth knew that the face Earth presented here would never change, save for the cycling of day and night.

Meanwhile John Smith was looking around at the sky, beyond Earth. 'Just trying to see Sagittarius. Is it visible from here, just now?'

'I'm not sure,' Jeorg said. 'Looking for the object at the Galaxy core? I guess I ought to know where it is, given the heat that thing is pumping out.'

Smith asked, 'Are there any fresh observations, theories about that?'

Elizabeth nodded. 'Some. More observation than theory, though we have some guesses. Its luminosity, its energy output, is measurable. To be so bright in our skies it must at least have the characteristics, the energy profile of a quasar – a galaxy core explosion. Our Galaxy's core has never been suspected of having the symptoms of a nascent quasar. Yet there's the evidence, that energy flow, measurable, and measurably increasing. And we think the rise is actually cumulative, exponential, like compound interest. And so it will grow . . .'

The Conservers glanced at each other.

Ariel Uwins said, 'And how long will this – heating episode go on for?'

'Well, we don't know,' Vasta said. 'Possibly it depends on the width of the, the *spot*, through which the Sun seems to be passing. Like an actor crossing an illuminated stage. How wide that is, given the Sun's own velocity in its orbit . . . The minimum guesses are in the tens of thousands of years. Hundreds, maybe.'

'And if this goes on? The exponential growth—'

'Worst case?' She shrugged. 'A doubling of the Sun's output after a thousand years, fifteen hundred. Earth then will be as hot as Venus is now. And some models say the atmosphere will be stripped off by twenty, thirty thousand years. You can imagine the interim stages as the process unfolds.'

'Ouch,' Ariel said. 'I hadn't known we'd learned that much. Although some of our stations had recorded it, analysed the rise too . . . Thanks for sharing that much. And we'll share in return; we do have some far-flung observation positions. The *Shadow* itself, out in the Oort cloud so beyond the solar wind; that might give up a little more data.'

Elizabeth nodded. 'Thank you. Well, we should share. We don't actually know what we're dealing with here. What the Sagittarius object is, or what it will become – or what the anomalous object we are still calling Nine might be – or indeed what the existence of the creature discovered within it might imply . . .'

John Smith grunted. 'I know it's controversial among scientists, but I for one believe there *has* to be a connection between the various phenomena. The coincidences alone – just as we reach Nine, and discover this creature they're calling Feathers, along comes the lighting-up of this beacon in Sagittarius.'

Elizabeth said cautiously, 'Yes, the timing is extraordinary, but actually it's hard to see a causal connection. Remember that the core lighting-up must have happened twenty-five thousand years ago, as it's at the Galaxy hub. Twenty-five thousand years before we found this alien in the Oort cloud. So the lightspeed limitation eschews any connection between the two events—'

'You speak as a scientist,' John Smith said. 'Forgive me. I'm a lawyer, of sorts. I got that from my grandfather, who was in the law down on Earth. So I trained up too. Mostly diplomatic and commercial wrangles but some criminal work. The Conservers are a new movement, relatively, so lots of new law to be developed.'

Uwins smiled. 'Including novel aspects of criminal law. Contrary to popular belief on Earth, we Conservers aren't all saints.'

'You speak as a scientist, Doctor Vasta. But I think as a lawyer. And I usually assume that there are aren't too many accidental coincidences at the average crime scene.'

Elizabeth frowned. 'This isn't a crime scene.'

Smith looked up again, seeking Sagittarius. 'Not yet. So, shall we find somewhere to sit, eat?'

14

As their hosts settled them at a table, Smith went to order food
and drink at a central station.

Smith returned with a tray laden with transparent flasks —
Vasta saw what looked like coffee, tea, some clear water — and
some kind of biscuit. The drinks were covered and equipped
with straws; all the food and drink containers and wraps were
attached to the tray with some kind of sticky pads.

There was a short, awkward interval as they took drinks,
flipped open packets.

Ariel spread her hands. 'We Conservers live simply, but comfortably, all the way out to the Oort cloud — even if we have to
make compromises with technology to survive here, in space.
I'm quite sure you are familiar with our philosophy, outlandish
or controversial as it might seem—'

Elizabeth waved that away. 'Most educated people on Earth
know about the Conservers, and what their values are, their
goals. And appreciate them. To — conserve. Not to waste resources needlessly.'

'But it's more than that,' Ariel said. She looked up at the sunlit
windows above their head, shedding light on the vivid green
grass. 'Just a little sunlight is all we ask, and we tap the solar
wind, which would likewise disperse into interstellar space.

That and what falls *into* the Solar System, extrasolar comets, the interstellar wind. Everything else we keep, we save, we recycle. Entropy will wear us down eventually – that's inevitable for all inhabitants of this universe of ours – but that is how we are making our shot at longevity, if not eternity.'

'And so,' Jeorg said, 'you are happy to send out missions like the *Shadow*'s, which took energy-starved decades to reach its destination. And were the children of the first crew just as happy to accept a life of no-choice servitude aboard that slow little ship?'

Elizabeth covered his hand. 'Only one child.'

She knew that this question – about the rights of children born during long-duration ship voyages, or trapped for life inside extremely isolated habitats – was one of the most difficult ethical problems of the age. One twenty-first-century thinker had claimed that the pioneer generations born in space would be the first humans to be raised in cages.

It was an irony that since the launch of the *Shadow*, sleep-chamber suspended animation had come along by leaps and bounds. If they'd waited a few decades, the *Shadow* crew could have slept through the whole thing. That single child need not have been born . . .

In this case, anyhow, the experiment had evidently worked.

She said, 'I do know that it was one of those born on the *Shadow*—'

'Actually the only one, I believe,' Ariel murmured.

'She was the first to find the – feathered humanoid – when Nine was explored.'

Ariel nodded. 'And we believe it's her who is doing the most in terms of making some kind of contact with the creature. Whatever it is.'

Vasta nodded. 'Anyhow, months on from that first contact, the reports are very encouraging. Good work. But, going forward, maybe we can help each other.'

The lawyer took another biscuit, frowning. He said, 'So we come to the point of the meeting.'

Ariel, though, seemed sympathetic. 'Help each other how?'

Vasta said, 'Why, help each other through the fall-out of the discovery. The encounter with Nine, the revelation of its true nature, the mystery of the feathered humanoid – *and* the quasar-like object that has suddenly erupted at the heart of the Galaxy.' She nodded at Smith with a smile. 'And my thinking mirrors yours, John, scientist versus lawyer regardless. With all respect to my scientific colleagues, the safest thing for the *politicians* to do for now is to assume these things *are* connected. And to handle them that way. And there could well be some connection – even aside from the weird synchronicity of the timing.'

John Smith nodded. 'OK. But I note you say *the* discovery rather than *your* discovery. The Conservers' discovery?'

Careful, Elizabeth. These are righteous people you're dealing with. And smart. Isolated but not naive. Otherwise they wouldn't have been sent out to represent their culture. Also Smith is a lawyer.

'True enough,' she said. 'And – for now, I'm speaking for the united governments of Earth – we fully recognise that discovery, and applaud the way you have handled it so far, and the way you have shared the data – beginning with the very fact of the existence, the nature of Nine.'

Smith smiled. *'But.'*

'But, how *are* we to handle this going forward? And by we, yes, I mean all of us, all of mankind – for all mankind is going to be impacted by this, even if this bird-like creature, Feathers, is not what she seems to be, even if the quasar object were to switch off tomorrow as mysteriously as it appeared. There will be aftershocks, even if only philosophically. We will all be affected. And meanwhile your brave sail-ship is light-days away from even radio contact. We have to get resources out there to support it, and the ongoing situation.'

Smith nodded. 'And again, when you say "we", you mean "you". Earth.'

Jeorg North smiled. 'Are all lawyers so cynical?'

Elizabeth touched his arm. 'It's OK, Jeorg. This is a difficult situation – but a very important one, clearly. So they sent me, a scientist rather than a diplomat, to start these talks because of the very complexity of the situation in scientific terms alone.'

'Or,' Smith said, 'as a cover for Earth's true intent.'

Elizabeth was growing irritated, and thought she might as well show it. 'Well, what would you have us do, John? Nine is a fact. The humanoid is a fact, our encounter with it a strange, unexpected first contact. Even the quasar is a fact, connected to these things or not through the weird coincidence of its timing. And that rapidly increasing heat output, if it goes on, will imperil us *all*. These are givens. We have to handle this as a species.

'And what I think you ought to see is that the human race as a whole has a much better chance of handling this well if you allow Earth to help. Again you'll probably dismiss this as a cynical ploy, but you must see that modern Earth's values are much closer to yours than, say, the Lunar Consortium's are.

'I've seen the economic models myself. Even helped develop some of them. There *must* be growth, economically, with time, and an expansion of resource usage. There we agree with the Lunar Consortium and their industrial-revolution style expansion plans. But we, of Earth, have no ambition to expand endlessly. Our strategy is simple. We want to restore Earth as a living planet, with *all* its natural sunlight energy fuelling life – a healthy, restored biosphere. But we *also* want to develop a strong technological civilisation. And so the plan is to build that infrastructure in orbit, using the helium-3 resources of the Solar System—'

'The Kardashev project,' Uwins said. 'I've heard of that.' She smiled. 'In a disapproving memo from one of our think tanks.'

'Well, the numbers make sense. Oh, all the helium-3 on the Moon would only power that kind of civilisation for a few *weeks*. But Saturn, for example, has enough of the isotope to power us for *fifteen thousand years* – and Jupiter twice as long again. And by then I guess we'll think of something else . . .

'That's why I believe you ought to accept the Earth's offer of support as we – you – handle this strange project, this anomaly at the edge of the System. We do think you are close to us culturally. You seek to prosper eternally; we plan for a mere thousand generations! Maybe you could even learn from us – I'm certain we could learn from you.' She sat back in her floating chair, her feet tucked behind a safety bar under the seat. 'Well, I guess that's my pitch. *Let us help.*'

There was a brief pause.

Elizabeth was distracted by voices in the distance. Children playing. She looked over that way, and observed that you could throw a ball a heck of a way in zero gravity.

Then Ariel Uwins slowly clapped her hands. 'Well said, Adviser.'

Elizabeth held up her own hands. 'I'm not so good at irony. If you *are* being ironic?'

'Not at all. That was a good pitch. I think we'd be convinced even if—'

Jeorg said, 'Even if what?'

Ariel Uwins sighed. 'Even if we hadn't decided to ask for your help anyway. Oh, of course we were going to turn to Earth – certainly in favour of the Lunar Consortium and the like. Personally

I feel reassured that you were diplomatic enough to ask if we *wanted* your help before just barging in.'

John Smith laughed, a dry and oddly calculated sound, Elizabeth thought.

Smith went on, 'Well, yes, that's marvellous. But we're not done just yet. We still have issues to resolve. The most immediate being, it seems to me, *how* can you help us? As we said, all the action is light-days away. Our ship out at Nine took a generation to get there.'

'True,' Ariel said. 'We can advise all we want, but unless we can get resources out there on the spot it's not going to make much difference . . .' She looked at Elizabeth. 'Unless you're going to tell me you have a secret wonder-ship capable of velocities comparable to the speed of light . . .'

Jeorg North smiled. 'Not quite that. But we do have the *Cronus*.'

Ariel shook her head. '*Cronus*?'

John Smith frowned. 'Even *I've* heard of that. Your big fission-powered ferry, that's been to Saturn and back — how many times? Ah — and is this why you've brought along a deep-space pilot — no less than Jeorg North, conqueror of Ceres?'

North just shrugged.

Smith went on, 'Possibly I know more about your technology than is healthy, but isn't *Cronus* a big *slow* ship — and it is powered by nuclear fission, correct? Designed to bring home various products lifted from the atmosphere of Saturn. Methane — helium-3, of course . . .'

Elizabeth knew that Ariel and Smith must understand this much very well, as some Conserver factions were already at Saturn, engaged in a study of the feasibility of low-impact resource extraction projects.

'That's been the idea,' Elizabeth said. 'Yes, *Cronus* is a big slow scow — actually I think it's more like a luxury liner. The tourist trade is healthy, believe it or not. Zero gravity gyms, if no ballrooms . . . It's in lunar orbit just now being refitted, but—'

'So what?' Smith asked. 'Why are we talking about this ship? Isn't it six years to Saturn aboard her — at least?'

'About that,' Jeorg said.

Smith pressed, 'Saturn is ten astronomical units out from the Sun. Ten times Earth's distance. Whereas Nine is seven *hundred* AU out. Which, at *Cronus*'s velocity, would take, what, over four *centuries*?'

Elizabeth smiled. 'We have a plan to get there quicker.'

Uwins saw it. 'Ah. You have something new, right? I've heard of this, I think. Conservers do gossip, you know. *An interplanetary-capable fusion engine*? And that's your plan? To refit *Cronus* — oh. Helium-3. Hence all the hints. You're going to burn helium-3, extracted from Saturn? Why, you could reach the stars with that stuff, let alone Planet Nine.'

'You've guessed it. The project's already underway. The *Cronus* will set out for Saturn in a month or two — under its old fission drive. Six years to Saturn; we can't get around that. And *there*, we plan, she'll be loaded up with helium-3, finally fitted with the fusion drive, hopefully with its own development complete—'

'And then, just *five more years* to Planet Nine,' Jeorg North said.

Elizabeth's smile widened. 'And we'd like you, or other Conserver guests, to come with us, as we set out to reach the heroes you sent out so long ago, so far away.'

Smith and Uwins seemed stunned.

Vasta nodded. 'I'll take that as a tentative yes. I think I've said enough! And now — look, in the interest of cross-cultural partnership, could we see some more of this place?'

Uwins grinned, but still confused. 'It would be our privilege . . . Are you serious about this offer?'

'Oh, yes . . .'

Later, of all of them, Jeorg North thought he might have come out of the meeting best.

He knew he was no diplomat – he was a mere pilot, and, hell, he didn't have the imagination or the know-how to take in all this cosmic-meddling stuff. He knew he was only being used as a prop by Elizabeth Vasta, a symbol of Earth's interplanetary reach.

But he had his own ambitions. He *was* a pilot, with a high reputation – but Ceres was receding into the past now.

And a refitted *Cronus* would give him the kind of command he had needed now.

If only because this odd little jaunt to Planet Nine could just become the precursor to what he dreamed of above all.

To captain the first interstellar mission. What finer goal could there be?

But, over the next few months, it didn't turn out quite that way for Jeorg North.

And, after that, his plans changed.

So he went to the Moon.

15

Matt Kord, coordinator of the Lunar Consortium, decreed that, on arrival, at first their visitor from Earth would be held at the quarantine facility at Port Tranquility, where his shuttle from orbit was to land. Jeorg North was an irregular arrival, after all, with permissions apparently obtained for this visit by irregular means: probably through buddies, even hero-worshippers, in the Earth-Moon ferry pool. So Kord decreed North was not to be allowed any further than decontamination until he was satisfied North intended no harm to the Consortium and its facilities.

But as he and Doria Bohm, his restless, troublesome, rebellious assistant, rode the surface transport to the port, and then endured the mandatory fifteen minutes' surface-to-surface quarantine checks before being allowed into the decon centre, Doria did nothing but argue.

'Look,' Doria said, 'this man, Jeorg North, is one of the Earth's most prominent spacecraft commanders. His mission to Ceres—'

'We all know about Ceres. That is why I'm coming out to meet him in person, you know. Even though he smuggled his way out aboard an empty cargo scow from the space elevator . . .' As Doria well knew, Kord suspected. She had her own sources.

'And,' Doria said, 'we do know that North isn't just some other pilot. In recent times North has had the ear of the ruling councils down there, including President Mason and her science adviser, Elizabeth Vasta. Something to do with the Planet Nine business, we think. And now he's turned his back on all that and has come to us – all the way out here to the Moon from Earth. Just think what he might have to offer!'

Kord eyed her critically.

Doria Bohm had long been a high-up in a loose association of rebellious factions, here on the Moon – rebellious against Earth's control. Which was why, after the immediate fall-out of the extraordinary events at Planet Nine, Kord had recruited her as a sort of vice-coordinator. Sooner that than have her outside, throwing criticism in.

And, as it happened, she had turned out to be surprisingly competent. Bohm was full of energy, super intelligent, and dedicated to the cause which he supported himself: economic and legal freedom for off-Earth communities, starting with the Moon. But—

But she had different methods from Kord's. And now, today, she had the look of one of her loose-cannon days. *Deep breaths, Matt . . .*

'Doria,' he said, 'you just don't get people.'

That shut her down. She fingered the disc of black lunar obsidian at her neck, visibly calming herself. 'I don't? How so?'

'We need to take this cautiously. I know what you're thinking. You see an opportunity. I think *he* sees an opportunity. We *could* attach this very competent man to the mission of the *Aquila* – well, the proposed mission . . . But it would be a risk.'

And she seemed surprised that he cut to the core of it so quickly.

They had discussed this before, however. If Earth developed a helium-3 drive, and was thus able to get a ship out to Planet

Nine and its wonders soon – meaning within a few years rather than decades – then, it seemed to most thinking people, the planetary authorities would be likely to be able to dominate the Solar System for centuries to come. It would be a home run – in the jargon of an old sport that had adapted surprisingly well to lunar conditions, Kord sometimes thought.

But *if* the lunar engineers could modify their own fastest ship, the *Aquila*, meant for Earth-Moon transits – *and give it the capability to get to Saturn*, almost as quickly as the *Cronus* on its loop out . . .

The argument was simply that by having a presence there, the Lunar Consortium could present itself as a significant player, now and in the future. There was no intent to attack, or disrupt, either *Cronus* or the operations at Saturn. And the fact that *Cronus* would have to be re-equipped with fusion technology and refuelled at Saturn, before going on to Nine, made some kind of intercept mission all the more plausible in terms of timing.

All this was tentatively planned; already modifications to *Aquila* were underway. It was the Consortium's most covert operation just now, and the most audacious – or foolhardy. A mission breaking all interplanetary flight protocols. All to get a piece of the action of the outer planets, even Planet Nine, perhaps. It was, in Kord's eyes, a mission full of risks, technical, political and human. But, he knew, it was also a mission which might just about achieve its technical and political objectives, a break-out from the legal and technological framework that contained the Consortium.

However, they needed a top pilot to handle the mission.

But— *Jeorg North*?

'This is already a huge gamble, isn't it? Every way you look at it. And now you want to involve this man, North, this rogue?'

Doria was frowning. 'Rogue? All that matters is his utility. All that matters is that he's the best qualified deep-space commander there is, as was proved by—'

'The Ceres mission, yeah, yeah. Not to mention his huge experience of the Earth-Moon-Mars circuit. But why is he *here*? What does he *want* . . . ?'

She seemed confused by the question.

You are so naive about people, Doria. Maybe all the generations brought up in the tiny human community of the Moon are like this. Socially – deprived.

He sighed. 'Look – *you* see this man, Jeorg North, purely as an asset. What could he offer us, offer *you*? But he's not just an asset; he is a human being following his own life trajectory, his own goals. Just a few months ago he was working closely with the World President's own science adviser, wasn't he? And now he's betraying his own world, his own culture. So why should *we* trust him? What does *he* want here?'

'Well, it might be a noble motive for all we know—'

Kord shook his head. '*For all we know*, it might be something to do with the messy divorce he's going through. Ha! You didn't know about that, did you? You ought to try to cultivate people, contacts, if you really want to make a difference, Doria. North's husband is a hot shot pilot too . . . So what's the intersection of *our* goals with the goals of a super-pilot from Earth who's maybe been thwarted in his ambitions by his own spouse? Is he really in the right mindset for something like this?'

She looked at him sceptically. 'And that's why you've kept him stuck in quarantine for so long?'

'Only a few hours—'

'Several hours longer than the minimum set-aside . . .'

That was true enough. But that had at least bought Kord some time to try to find out for himself through various channels, public and otherwise, *why* this Earth hero should suddenly become a rebel.

He shook his head. 'Too damn much going on, and too fast. Look, Doria – this is a strange time, a fragile time for all of us. Especially given the quasar heating.'

She grunted. 'There is no "us" as far as we and Earth are concerned about that. We're dug down in the regolith; they have a wide-open unprotected biosphere.' She peered out at the bare, dead lunar ground, the black sky, the sharp shadows cast by a rising Sun. 'Their oceans might boil. *We* can just spin off a few more reflective sheets from all our lunar aluminium stock—'

'That's callous. And don't be naive. We still depend on Earth for vitals. If Earth went down, we would follow pretty quickly.'

'Well, even so. We can't let ourselves be intimidated by that kind of possibility.'

'But you have to look at the wider context. In terms of the human factor too. Jeorg North isn't just a pilot, he's not just an asset to be controlled. He's a human being who's hurting, evidently. And *something* has brought him out here. Some kind of angle that has come out of the wider picture. Nothing to do with our own goals, that's for sure. And that's what we have to figure out before we make any kind of recruit of him.'

She snorted. 'And then what, we give him a counselling session and send him home?'

'If necessary, yes . . .'

'So I'm to treat this as a learning experience in the art of politics?'

He said nothing more. Just stood there, holding her in his stare.

'I'll follow your lead,' Doria said at length, submitting.

'Thank you. Although I have a feeling we may both end up following Jeorg North's lead.'

She grinned. 'All the way to Saturn? Or beyond? I'd take that trip.'

'One step at a time, Doria. One step at a time . . . I believe he's going through decon. Let's go see him.'

The Tranquility base's main decon facility was a roomy but self-contained habitat, situated not by chance at the heart of the nearest thing the Lunar Consortium had to a tourist destination. From here there were daily tours to the historic Apollo 11 site, where you could also see modern history being made with the tremendous helium-3 regolith-scraping machines in action – the regolith of historic Tranquility being, by chance, a comparatively rich lode.

In the onsite hotel there was even a bit of luxury, though that wasn't saying much, Kord reflected. The Moon was a world of sparse treasure and monumental labour. Indeed the colonists couldn't *afford* much more luxury than this, thanks to the economic vice Earth had on them. Tranquility was just one, very visible, symptom of that vice, and maybe that was appropriate. Symbolic.

Anyhow, they had nowhere else to keep an ambiguous visitor like Jeorg North, deserter from Earth.

Kord and Bohm found him, alone, still in the main decon tank. There were no staff on duty with him; the facility was fully automatic.

He was doing some kind of calisthenics, it seemed, lying on his back, folding his body into a ball with arms wrapped around the knees, and then opening out to a stretch, legs straight out. Over and over. North was a short, stocky man – well built for the confines of spaceflight and off-planet living, Kord thought. Strong, though, that was evident. His skin, dark, was slick with sweat.

All this before panoramic windows that showed a panoply of stars, and illuminated crater rims on the horizon that gave a hint of the sunlight of the long lunar morning to come.

Now he noticed them. He rolled to his feet, grabbed a towel, and grinned confidently at the visitors.

Kord, glancing over, found it easy to read Doria's expression. *Look at him. Think what he's already done. We need a person like this if we're going to take a semi-experimental craft to the outer Solar System – and to deal with rivals from Earth on the way.*

But Kord remained to be convinced. And so, he suspected, on some deep level, did Doria. All that in a sharp glance. In some ways they were learning to work together, the old fart administrator and the clear-eyed young rebel.

As two of them entered the room, North relaxed his posture, reached out for a wall rail, grabbed a towel to mop his face and neck.

Doria made the introductions. 'Sorry to keep you waiting, Jeorg. This is the coordinator of the Lunar Consortium—'

'Matt Kord. Sure. I'll eschew a sweaty-palm introduction. And, nice to meet you too, Doria, in person. I like your pendant.'

That disc of lunar obsidian at her neck. Doria touched it, self-conscious.

'Elizabeth Vasta has one similar. Different stone, I think. Wears it all the time. Funny coincidence! Name-dropping, I know. And I also like your rebellious spirit. Read some of your articles back home. About pushing ahead with lunar independence, bending the old space treaties?'

She shrugged, apparently embarrassed. 'I do what I can—'

'You do have sympathisers on Earth, you know. Is she your local-hero rebel, Matt? Keeping her close to your politico chest?'

Kord tried not to react to that. 'We don't all play such games, pilot North. I'm an employee of the Lunar Consortium. A coordinator. A manager, not an Earth-style President, still less a monarch. There are few of us on the Moon—'

'And probably as many opinions as there are people,' Doria put in.

Kord said, 'We believe in cooperating, here. Creative conflicts only.'

North grinned. 'And I wonder how true *that* is. In my experience people are people, wherever you go.'

'Well, we're here to listen to your opinions, Captain North—'

'Call me Jeorg. Let me gather up my gear.' He did so, stuffing a bag with quick, brisk movements. 'You know, I came up on one of your cargo boats, returning from cislunar. Asked what they were carrying.'

Kord knew. It was no secret. The ship had been accepting a cargo of liquid nitrogen for the Moon bases, in exchange for a *much* less valuable load of helium-3 destined for Earth.

'Sums up the basics of Earth-Moon economics, doesn't it?' North said, with a goading tone. 'Helium-3 for nitrogen. Helium-3, the lifeblood of this rocky world of yours – your most precious commodity, laboriously scraped out of the lunar ground. But you have to give it away in exchange for a scrap of what every one of the Earthbound breathes in and out, for free. If there were any justice—'

Kord cut him off with a gesture. He thought there was nothing subtle about the way North had picked up that cue and run with it. 'We know all this, and we don't need to be reminded of it. And whatever went before, the situation is changing, isn't it? Because of Planet Nine—'

'And the quasar,' Doria said.

'Which is what I'm here to discuss,' North said. He hefted his bag. 'Shall we get out of here?'

*

Kord led them out of the decon area and through a more public zone in this tourist-friendly spot, a meet-and-greet area with a corner set out with tables and chairs. The furniture was all very lightweight, to show off the Moon's low gravity to new arrivals – or to visibly remind them of it.

A small serving bot slid silently over the floor towards them.

North slowed, sniffing the air. 'Is that coffee? And I'm hoping not the tepid slop they serve you on the translunar flight.'

Kord grinned. 'You want to stop here? We can talk as well here as anywhere. Sooner that than to bundle you off one vehicle straight onto another.'

'But, security?'

'You've already been passed. The place is swept daily,' Doria said. 'Mostly for reasons of commercial confidentiality. This, Tranquility, is a port, legally and in practice. A lot of deals are done right here, you can imagine. Or signed at any rate.'

'Ah. This is where the oligarchs of Earth put the final squeeze on you innocent lunar folk, before they head straight back for the shuttle home.'

'Something like that,' Kord said dryly. 'Come. Sit. Dump your bag. And tell the bot what you want . . .'

North asked for coffee, but Doria made a side order for him of a glass of pure water.

'Lunar water,' she said when the order arrived. 'Or rather, comet debris, collected from the permanent shadow at Shackleton crater. It's less scarce than helium-3 at least – we have a gigatonne of the stuff.'

North nodded, as if impressed. 'Cheers.' He raised the glass, sipped. 'Good enough. And I guess I'll be returning the gift through the recycler later on. So, to business. You know why I'm here. The prime cause anyhow.'

Kord said, 'You mean the anomalies at Planet Nine.'

'Right.' North ticked off items on his fingers. 'The — artefact — that Nine itself turned out to be. The creature they found, Feathers. Probably now the single most famous entity across all the worlds of mankind. And, not least, whether it's all related, or not, the quasar event at the heart of the Galaxy. OK.

'And from the beginning of this new phase of our lives I've been troubled by the way you people are being shut out of the argument. I'm serious. I'm from Earth, but I'm closer in spirit to pioneers like you.' He swigged more water. 'Of course Earth has a lot on its plate just now, other than business as usual. The global heating — I presume you see the data from the Earth governments?'

'Also our own observatories,' Kord said. 'The big farside tele-scope farms. We do share it all, especially given the critical nature of all this — for all of us. But that may be more significant for Earth than it is out here, actually. At any location on the Moon we're used to living with huge, unshielded swings in the sunlight intensity. No atmosphere, you see. But Earth has all those elaborate cycles of mass and energy, circulations of air and water and heat, those elaborate seasonal changes, all driven to a fine degree by the Sun's heat. So that extra fraction already makes a difference. And that may be just the start, as far as we know.'

Doria nodded, with what looked to Kord like genuine sympathy for the hapless Earth dwellers. 'You've just come from Earth, Jeorg. How bad is it so far?'

North shrugged. 'I only follow the news. There are already fears that the big farming areas are drying out. In parts of North America, you know, it's *still* the case that much of the water for arable land is drawn from aquifers. All over there's been water rationing: in China . . .'

Doria nodded again. 'It's like the climate-crisis generations all over again. My family had some tales to tell about *that*. I guess most people did. Here, we could just dig in for a while, Matt is right. But we aren't safe here. Not fully independent, not yet. Everything leaks, on the long term. If support from Earth folded – well, we wouldn't last long.' She glanced at Kord. 'I do understand that, you know. And Earth knows it, of course, and it's always been a lever.'

North smiled, encouraging her to speak, to say more.

Kord was becoming more and more wary of this man. He still couldn't spot North's true motives.

But Doria seemed oblivious to such subtleties. She said now, 'There's also the question of the humanoid on Nine.'

'*Feathers*,' said Jeorg North. 'You should have been down on Earth when the news broke about that. Among other things, it's our first encounter with extraterrestrial intelligence – indeed, extraterrestrial life. She's an enigma from beak to feathery ass. Nice open questions, and there are plenty down on Earth rushing to provide answers, of one kind or another. Usually not too scientific, though.'

Kord nodded. 'I heard about this. Religious reactions too? I mean, a birth without parents? Even Jesus had a biological mother . . .'

'You've not had that here?'

Kord considered. 'I think people here, those born here and immigrants too, are less – religiously inclined – than folk on Earth. That's my personal impression. On Earth you are standing on a world that wasn't made by humans, and even now has been little modified by humans, save for the worse: all those extinctions, the fouling up of the environment. Here, it was different. Here we didn't start with a living world and trash it; here we are taking a dead world, if you like, and making it live. We don't *need* to believe any god made this world.'

Kord smiled. 'She's right. Nobody here is praying to Feathers yet.'

Jeorg nodded. 'Nobody on Earth either. But they are sending out a ship, right? The *Cronus*. And if they win that undeclared race, if they get there first – if they can capture this exotic technology, whatever it is, and this religious icon, Earth may have made a decisive move. Never mind squabbles over duties on a race of helium-3, or an embargo on nitrogen exports to the Moon. A move that could cut off the extraterrestrial future for good.' He looked hard at them both. 'Don't you see the *threat*? Don't you see the *opportunity*, if you can get out there and at least match them in the race?' He sneered. 'Or you could always go join the Conservers, and live off scraps for all eternity.'

Kord saw that he was becoming aggressive, forceful, so carried away was he with his own argument. Kord found this manner repulsive, in fact. Which wasn't to say he mightn't be right.

But Doria was scowling, intense. North's arguments did mirror the views of many lunar colonists – especially the young. North had got through to her, and he knew it, Kord saw. He had recognised the half-tamed rebel in her, and was now reaching out to that rebel.

And Kord wondered, not for the first time, if, in bringing her into his own minuscule administration, he had made a strategic error.

But still, it couldn't be denied that everything was in flux. What did he want himself? What did *he* see as the way forward?

Play for time. He sensed that generations of bewildered politicians and managers and administrators were whispering in his ears. *Bluff. Keep them talking.*

Ask him what he *wants.*

'So,' Kord said at length. 'Jeorg North, you are here on a mission. Evidently. But why come here?'

North grinned. 'I think you know. Because you have one ship here that I believe is capable of catching, even overhauling, the *Cronus*. At least as far as Saturn. Even now you're fitting it out for the trip.'

Kord had been expecting that. He played for time. 'You mean the *Aquila* – you know about that? How?'

He shrugged. 'I'm a top pilot. Pilots talk. I know about ships, Earth's or otherwise.' He grinned again. 'I always fancied taking the *Aquila* for a trial run . . . Look, you have a ship that will at least get you into the game of – well, whatever follows when *Cronus* reaches Saturn. So I believe. It's always served as a cislunar freighter but is capable of much more than that. Your pilots, too, probably never go further than the Lagrange points. But in me, you have an experienced commander capable of getting you *out there*. Because I've been out there. All the way to Ceres, remember.' He leaned forward. 'This is the pitch I made to your colleagues, like Doria here, but I do understand it's your decision to make.

'You need to get a ship to Saturn. You have the ship. Let me fly it.'

Doria turned to Kord. 'He's got me halfway convinced, Matt. Why not? Show him the *Aquila*. See if he can live up to his promises.'

'Or his boasting,' Kord said.

He considered North again. He found it hard to believe that a man like this gave a damn about the political future of the Solar System, still less that of the Lunar Consortium, which must seem to a denizen of Earth to be a small, scruffy operation. If that wasn't his motive, though, then what?

But on the other hand Kord had no other way he could see of involving the Consortium in the events at Saturn, and whatever might unfold from here.

'I'll make a deal,' he said at last. *Or play a gamble*, he thought.

The way North looked at him, sharply, eagerly, convinced Kord he had made the right play. *Still in control*.

'What kind of deal?'

'If we show you the *Aquila* – and if you still honestly think you can handle such a mission as we've discussed – then you have to answer me, truthfully and fully, one question. Is that acceptable?'

'What question?'

'You'll find out.'

North grinned widely. 'Acceptable and accepted. Now show me your treasure.'

The *Aquila* was an experimental ship, Kord knew. Its purpose was to demonstrate a relatively independent means of transport and communication – independent of Earth, at least. A craft built of and fuelled by lunar materials almost entirely, both for structure and propulsion, and constructed by lunar industries.

And it worked. It had made a few runs in the environs of the near-Earth asteroids, camouflaged as much as possible. Earth probably knew about the existence of this ship, but, he was confident, didn't know its capabilities.

Test runs over, for the time being it had been returned to a dry dock, a grave-like pit dug deep into the substance of the Moon – only a short journey from the Tranquility public area. So that was where they took North now.

And when they delivered him to the dock, North was clearly transfixed.

The bay was spacious, deep, and brilliantly lit, with the *Aquila* lying at rest in a cradle. A conveyor belt took them slowly along a pressurised, glass-walled corridor, paralleling the length of the

Aquila, with North peering at the craft, barking out technical questions at Doria.

The main body was a hundred metres long, around fifty wide, aside from fold-out radiator panels that would extend past that limit once in space. The lightness of the ship's framing and inner supports, and the lack of a solid hull, made it easy to see the detail. It had a roughly cylindrical arrangement, with major components of different diameters connected by struts. At the centre was a gleaming sphere, at the rear a cluster of nozzles.

'That small compartment at the nose is the control room,' Doria said softly. 'You can see rocket clusters for braking, around the nose. They make a hell of a racket in the cabin when they fire, by the way, the noise passing through the frame. Behind that, electricity storage cells, then that big section contains the propellant tanks—'

'What propellant?'

'Hydrogen. From Shackleton water. The main crew quarters are *inside* the tank cluster—'

'For radiation shielding?' North asked.

'Correct.'

'That big sphere is the fission engine?'

'Correct again. Behind that you have the drive units, basically hydrogen rockets. Fusion fuels, like helium-3, deuterium, are scarce on the Moon – and Earth buys all it can. But what we do have are heavy metals in the same relative abundances as Earth. That includes a hundred million tonnes of uranium – not that Earth will buy any of *that* any more. But we figure we have the uranium to support hundreds of thousands of missions of this scale.' She grinned again. 'We aren't as rich as Earth, or its colonies, such as Saturn—'

'But you're pretty smart at making use of what you've got. I get it. And this baby would take us to Saturn—?'

'In six years, by minimum-energy trajectories,' Doria said. 'Easily matching *Cronus*. She has already launched, but we're confident *Aquila* can overhaul her. "Aquila" means "eagle", my friend, and this eagle will fly straight and true.

'And once we're there, the Consortium will have a presence as far as Saturn at least, and then . . . Well, we'll see. Plenty of time to figure it out from there. At the very least they'll know we're coming.'

North nodded, looked around once more. 'You know what you're doing. And this is a fine ship.' He extended a gloved hand to Kord. 'If you'll have me, I'm in.'

Kord shook his head, withholding his own hand. 'Not yet. Now you have to answer me that one question, truthfully.'

North frowned, dropped his hand. But he nodded.

Slowly, Doria led them out of the bay.

'One question,' North prompted Kord as they walked.

'Tell me, then – *why do you want this*? To leave Earth, your home, your world – to betray it, in a sense, in this way? We know you have pretty senior contacts. And no more guff about the Lunar Consortium's relative economic disadvantage and whatever. Why does it matter to *you* that you should be on this ship?'

North hesitated, sighed. 'OK. Because I had a tentative posting on the bridge of the *Cronus*, when its six-year mission was hastily put together. *Cronus* to Saturn, and then beyond to Planet Nine. I say tentative. The posting was promised to me by the World President's science advisor herself. And I didn't get it. The posting. I didn't get the gig. *My husband did.* Now my ex-husband. Bheki Molewa. He had better contacts, frankly. And he used them to cut my heart out. Look him up. Bheki Molewa. Is that enough for you?'

There was a stony silence.

Doria frowned. 'That's *all*?'

Kord believed him implicitly. He laughed. 'On such details, the destinies of billions depend.'

Doria looked bewildered. 'This is why I'll never understand people, for all your tuition, Matt. So. OK. You're in. Shall we take a look at the specifications . . . ?'

Year 4

AD 2259

16

The day they found the nest was about four years after the discovery of Feathers herself — and about four years after two craft from the Earth-Moon system began their race to Saturn.

But it started for Salma pretty much as every day had since that discovery — or anyhow since the *Shadow* crew, and Feathers, had settled into a routine, of sorts.

Not long after finding Feathers, and with the crew of the *Shadow* evidently going nowhere soon, they had migrated en masse onto the transformed Planet Nine, with its vast, roomy but featureless surface — and, they confirmed, the safe lack of a radiation environment. Here they had set up an airtight habitat, improvised but well-lit and spacious, all powered by a small reactor scavenged from the ship.

Even in this extraordinary environment, they soon settled into a mundane cycle of chores, maintenance, science observations, and long-distance communications with Conserver bases and other human outposts — even Earth itself, given the interest in their adventure across all the factions of mankind. Elizabeth Vasta, science adviser to President Mason herself, was a frequent contact, despite the long time delays. All of this was punctuated by a routine of exercises and diet supplements devised by Meriel to get the crew used to Earthlike conditions after decades in microgravity.

As to the bigger picture, they still didn't know who Feathers was, or where she came from, or the meaning of her existence in this universe – if *universe* was the right word any more. And they weren't likely to learn much more of the wider picture, not yet. The governments of Earth had evidently unified enough to launch a joint mission to Nine, and had insisted the *Shadow* crew did no more meddling – such as poking Nine itself with any more fake Hawking radiation – until the *Cronus*, for now still en route to Saturn, finally got here to Planet Nine eleven years after the discovery.

It was an extraordinary location, an extraordinary situation – to live on Nine, *on* a strange relativistic artefact. But Nine, for all its ambiguous and baffling properties, just sat there, and you got used to it.

On the other hand, Feathers, just as ambiguous and baffling, *did* stuff, and the crew had to react, deal with that, cope with it. Soon Feathers wasn't just an anomaly, a science study. She was part of their lives. Part of the family, Boyd said.

As for Feathers herself, Meriel took it as a good sign that she had generally become more active with time.

She liked to play.

That was the bottom line, and as far as Salma was concerned play could only be good for her – and, luckily, Captain Hild agreed, as did quasi-doctor Meriel. So the crew was mandated to play too, and play nice.

It had been immediately evident that Feathers was an intelligent, emotionally complex being. You could see that in the constructive nature of her play, and in her evident attempts to communicate in her very avian chirps and trills – sometimes long symphonies of such sounds – which the *Shadow*'s computer banks were doing their best to interpret, without success so far.

And her intelligence showed too in ways no machine could

have detected. Especially in the way she responded to Salma, as she had from the moment she opened her very bird-like eyes. She soaked up empathy, and tried to return it too – by bringing Salma bits of food, for instance.

Even so, in the beginning she had been very quiet, still – shy perhaps, although Meriel had counselled against reading too much into the body language of such an alien creature. And sometimes she retreated into herself. She would be content to be with Salma for long hours – and only Salma – especially after sleeping. Or sometimes she would just sit, while Salma got on with other things – personal stuff, like sorting out her clothes, or changing round the furniture in her space in their improvised surface habs, even productive work. And when Salma slept, Feathers would crawl into a corner of Salma's toom, sometimes sleeping herself, sometimes simply quietly waiting. This never troubled Salma.

At other times, though, Feathers would sit quietly with Meriel. She seemed to have a bond with the healer who had patiently worked out how to feed her and fix her minor injuries. Meriel said that she was second favourite and was happy with that.

Or Feathers would just wander around, usually with Salma at her side, watching the business of the other humans with her wide, black, enigmatic eyes.

The rest of the six-strong crew mostly tolerated this behaviour, though Salma thought that Boyd, the oldest and most stuck in his ways, found Feathers' watchfulness a little creepy – especially as he couldn't read her expressions. He would say, 'What is she *thinking*?'

At the other extreme of engagement, Feathers liked to run races around the habitat with the youngsters, Salma, Zaimu – races which, super-fast on those skinny, very reptilian legs, she always won.

After the first couple of years the small hab dome they'd set up to live in, adapted from an inflatable module for use during the spaceflight, had clearly become much too small for her. Feathers just couldn't run far enough away, find remote enough locations for her stashes.

Well, Feathers had become the mission's priority, along with the ongoing monitoring of Planet Nine. And so, guided by lightspeed-delayed advice from specialist teams at the various Conserver stations, the crew had quickly constructed a much wider habitat around the old structure's core technological suite, with its life-support systems. Improvised from more cannibalised components from the *Shadow*, the new hab evolved into a spacious multiple tent, essentially, but with inner panels and closed-off sections, so there were plenty of places for Feathers to explore and hide – and fall back shelters in case of leakage.

The development inspired some grumbling from some of the crew, especially old Boyd, and especially since chunks of their solar sail had been used, or misused, in the construction. But that didn't matter any more; the *Shadow* was never going to leave Nine, Hild would say patiently. The *Cronus* would soon be on its way, and eventually they would all be taken home in style, Conserver conscience or not.

And in the meantime Feathers had evidently loved it all, using the new spaces to wander, explore – and hide still more stuff.

But by now, four years after her retrieval from the mysterious interior of Nine, Feathers was changing. Her behaviour now was often more like an older child, or a young adult – 'that kind of awkward transition age', as Meriel tentatively put it – and the games she wanted to play had become ever more elaborate, her runs and explorations more energetic, faster, longer, although she was never far from Salma for very long.

And, at some point, she had started to take stuff away with her.

Nobody noticed this at first. Eventually Salma and Meriel found what she was doing.

She was building evidently meaningful piles from discards – mostly old clothes and tools and empty food packs – sometimes out in the open, sometimes hidden in corners of the habitat. These trophies were carefully selected, but were generally just recycler-heap junk to the crew, a distinction she learned quickly once Hild had carefully instructed Salma to show Feathers what was vital and what wasn't. Salma kept an eye out even so, just in case something important did get lost in the kipple heaps.

All these behaviours seemed *natural*, as far as Meriel could tell, so she said, given this was the only member of her species humankind had ever encountered.

Feathers was evidently growing into a healthy, fast-moving, roaming, exploring creature, putting her own stamp on the place in her own way. But she did change with time, it seemed to Salma.

Mostly, Feathers started to become a little more solitary.

More often now she would build her heaps of stuff alone, even more well hidden in some corner of the habitat. They were more orderly too, often circular in form, or arcs of circles. Sometimes she would show the results to Salma or Meriel, sometimes not, though she was not yet hostile to Salma coming to see what she was doing, or to accidental discoveries by the rest of the crew.

One day in that fourth year – a day when she had hardly seen Feathers at all – Salma talked this over, not for the first time, with Meriel.

And Meriel just shrugged, as usual. 'All we can do for now is keep an eye on her, and let her develop at her own pace, her own direction. As we've done from the start. Just keep her safe; stop her from getting frustrated, if you can. We don't know enough about her physical needs to be able to intervene safely, let alone her psychological needs . . .

'Why, if you think about it, we don't even know how *old* she is. Either in absolute time or relative to humans – or even relative to birds and bird-like creatures on Earth, which is what she most resembles. She *has* grown in the four years since we found her – I can measure that, at least, and I do every ship's day – but that growth *rate* is slowing, it seems to me. So she might be like a human adolescent. Topping out. Or not. We have to be wary—'

'Of making simplistic parallels,' Salma trotted out. 'Concerning a being from an entirely different biosphere.' She held up a finger and spoke pompously. 'Indeed, from an entirely different evolutionary trajectory.'

Meriel grinned, self-deprecating. 'I do *not* speak like that. Well, at least it's sinking in.'

This time Salma did have a new question. 'You've measured her growth rate. Can you, umm, project that back? Can you *guess* how old she is, at least?'

Meriel pursed her lips. 'Good question. Answer is, yes, we can guess. But you have to be aware it is just a guess. We have four years of observational data, and absolutely nothing on her development before, and no comparison specimens to learn from. I know you don't like me using the word "specimen". I can tell you her overall growth rate must be faster than a human's. Maybe twice as fast. But, given she hasn't grown twice as tall since we found her, or doubled her mass, most of her growing must have been done before we encountered her. I think I'd tentatively put her down as equivalent to a human eighteen-year-old. Just coming out of an adolescent growth spurt. But in calendar years I'd say she is no more than nine, ten.'

'Does that mean she's *living* twice as fast as we are? I mean—'

'Don't go jumping to conclusions,' Meriel said cautiously. 'If I was a real doctor, let alone a real biologist, I probably wouldn't speculate away like this at all. But . . . we know that her anatomy is more like a bird's than a human's. Her physiology is fast, high-energy, compared to ours. But birds can live for many years in the wild, back on Earth. Albatrosses, ostriches, big birds like that, may live three or four decades.'

'Humans live twice that long, if they get the chance.'

'Yeah, but remember that birds do use up a lot of energy in flight, and there's a lot of wear and tear on the muscles and so forth . . . I know even less about birds than I do about humans. And still less about Feathers, who is some kind of bird-analogue from someplace else, not really a bird at all.'

Salma tried to think that through. 'But if she's growing old twice as fast as I am,' she said slowly, 'maybe she was *younger* than me when we found her. Now she's effectively *older . . .'*

'Don't think too hard about it. We don't *know*; we only have this one specimen, who only just seems to have grown to adult-hood herself, or near it.' She reached over and touched Salma's shoulder. 'Don't fret it. Just keep on doing what you're doing, which has been the right thing from day one. Just be with her. Make the most of the moment . . .'

Because Earth is on the way. Because this moment may not last for long.

They sat thinking that over a while, in silence.

Salma knew that the rest of the crew – the more thoughtful of them at least – spent a lot of time thinking hard about Feathers too, and the mystery of her weird origin. They could hardly fail to do so, given they had been living out here on the edge of the Solar System, four light-days from home, with 'possibly the most baffling conundrum since the dawn of the scientific age', as adviser Vasta had once put it. 'And it's got us trapped out here,' as Boyd had added.

That remark about a trap was valid, inasmuch as they had been pretty much mandated to stay on the spot and observe the various conundrums of Planet Nine until the much better equipped and staffed *Cronus* showed up.

But now the crew all seemed to have mixed feelings about that too. Nine was *their* prize, won after decades of travel. These were their discoveries. Salma herself felt dismay at the thought of 'some vast gaudy liner turning up with a cargo of celebrity scientists', as Boyd put it. While she wanted to understand more about what was going on here, she also didn't much like the idea of a circus like that arriving at what had come to feel like home, for all its remoteness, all its strangeness.

Her home. And Feathers'. What would become of *her* when the *Cronus* arrived?

A soft bleep; she checked her wrist. 'Hey, lunch time for Feathers.'

Meriel glanced around. 'And she's out of sight. As usual these days.' She stood, stiffly. 'You want to send out a drone?'

'She doesn't like drones. I'll go find her.'

'And I'll help you search. You go clockwise . . .'

It turned out that Meriel found Feathers first this time, and brought her back to the heart of the hab, where the rest of the crew were gathering for their own lunch.

Captain Hild had always insisted that everybody show up, unless unavoidably detained, at meal times each working day. They had been effectively grounded for years and a strict ship's schedule wasn't necessary, but still Hild kept to a regular timetable, and she used meal times in particular as three opportunities a day for them all to gather. Good for the morale and team spirit of a good-natured but cynical crew, as Hild had quietly described it to Salma.

And from the beginning here on Nine, at Zaimu's suggestion, Feathers had joined the group for their midday meals.

Today Meriel and Feathers were the last to show up, a little later than Salma. Salma sat on a chair improvised from a packing case, at the hub's low table, scavenged from the ship.

Feathers settled willingly enough – on the floor. As usual she eschewed the crew's chairs, though one was always brought out for her as a courtesy, as Salma had insisted from the earliest days of this strange arrangement, so Feathers wouldn't be left out.

The crew's food was briskly set out on the table, by Boyd and Joe today, their turn. It was the usual high-protein, low-fat meat and cheese substitutes from the recycling system, with authentic green vegetables laboriously grown in the hydroponics bays by Meriel – when she had time for her day job, as the supposedly part-time doctor insisted.

Meriel and Salma tucked in hungrily, having put in some exercise tracking down Feathers in the depths of the habitat. Joe the comms guy, sweating, had evidently been working out, probably as per the rota Hild had set up as soon as they had settled here for what was evidently going to be a long duration. Boyd filled his face, as he put it, in the way he always did, as Salma had long observed. Zaimu ate more slowly, picking at his food, as *he* always did.

The six of them. And Feathers.

She sat on the floor with her long, scaly legs up against her chest. And as usual, before she turned to her own food, she explored some of the human supplies, feeling stuff, taking it apart, even chewing a little of it.

Salma and Meriel had talked this over from the start. Evidently Feathers was an intensely social creature, even if in this setting the other social creatures around her were so strange, their food so unpalatable. Salma and Meriel had persuaded the rest to keep up this gentle imitation of the kind of feeding group Feathers seemed to need, instinctively, wordlessly. They had been supportive – welcoming to a stranger. Meriel assured everybody that she made sure the human food Feathers sampled would be no more than roughage for her, with little or no useful nutrient content, harmless. Water to drink was fine . . . They all took care not to eat the fragments Feathers had handled, though.

Her own food, researched and synthesised by Meriel, looked like seed, or like animal flesh, or some kind of pulpy vegetable, much of it softened with water – and the water was the only authentic, non-manufactured Earth like ingredient. Feathers would nibble and suck at this stuff, her beak working quickly, her head ducking down to take a mouthful of food and then rising up as she swallowed, all the time gazing at the crew as if they intended to steal it. She never seemed more bird-like than when she ate, people said – people who had seen birds for real.

To get this far, Meriel had thoroughly analysed Feathers' organic chemistry. She had her own distinct suite of amino acids and proteins, different from any human, indeed any terrestrial bird – and Meriel had synthesised a range of food products on that basis. There had been a period of experimentation with what Meriel called her chemistry set, tweaking flavours and textures and above all nutrient value. The final food package was essentially based on a kind of reverse-engineering of Feathers' own digestive system, and her waste. Meriel had tried to replicate what she *thought* that digestive system was designed to process as input, given her output waste as a clue.

It seemed to work. Feathers cautiously tried out each resulting foodstuff, accepting or rejecting. But her tastes seemed to vary;

sometimes she would reject what Meriel had presented to her before.

But as she had grown the cuisine had had to evolve. Sometimes Feathers' weight had dipped alarmingly for long periods, before beginning to recover as Meriel got her act together once again.

Even so, to be able to nurture such an alien creature at all, from scratch, seemed miraculous to Salma.

Meriel was modest about it. She said that Conserver life-support systems and their recycling capabilities were already the most advanced of any human society's, even Earth's. The systems depended on a principle called 'molecular sustainability', she told Salma. In a closed life-support system, by now a centuries-old spaceflight technology, human waste products – exhaled breath, liquid and solid wastes – were broken down at the molecular level into nutrients for crops and edible organisms such as yeast, along with oxygen and water extracted from the air.

So, once Feathers was eating regularly and producing waste regularly, a similar closed-loop recycling regime could be set up for Feathers' benefit, with her own waste passing through a series of scratch-built bioreactors: mechanical, adapted from human analogues, impressive novel creations designed to mirror the biological systems and processes Meriel had defined in Feathers' own body.

All these experiments and achievements were based on principles and technologies that had been given freely by the Conservers to the crowded nations of Earth, to help sustain what was still, after all these decades since the twenty-first-century crashes, a hungry planet. Now all this careful understanding was being adapted to support an isolated alien. For Feathers, these laborious experiments had evidently worked – eventually. And Salma, young and naive as she knew she was, had been amazed as she had come to understand to learn what the feat of feeding Feathers actually amounted to: Meriel was essentially synthesising the products of an entirely alien *and unknown* biosphere.

But the food produced for Feathers certainly did not look, smell or taste like human food. It was off-putting if you sat too close while you ate.

And, as the crew queasily discovered – though she did defecate in pretty much the same way as a human – Feathers did not eat as a human did. She used her wings.

Salma had discovered, by looking stuff up when she had needed to, that on Earth birds' wings were a kind of degeneration, or remodelling, of the *hands* of four-footed land animals. One long, heavily evolved finger had become the spine of a wing. Feathers had something like that; she was like a flightless bird – though in her case the wing-hands were evolving back *into* hands.

So when she reached for her food, Feathers would fold her wings down over the plate, and the hand-like aspect took over, scraping at her plate with long, bony fingers evident beneath a sheen of feathers.

Even that wasn't so odd for observers, compared to when she kicked off the boots Hild insisted she wore, to reveal feet with claws. The boots were intended to save damage to the habitat fabric, rather than to Feathers' feet.

And with the foot-claws she would just grab food and lift it to her mouth. All this with a smooth, continuing rustle of feathers, over her wings, her back, her chest. But at meal times, this could be pretty distracting.

Salma found that if you thought of her as a bird when exhibiting bird-like behaviours, and human when showing human-like behaviours, it didn't put you off so much. Mostly that worked OK. But eating with her was always a challenge.

Sometimes Feathers got through her meal quickly. Other times she would stay, as the slower humans ate and talked. Stayed to be one of the group.

And Salma, still the closest to her, would try to include her in the conversation, if she could. She used simple props, and pointing. Today for instance old Boyd asked if he could finish off a shared pot of rice, and the rest joshed him, and he went into his Feathers-friendly routine. *Props and pointing*: the food in the pot, Boyd's mouth, he mimed chewing, patting his belly, while Zaimu mimed the growth of a big fat belly. Salma watched Feathers as they went through these pantomimes – those big black mirrors of eyes that she had – and she seemed, to Salma anyhow, to understand at least some of it.

Starting from Boyd's clowning and other such situations, Salma had tried to work out a simple sign language for them to share, based on human analogues she looked up. *Please* and *thank you*: a touch of the wing-hand to the mouth. *Hungry*: pat the belly. *Sore*: shake wing-hand and rub the affected part. *Sad* and *happy*, folded-in wings versus wide shakes, natural enough gestures. More invented or improvised signs for food, cold, hot. Sign-names for the crew: Salma's, worked out by Feathers, was like a cuddle, wing-hands wrapped around the body.

But today Feathers didn't respond to Boyd's clownish signing. As soon as she had finished her meal this time, she touched her mouth with one wing, flapped the other wing away from her body.

That meant, *Can I go please?*

Salma checked with Hild, who nodded.

Feathers knew what that meant now. Nimble, fast, she stood, jumped away from the table, and ran off into the distance of the tent, soon disappearing into its artful folds.

*

Hild sighed. 'And then there were six. She does seem a little more restless than usual. And why run off, why always get as far away as she can?'

Meriel shrugged. 'She's collecting stuff again – bits of waste, wrappings, a few dishes from the meals.' She glanced at Salma. 'She's just putting together more stashes of some kind. Sal and I have kept an eye on it, making sure she doesn't take anything necessary. Or dangerous, to her or the mission. As ever.'

'Right,' Boyd said with a laugh. 'Don't want her tunnelling out into the Oort cloud! Ha!'

Not for the first time, Salma felt defensive about Feathers. 'I doubt that she's so dumb. Even if she hasn't got inborn instincts about the presence of vacuum, of its dangers. Why should she . . . ?' But even as she defended Feathers she was aware that her behaviour lately had been more erratic than usual, more brusque. Restless. Maybe she'd come back to her old self. But Salma wasn't sure.

She caught Boyd's eye. For all his robust humour, he was a people-watcher, and knew her moods. Now he shrugged. 'She needs watching, is all.'

Hild was fiddling with a water glass. 'That's for sure, but maybe we should be doing more than that. Something more analytical. We are coming under increasing pressure to start providing some kind of answers about our situation out here.'

Boyd snorted. 'Before a bunch of space-sick groundhogs show up in their luxury boat – if the *Cronus* ever makes it out here at all.'

'Oh, grow up,' Hild said, sounding weary. 'You know that the Conserver council has agreed to that as a joint scientific mission. But in any case they won't be here for years more yet, even if their fancy fusion drive works to spec. For now they can consult all they like, but it's us who are on the spot – and maybe we've still got the chance to shape the agenda. The science agenda at least. I've asked you all to put in some thinking on this, even if it's not your speciality. Has anybody—'

'I have something to say,' said Joe Normand, raising one finger.

Salma found she was surprised to hear Joe speak. As Boyd had remarked more than once over the years, for a comms guy he was remarkably uncommunicative. Still, here and now, that finger.

If Hild was amused, she didn't show it. 'Go ahead, Joe.'

'OK.' He looked up at the hab roof, locked his fingers behind his shaven head. 'So we've been studying what we can of Feathers' nature. Her anatomy and so on. And I've been wondering what else we can figure out about her world, her background. Just from what we observe of *her*. I mean, her home is evidently Earthlike to some extent. She's comfortable in the gravity here, she shares our biochemistry—'

'Our *type* of biochemistry,' said Meriel. 'But, yes, hers must at least be a water world like Earth, carbon chemistry, amino acids—'

'Sure. But how *much* like the Earth? How different? I checked out some of your results, Meriel. All those tests you've made over the years. She's human-like, but not human, evidently. Consider her skin, for instance.'

Boyd snorted. 'Her skin? What about it?'

'Well, think about it. What's the *point* of skin? Aside from holding in your insides, it's a barrier, a suit of armour against the outside world. Right? *Our* skin has to exclude microorganisms, toxic chemicals, radiation from a nearby Sun – alpha rays, ultra-violet to some extent.

'But, I can tell you, Feathers' skin is sterner stuff. Meriel, you took scrapings for samples, put it through various tests. I took a look too. Feathers' skin is a *lot* tougher than ours. It can't entirely keep out the harder forms of radiation – gamma rays, X-rays – but it does a better job than ours. Also, if damaged, it repairs itself quickly and more effectively than our own skin. Again, something you proved, Meriel, by snipping out bits of it and watching the tiny wounds heal.'

Meriel nodded cautiously. 'Hmm. Now you mention it, I did record that it healed up remarkably quickly. And actually seemed tougher over the old wound, I guess a response in case of some kind of repeated harm.'

Joe nodded. 'And also, have you taken a look at the feathers themselves? They're pretty robust. Not just there for flight, I think. Or rather, I think the flight feathers have evidently evolved from some kind of scaling – like in our birds – and they've retained some features of those scales. And, I'm extrapolating here, I think those scales were pretty tough too. An extra layer of protection, of shielding.'

Meriel nodded. 'Shielding from radiation?'

'That's what I'm thinking. And maybe if you did get badly irradiated, maybe you could shed the feathers, or the scales, just walk away, leave it all behind like a contaminated hazard suit – or like a snake shedding its skin – and grow more.'

'Well, that's a stretch—'

'OK. Here's another one. I think those feathers might also be *photosynthesising*, just a bit. I've run a few tests on discarded feathers, under sun lamps. Hard to prove when detached from the body, and I'm guessing at the stellar spectrum they are adapted to. But I think the feathers continue to grow a little *even after detachment*. Maybe they're actually some kind of symbiotic organism—'

'Hmm.' Meriel was pursing her lips. 'Good observations. Seems like I missed a lot. But I am a food scientist by training, you know. Not a biologist, still less a xenobiologist—'

Hild grinned. 'I want your resignation on my desk in the morning. For now let's listen some more to the comms guy. What else, Joe?'

Joe shrugged. 'So, *our* skin – in part – protects us against the hazards of living near *our* star, the Sun. That's what it evolved for. So I thought it would be fun to figure out what kind of star Feathers might have evolved close to, given *her* natural suit of armour. And on what kind of planet.'

'OK. I buy it. Your conclusions?'

'Maybe a smaller star than ours. Or an older one. Even a red dwarf, like Proxima. So the origin world would have to be closer to the star, to be in its habitable zone – the right temperature for liquid water to exist on the surface – but, being that much closer to the star, you're in a bath of more intense radiation, so there's a need for more protection.'

Meriel said, 'Well, that's good thinking—'

'For a comms guy?' Joe said.

'I never said that. Or implied it.'

'But there's more. I mean, this whole episode isn't just about planets and biology and stuff. It's just – maybe it's because I *am* the comms guy that got me to thinking a different way about Feathers. I mean, not thinking of her as some exotic beast, like you, Meriel, or even as a person, as you have, Salma, to your credit. I mean I don't *not* want to think of her as a person, a sentient being.'

'But—'

'But, I'm the comms guy. *And I started to think of this whole situation in terms of communication.*'

That created a pause.

A little more uncertainly, Joe went on, 'Because that's what all of this is about, isn't it? The Planet Nine artefact, the beacon, that drew us here. We are summoned, we come.

'And as soon as we get here, Feathers gets — shoved — into our universe. *What can she represent but a message* — or a whole bundle of messages? It's not just that she's got some similar-but-different biology from us, though I suspect we haven't got to the bottom of that yet. She's different — she's bird-like, obviously — but *why so close to the human form*? That can't be inevitable. Look at the range of body plans on Earth, from the insects to the cephalopods . . .'

Hild nodded. 'I remember us discussing this kind of idea when we first found here. And it still makes sense. There must have been some *deliberate* choice, to — insert — something with a vaguely humanoid body plan, to find a world with vaguely humanoid inhabitants. A selection based, in turn, on some kind of observation. Of *us*.'

There was a long pause, Salma thought, as this strange idea sank in.

'OK,' Boyd said, 'but so far as I know the only message *we* sent was that blast of Hawking radiation we bathed Nine with, that made it open up in the first place. And there was hardly any data in *that*, or none we supplied anyhow. It was essentially an echo—'

'But they may have been watching us for ages,' Hild said.

'Yeah,' said Joe. 'And we do keep saying we're looking at another universe here, somehow joined to ours by Nine — and maybe by the centre of the Galaxy. Who's to say time runs at the same rate *here* as over *there*? Maybe in their time frame, once the bridge was made by Salma's signal echo, they've had a thousand years to study us, and—'

'And to manufacture Feathers,' said Meriel. 'Or maybe to *breed* her.'

'More likely to find her,' Hild said. 'If this other universe is rich enough to breed such creatures . . . But how rich would that have to be? How extensive, to have come up with a bird-like creature that's so close to our primate body pattern? Presumably by chance. Hmm. I'll have to think about that.'

'Anyhow,' Joe pressed on, 'however they got hold of Feathers, however they selected her, they evidently believed her existence, her characteristics, were enough to deliver to us the message they wanted. Without words, I guess.'

'Yeah,' Boyd growled. 'And I think I know just what kind of message this is. I'm older than you guys; my grandparents lived through the Holy Wars that came after the climate collapse, and told me about it.

'I think you're on the right lines, Joe. And I think there's an analogy with religion. You see, I don't think this is a message as such. The meaning of it all. I think it's a revelation.'

There was a startled silence.

Salma, frankly baffled, looked around the table at her crewmates. They all seemed to react to that word pretty strongly, Hild shaking her head, Meriel almost laughing – or sneering.

Joe Normand said, 'You're not serious, Boyd. We're technologists. Scientists. Conservers. Our whole society is scientific. To use such language as that—'

'I don't even know what it means,' Salma said, hoping to deflect an argument.

Hild eyed her. 'Well, you have been brought up on this tub. We always tried to ensure you learned about the wider world, about humanity in the round. And that included religion. Revelation is a religious term, generally speaking, I'd say—'

'OK, OK,' Boyd said. '"Revelation" is a loaded word, but isn't faith necessary even in scientific thinking? I mean, what you need if somebody shows you the double-slit experiment and tells you it's the key to the multiverse? I'm older than all of you. I was born into a post-Catholic family. The Vatican was a smoking ruin not long before I was born. But some of the sects that came out of the ashes – almost literally – tried to preserve some of the Church's relics. Its teaching. At least the historical stuff. So now it's all reviving, for better or worse . . . Some of the other faiths suffered similar harm, might achieve similar recovery.'

He turned to Salma. 'Look, kid – a "revelation" in these terms is when God intervenes in the world. It's like a sudden injection of information into a human culture, from outside. Maybe you have a prophet with a head full of a new way of looking at the world we live in, and at the wider context of what comes before and after our lives here, and society is upended.

'So in the Christian faith you had Jesus, a man, but bonded to God in some way, and able to deliver a new message – a new way of looking at the world. In that case the message *did* change the world, for better or worse, largely thanks to an empire that adopted it, and when it survived that empire's fall—'

Joe snorted. 'You're not suggesting that God is inside Planet Nine, or on its other side in the multiverse, or whatnot? Or that Feathers is some kind of ornithological Jesus?'

'Not at all. Although she came from a virgin birth, kind of—'

'*Not* helping,' Hild said. 'Though others on Earth have observed the parallels.'

'Sorry. OK. What I *am* saying is that right now a mass of new information is being injected into our world, into our minds, from outside. The proof we now have of the existence of a multiverse *alone* qualifies as that much. And, the arrival of some kind of being, from outside our universe altogether so far as we can see . . . Feathers isn't Jesus, no. I mean, she's just *there*; she seems to have no verbal message to impart.'

Meriel seemed to be trying to think that through. 'So Feathers is some kind of – mute prophet? Is that what you're saying?'

'Well, isn't it possible? Is that why she was sent here? We guessed from the start that her very existence, her biology, is evidence of a universe beyond our own. Sitting here we've been able to figure out some aspects of where she came from – or we can guess, anyhow. One point you haven't made yet, by the way, is that the laws of physics on her . . . side . . . must be more or less compatible with ours. Otherwise her very substance couldn't survive here.'

Meriel nodded. 'Damn good point. So maybe it's all a kind of psychological softening-up – or part of a slow reveal.'

Hild said eagerly, 'Yes. That actually makes sense. Even if you drop the religious connotations. I mean, the base idea that we've been given Feathers to prepare us. Prepare us for what, though? We've been here four years and we haven't yet figured that out. Not a glimpse.'

Boyd snorted. 'If only Feathers could tell us. Some prophet who can't even speak our language.'

Hild snorted. 'So, how easy do you want first contact to be, old man . . . ?'

Salma made a quick time check. She realised that Feathers had been away, alone, for longer than usual. She had rushed her food too. She was often restless, but this was unusual.

Maybe something was wrong.

She stood up. 'Sorry to go. I think I'd better check on Feathers. She's probably just at one of her heaps of stuff, but—'

Meriel stood too, more stiffly. 'I'll come too. Especially if she's suddenly a being of cosmic importance.'

'She always was,' Boyd said gently. 'Even if she doesn't have a beard and a halo. Go find her.'

They went.

*

They split up, Meriel going right, Salma left.

Feathers' 'heaps of stuff' were mostly in the shadows, at the outer edges of the improvised dome. By now the entire perimeter was marked by evenly spaced collections. As she searched, Salma took a little more time at each one than usual, even sifting through the bigger piles to make sure Feathers wasn't hiding somewhere. It really was rubbish, bits of habitat fabric, discarded clothing mostly ripped to shreds, some vegetable and plant material, mostly dried or rotting . . . The crew had no more stuff than they had brought with them in the *Shadow* into this place. Little was wasted, or thrown away. Still, with Salma's silent endorsement, Feathers had managed to assemble of fair-sized heaps of the stuff.

Meriel found her first. Softly, she called across the hab to Salma.

When Salma got there, she saw that Meriel was down on her knees, with Feathers held in a firm embrace. They were sitting close to yet another heap of debris. Feathers had her face buried in Meriel's chest, and her body was shuddering, the limbs jerking – her feathers ragged and rustling.

Salma stood helplessly. 'What's wrong?'

'Take a look.' Meriel waved one hand at the heap.

Salma took another step forward, looked down. 'I can't see . . .'

'They weren't fertilised,' Meriel said. 'How could they have been?' Meriel was visibly angry, though she cradled Feathers with her usual gentleness. She raised her head to the sky beyond the habitat roof. 'This is a prophet, is it? Is this cruelty worth it, just to send a damn message to us? Show yourself, you coward, you bastard, whoever you are. Whoever is responsible for *this* . . . Ha!'

There was no reply. Still Salma didn't understand.

Feathers stirred, still limp, and moved over to Salma, and — just as when she had first been discovered — she snuggled deep into Salma's arms.

And now Salma saw them, in the nest. Still glistening with some kind of mucus on their shells. Each about the size of the baseballs Boyd used to throw for her as a child.

Three eggs.

Meriel seemed disgusted. 'I wonder what the brains on *Cronus* will make of this . . .'

17

And on *Cronus* at that moment, most minds were distracted by the ship itself, a strange new environment – even after four years aboard.

That was especially distracting for Ariel Uwins and John Smith, Conservers.

Their whole lives had been dedicated to a creed of universal parsimony, of economy, of eschewing the wasteful use of any of the Solar System's resources. And yet – so soon after their compatriots had made their extraordinary discovery at the edge of the Solar System – they had committed themselves to a six-year cruise on a luxury liner.

Because that was what the *Cronus* was, there was no doubt about it. And over these years of the six-year journey to Saturn, John Smith had had to spend a significant fraction of his time half-apologising for his presence on this huge bauble of a craft. Somehow the excuse that this was the *only* way anyone was going to get out to Planet Nine soon – and that only if a highly experimental fusion drive, to be fitted and fuelled when they got to Saturn, actually worked – didn't wash. Not for the conscience of a Conserver.

Of course most of the passengers on this mission were working scientists and engineers and politicians, or lawyers and

174

philosophers and journalists, and their assistants. Cosmologists and physicists keen to study the anomaly that Planet Nine had turned out to be. Astronomers hoping to find links with the peculiar, damaging quasar-like phenomenon at the heart of the Galaxy.

And, most interestingly to Smith, amid all the cosmic special effects, various experts longing to study the peculiar creature the *Shadow* team had discovered: the 'human pterodactyl', as some of the trashier media outlets described her. Biologists and biochemists, travelling to investigate her deep makeup (if it really was a 'her', as the *Shadow* crew insisted). Linguists to puzzle out her language, if she had one. Palaeontologists, to consider parallels of her peculiar avian-like descent to be found among the complex trees of life on Earth. And, yes, theologians of many faiths, eager to work out the spiritual meaning of Feathers' arrival and existence. Religion had retreated in the dark years after the peak climate-crisis years, a global calamity that evidently had nothing to do with any god. But still the ancient faiths had never gone away – and as there were, across Earth, evidently faith-based reactions to the situation at Planet Nine, John Smith had spent some of his waking time studying the Christian Bible and other holy works.

As for the other lawyers on this mission, Smith tried to keep out of their way – but the fact was he was the Conservers' only legal representative here. And there were plenty of legal aspects to be discussed with other groups and representatives about the situation, not least ownership of territory and intellectual property, given that it had been a Conserver vessel that had been first out to Nine to make those discoveries.

The Earth governments continued to insist that anything beyond their own world's atmosphere was a common good – and, therefore, Earth's to 'protect'. Long and sometimes heated arguments over these principles were held even as the great craft had begun its years-long drift away from the sunlight – though not away from the glare of prying eyes of cameras, and plenty of media outlets were represented aboard.

But as Earth had receded and the longueurs of the voyage had cut in, many of the journalists had grown bored with filing such reports from this ark, apparently suspended as it was in deep space, and had turned their attention to the individual passengers. Even John Smith had been interviewed a few times, though it seemed that the Conservers, in person and in terms of their mission, were generally judged too dull for the news-hungry masses of Earth.

And when that first flurry of activity died down, and the scientists caught up with their literature, and the journalists began writing the novels, screenplays and game-world scenarios they had never had time for, and the crew quietly monitored the health of the enormous craft and its human cargo . . .

And *then*, tiring of work, people turned to leisure.

As best they could at any rate, given a complete lack of gravity aside for a few therapeutic centrifuges. That lack made sports and exercise problematic or challenging for the novice – as was energetic sex, Smith was told. You needed practice and tips from experts . . .

Soon, it seemed to Smith, the hardest-working people aboard had been the crew who ran the great globe that was the ship's passenger section, doing their best to keep the passengers fed, watered, and exercised, if not entertained.

After a few more months, predictably enough, there had been a rash of affairs, some open, some fairly clandestine, and probably others he had seen no sign of at all.

But then, as the odd little community of the ship relaxed still more, people had started to mix a little more widely.

Smith himself struck up friendships with a group of space-

elevator engineers, who had cut their teeth on the great installation at Earth, and were now heading out for a full decade's
assignment, serving as relief on the still more monumental bean-
stalk at Saturn. Even the youngest would return middle-aged,
but financially secure for life. Other technicians were specialists,
there to support the replacement of the *Cronus*'s fission drive
with the new helium-3 engine.

And the youngest of the latter group, a dark, intense woman,
mentioned she was something of a chess player. That gave Smith
an excuse to haul his own handsome set out of his room and set
it up in the public areas – handsome and an antique, but adapted
magnetically for zero gravity. At first they played daily – until
Smith detected a subtle flaw in her defence strategies, and the
games became one-sided.

All this socialising, this work and play, was set against a background of staterooms, lounges, halls, dining rooms and other
facilities that seemed to have been designed by plundering some
of the more decadent eras of the human past, from Roman-era
banqueting halls to the extravagant luxury of the wealthy classes
of the nineteenth and early twentieth centuries, and even the
carbon-spewing techno glitter of the early twenty-first. And in
particular there were quaint, deliberate echoes of the decor of
the ocean liners of the early twentieth century: their staterooms
and dining halls, and ballrooms where virtual orchestras played
at high tea . . .

Through all this John Smith drifted, mostly alone.

Ariel Uwins, formerly ambassador to Earth, the only other
Conserver he had knowledge of on this trip, had quickly declared herself bored and faintly disgusted by this monument to
wastefulness – a monument to the resource-eating greed that
had characterised much of humanity's hegemony of the Earth,
and now most other worlds as well.

177

And so, after a couple of months, Ariel had ducked out entirely.

Several Conserver-tech coldsleep pods had been loaded aboard the liner. This was a technology developed to maturity only *after* the departure of the *Shadow* on its decades-long mission – which otherwise, Smith reflected, would have banished the *Shadow* crew-person Salma to non-existence, or at least relieved her of a childhood and adolescence in a cage of a spacecraft.

Had he asked, John Smith could have used such a pod, and he had toyed with following Ariel. But, for a while anyhow – a guilty conscience, over the fate of Salma? – he had stayed out.

He did find a few refuges. There was a Mars suite he rather relished, where you could simply sit and watch as the Sun crossed a simulated pale brown sky, and the thin winds moaned softly, and lonely rover craft made their agonisingly slow way around some dry lake or other. All of this was recording or simulation, but at least authentic, and he knew that at least some of Mars had been left relatively unharmed, despite the industrialists' rush for Martian aquifer water since the late twenty-first century.

And *Cronus*, drifting inert in the dark, was an ideal platform for deep-sky astronomy – even with nothing but the naked eye. Its engines had been silent since they had pushed the great ship out of Earth orbit. In fact the main engine had required only a single forty-minute burn to put the ship on a long, slow passage to Saturn. This was a 'Hohmann trajectory', as it was apparently known in the trade, slow but efficient in fuel consumption – about the only resource-efficient aspect of the whole mission as far as Smith was concerned – and the only way to get such large payloads to Saturn until fusion engines came on line.

And so, in the stillness, there were usually a good number of astronomers and cosmologists and other observers, professional and amateur, crowding out the various space-facing observation galleries. Smith enjoyed the astronomers' taciturn company, and they tolerated his presence, perhaps welcomed it, recognising a Conserver's instinctive aversion to wasteful disturbance in all things.

So they sat, amateurs and professional sky-watchers alike, mostly in silence, following the evolution of the quasar-like beacon off in Sagittarius.

As yet more months passed Smith began to explore more adventurously, away from the core of cabins and entertainment facilities.

And he began to appreciate the scale of the craft, at least from the inside.

The *Cronus*, never intended to land on any planet or moon, was a mighty dumbbell in form, with two vast spheres each some hundred metres in diameter. These were connected by a spine itself some hundred metres long, along which were draped radiator panels to dump waste engine heat – square kilometres of them. Roughly speaking, one of the spheres contained the habitable quarters – everywhere the passengers were allowed to roam – along with tanks of propellant for the engines, liquid methane. The second sphere, safely attached at the other end of the ship's spine, contained the huge fission-drive engines themselves, with more propellant, and a store of lunar uranium to feed the reactor complex that powered the ship's propulsion and other facilities.

Smith took more than one tour of these vast caverns of technology, in person in the more accessible areas, and as a virtual tourist elsewhere. So he visited the big fission reactors which, when necessary, were capable of the ten gigawatts or so which powered the propulsion engine and the ship's inboard facilities – enough power to sustain a city of a million people. The basis of the engine's operation was to heat a gas – all that methane – and blast it out of super-cooled nozzles, thus driving the ship forward. At launch, he learned, the ship had had an all-up weight of about fourteen hundred tonnes, of which about nine hundred tonnes had been methane propellant. By comparison the uranium supply was measured in mere kilograms.

All this surprised Smith with its apparently primitive nature – it was a design that might have been dreamed of, if not actually realised, two or three centuries earlier. But his Conserver's soul was soothed to learn that the design had been driven by a question of available and plentiful resources. Such as uranium, of which there was plenty to be had on the Moon for the fission engines, and indeed methane, of which there were thousands of gigatonnes on Earth, in the atmosphere, or trapped in layers of ice under the oceans. Methane was in fact a ferociously potent greenhouse gas, and essentially Earth was well rid of it – as long as the heat generated by its removal was <u>less</u> than the methane could have captured if left alone. And, thanks to Earth's space elevator, that could now be achieved.

Anyhow, this 'steam rocket', as the engineer and guide showing the passengers around affectionally called it, was good enough for the job, even for getting as far as Saturn.

But no further, as Smith knew. This ship, given its current propulsion system, able in nearly six years to reach Saturn, would take some four *hundred* years to get out to Planet Nine – and then would be unable to return without refuelling.

Which was why, at Saturn, this grand old boat was going to be fitted with a new engine entirely, some components of which she was carrying in her own hold. If all went well – if that huge upgrade held, if the whole cobbled-together monster didn't blow up on the pad – she would then take a mere five more years from Saturn to Planet Nine.

*

John Smith lasted a full three years before he felt he had seen it all. Nothing much changed, after all, save the slow, potentially lethal brightening of the quasar beam.

Three years, during which he gloomily followed reports of the slow but relentless increase in the heating of the Earth – as of the rest of the Solar System – and news of conflicts inevitably beginning to spark.

Early flashpoints came between countries and communities who shared a common river: the Nile, the Mississippi. Desertification was increasing such places as the Sahel, and the Gobi, neighbouring the encroaching deserts – there was even deepening aridity in America's Great Plains.

And out of such areas, heading north or south, a slow seeping of migrants was forming up, an echo of the desolate days of the late twenty-first century.

Three years, by which time he had heard the resident orchestra – modelled on that of the *Titanic* – run through its repertoire at least forty times.

Three years, after which he gave up, and committed to cold-sleep at last, thinking of the first words Ariel would doubtless say to him on waking.

'Told you you'd give in . . .'

Year 5

AD 2260

18

It was in the fifth year of their sojourn on Nine – their last year alone before *Cronus* was due to arrive – that Feathers began to sing.

The crew had their first serious discussion about this one evening, as Boyd and Joe slowly assembled the supper.

Feathers was sitting on the habitat floor, rather than at the table where the rest gathered – as she usually sat, *with* the group but a little way *away* from them. Sometimes, now, she sang softly. As she did tonight.

'Here she goes again,' said Hild. 'Always sounds to me like a contralto imitating birdsong. Have we got any better ideas on *why* she sings?'

Joe just shrugged.

Feathers did have her little private habits, as they had discovered over the years – including more she had developed as she grew. And private places to retreat to, nest-like. She preened a lot, as most birds did – so Salma understood, given that she had never seen a bird in the flesh herself.

But, preening in privacy or otherwise, Feathers generally still seemed to like to hang out with the human group, and especially Salma. She *knew* she was different, everyone assumed, yet she clearly knew them as individuals, and responded that way.

And by now she even had her own bird-call names for them all – so Joe the comms guy had determined, by patiently recording and analysing her song.

There was plenty of linguistic content in her songs, Joe informed the group. It was evidently expressed in a complex language, but its meaning eluded him – he had no referents to begin to translate it. And it was a mystery where that language had come *from*. Had she been born with it?

Joe could only guess at what her names for them all might *mean*, in her own language. 'Good-looking young guy,' he would josh, pointing to himself. 'Grumpy old guy,' for Boyd. 'Big sister,' for Salma.

Meriel said she now believed that Feathers had been very immature when they had found her – not long out of the egg, but after a growth spurt.

'So my best theory is that she was *born* with it,' Meriel said. 'The language. Why not? Our babies are born with the ability to cry, a very basic message to attract attention from their mothers and other adults. But we learn true languages pretty quickly. All of it evolved from some kind of repertoire of chimp hoots, probably.' She glanced around, at Boyd. 'In some cases devolved.'

'Ouch, cheap shot from the plumber there,' Boyd grinned back.

'Yeah, yeah. Well, what if evolution has gone a little further in the case of Feathers? What if you could be born *able to speak*, able to tell your mother you want changing rather than just hollering? You might think that in a sufficiently old species, in a sufficiently tough environment for survival, that kind of facility might evolve. Based on some kind of optimally efficient coding of sounds, gestures . . . Although a lot of babies might have to suffer before the parents caught on.'

Joe the comms guy said, 'Well, *my* analysis shows her song language is sophisticated, all right. I could bore you with stats on the complexity, the cross-correlation of internal structures, the entropy gradients . . . Put simply, I believe her language, as evidenced by the songs, is *more* sophisticated than ours, by about the same kind of ratio as *our* languages are more complex than those of dolphins, or whales.'

Boyd frowned. 'I thought dolphins were pretty smart.'

'Well, to be fair there's a lot of gestural content, movement – like dances – with the dolphins. But they're basically bluffing, believe me . . .'

Now, as Feathers continued to sing softly, her 'voice' some-where between a high-pitched human tone and a gentle, trilling whistle, she sang a phrase which Boyd had tried to learn.

He whistled it back. 'Damn. Nearly got it right that time.'

But Salma thought she could see how Feathers responded, with a kind of opening of her body towards Boyd, a slight splaying of the feathers. That was a smile, for Feathers.

Joe shook his head. 'Let's face it. Five years on, we're no nearer understanding her. Not beyond the obvious – shrieks and cries when she's alarmed or in pain, that softer trilling when she's content. I can tell you how complex her language is in terms of the internal structure, but I can't tell you what it means. Not without doing a lot of much more structured experiments—'

'And since we're here to protect her,' Hild said firmly, 'that ain't going to happen any time soon. When the *Cronus* gets here in a few years' time, maybe their experts will be able to analyse it—'

'Without stressing her,' Salma said.

'We know, kid,' Boyd said now, grinning, rubbing her back gently. 'We all feel the same under our gruff exteriors. She's family. We'll take care of her.'

'Boyd, I've been advised not to kiss you without a course of jabs.'

He guffawed, and pulled back. 'Back to my gruff exterior.'

'Still, though,' Zaimu said thoughtfully, 'before Earth takes over, I wish we could get further with our own hypotheses about Feathers' existence, and why she is here at all. I don't think I ever bought the idea that she's here to deliver some kind of message. I mean, not literally, not some sermon she's somehow memorised, or maybe has coded into her neural architecture somehow.'

The John the Baptist hypothesis, they had eventually called it, following discussions going on across Earth and transmitted out to them.

Zaimu went on, 'Remember, I was with Salma when we found her. Salma and I, down on Nine. And I thought we could recognise her emotions at least, pretty clearly, with or without signs, language, even her songs. Right from the beginning. She was scared. Bewildered. Whatever. It was obvious. But when we brought her back to the *Shadow* and took care of her – OK, especially Salma – she opened up. Her body language stopped being so defensive – and then the songs. She was always being social, or trying to be, is what I think of that. Not delivering some awful warning encoded in her genome. Or whatever.'

Salma grinned. 'She's done even better since we learned to whistle song fragments back. We are lousy at it, but we keep trying. Yes, that's my theory too. Her songs are all about being social. Not awful warnings, or sermons. That's all. Isn't that enough?'

'Hell, no, kid,' Boyd said gruffly. 'Because *why* the hell, in that case, has she been thrust through some kind of portal from another universe to here? Just to say "hi"? I mean, what we thought was a black hole unfolded – a *black hole* – and there she was. The whole set-up needed intelligent, technological parties – like us, but more powerful – to make it work. But out came – *this*. Why would you do that, why send her, if we were *not* to take away some kind of meaning – some kind of data, a complex message? That's what I've always believed. She must have some kind of message from ET *somewhere*, even if it's encoded in her DNA or her neurones—'

'She doesn't have DNA,' Meriel said, 'not quite, and not quite analogous structures to neurones.'

'Yeah, yeah. But all I'm saying is that I still believe some day she's going to open up and deliver The True Message. Hell, I don't know. Maybe she'll just sing it. Or fart it out.'

Zaimu leaned forward again, Salma saw, grabbing the initiative. 'Whereas *I* don't believe she has a "message" of that kind at all. As I keep saying, I was there from the beginning, with Salma.' He glanced around. 'None of you lot were *there*, at that moment. Everything you got was second-hand, our reports at the time, verbal and images, all before you got to see the reality. Everything was – filtered – for you, by our first reaction to her, and by her first reaction to us, I suppose. *She had already adapted.* And so *our* experience of that moment of first contact was the most authentic it could possibly be.'

Boyd snorted. 'OK, wise guy. How jealous I am. So before you write your autobiography, what did you take away from that precious, unrepeatable first contact?'

'That I don't think she has a message,' Zaimu said. 'As I just said. Not as you mean. Her songs are just – social, I think. And no, I don't believe there's anything clever like inscriptions in her DNA. Nothing so *literal*.'

'Then what's the point? Where's the message? If there's no – signal—'

Zaimu shook his head. 'I believe her *presence* is the message. Her very existence. Her nature. Here, in our universe – separated from whatever lies on the other side of Planet Nine, if it really is a portal from someplace else. All we have to do is figure out what that means.' He glanced at Hild. 'And, Captain, I remember saying you something like that on the very day we found her. That the very fact that she *looks* quasi-human is itself a message.'

Hild smiled. 'Thanks for that. But we never followed up that thought, did we?' She stood up. 'OK. Well, we've had the years we've been stuck here to figure it out – or at least to observe. Maybe we can beat up that idea a little more for a while?'

Meriel snorted. 'And before the *Cronus* and its boatload of eggheads shows up to tell us we got it all wrong.'

'You got it. Five minutes. Bathroom breaks only. I'm looking at you, Boyd. Then, back here and we push it until it cracks, or we do.'

When they got back, Meriel, a little grumpily Salma thought, grabbed the floor, and started to summarise key points of Feathers' anatomy.

'If there's anything in the notion that Feather *is* the message, well, let's look at *her*. Salma, maybe you could help keep her calm and happy in the meantime . . .'

After the first discovery, it had taken a while for Salma to persuade Meriel that she shouldn't use Feathers as a specimen: no pointing or jabbing or handling. Feathers was always visibly unhappy to be the centre of that kind of attention. Maybe some kind of prey reflex, they had speculated. All those predatory human eyes fixed on her, human claws grasping.

So, as Meriel spoke, Salma was careful to make eye contact with Feathers, to smile, to stroke her back, downwards the way the feathers fell – a gesture she had relished from the start.

'As you all know,' Meriel went on, 'she's essentially, well, bird-like in many ways. There's the basic body structure, more or less like ours – the skeleton, the soft tissues, the outer skin – with, in her case, feathers. She has a lightweight skull and skeleton – and light bones generally are typical of birds. Strong but not massive, full of struts and cavities – evolved for flight. This is even though Feathers herself is flightless, her wings having evidently devolved back into arms, or hands.'

Zaimu put in, 'So, if you think about *that*, she's the product of a *lot* of evolutionary change, of time. To grow wings and then lose them. She comes from an *old* biosphere – older than ours, perhaps.'

Meriel nodded grudgingly. 'Good point. Back to her anatomy.

'She's strong, especially her upper body, with big muscles evidently evolved for flight anchored to her breastbone. Her arms are winglike still, especially when she spreads them – you can see the feathers, rooted in what must have been an aerodynamically efficient way, once. By now the flight feathers, and others, have evidently evolved into a kind of down – but still tough, resilient. As Joe suggested, they serve as a decent radiation shield for parts of the body. And there's very complex chemistry in there, the feathers' layers. I'm still trying to determine if she actually photosynthesises . . . I mean, if her outer skin and feathers are full of something like chlorophyll, that can take energy direct from sunlight.'

Boyd looked sceptical, but intrigued. 'A photosynthesising animal. In terms of exploiting the sunlight energy, a very efficient arrangement, if you cut out the middle man – or the middle vegetation. Even if it means a lot of sunbathing. I could get used to that.'

Zaimu went on, 'And look at her frame. She's very muscular, and very smart, with a brain as large as ours – in fact, more convoluted, more structured. Oxygen breather, of course, with big lungs behind that breast bone, and a big brain to support . . . Her heart – or the analogue, it's a *series* of pumps rather than just one, like ours – circulates blood very efficiently, and that bloodstream is also more efficient at carrying oxygen than ours is, into the bargain.'

Hild said, 'All good points. But what about the real basics, though? The *four limbs*. What can we infer from that? I mean, on Earth the basic tetrapodal body plan goes back to the first ancestral amphibian that crawled out of the ocean onto dry land, doesn't it? Four limbs, a head. And out of that came the dinosaurs, the birds, the mammals . . . What if those common ancestors had had six legs, or eight? Or two? Did it have to be four? Why should Feathers be like us in *that* way, two legs to stand on, manipulator arms, a head—'

Meriel shrugged. 'Maybe the upright four-limbed design is optimal for intelligence in some way. Two manipulator arms, two legs to run away, and to stand you up tall so you can see far with the optical gear in your head. Maybe you don't *need* more limbs than four.'

Boyd snorted. 'You're trying to say the human body plan is *inevitable* if you want smartness? Tell that to the octopuses.'

Hild nodded. 'OK. Keep speculating, keep picking holes. We're trying to figure out why *this* being, with *this* body design, has been – presented – to us. Maybe nothing about our evolution was *necessary*, even if it had to deliver smart tool-making creatures. There's something about her anatomy, her deeper nature, that – well, maybe *that* is the message we're supposed to get. Boyd made a good point. Why is she a bird and not an octopus?'

Meriel nodded. 'Good. So let's follow that line.'

'How could our evolution have been different?' Meriel asked. 'If we can map that out we might get some idea of how – unusual – it is that Feathers here is so like us. Even if not identical.

'And we probably have to go back through the history of life on Earth to figure that.' She sighed. 'On which I'm the nearest to an expert, so I'll keep talking.

'You know that our genetic code is run on DNA, a big molecule which in turn is assembled from a set of amino acids.

'And as you know, Feathers' biochemistry is also built on amino acids, but a different set. There are a *lot* of aminos to choose from, but presumably only some large but finite group of those sets that will work to support life. But we do know of lots of theoretically possible variants on our own system – stuff that could potentially support some form of life. The biochemists call it "protein space", I believe.

'Anyhow, if you want to base natural evolution in some environment on *any* selection of those complex carbon molecules, you have to have some kind of medium, like water, and some *process*, to deliver those big molecules into a place where a genetic system could self-assemble.

'Imagine the young Earth, still roiling from the big final bombardments as the planets formed. There would have been a murk of carbon and nitrogen chemistry delivered by comets and such – ammonia, carbon dioxide and water. And we know that amino acids – even RNA, the first replicator molecule – can form by chance, for example if a warm puddle, or even a mist, is hit by lightning strikes . . .

'Then you have to have it all stirred up or forced into contact, maybe through being trapped on clay surfaces, or concentrated in a drying-out tidal pool. And *then*, presumably if you are lucky enough, all this concentrated sludge starts to self-assemble into structural units, proteins, alongside some kind of information-retaining structure like DNA, which is itself an assemblage of amino acids. The components of the machine *and* the blueprint.

'And *then*, when you have a structure that is capable of self-replicating – even if slowly and clumsily in the beginning – you have the beginnings of life. Natural selection gets to work right from the off, as the marginally better replicators out-breed the lesser.

'Nobody knows if this *had* to have happened at all. Was it inevitable? If so there could be life everywhere there's a world even remotely like Earth: heat, carbon, water, nitrogen. This is still speculative, after centuries of study.

'But surely, however life came about, you have to have *some* process like that, you see – *mesobiosis*, they call it, chemistry becoming life, life from lifelessness – or at least the components of life.

'*But*,' she said heavily, 'it doesn't seem to be the case that our specific kind of coding and reproduction system, *our* DNA design, is the only one that could prevail. Protein space, remember?

'Look, you need around twenty amino acids to make a protein, and there are a hundred different proteins in nature – our nature. But there are a lot of different combinations of acids you could pick out, one by one, until you get to twenty – always supposing you have to stop at twenty.' She thought that over. 'I suppose in principle you could have a hundred to power twenty different protein designs – umm, that's *ten thousand trillion trillion trillion*.'

'A lot,' said Boyd.

'A lot. Of course they wouldn't all be functional . . . Hmm . . . Just thinking that through. How many stars in our universe?'

Zaimu checked. 'A mere ten billion trillion.'

Boyd snorted. 'Wimpish. So there are more *types* of protein than there are individual stars in our universe, many orders of magnitude more. So there's no need to imagine that every possible combination of twenty-fold protein sets has been tried out, anywhere in our universe – no need to imagine our particular set of proteins and aminos and DNA types is in any way optimal, the best. Our set has emerged from natural selection, so it does its job pretty well, but there *must* be many other designs that would work still better, out in chemistry-set space. And Feathers' DNA? Or whatever she has?'

Meriel shrugged. 'Similar to ours, broadly. A subtly different corner of DNA space, and I haven't figured it all out—'

Boyd said, 'Good job. You've got to leave something for the geniuses on the *Cronus* to work out.'

The rest chuckled.

Salma joined in, but didn't really get the joke. *Billions and trillions . . .*

She often felt more than a little out of her depth in fast, high-information conversations like this, even when the others made an effort to include her. Sometimes she was very aware of her lack of any kind of formal schooling, which she knew, because they told her, all the rest had had. Still, she could joke, join in their laughter.

And Feathers stirred, hearing Salma's voice, the chuckles, and made the soft clucking sound that Salma had come to associate with pleasure. Salma grinned and rubbed her back.

Boyd leaned forward now, took more coffee.

'Maybe we're looking at this the wrong way up. It's easy to concentrate on the differences. So she has a different genetic-chemistry makeup. So what? Maybe that doesn't matter so much. In what ways is Feathers *like* us?'

Meriel shrugged. 'OK, another good question. Well, she's an evidently intelligent creature, who has evidently emerged from an evolutionary process. Natural selection, like ours in some way.

'To evolve at all, you have to have some equivalent of DNA, a record that defines how to build another little Feathers. As you say, Boyd, the precise medium may not matter. 'But you have to give the DNA-analogue room to play, to pass on traits to offspring. You have to be a creature that *has* offspring . . .'

And she glanced over at Feathers. Salma knew everybody would be thinking about the sad little eggs she frequently laid now, unfertilised, pointlessly hidden in improvised nests throughout the habitat.

Meriel said, 'But that offspring has to have differential levels of fitness. Meaning, fit to the environment you find yourself in. And you need some kind of selection process to weed out that fitness – like our natural selection, evolution. So, just by chance variations of the genes, you get a bunch of little Feathers, of whom some are a little better at flying, say, than their siblings. And maybe that enables them to do just that bit better at surviving than the groundhogs, and so *their* genes survive a bit better, proportionately. And the same process occurs in the next generation – fly better, you have more kids. Pretty soon everybody's flying around like nobody's business—'

'Until the hawk comes along to take out the chicks,' Boyd growled. 'But why get *smart*?'

Meriel said, 'Fair question again.'

'On a roll,' Boyd murmured.

'There's a huge cost. I mean, to become smarter, in our kind of body plan anyhow, you need a bigger brain, and supporting networks – senses, nervous systems, stuff that allows the brain to take in information and then act on it by giving the body orders. But all that is expensive, in terms of energy. So, yes – why get smart at all?'

'You can make better weapons,' Joe suggested. 'Better than

the claws nature gave you. Better tools all round. Your chances of survival must be better.'

Meriel pressed on. 'OK. But it's more fundamental, more powerful than that. The smarter you are, the more you learn and remember, the more you can predict the future – you can guess where the food is – and ultimately even control your food supply, by becoming some kind of cultivator. A farmer. Like humans, and some ants by the way. And with language, when you get around to inventing that, you can pool your intellects, and achieve stuff no one could achieve alone, or even with a few immediate family, like a chimp pack. All of which gives your genes a still better chance of propagating than the other guy's.'

Boyd said, 'But then you have to go and spoil it all and invent stuff like intensive farming—'

'Right. You win until you get to the point where you are despoiling your environment, and even then if you're smart enough you stop . . .'

'Hm,' said Hild. 'It does make you wonder why intelligence isn't even more widespread than it is. In Earth's biosphere, I mean.'

Meriel shrugged. 'I'm no expert, remember. But there is plenty of intelligence rattling around on Earth – the birds, for example. Their song is pretty elaborate, their flocking, their nesting behaviour pretty intricate. You ever try to make a bird's nest as a kid? . . . I guess most of you never got the chance. Anyhow, you end up with a handful of straw. The cephalopods, like the octopuses, tend to be solitary, so they put together fantastic gardens of stuff that does nobody else any damn good at all. And there are lots of collective intelligences, without any single over-brain, or consciousness, at all. Like the ants, with hives like intricate, self-assembling machines. They do pretty well—'

'OK, OK,' Boyd said. 'But look, with all due respect to the

octopuses, *we* aren't just smart. As we said before. We are the only intelligent species to have deliberately, if dumbly, screwed up the whole planet – and then, maybe more significantly, rebuilt it again. The climate-recovery decades, all those heroic stories we heard at school . . . And after *that* we have been the only species to get off the Earth – aside from a few bugs that may have hitched a ride to Mars on splashed-off meteorite debris.' He waved a hand. 'We are the only species to have built spacecraft, to come out to places like this . . .

'But now, evidently, here's Feathers and her folk. And they have evidently done something similar. Broken out of their world. Gone to the stars. Gone even further, if that black hole is any clue . . .'

Hild asked, 'So what are you getting at, Boyd?'

'*What are the odds?* What are the odds of another tool-wielding, world-shaping intelligence showing up in this galaxy of ours? And on top of that, what are the odds of it looking even remotely like us, as Feathers does? And what are the odds of it showing up here? And what does it *mean* . . .' He ran down. 'Ah, hell. I think I'm getting out of my depth here.'

'No, no.' Joe started tapping eagerly at screens. 'It's a good question. Because we might be able to use this line of thinking to estimate how far Feathers here has come.'

Meriel looked sceptical. 'Convince me.'

'I'm trying to dig out some data, such as it is,' he said, staring at his screens. 'There used to be a theory about this, you know. Centuries back, when we knew a lot less about life in the universe, or the lack of it, than we do now. It used to be thought that the human body was such a natural winner that the sky was *bound* to be full of human-like forms: the hands, the brain, the vision equipment on top of an upright frame . . . Yeah. Here it is. They called it *convergence*.' He stressed the word. 'The idea was that maybe there was only one basic useful design if you wanted to make a planet-builder. That is, the human design.'

'Get to the point sometime today,' Hild said, not unkindly.

'OK. The point is that not all lines of evolution will *yield* such a planet-builder.' He tapped his screen some more.

Salma saw numbers scrolling.

'Consider this. There are thought to be a *trillion* species on Earth right now.' He looked up. 'Impressive. Even the climate-collapse mass extinctions didn't make much of a dent in the overall numbers, although most of the glamorous species went, or survived only in zoos . . . But it's thought that over time about ninety-nine per cent of all species that arose on Earth have gone extinct. So that's a total of a *hundred* trillion species on Earth. I imagine that number gets fuzzy when you work back through the tree of life to the beginning and species merge and split . . .'

'The *point*, Joe?'

'Sorry, Hild. Here's the argument. So *one* in a hundred trillion species on Earth, us, turned out to be planet-shapers – and *we* showed up late in Earth's evolution, a couple of million years ago out of four billion or more.

'Now, what if you take that as a ball-park estimate for the chances of *any* planet evolving technological life like us? At least one species?'

'One in a hundred trillion,' Boyd said. 'OK, I'll buy that. How many planets in the Galaxy?'

Joe checked his screen. 'A lot less than a hundred trillion – more like forty billion habitable. Just an estimate, of course.'

'Umm. OK. So how many galaxies for a hundred trillion planets?'

A quick on-screen calculation. 'Twenty-five hundred. Wow.

That's the size of a supercluster. A hundred million light-years across. Maybe more.'

There was a silence after that.

'So,' Boyd said, 'to an order of magnitude, we could have expected Feathers here to have had to travel a journey the scale of a supercluster—'

'Just to find one other tool-wielding, planet-scarring culture like our own. But it's worse than that,' said Joe, staring into his screen. 'I love playing with numbers like this. She hasn't had to find just another tool-making culture. To make this visceral connection with us, *she's had to find one which is humanoid in body form* – like her, more or less.'

'Wow,' Hild said. 'And what are the odds of *that*?'

Nobody knew.

Boyd said, 'Let's make a wild guess.

'Humour the old guy. Suppose it's about the same order as the odds of finding such an intelligent culture in the first place. Just suppose for now; the super-brains on *Cronus* can come up with a better guesstimate when they get here. But for now, if you multiply the culture number times the body plan number—'

'It means another factor of a hundred trillion,' Joe said. 'You'd need to search a hundred trillion times a hundred trillion planets . . . These numbers are absurd. There are thought to be around a billion trillion planets in the universe. Shit. There are too few planets in the entire damn universe to make that a worthwhile bet.'

'Then how many universes?' Hild snapped.

'How many universes? What does that even *mean*?' Joe looked discomfited, but made the calculation on a screen. 'Ten million, it says here. Ten million universes the size of ours . . .'

'Or,' Boyd said quietly, 'if our universe was ten million times *older*, it might be a fair bet.'

That made them think, Salma realised.

'Umm.' Joe pawed at his screens. 'Ten million times older . . . A hundred thousand trillion years? That far in the *future*, our universe will be a dark place, all the stars burned out . . .'

Hild said, 'You know something – I think we made some kind of breakthrough here. Even if my head's spinning—'

'Mine isn't,' said Boyd. 'I think we got an answer to the question we started off with – even if these are just guesses, if the actual numbers we're quoting are speculation. You said that even if Feathers doesn't have a literal message, something to tell us directly, then maybe her very presence here *is* the message.' He looked around. 'And that message is that we're dealing with something from outside our universe. From somewhere else. Some other place that's very big, or very old. Or both. Something, or somebody.'

The mood was sombre now, Salma realised. Hild muttered something about writing all this down, sending the conclusions back to the Conserver bases . . .

Boyd nodded. 'And what we have to figure out now is what that somebody *wants*. And what it will cost us.'

Feathers, evidently sensing the change in atmosphere, wriggled over to Salma.

Salma held her tight.

Year 6

AD 2261

19

In the final months and weeks of the six-year flight from Earth, John Smith had intended to spend his time at the windows of the big viewing lounges that occupied much of the equator of the passenger hull of the *Cronus*. In fact, he'd scheduled to have himself woken out of cryo six months out from the arrival of the *Cronus* at Saturn, for that very purpose.

Only to discover that from here Saturn was still no more than a pinprick of light. And *then* to discover that six months was a hell of a long time if one was confined with little to do, even after a years-long sleep.

It did occupy a few days, but no more, to catch up with the news, and with downloaded messages and technical papers from his own office on Earth, and from the Conserver home base at the heliopause. Most of the messages concerned the science of Planet Nine, and global curiosity about the creature called 'Feathers' — against the background of the quasar's steadily increasing and malevolent effects on the Earth.

As the years had passed, the intensity of the heat in which Earth and the rest of the Solar System was bathed had continued to increase. By now the increased heating amounted to an extra day's sunlight load per year. It still didn't sound much, but year on year more of that energy had to be absorbed by the planet's various natural reservoirs: the air, the land, the oceans. Year on year that additional load grew, slowly but exponentially increasing. And the fragile, barely recovered systems of Earth – living, climatic, geological – and political – were increasingly feeling the strain.

It was a paradox that off-world colonies, including on the Moon, fared better than the home planet; out there all you had to do was throw a few more layers of reflective insulation over your habitat. But, tentatively, slowly, cautiously, the space industries were responding, such as with the floating of huge new reflective sails over the planet to deflect the increased insolation.

But there was more urgent news. In particular, Smith discovered with faint alarm, a high-performance Lunar Consortium ship, the *Aquila* – eagle-fast as its name implied, he supposed – had been detected apparently pursuing the *Cronus* out towards Saturn, following much the same trajectory, and would arrive at about the same time. The *Aquila* had evidently run silent and dark for most of its six-year mission, shadowing *Cronus*. Now, evidently, it was out in the open, and it was an unsettling development.

Nobody on Earth or in the Conserver councils knew what the mission of the *Aquila* was; despite heavy diplomatic pressure the Consortium refused to say what it was up to. There was nothing to be done about it.

Yet another watching brief, in what felt like a slow-moving, Solar-System-wide crisis to Smith, despite his own long sleep interval.

So that was the news. All the updates consumed and absorbed. *Now what?*

He explored the ship, once again.

Only to find he didn't actually know anybody well among the currently non-sleeping passengers. There was a logic to that.

Those he met now had mostly been sleeping in his own early period of wakefulness.

Even Elizabeth Vasta, senior science adviser to the top layer of Earth's multinational government, was absent. He knew that *she* had put herself into cryosleep a mere three weeks after launch from Earth high orbit, and, he learned now, intended not to wake until three weeks before the destination. Probably sensible. He even considered asking to be put back in the sleep tanks himself, only to find that the medical advice was against submitting oneself to another dose of cryo so soon after the last.

So he was stuck here, trying to get some work done – trying to find useful work to *do* – trying not to feel too guilty about another dose of opulent living, unwanted and unearned.

Guilty, yes, that was inescapable.

John Smith was a dedicated Conserver partly because of his own background. He had grown up in the slums of New Los Angeles, a legacy now carefully hidden beneath a layer of education and cultivation. He had come to understand that one result of Earth's one-time addiction to uncontrolled economic growth had been such wells of impoverished misery.

Smith had been lucky in the education he had received from various charitable institutions – some Christian groups, battling the general post-climate-crash downturn in religious activity, and he had done a lot of Bible studying because of that – and including, most valuably as it turned out, a mission to Earth from the Conservers themselves. In time, and perhaps as a reaction to all that had gone before, in his own life as well as what he had seen of the world, he had gladly accepted the Conservers' quiet philosophy, their obvious logic, their teachings, and the practices they preached. The basic message was after all simple. *The Solar System looks like a big place to expand into – but so did the Earth, once . . .*

And so he knew that hurling this big luxury hotel across ten astronomical units was a gross misuse of the common resources of mankind: a waste of materials and energy, as well as of the many, many hours of labour it had taken to design, build and crew this thing.

But he also believed that the astonishing discoveries at Nine justified the full attention of mankind, including, for once, the expenditure of such huge resources. The moral compromise had to be made; the mission had to be achieved.

And there was wonder to be cherished. At last, as the long journey of the *Cronus* drew to a close – even though many of the onboard experts continued to look out at the quasar speck in the deep sky – as Saturn finally loomed ahead, for Smith there was only one show in the heavens.

John Smith knew the basic orbital geometry of the Saturn system.

You had the planet itself, a gas giant more than ten times the width of the Earth, turning on its axis in an unreasonable ten hours: it spun so fast it was visibly flattened by rotation away from a pure sphere. The sunlight was dim here, almost autumnal. Saturn was ten times as far as Earth from the Sun, so its sunlight was only one per cent of the intensity of that at Earth – but still the light was better, more useful, than Smith had expected.

And in this September light you could actually see, via simple telescopes, the elevator hub: a speck shining bravely about the planet's radius above the clouds, though the thin thread of the elevator cable itself, dipping into those clouds, was invisible as yet.

That hub was the destination of John Smith and the *Cronus*.

The timescale for the final approach was set by the ten-hour spin of the planet itself, which was matched by the hub's orbital speed. So it took a few hours of manoeuvring for the *Cronus* to sweep in from interplanetary space, heading for that elevator hub.

A thrilling few hours, more grand spectacle.

The first encounter was in fact with Titan, Saturn's largest moon, where the ship's drive was squirted to gain a gravity-assist boost – an 'Oberth manoeuvre', apparently, stealing a little of Titan's own orbital energy to slow the ship down and help it lodge in the greater gravity well of the giant planet. And at closest approach to Titan, a world in itself, Smith and his fellow window-watchers peered out.

Titan was known to be rich in useful resources. Even its air was mostly the super-useful gas methane, relatively cheaply extracted from the moon's shallow gravity well, and employed as propellant by ships such as the *Cronus* itself before its helium-3 refit. But, under international law, Titan as yet had been left largely unexploited and unexplored, save for a few automated probes. That was because of Titan's similarity, as it was perceived, to primeval Earth. Even if it had no life itself, Titan as a model of a prebiotic Earth like world could be hugely scientifically valuable, if only as a comparison: *this is how Earth was, once . . .*

John Smith knew that the Lunar Consortium chafed at such restrictions, and had put forward proposals to mine Titan more extensively, going beyond the scoop-mining of methane from the top of its atmosphere, to taking nitrogen from ammonia layers deeper in the air and on the ground, and eventually digging into the moon's water-ice core. This would disrupt the moon's scientific value permanently – and, if some kind of life did linger in Titan's cold oceans, an early extermination could follow, perhaps even without discovery first. Earth believed in a cautious expansion of industry in such realms. The Conservers meanwhile argued for *no* industrial expansion into the Solar System.

In this case the resolution of the conflict had played out well, Smith thought. With the coming of the Saturn space elevator, even the aerial mining of Titan's methane was to be largely abandoned, in favour of extraction of the gas, and others, from the upper atmosphere of Saturn itself presumed lifeless.

And for now, after a close encounter lasting just minutes, Smith was pleased to see Titan sail by, barely perturbed by this latest invasion from the bright heart of the Solar System.

While *Cronus* descended ever deeper towards Saturn and its rings.

Titan orbited at some million kilometres from the centre of Saturn – and so was in fact well outside the ring system.

And, once within Titan's orbit, John Smith and the rest eagerly peered out of the *Cronus* windows for a first glimpse of the next great spectacle.

The rings themselves extended around Saturn's equatorial plane from an inner edge at a few thousand kilometres above the cloud tops – only a tenth or so of the planet's own radius – out to around a hundred thousand kilometres.

Smith had seen the rings from further out, a belt of ice fragments orbiting the planet and shepherded into neat concentric circles by the moons' gravity – a spectacular arrangement that had looked oddly artificial to Smith. Now the ship was much closer in and tracking Saturn's equator, which was the plane of the rings too – so all that was visible was a scratch of light, a fine line before the planet. This was the ring system seen edge-on, the individual ring fragments too small and distant to make out.

But the ship needed to sail no further across the plane of the rings than its outer edge, Smith knew; the orbital mechanics demanded that the hub of any Saturn space elevator had to be in the world's equatorial plane – and, a hundred thousand kilometres above the clouds, actually outside the inner ring system. And the cable to which it was attached had to be that long, or longer, to reach down from hub through the rings and into the clouds of the planet itself.

The scale of all this was tremendous. The stately approach went on, another hour passing, and another. Smith may have dozed a while.

And after his last waking, he found a larger body loomed before the ship – a body that shone bright blue, the blue of an Earth sky, even if the wan sunlight didn't really do it justice, Smith thought. A human-built body amid this grand natural ballet.

This was the Saturn elevator hub.

The hub itself was a rough sphere, dotted with what looked like small rocket clusters – perhaps even missile launchers. That wasn't necessarily militaristic. The hub spent its life outside the main ice-swarm rings, but a collision with even a small rogue fragment could be lethal. Smith guessed he was seeing a collision-avoidance attitude control system – maybe even some kind of weapons system to break up ice chunks.

Extending from that central spherical structure, he saw a line of sky blue, the elevator cable itself, arrowing horizontally, from his viewpoint, in through the ice of Saturn's rings, straight down into the cloud layers of the planet. The cable did not reach down to any solid surface, unlike Earth's elevator; instead the line terminated in a heavy factory installation, suspended deep in the complex air.

The whole immense arrangement seemed oddly parasitic, Smith thought. But then humans were indeed draining a little of the lifeblood of this huge world, as if taking a medical sample – or as if sucking out sustenance like some tick on a human skin.

And it was startling to see this strange human colony, this human gadget, suspended in this extraordinary sky, so far from home. Smith felt a surge of pride in the achievement, a reaction to which his Conserver conscience only mildly objected. If you were going to go dipping into Saturn for its resources, this was about as non-disruptive as you could get.

And John Smith from the New Los Angeles slums could not help but be thrilled at the sight.

20

When the *Cronus* finally reached the elevator hub, the first step was to anchor together the two massive bodies, hub and ship, with rigid struts. Then transparent tunnels were attached to airlocks, through which passengers and freight could pass in either direction — tunnels through the vacuum.

When that was done, they all had to be brought off the ship, John Smith learned, in order to give the maintenance crews and their bots the room to work — and for the refit of *Cronus* with its new fusion propulsion system. Already small ferry craft had come sailing out to empty the ship's hold, and crew and specialised machines had begun dismantling its now-outmoded fission-powered engine.

It didn't take long for John Smith to pack up the gear he would need during his brief stay on the hub. Most of his already modest bundle of possessions would stay on the ship, to which, of course, he would return after its fitting-out for its even more extraordinary journey onwards.

The passengers were taken off in small groups — small so as not to overcrowd the facilities of the elevator hub itself. Which wasn't nearly so roomy inside as it had seemed from outside, Smith learned when he got there; the habitable spaces were swathed in layers of ice-fragment impact shields that were thicker than he had realised.

Still, there was a zero-gravity melee as the *Cronus* passengers were shepherded through a final security and quarantine barrier and into the reception areas.

And it was during the crowding of the debarkation process that Smith ran into Elizabeth Vasta.

Smith hadn't seen Earth's top science adviser since she had put herself into cryosleep only weeks after the launch. Now her black pearl pendant, a relic of life from Earth, gleamed in the pale light of Saturn, as she casually gripped a rail to keep from floating around.

She grinned at him. 'So, John, good to see you. Good long sleep?'

'Not so deep or so long as yours.'

'I do have a twinge of guilt at not keeping you company. Although I do know you Conserver types are a little anti-social.'

He frowned at that. 'I'd prefer, reserved—'

'Reserved or not, here you are, Mr Smith.'

A tall, gangling man in a crisply creased coverall approached them. Shoulder flashes, John observed. An officer.

'And, as the most distinguished guests among this shipload, Professor Vasta, Mr Smith, I'm here in person to tell you you're very welcome. I'm Emmanuel Caspar. Commander of this installation. Please, come this way.'

After perfunctory handshakes, Caspar led them with easy pulls along hand rails on a slow zero-gravity traverse through corridors still crowded with passengers and station crew.

Pale, with thinning red-brown hair, maybe mid-thirties, Caspar looked friendly in a professional sort of way, Smith thought.

Caspar said now, 'Formally, I'm a commander in the United Earth Air Force – as you probably know . . .'

214

They had known. Caspar's coverall was a lighter blue than the standard issue to the crew at the quarantine barrier, Smith noticed now, maybe a sign of rank. He thought Caspar had an accent Smith had learned, in his time on Earth, to call European English – the light tang of a language familiar but not one's own.

All the while Caspar led them on, he was evidently sizing them up, and their fellow passengers. Smith had the feeling that one false step would have this Commander Caspar throwing them in a cell with little compunction. But then this station was far from home and an obviously fragile habitat, so lifeboat rules must apply, and commanders and captains had to be harsh when needed.

'I've had the luggage you'll need while on the station sent to your rooms.' Caspar grinned. 'Including your chess set, Mr Smith. A luxury?'

'John, please – how would you know that? Oh, the cargo manifests.'

'I always do a search, to find players among newcomers. My son Fabio plays the game. I don't, sadly, or not well enough – not since he passed the age of five. Ten years old now. And not enough chess played here. Maybe you could catch up with him some time?'

Vasta seemed surprised at that. 'Your son is here?'

'Plenty of families up here, Professor Vasta. The station is fifteen years old already, though the methane extraction operation hasn't been operating that long. And I'm sorry to be hurrying you, but there are some pretty unique things you need to be shown while we have the chance . . .'

A spatter of red lights lit up on the ceiling and walls, and a softly spoken voice issued an evidently automated warning. And then came a loud, multiple *clang* that made Smith start.

Caspar didn't lose his rhythm. 'That's just the decoupling,' he said, shepherding them along. 'Nothing to worry about. The

Cronus detaching from the hub – already, and on time, I'm glad to say: we are keeping to an aggressive schedule to get this project done. *Cronus* is straight off to the jig factory for her refitting. For now she's not accessible, but don't worry, your ride onwards is in good hands. But first—'

They came to a lounge, hardly a tenth as spacious as some of the big spaces aboard the *Cronus*, Smith thought, but comfortable enough – certainly for a man used to Conserver chic.

But the view out made up for the lack of room. Or rather the view *down*, through a crystal-clear floor.

In this lounge there were chairs fitted with loose belts, and bars for legs to wrap around, and glass tables with covered bowls of some kind of snack, and bottles and flasks all held in place by clips and straps. A zero-gravity lounge, like those on the *Cronus*. But as they sat, Smith saw immediately that you were meant to sit at these glass tables and look *down* through the transparent floor.

Where the clouds of Saturn roiled. The ring system, seen edge on, was that now-familiar straight-line scratch across the sky.

And, looking down, hanging here above the air, Smith immediately picked out the elements of engineering that justified the routine existence of this place. He saw a fine line arrowing down into those clouds, evidently the space elevator cable itself – or rather cables, several of them, presumably some for lifting and lowering, some for power transmission, others as some kind of emergency backup perhaps. Cables made by humans and their machines, anchored by a knot of industrial technology, and plunging down through the rings and into the air of the planet.

Smith had seen Earth's space elevator. This huge structure, mining the clouds of a gas giant, dwarfed anything terrestrial. It was an audacious concept from this angle, a remarkable sight – thrilling, even for an instinctive Conserver.

Caspar let them just look for a few moments. Then he opened a small cupboard under the nearest table. 'Champagne? Coffee? Both? Captain's privilege . . .'

Neither Smith nor Vasta felt like talking, evidently, as Caspar served the drinks in bulb flasks. Sitting here, Smith did feel oddly exhausted, in fact – some combination of his extraction from an environment he had been stuck in for six years, the shock of new faces . . . Conservers were supposed to live quietly, he reassured himself.

The champagne felt flat, and the coffee lukewarm.

Vasta too was a little subdued, though she was better at hiding it than Smith, he thought.

Caspar was sensitive enough to see their reactions, and rather than force them to converse he took the lead. 'I know how it feels to be suddenly suspended in all this – spectacle. Overwhelming. And the scale of it is profoundly un-Earthly. But it soon becomes business as usual. I was mostly ground-based – I mean, Earth-based – before I applied for this job. It requires more diplomacy than many postings, what with representatives of so many agencies, nationalities, corporations, all working, living and playing up here. And specialists from cable engineers to biologists looking for life in the clouds. As for the military side, I can leave that to the lower ranks save in emergencies.

'Life here isn't as comfortable as it might be. This is an outpost, far from home. But people do *live* here. This is my twelfth year on the station, fifth as commander. We get by. My own son is here – Fabio—'

Smith smiled. 'The chess fiend.'

Vasta looked at Caspar more closely. 'His mother too?'

'Afraid not. She left a few years ago – on one of the regular transports. There have been more of those recently; a lot more propulsion engineers and related workers have been brought here for the rebuild of *Cronus*, as you can imagine. And a lot of planetologists and other specialists have been sent back to Earth to make room, mostly volunteers. Lynette . . . was never happy here. The confinement, I think. Whereas I—' He waved a hand. 'I think I've found a role here.'

Vasta said, 'But — Fabio, was it? What of him?'

'We gave him the choice. To stay or go—'

'He had to choose his father or his mother? At, how old, *seven, eight*?'

Caspar looked increasingly uncomfortable, but he was standing his ground. 'We are a deep-space society now, Professor Vasta. Such dilemmas are hardly unique. Why, separated families may become the norm in the future — but the sooner we get faster links between the planets, the more human the Solar System will become, those family ties less disrupted. But as to the present project . . .' He turned to look out of the windows. 'How could I give up all this? And the chance to work on a ship like *Cronus*, on such a mission?'

Vasta and Smith exchanged a glance. That was the end of that topic, Smith thought.

They followed Caspar's lead in turning back to the windows.

Caspar went on, 'I wanted to bring you straight up here to view the scene of the crime, as it were. Orientation. Because the station at the other end of this tether is collecting what you've come for.'

Smith peered down. Now he saw clusters of tanks, in hexagonal arrays, attached to the cable along its length, each slowly ascending from or descending into the clouds of Saturn. 'Ah. That's the helium-3 for the *Cronus*, is it? The fuel for its fast mission to Planet Nine.'

Caspar nodded. 'Well, along with other useful gases. In normal operations, of course, the *Cronus* crew would already be taking on board the methane propellant they would need for the long, six-year journey back home to the inner System – and we would have already hauled *that* up the elevator cable from the clouds below. Now we are extracting the helium-3 that will enable *Cronus* to go much further and faster, to reach Nine in a reasonable time. But even after this mission, the helium extraction process is going to be a bootstrapping arrangement that could lead to very large industrial complexes here indeed – and ultimately transform the prospects for Earth itself.'

Vasta nodded. 'The Kardashev project . . . I've heard of that. Still a long way off.'

'True. For now. Of course everything we do needs power, and even out here it all starts, in fact, with the Sun.' He pointed upwards.

Smith and Vasta looked up now, through a transparent section of the roof. And Smith saw what looked like a flower, a stalk with petals, shining dimly in the low sunlight – or rather he saw one edge of such a structure. Huge in scale, evidently.

'Solar energy capture?' Vasta said.

'Correct. We are ten times as far from the Sun as Earth, so – inverse square law – you need a hundred times the area of solar cells to capture the equivalent power. But we have the room for that. This isn't the crowded low orbit of Earth . . . That solar sail, around two kilometres across, was built for the operation of extracting methane from Saturn's atmosphere – for now. Soon we will be switching over to the helium-3 extraction, of course.'

Vasta frowned. 'I can't do the math in my head. I've probably slept too much the last six years . . . A power plant that size ought to yield about twenty megawatts, with decent efficiency?'

'About that.'

'And the methane extraction rate?'

'Not so easy for you to guess, I'd think,' Caspar said. 'But maybe faster than you might suppose. We believe we've a smart design in terms of exploiting the environment down there.

'The cloud composition changes with depth, you see. In the uppermost layers you have mostly ices, ammonia, along with traces of water, methane. But hydrogen and helium are both gases. To get at the methane easily, we send our miners a few kilometres deeper into the air, where the temperature rises a little, and we come to a sweet spot where the temperature is about a hundred and sixty below the freezing point of water, pressure about seventy per cent Earth's atmospheric pressure. *There* you have an environment where hydrogen and helium are both *gaseous*, and ammonia and water are both *ices* – but methane forms *liquid* droplets. So all you have to do to separate out the methane is to collect the *only* liquid component at that level. In fact the energy we need to lift the methane out of the deep atmosphere is the main cost – even though to sieve out one kilogram of methane you have to process over two hundred kilograms of air.'

'Very elegant,' Smith said. 'But now you're switching over to extracting helium-3. Which I imagine is more of a challenge.'

'True. But we've already had six years, since your launch from Earth, to figure out a way. And, given how crucial helium-3 is going to be to the Earth's economy some day, even aside from the *Cronus* mission – so I'm told—'

He glanced at Vasta, who nodded.

'The principle is the same. We just need to go deeper into the atmosphere. Helium-3 is as abundant here as it is anywhere in the Solar System. Far more abundant than on the Moon, of course. But still to extract a kilogram of *that* stuff from the clouds you have to process, not two hundred kilograms of air as with methane, but six hundred *tonnes* of it. In this scenario the energy cost of extraction from the air is much larger than the lift to orbit costs – three times as much. But, hey, the solar energy is free. As I understand it, for a return trip the *Cronus* will need around five hundred kilograms of fuel, which will have taken us a hundred days to extract, allowing for inefficiencies, given our twenty-megawatt power plant. Some of it we already have in store.'

Vasta nodded again. 'I do know they're going to take a lot longer than that to fit out the *Cronus* for this halfway-to-the-stars trip, in your improvised shipyard.'

Caspar said, 'But it has to be done. To get to deep space. I fully accept the logic of the mission. We have to get boots on the ground out there. We know the situation out at Planet Nine is – compelling, if not urgent.'

Vasta snorted. 'Compelling? More than that. If it has anything to do with the quasar and the effects on Earth – yes, getting us out there is damn urgent.'

'I do understand,' Caspar said calmly. 'Which is why we've got started already. Come, follow me. There's a better view from another lounge. We are quite the nest of engineers here, always busy . . .'

He pushed out of his chair, and Vasta and Smith followed.

It was a tough little trek. Caspar set a fast pace through a maze of corridors, and Smith felt that both he and Vasta tired quickly. *Should have slept less and exercised more en route.*

But aside from that it was bewildering to be in a new place after so long confined to the ship, large as that great vessel had been. Not only that, as they approached the apparent destination, there were crowds to push through, both of Hub staff and *Cronus* crew, busy, Smith supposed, with the handover of crew to fusion-propulsion engineers.

But Caspar was the base commander, and people magically

cleared out of his way, especially with two high-status guests in tow. That magic still worked when they got to the observation lounge he wanted.

And when the guests were delivered before another big picture window, Smith immediately saw what he meant by a better view.

'That,' Caspar said, 'is what my teams call a jig factory . . .'

Saturn below, starry sky above, the brilliant, perfectly flat line that was the ring plane edge-on. And there, hanging in space, a few kilometres away – magnified by the window – Smith saw the *Cronus*, that now-familiar dumbbell configuration.

He reminded himself just how big the thing was: the two large spheres each more than a hundred metres in diameter, the total ship length a third of a kilometre. But there were other components drifting in space now, besides the main hulk, some of them huge themselves.

And the ship as a whole was moving, but evidently not under its own propulsion system. Smith saw little sparks of light coming from small ferry craft, now docked with that enormous hull – a fix-up to enable precise short-term manoeuvring. People were moving around the hull too, some in suits with long, fragile-looking umbilicals, some flying independently with flaring backpack rockets. From this distance they looked like ants. Flying ants. Or glow worms perhaps, he thought.

And this industrial swarm was guiding the huge ship *into* an even larger form, a rough rectangular frame of struts and girders, longer than it was tall. A box big enough to hold an interplanetary spacecraft.

Caspar watched his guests, grinning. 'That, my new friends, is a jig factory. Essential bit of kit for assembly in space – or disassembly. Keeps everything lined up, you see, in the absence of gravity, as you put it all together. I've seen this kind of manoeuvre before. Never palls. Beautiful, isn't it? In its way. An elephantine ballet.

'Well. I think that's enough for today. Shall I show you to your rooms?'

It took only a month for the *Cronus* to be refitted with its new fusion-fuel interplanetary engine. John Smith saw it all.

And, aboard the Consortium ship *Aquila*, Jeorg North, glaring into high-definition scopes, was there in time to see it finished. Or should have been.

21

'Can you see it yet?'

'Not yet, damn it . . .'

Jeorg North was in the nominal pilot's seat in the *Aquila*'s cramped bridge. Indeed he was nominal ship's commander, given that the crew of this adapted Earth-Moon ferry numbered just two, for this stretch mission to Saturn.

His only companion was Doria Bohm, herself a leader of a diffuse rebel faction on the Moon.

Few of the Lunar Consortium's ruling elite, such as it was – even those who had strongly approved of the mission of the *Aquila* – had been overjoyed about this choice of crew. Especially since Jeorg, their pilot, a defector from Earth, had a connection by marriage to somebody who was actually slated to be on the *Cronus* when it was sent to Planet Nine.

That, Jeorg admitted, was a strong, if not the only, motive for his volunteering for this mission: to get back at his husband, Bheki Molewa. Bheki, who had jumped at the chance, when he was surprisingly offered it, of riding the *Cronus* to Saturn, and then on to Nine. Without a backward glance, it felt like, at his husband of a decade.

Their divorce had been done in a helium-3-fast flash.

Well, however Jeorg and Doria had got into this ship, it had been one heck of a ride so far. A rebel pilot from Earth and a rebel lunar – both highly motivated to do this, if for different reasons, and somehow they had gotten along during the *six years* of this mission, shadowing *Cronus* all the way . . .

But a glance through the various views of their target drove home to Jeorg that the journey wasn't over yet.

'If you want pretty views of Saturn, I've got them,' he said. 'But the elevator hub and all the stuff going on around it is a blur. Still too far out.'

'We're doing our best, Jeorg. And so is this beat-up bird of ours . . .'

She was right, of course.

The *Aquila* had been designed as a Moon to Earth-orbit cargo ferry, in essence – but with the capability to go further, the asteroids in particular in mind. Its acceleration was not much less than that of the *Cronus* – both based on the same uranium-fission technology – and it had been able, just, to match the much larger ship in making this long, slow, mostly unpowered transfer from Earth to Saturn. But still, it was a rattly bird, a floating coffin, compared to the roomy liner they were chasing, and Jeorg, despite long periods of cryosleep, was old enough for the rattling to be a pain, and to suffer at long confinement in such a small craft.

Doria, absently stroking the obsidian-disc pendant at her neck, looked over his shoulder at various consoles. 'Still too far out – that's not good enough. We don't have a rendezvous solution yet. The predictive algorithms must be able to do better than that. I mean we know what we're looking for. The *Cronus*, in a damn jig . . . It's pretty hard to miss.'

'Yeah. But what we need is a precise location, a precise pre-diction of when they're going to launch the damn thing, so we know when to close in and *be* there, and for that we need detail.

Ah, I've tried long enough. You take over if you think you can do better.'

Ill-tempered, scratchy, cooped up in this tiny ship, he loosened his harness and pushed out of the chair – but came out clumsily, scraping his leg. Feeling a little groggy too. That was the effect of the thrusters, he knew.

Doria laughed at his scrape. 'We'll make a spacer of you yet, Earth boy.'

But before Jeorg could dig out a suitable response – indeed one he hadn't used before, after the years of the voyage – Doria held her hand up, staring into the monitors.

'Actually I think I have something. Imagery's getting a little sharper. Yes, I think it's extrapolating a formation from what must be the jig frame lights, and the lamps on the ship itself, on *Cronus*. And—'

'Just tell me . . .'

She hesitated. 'Let me verify . . . We've found her. The *Cronus*.'

'Shit.'

He copied over the image to his own monitor, examined it, magnified it.

'There she is. In her jig. At last. We're going in.' He began to clear his board in preparation for a high thrust burst.

Doria said nervously, 'And then they'll know we're here, won't they? And where we are.'

'Good,' he snarled.

When the news of the intruder broke, several days after their arrival here, John Smith and Elizabeth Vasta were in the elevator hub, watching the final stages of assembly of their enhanced ship, after which would come her cautious backing out of the jig frame.

They both knew how close the *Cronus* was to launch – or

relaunch, rather. In the final days and hours they had spent much time in the hub's restrictive viewing lounges, watching as much as they could. A project, Smith thought, that sometimes looked like a high-tech artist's caricature of a kicked-open ants' nest.

But Smith knew that Elizabeth Vasta hadn't much enjoyed watching the transformation – for aesthetic reasons.

She said now, 'I take it you've actually seen what those engineers have done to that beautiful ship of ours.' They'd both been given tours, mostly virtual, of the modified sections. 'The *gutting* of it . . . '

He smiled. 'It does feel like ours after six years, doesn't it? But with the right attitude, it can seem just as beautiful now . . .'

'Oh. Here she comes.'

They both peered out. The slow withdrawal from the jig was cautiously, agonisingly slow.

And the ship emerging from the jig's cocoon of struts and panels had indeed been radically transformed.

Smith clearly recalled its elegant dumbbell shape – the two big spheres, the long spine – all of it surrounded by a forest of sails, solar panels and waste-heat radiators. The forward sphere that had been their home for six years.

That had all changed.

As soon as the ship had been backed into its jig factory, the rear sphere, housing the fission engine and much of its uranium and methane fuel, had been detached and dismantled. The very anchorage at the end of the spine had been much changed.

And now onto that rebuilt anchorage had been attached a new engine entirely, based on a new, ultra-modern reactor burning helium-3 fuel. But the reactor itself, even the fuel tanks, all of it was difficult to see, dwarfed as it was by a huge new engine bell, that, unlike the old, modest fission engine nozzles, challenged the dimensions of the craft as a whole.

Smith pointed now. 'Look at that. An engine nozzle the size of a cathedral.'

Vasta grinned. 'I guess you've seen more cathedrals than I have. But that's a good comparison, yes.'

'Maybe this is *our* cathedral, our way to reach God, not through prayer, but by going out in a huge ship to the edge of the Solar System, and meeting Her?'

She winked at him. '*Her*? We in government keep all comparisons of the creature they call Feathers with gods or other supernatural beings strictly under wraps.' She looked again out of the window, at the much-evolved ship in its cradle, the industrial movements around it. 'All in just a month. Though I suppose you have to allow for the preparation time we never saw, before we got here.'

He smiled. 'And now you can fly to the Oort cloud, and bring back Feathers to Earth – where, though? The world government chambers at Geneva? Like Pocahontas in London?'

'Who?'

'Or Saint Peter in Rome, if you want the religious connection . . . though that didn't end well. Never mind.'

'That's the plan, roughly. That's if the damn quasar doesn't melt the Alps before we get home – or even melt *us*. Our ships, I mean.'

'Have you heard yet who the captain is to be, by the way?'

She grinned. 'Hadn't you been told? Commander Caspar.'

'Oh.' He pondered that. 'Commander of the elevator community itself? Should that surprise me?'

'Well, he wanted the job, and nobody here outranks him, either in the elevator hub or aboard the *Cronus*. He's made sure he's been all over the works in progress on the ship itself – in fact I found, looking back, he was even heavily involved in the specification, scheduling and equipping of the operation since long before we got here. I've seen the paperwork. Maybe this has been a long-nurtured ambition.

'He's had no complaints from the crew of the *Cronus*, including the current captain – I suspect that she was told direct from Earth that she would be standing down in favour of Caspar, that she would be going no further. But it all still depends on us getting the *Cronus* refitted successfully and on time.'

Smith frowned. 'What about Fabio? His son?'

She smiled. 'Your chess partner? I'm not sure . . .'

That was when the alarm sounded. And Caspar's own voice boomed over the links.

'All hands. We've got a problem.'

They stared out of the windows.

And their screens flickered, and filled with images and data concerning a craft John Smith immediately recognised.

The situation became clear quickly.

Once the hub's hazard monitors, checking for rogue ring-ice fragments, had picked up the signature of the *Aquila* – as soon as it came out of hiding and lit up its engine – the automatics had started to track the intruder's trajectory.

And when it appeared actually to be on a collision course with the *Cronus* in its jig – or at least heading for a close pass – alarms blared.

Smith and Vasta downloaded all the data they could, trying to understand. And soon enough they found more, higher-resolution long-distance shots of the *Aquila* itself.

Vasta grunted. 'It's one thing knowing that this craft has dogged *Cronus* all the way from Earth. It's quite another to *see* it.'

Smith nodded. 'And it doesn't help matters that the *Aquila* has no grace, none at all. That rough, blocky, cylindrical shape – it *looks* like a weapon to me, a missile, a crude club—or even a forearm with a clenched fist. And do you think they actually *are* implying some kind of threat?'

Vasta was rapidly following feeds: visual, audio, text. 'Well, they're saying nothing for now. The crew here take it that way, it seems. Emmanuel Caspar certainly will, I think. He'll be preparing for the worst. I know the authorities have been working on this, even over my head—'

'Pretty high up, then.'

She gave him a look.

'I think there must have been attempts to resolve this situation long before it reached us, here. The governments, and President Mason herself, have long been fretting about the relationship with the Consortium. But they haven't *done* anything.

'When the *Cronus* mission design was published, the Lunar Consortium wanted in. Their demands seemed reasonable. At least to be able to provide witnesses, participants, even just as passengers. They even referred to bits of history. Precedents. The Apollo astronauts, first to the Moon, claimed to be going there on behalf of all humankind. Even if that itself was all a geopolitical stunt on many levels.'

'So what's their purpose now? This Consortium ship, chasing us across the Solar System—'

Vasta shrugged. 'There is some intelligence – it says here – that they just want to have a presence in this mission. Here at the launch, if nowhere else. Just to show they have a right to be here.'

And is it plausible that that's really all they want?

Smith hesitated, not sure if he should meddle. He was a Conserver; all these political tensions between Earth and Consortium had nothing to do with him. But this was a big moment; when else could you speak freely?

He said cautiously, 'There is a way they can ensure they won't be left behind by *Cronus*. Not if they can stop it flying.'

Vasta raised an eyebrow.

And Caspar, evidently juggling feeds, chimed in. 'I heard that. Sorry, I feel the need to keep you online, Advisor Vasta. Mr Smith?'

Vasta called, 'Commander? Can you project the *Aquila*'s trajectory?'

'Sure . . .'

He hesitated. Taking a long breath, Smith imagined.

'It's actually a collision course now. Shit. I can't believe . . . You think they might actually try to harm *Cronus*? I mean, the possible consequences – not just the political – the physical harm could be immense. You're talking about two nuclear engines here, coming together . . .'

Smith thought fast and hard. *Don't make it worse, John.* 'We need to find a way to stand all this down. Look – it seems evident that the Consortium want a stake in this project.'

Vasta looked at him. 'That's obvious. So what are you suggesting?'

Smith shrugged. 'Give them what they want. Even now. It only need be a token. Maybe even get one of their own, one of the crew of this *Aquila*, onto the *Cronus*. We have time to resolve this. Umm, I see from the readouts that the *Aquila* will be here in hours, collision course or not.'

Vasta said stiffly, 'A presence on the *Cronus*. That may be politically awkward at this point.'

Smith pressed, 'You could make a case for welcoming them, scientific, diplomatic. The Consortium does represent a new branch of human society – just as I do, I guess. *I'll* be aboard, representing my own faction—'

Vasta shook her head. 'You Conservers live out in the Oort cloud under huge solar sails. You do *not* dig fission fuel and such

231

out of the face of the Moon; you are *not* in a position to throw a city-killer chunk of Moon rock at the Earth at a few days' notice.'

He smiled. 'I'm not sure if I should feel flattered by that, or not. But isn't that all the more reason to reach out to the lunars? Even at this late stage—'

She waved a hand. 'Maybe. I'm glad it's not my decision to make . . .'

'But maybe it is,' Caspar snapped. 'Or mine anyhow. Given the lightspeed delays to comms with Earth. If things happen too quickly, we're on the spot . . . I need to deal with this. And I may need your backing, Advisor Vasta.'

'You'll have it.' And, distracted, Vasta turned to peer into another of the monitors.

Looking over her shoulder, Smith saw another angle on the *Cronus* – with the Sun's low illumination heavily enhanced, and a number of guide lights on the jig structure and the ship itself shining bright.

He had the feeling something had changed. He bent, trying to see. 'Elizabeth – I thought I saw something . . .'

Vasta had leaned away, looking into the distance. Thinking. 'Maybe you're right, John. Maybe we can make this work. If the *Aquila* can get here before we launch the *Cronus* out towards Nine in three days' time . . . I imagine we'll handle the diplomacy, the clumsiness of the move. We're all a long way from home.'

Caspar grunted. 'We'll give them a good viewing position for the launch. And beer. Consortium types always like beer. But they are *not* getting a berth on my mission— not after this – ah. Wait, please.'

His image disappeared.

'*Elizabeth.*' John didn't take his eyes off his own screen. Tried not to blink, to verify that the small motions he was perceiving were real. 'Look at this.

'I think the *Cronus* is coming out of the jig.'

Vasta snorted. 'Can't be. That's days away, by the published schedule. If it is moving it ought to be obvious . . .'

But Smith leaned forward. 'And so it is, now I see it.'

'Shit.' She pressed a button. 'Commander Caspar? Paging Commander Caspar. This is Elizabeth Vasta, Please respond . . .'

Another screen lit up with Caspar's face.

Where Caspar had seemed angry before, now he looked – excited. Smith thought. Energised. Pleased with himself.

'Elizabeth? I can guess why you're calling. I should have told you, but . . . *We accelerated the schedule*. We've been working towards this for weeks – after all, there wasn't much to finish up, and it wasn't hard to lose a few days in the final test plans. It was a snap decision, and you can see we're moving already—'

'Hmm. I'm not sure the quality review panels are going to be so sanguine.'

'Orders from the top, actually, Elizabeth. Authorised by the President, ultimately. So I was told.'

'I wasn't—'

'Standing orders, in case the Consortium or any other malefactor tried to meddle with the mission. We get the ship out of there and to safety. Well, this is one hell of a meddle.'

'Damn it,' Elizabeth snapped. 'Why wasn't I consulted about this?'

'Because of the time lags, I'm in operational command,' he said, speaking quickly now.

John Smith was following all this, but slowly. 'Oh. So to avoid any chance of the Consortium people impeding the mission, in the middle of this chaotic situation, you're actually going to try to launch ahead of schedule—'

'Ahead of the *public* schedule, yes.'

'So you can get out of here before the *Aquila* even arrives? All to make sure the Consortium stays shut out?'

'It's not much of a plan, but it's all I've got. It should work. If we can get away now, they won't have the delta-V for a catch-up manoeuvre. You know how underpowered their little fission ships are.'

John put in, 'I don't know anything about that. But I know what hubris is, Commander. Talking this out may be a better option that some dangerous physical stunt.'

'Well, my team made the recommendation, and I accepted it. Advisor Vasta, again I hope you will back this as in the spirit of my orders, secret and otherwise. Look, to practical matters. Even with the accelerated schedule it's still days until the launch proper – until engine start. From that point the schedule will proceed as before. All we've cut is the final prep time. Get the *Cronus* out of there quicker. The immediate implication for you two is that you need to be ready to transfer to the *Cronus* today.'

Vasta threw her hands in the air. 'Have you any idea how many meetings I'll have to cancel to achieve that? . . . OK, Commander. I do, officially, think this is crazy, by the way. You have my authorisation. I trust you.'

Possibly mistakenly, Smith thought, but didn't say so out loud.

'Prepare for departure . . .'

On the *Aquila*, leaked voice comms and a few images had by now made the hub commander's strategy all too clear.

Jeorg tried to keep a lid on his anger. He wondered if his ex, Bheki, was at the controls of *Cronus* right now.

'The bastards,' said Doria. 'They're moving out. They tricked us over the timing.'

'You can say that again.'

'You think they planned this from the start?'

'Maybe. They didn't see us coming, but they must have had an early launch baked into the schedule as a contingency right from the off. Maybe in case of some other disaster, some natural horror show . . .'

'Damn.'

Doria was monitoring message chatter, he saw.

She said now, 'You know, there is a *lot* of complaining going on out there. At Saturn, I mean, at the elevator hub. About the early launch – not so much the commanders, but lower down, some of the engineers, the logistics people, even some of the passengers. It could be that we surprised them after all. They thought we couldn't get here, even late in their planning. Yet here we are. They're all having to rush to get ready before we close in, which isn't healthy, in terms of engineering integrity. Oh – and there are some who actually think we should be given a chance.' She looked at him. '*A place on the ship*. That's my reading. We can download all this to the Moon and get a proper analysis. If the Moon can talk to the Earth councils—'

'Too slow,' Jeorg said. 'I mean, yes, let's do that, but you're looking at an hour each way to send a message at lightspeed. And the sooner we make a decision about what the hell we do, the better. I mean in terms of changing our trajectory.'

They looked at each other. They both knew that the earlier such a change was made, the less fuel it would require, and the more options they had.

She seemed worried.

Well she might be, Jeorg thought.

'So,' she said, 'what are you saying?'

'What I'm saying is that we have to do something right now.' He grinned, which he knew was a brutal expression. 'We came out here to make a rendezvous with *Cronus*. Well, let's make it.

'Prepare for manoeuvres.'

22

'Prepare for departure.'

The command rattled around the Saturn hub, the jig – the *Cronus* itself.

Within the hour, with startling suddenness given the scale of the operation, the loading of passengers back aboard the *Cronus* was to begin.

For John Smith, this was shocking. Disruptive.

He found, in fact, that he didn't much feel like leaving this fairy-tale tower above the autumnal sea of cloud that was Saturn, with this odd little community of people, working on their odd tasks, steadily and productively, so far from home.

And Smith had had a private agenda here, after all, even leaving aside the Planet Nine issue – he was to test the legality of the extraction of resources from Saturn by a station under Earth government authority.

It was a good project for a Conserver and a trained lawyer. You couldn't take a breath in this universe without using up some useful matter, some energy. You could always be moderate in that usage, though. And the Conservers, who strove to take nothing at all from the world, who tried to get resource extractions from finite caches banned altogether, represented a higher level of conscience, Smith believed. Indeed, a higher consciousness.

But all that was abandoned now. Mere hours after the detection of the rogue Consortium craft, crew and passengers for the mission to Planet Nine were being summoned to the *Cronus* for final boarding.

Including John Smith. Saturn was done for him now. He dashed to his tiny room in the hub, grabbed all he could, and headed for his designated departure point.

Smith was to be taken from space-elevator hub to spacecraft hull in a small ferry craft: no more than thirty metres long, it was so small that crew and passengers shared the same cramped cabin as the pilot and co-pilot. He took some comfort in knowing that much of his luggage was already back aboard *Cronus*.

At the gate he was led aboard and buckled up by a nervous young cadet, who anxiously reassured Smith that these small craft were powered by fission engines. 'Old and very reliable technology . . .' Smith listened carefully, and to the safety precautions aboard, especially about an airtight plastic refuge bubble under his seat.

As it worked out, for him the crossing was smooth, the departure from the hub, the docking with the *Cronus*, both seamless.

When the hatches were opened Smith found himself being led, or zero-gravity hauled, from ferry to liner through a short, transparent transfer tube – unwisely transparent given the giddy views, he thought after the fact – guided by one crew person and a couple of bots. He feared nausea in this transparent tube, but in the event the astounding view outside, of Saturn, didn't distract him. He did peer out, though, just on the chance that he might spot the intruder that was causing so much chaos, so much rush.

And he was already starting to think of the five years' journey ahead of him out to Nine much as he now looked back on the six years from Earth to Saturn – as if he were to be imprisoned in another unusual hotel with a useful library. He'd got through it before; he would get through this next adventure. And then, in the end, could come wonder. *Planet Nine, surprise me.*

He tried to focus on the here and now.

Once through the transfer tube, his nervous young guide led Smith to his cabin, and went on his way.

Smith moved in. And, once alone, he discovered that the passengers, once safely in their cabins, were instructed to stay there while launch preparations continued.

There were contingency stashes of food and drink, plenty of information inputs. But the sudden isolation, the quiet, was eerie.

He unpacked perfunctorily.

And, suddenly, when he had finally stopped moving, for now, he felt overwhelmingly tired. It was like his boyhood city life, oddly; if you found a place of safety and stillness, you used it. And fatigue, perhaps the result of stress, consumed him.

He slept for a few hours.

Until he was woken by a knock on his cabin door.

The monitors showed him it was little Fabio Caspar, ten years old, son of Emmanuel Caspar. Smith had known it was Fabio. On the hub he had always knocked on the door the same way, when he came to play chess.

Smith opened the door, carefully not looking down, looking left and right along the corridor. 'Nope, nobody there. I'd better get back to my lawyerin'—'

Which was little Fabio's cue to float up into the air in front of him, wave his hands, and – a bonus in weightlessness – make a mid-air somersault. 'Down here, Mr Smith!'

And Smith jumped backward, this time nearly knocking his

head on the unfamiliar door frame. 'Oh, there you are—'

'Here I am, Mr Smith, here I am! Can I see your new room?'

'Well, I think it's a cabin, strictly speaking.'

Fabio came in, sniffed, gazing around at the half-sorted clutter. 'Not much space, is there?'

'It'll be weightless for most of the journey, I'm told, and that makes places seem roomier, like on the journey out—'

'I saw your old room. Better than this one! You had your own shower!'

'Well, that's true—'

'And you haven't got a window! Even though you have a room up against the pressure hull.'

He sighed. 'Well, that's true too—'

'In the old ship all the rooms by the hull had windows, didn't they? Just little round ones in case they blew out.'

'They were called "portholes" . . . Well, Fabio, it's all different now. I mean, this part of the ship—' This was the 'southern hemisphere' of the ship's big forward sphere. 'This used to be all fuel tank. Now they don't need so much fuel because they use helium-3, and you get a lot more energy out of that . . . You know all this. Anyway my old room got knocked down. Where it used to be there are big steel struts now. They had to make the whole ship stronger, lengthways anyhow, because of the new engine's higher thrust—'

'I'm going to be sleeping in my dad's room tonight. So I won't get lonely in a strange place. But I've still got my old room on the hub.'

'I know . . .'

The Caspars weren't the only family aboard the Saturn hub, and not the only family to suffer repeated separations. The long journey times from Earth had made this a posting for inevitably long stays, and so accommodations for families had been planned in from the start, as were schools and dedicated medical facilities for children. That was one reason the hub facilities were so roomy, Smith had soon learned; there were plans for still more expansions, still more families. This was a nascent colony, not just an industrial site.

But now Fabio's father was going to be away for a long time – longer than he imagined Fabio could understand, not yet. Because Emmanuel Caspar, hub commander, having already served several years on a mining operation that was evidently running well, had grabbed the chance to captain the rebuilt *Cronus* on its mission to Nine, and the adventure and glory that would follow. And that meant that Caspar had to leave behind his family, his little son alone on the hub, for ten years at least.

Now Smith looked down at the lively bundle that was Fabio. Evidently Caspar felt it was worth it, the coming separation. Something ached in Smith's heart.

A soft chime echoed through the ship's corridors.

Smith asked gently, 'Isn't that the summons? All ashore that's going ashore —'

'It just means the *Cronus* is ready to get out of the jig frame. My Dad told me.' Fabio executed another perfect mid-air somersault. 'Can we play chess, Mr Smith?'

'I'm afraid there isn't time, Fabio. Not now. You have to let your Dad take you back to the hub and your cabin, don't you?'

'Before he goes away.'

'Yes. But, look. You'll be talking to your Dad every day, won't you? By the radio?'

Fabio looked vaguely sulky. 'Not when the time lag is too long. It will be days and days.'

'Yes, all right.' Smith felt oddly desperate. Sorry for the child. He said, 'But we could still play chess, couldn't we? You and I. Even when we're far apart. Over the radio. One move a day. It could be sort of exciting. But we can play faster at the start of the mission, when the lag's not so bad.'

'We could play ten games,' Fabio said now. 'All at once. A different one every day. Then it would seem like we were playing all the time.'

Smith smiled. *Until you grow up a little more and forget all about the old man who played you at chess.* 'Smart idea. All right. Let's do that.' That soft chime again, a little louder. 'But now I think you do have to go, Fabio—'

'I'm going back again to the hub on the last ferry. My Dad's piloting it himself, back and forth. He says he wants to say good-bye to everybody. He says I can ride with him.'

'Well, that will be a treat too. I'll look for your ferry out of one of the big picture windows.'

'I'll wave! I'll get Dad to wave!'

'Not if he's piloting the ferry,' Smith said with mock horror. 'Don't worry. I'll wave back.'

Fabio hesitated for a second, then he clumsily hugged Smith, released him, and bounded off down the corridor, an extraordinary mixture, Smith thought, of lively kid and microgravity freedom.

Then Fabio called back, 'Pawn to king four, your move!'

And as it happened, as Smith would learn later, at that exact moment aboard the Lunar Consortium craft *Aquila*, Jeorg North was also thinking in terms of chess moves.

23

The *Aquila* crew, flying dark, had their own strategy, their own schedule to keep. A grand gesture to make, Jeorg mused. *Then* the locals would know they were here. Which was the whole point.

And there would be nothing the locals could do about it. *Aquila* had no fusion drive but was pretty fast on the scale of the scattered structures around them now: the Saturn hub complex, the *Cronus* in its jig factory, other technological islands, the small ferry ships that passed to and fro. All of it set out like pieces on a chess board, waiting for a move to be made.

With the *Cronus* sitting like a big fat rook, or bishop, surrounded by enemy pawns.

'Yeah,' Jeorg muttered. 'Just a chess move.'

Doria glared over. 'What's that?'

'What?'

'You said, "chess move". You do mutter when you think too hard. Bad habit on a covert mission.'

North knew that she might have added that he muttered, unconsciously, when making love, too. They'd only tried that a couple of times during the long, boring run out to Saturn; it hadn't worked out for either of them — and, yes, not helped by North's wavering concentration. Plus the fact that he missed

Bheki, despite all that had passed between them.

Now he shrugged. 'Our plan should work. Such as it is.'

The plan being to make a visible protest against the Consortium's exclusion from the Planet Nine mission.

Their best idea was to make a close, fast flyby of the revamped *Cronus* before it set sail for Nine – and the whole of the Solar System would see the stunt, and learn about the injustice that inspired it. Like one big swooping chess move, he saw now, boldly bringing a bishop or a rook into the action, one end of the board to the other.

But at this climactic moment, after years of brooding, Doria seemed to lack faith.

She said now, 'Well, so what if we do it? I'm just thinking that even if we do pull off the close approach – even if we somehow confirm that we ought to be a player in this – we've lost already. We got shut out diplomatically at the beginning of it all. Since then we've always been one step behind.'

North grunted. 'Well, if I'm honest I thought they would screw it up and give us time. That their rebuild job on the *Cronus* would overrun. We could have turned up with the thing still in dry dock, and once we were on site we'd have had a case to press for representation – at least one rep from the Moon on *Cronus*, whatever the rank. And the time to make it. Even the fancy Earthbound lawyers we hired thought we had a case for involvement, *if* we managed to be on the spot – it would have been hard for them to turn us away, even in the eyes of their own public. Mankind ought to be united at a time like this, not divided. Go out there as a united front. All that crap.'

Doria snorted. 'Yeah. Maybe we could have asked for a tow out here. That would have been a great look, wouldn't it? Look, Jeorg, I think you're becoming – over-excited.'

'What?'

'I mean it. This is all personal to you, isn't it? You have to be the big guy out in front. Long before your final blow-up, you were Earth's hotshot pilot, the first to Ceres, right? Then Nine comes along, a much bigger deal, and this *Cronus* flight is announced, and you're a sudden convert to the lunar cause – and all because your husband is flying for Earth—'

'Ex-husband.'

'Oh, right, yeah, how could I forget? Discussing that distinction livened a whole year of this dumb trip. All because Bheki was getting a ride on the *Cronus* and you weren't. Suddenly you're a convert to the lunar cause, all so you could blag your way onto this mission. We've been over and over this. You're using up years of your life on this – gesture.'

'But it's not just that,' he said, as calmly as he could.

He turned away and peered into his monitors, at heavily magnified, much enhanced, extensively labelled images of the complex of hardware around the elevator hub station. 'The *Cronus* is already pretty much out of its jig factory . . . Damn it. Look, I do care about the issues. It's clear they've paid no attention to the protests the Moon made about the schedule. In fact, once they knew our course, our likely arrival time, it looks to me like they actually moved the schedule *up* to launch their ship ahead of time, just so there was no chance of any of us hitching a ride. The Consortium was purposefully excluded. But here we are anyhow.'

She said, 'Well, there's nothing we can do now.' More uncertainly, 'Is there?'

'Nothing we can do to get on that ship, no. But maybe we can still make a point. Show that Earth can't mess with us with impunity.'

He was aware of her frowning at him.

Bishops and rooks.

He thought about it for one more second, before deciding. To implement his fallback strategy, or not. To make the biggest play of his life, he realised. And if not for his own wounded pride, then for a cause, the lunars.

Or not.

Do it. You'll be famous, win or lose. And then—

'Bishops and rooks,' he muttered.

'What was that?'

Rapidly, he began to load a new set of instructions into the ship's autopilot.

Doria tried her own consoles and looked at him sharply. 'You locked me out. What are you planning, North?'

He'd done with planning. *Just act.* '*Aquila* is named for the eagle. And you don't screw around with eagles. To hell with creeping around in the dark.'

He pressed a button to initiate a sequence he had already loaded in, tested out, during a couple of sleepless nights while Doria snored. Agonising over. It was done—

The punchy fission engine went to full power. He felt the thrust at his back.

He imagined the hot plume of super-accelerated ions roaring out of the rear of the ship – along with a flood of energetic particles and high-intensity radiation that would soon be causing every sensor and alarm in the vicinity to start pinging.

And he could *feel* this heavy ship starting to move, he could *picture* the course he'd already locked in, as a shining line through space. A line that, before the burn, had been stretching harmlessly past the lumbering *Cronus* – a line that now, as the engine thrust went on, as the acceleration bit, started to sweep across space, to his right, as he saw it in his viewscreen.

Right, towards *Cronus*.

Rook to black Queen's eight

Check.

*

A comms status board lit up immediately.

Suddenly they were visible. A dozen monitor stations around the hub, the *Cronus*, even the empty jig factory, had already pinged them, demanding to know what North's intentions were, where he thought he was heading. This was even before his own systems showed alerts of potential collisions.

At first these signals were automatic, but after only seconds human voices joined in the clamour. Stern faces in the screens.

'Ha!' He felt triumphant already. 'That woke them up.' He shut down the audio, leaving the talking heads to yell silently.

And other screens showed that the complex bulk of *Cronus* and its support structures quickly loomed closer. Very quickly, much closer.

Doria was definitely anxious now. She glanced at her own comms board: text, more talking heads. 'We're already getting formal diplomatic protests, on top of the threats of imminent destruction from the security types.'

'Hah! They can't ignore us, at least. Look, stay calm.' He tapped in a screen to show projected courses. 'We've plenty of moves we can make.'

'"Moves"? What have you committed us to?' She leaned over to see. 'Shit, you're taking us in to the *Cronus* itself. We'll come within, what, a hull diameter? We didn't discuss that.'

'Well, would you have agreed? There's plenty of room. See? I'm fixing the closest approach now. I've made us as visible as can be, on purpose mind you, and they can *see* where we're going. They can *see* this is a gesture, not a threat of destruction.'

'You sure about that?'

'It's a symbolic threat. We're *missing* the ship, that lumbering hulk. We don't *need* to damage the damn thing to make our point. Which is, don't screw with the Consortium. Because we *could* hold up this mission as long as we like. Don't sweat it. This is check, not checkmate.'

She snorted. 'Believe it or not, Earth boy, the Lunar Consortium wants to get rich, not start a war. We want to work within the law if we must, change the law to a more equitable regime if we can. We do not threaten, we do not destroy . . .'

'I thought you were some kind of lunar rebel.'

'Well, I am compared to some. But I want to achieve practical results, not make hollow gestures. And there are limits—'

A blaring siren.

Screens lit up with red flashes now, and a sepulchral voice began to sound, evidently overriding their mutes. *'Collision alarm. Collision alarm . . .'*

North stabbed a mute button.

A second of silence, as they stared at each other.

'Can't be,' North said. 'I'm clearly missing the *Cronus.*'

They turned to their stations and paged through screens.

'There,' Doria yelled, pointing. 'Dead ahead. Not the *Cronus.* Something else.'

He turned to see it. Coming out around the curve of one of the big spherical structures.

It was a small craft, maybe some kind of ferry, coming out of the shadow, orbiting *Cronus.*

'That's not supposed to be there.' North hammered at his controls.

But the ship itself had become aware of the potential collision. Now attitude thrusters fixed to the outside hull squirted on automatic, each brutal thrust sounding, *feeling* like a giant slamming the outer hull with a sledgehammer. North and Doria were jostled and shaken as the compact rockets fired and banged.

And North glared at expanded views of that approaching

247

craft. It was just a short-range passenger shuttle, in this configuration at least; it must have cargo modes. Its roof was transparent – so as to show off the view to dumb tourists, no doubt – and he could actually *see* them, see that there were maybe a dozen people on board.

He stabbed the screen with a finger to get higher magnification. And even from this angle North recognised one of the crew. Emmanuel Caspar himself, commander of the elevator hub, at the controls of the craft.

And a kid beside him, looking straight up and out at *Aquila*, it seemed, his mouth open with horror.

'That's not supposed to be there,' Jeorg said again, weakly.

Doria leaned past him and, with her fist, hit an override propulsion-control button.

From Caspar's point of view, the ship that approached, falling from out of the sky, coming from behind the curving hull of the great forward sphere of *Cronus*, was a blunt, rough cylinder, with a dazzling flare of hot ions emerging from a huge exhaust nozzle.

Emmanuel Caspar knew it immediately. Yet he couldn't believe his eyes, just for a heartbeat, two. It was a famous ship to any pilot, a Lunar Consortium ship, and an advanced fission-engine design – a ship his crew had had to study as it had dogged the *Cronos* all the way to Saturn. It had to be the *Aquila* itself. Despite having come all that way, ship and crew had been denied access to the hub complex and to the *Cronus*, for reasons of diplomacy at higher levels than Caspar worked at.

Yet there was the *Aquila* anyhow.

Caspar, hub commander, was out of the loop. As his staff and the automated systems reacted to the intruder, here he was stuck in this limping little ferry. Piloting it just because he could. Just so he could impress his son on this last day together.

And here was *Aquila* falling out of the sky at him . . .

And he was right in its path . . .

'Dad? Is it supposed to do that?'

He'd done nothing at all for long seconds, he realised. *React, Emmanuel*.

'Strap in, Fabio.' Caspar tapped consoles. 'Emergency evasion! Execute.' He punched a smart button to verify his authority with the ferry's systems.

Emergency lamps flared red, as the ferry prepared to respond to the sudden threat from above with emergency manoeuvres.

Caspar braced. He didn't look back at the rest of the passengers. He just yelled, 'Strap in!' He knew that if their automatics had worked each passenger would already be cocooned by heavy straps folding out of their deep cushioned seats and closing around their bodies. He made sure Fabio was being properly restrained. He didn't have time to check further—

And he felt a jolt in the back. That was the big rear engines kicking in, as hard as they could. He was pressed back in his couch as the thrust built up.

And he dared glance upwards again.

That damn craft was still descending – but sliding sideways in his view, as the ferry's engines strove desperately to push him aside and out of *Aquila*'s way. Caspar knew the specs of the lunar ship well, had been enough of a flyboy himself to have studied its design and testing. The *Aquila* was six hundred tonnes of mass plus fuel, and *a hundred metres long*.

That was the crucial statistic.

This ferry's low-power fission engine was usually sufficient for the slow, cautious assignments around the fragile hub facilities it was designed for. It and its siblings had even been used to help nudge *Cronus* into its jig bay. The question was whether that feeble acceleration could do enough in the time available to shift the mass of the ferry through that crucial hundred metres, before the larger mass of the Consortium craft came falling down, down out of the sky, a slow-motion approach but with enough momentum to crush the smaller craft—

The exterior light shifted. He looked up from his screens. The *Aquila* was closer still, actually blocking out the sparse sunlight, even the pale brown glow of Saturn. And still closing.

Somebody screamed.

That seemed to open the floodgates. Other passengers screamed, yelled; he heard hasty comms messages being sent out, and he imagined terrifying messages being picked up all over the hub complex, even in the *Cronus*.

And still the light shifted.

There was nothing more Caspar could do.

Fabio sat silent, looking at his father. Perhaps too bewildered to be afraid. No, not that; Fabio was too smart. The kid knew what was going on. Caspar reached over as far as his own harness would allow and enfolded his son in his arms, leaning over him as if his own broad back could save the boy.

Inside the ferry the noises of screaming, yelling, proximity alarms all seemed to rise to a crescendo.

And then the alarms halted, suddenly.

Caspar realised he had his eyes clamped shut. He felt the warm body of his son in his arms, could feel him breathing.

He opened his eyes, sat up straight, glanced at his consoles. It was over, the closest approach passed without a collision. 'Not dead yet, damn it.' Without looking around, he called out to the passengers. 'All OK?'

A clamour of voices, a chorus of complaints, cries, demands for information.

But one clear report, a woman's voice. 'No injuries back here, Commander. And no visible damage to the hull.'

'Whoever said that, you just got commissioned. Now let's see what's going on.'

He had a feeling this wasn't over yet.

Working by eye and instruments, Caspar drew the ferry away from the site of the near-collision. And, even before he got fully clear, he looked back.

He saw the *Aquila* immediately. The craft's own attitude thrusters were flaring, evidently having pushed it away from its collision course with the ferry.

Shit. But it shouldn't have gotten so close in the first place. He knew there would have to be some kind of inquiry – even prosecutions. Even if the manoeuvre had been intended as just some kind of gesture of political protest, nothing justified *this*.

He was guiding the ferry gently now, gently, backing further away from the site of the near crash. He glanced at Fabio beside him. *He could have been killed. Still could.* Caspar felt his anger gathering into a knot—

The proximity alarm sounded again.

What now?

He followed the same reflexes – checked on his ship, his son, his passengers. Then he turned back to the instrument board, only to find a muddled picture, that proximity alarm but no imminent damage warnings.

Ah. But the danger wasn't to the ferry this time. He swept clear an area of the board, folded down other indicators, trying to make sense of the data.

Not a danger to the ferry. The *Aquila* had missed the ferry, yanking itself onto a revised trajectory, but in the process had set itself on another collision course.

With the *Cronus* itself.

Again he hammered his boards with warnings, snapped out

commands to the crew of the *Cronus*, to the hub base.

He hailed the *Aquila* itself. But there was no reply. And it was too late anyhow.

Alarms screamed again.

Aboard the *Cronus*, John Smith, in his own cabin, huddling in a survival suit – hastily donned following much-drilled emergency protocols – had actually watched the near-collision of the rogue ship with the ferry. And the ship was soon identified by the smart room's systems as the lunar craft that had been haunting the site, the *Aquila*. Of course it was *Aquila*. Ferry and Consortium craft had come close to a collision, but both, painfully slowly, had pushed their way away, apparently just in time.

And Smith felt his heart hammer in the aftermath of the near-miss. He knew little Fabio and his father were aboard that ferry, and no doubt Smith would be on at least nodding acquaintance with most of the other passengers. All of them, it seemed, spared by luck and good piloting, by Caspar on the ferry – and presumably, in the end, the lunar miners in their own ugly craft. Surely the approach of the *Aquila* had been meant as a threat, a gesture, not a suicidal attempt to crash. But something had gone wrong.

Well, collision averted. Maybe it was over.

But now he saw the further aftermath of the initial approach, slowly unfolding. He had a dread feeling that the *Aquila*'s pilot wasn't quite as careful, quite as watchful as they should have been. Because while Caspar's ferry fairly scooted out of trouble, away from both *Aquila* and *Cronus*, the *Aquila* itself, having completed a hasty avoidance manoeuvre away from the ferry, now lurched backwards – and was heading straight for the curving hull of the *Cronus*.

Straight for the main sphere.

Inside which Smith sat staring like an idiot.

Very belatedly Smith realised he himself could be in danger. But which way to run?

He yelled to the automatics, 'Show this room! This room, relative to the outer hull!'

A panel on the wall turned semi-transparent to show a three-dimensional map of this part of the ship, the interior within the spherical hull, a honeycomb of corridors and rooms and clumps of machinery: air-conditioners, elevators. All of this, of course, recently built inside a converted fuel tank.

And even in this display, outside the hull, a skeletal sketch, the form of the *Aquila*, loomed large. The *Aquila* wasn't heading for him, not for his part of the hull, he saw immediately. He felt a surge of relief, and of immediate guilt, for his sparing only meant that the danger was passing to somebody else—

The two craft closed very quickly—

And *Aquila* hit.

It was a soft, almost noiseless impact. A kind of crumpling.

John Smith, in his cabin, heard this through the fabric of the ship itself.

But after a couple of seconds he felt the room around him shake. He thought he was feeling a kind of deep, long-wave shudder, as the shock of impact travelled through the structure of the ship. And now he heard the fabric of this spherical hull groan, the screech of tearing metal giving way under the stress.

A gust of air, as if of wind, brushed his skin. Wind, in a spacecraft?

The images on his screens fritzed, and went down altogether.

Smith, alone in his cabin, sat silently for a moment.

Listening.

Feeling the breeze.

Think, John. If there were a major breach of the atmosphere-bearing hull, if whatever safeties were built into the ship and his own cabin itself were to fail under this gross damage, these could be his last breaths.

He should be counting.

Two breaths. Three. He counted, eyes closed.

When he got to ten, he opened his eyes. He could hear the continuing soft hiss of air cycling through his room. *Lucky. So far.*

He needed to know what had become of the rest of the ship.

He shouted into the air, delivering all the emergency reboot commands he could think of. It didn't take long before he got an image, of sorts, on just one screen. A corridor, empty. For long seconds that was all he got. The systems had become, unsurprisingly, unreliable, and he had to play around with more commands for some minutes before he got an external view – and while he did so he quickly realised this viewpoint must actually have come from that near-miss ferry, standing off from the main ship.

There was the ship's hull, that smooth, huge spherical flank. And he could see a complex shadow, sailing past that flank and out of shot.

He demanded his systems identify that intruder. He wasn't surprised to learn it was the *Aquila*. Flying in close to the hull – no, now flying *away* from the hull.

But behind it the hull was smooth no more, he saw. Illuminated dimly by Saturn's light, the layered hull had been cut through, peeled back.

And without its skin, the ship's inner anatomy was exposed. The area he was watching was a passenger section: rooms, ceilings, floors, recently installed in place of fuel tanks, all now exposed to space. In some rooms he saw light, from lamps, even data screens still functioning.

All this open to vacuum.

And people.

Many seemed to have no protection at all. They came drifting silently out of their exposed rooms, spilling into space. Some wriggled, helpless, as if falling from a great height. Others wrestled with the silver fabric of pressure suits, or the opaque blankets of emergency bubble-shelters, even as they drifted out into vacuum. It was like an ocean shipwreck, Smith thought, people in the water scrambling for lifebelts.

Many became still, after mere minutes, less.

And, only minutes after the crash, he saw more people coming out of other sectors of the great hull, but these were better prepared, sealed up in silver suits, emerging from regular ports rather than gashes in the hull. They started to work through the damaged area, carrying what looked like empty sacks.

Most of the spilled-out people were still by now – already – while others wriggled feebly. But, with puffs of attitude-control rockets, the vanguard of the suited ones pushed into the sparse, dispersing cloud of people, caught up with the stranded, one by one, and, whether they were moving or not, stuffed them inside the bags they carried. Once zipped shut, the bags seemed immediately to inflate. Air bags, emergency shelters – as Smith recognised from the drills he'd endured himself.

Some of these saviours seemed much clumsier than others, and Smith wondered if these were passengers rather than crew, untrained in whatever procedure this was, and yet having a go anyway.

Sometimes the rescuers were evidently too late. *Corpses in bubbles*. They tried, anyhow.

John Smith wanted to go out and help with this effort. There had to be something he could do, even if only to help those retrieved. But when he tried to leave, the door was locked tight. For safety's sake, apparently, his room wouldn't let him out. Well, if the cabin held its air, it was probably the best place for him to be.

Helpless, he turned back to the gruesome, slow-moving human spectacle in his screens.

And now a single human figure drifted by his apparent viewpoint – without a pressure suit, or survival bag. No rescuers nearby. This vision delivered a visceral shock to John Smith. It was hard to guess at an age from here, in this condition. It – she – looked female, young, under twenty maybe. He thought he knew her – a student. The passenger roster wasn't that large, and on this science vessel there had been few so young.

And she wasn't yet dead.

One arm lifted, shocking him. Then she lifted her hands to her throat, pulling at the neck of her top. She kicked in the sharp vacuum. She struggled, kicking, clawing at her throat, her mouth wide. Her actions, jerky, hasty, contrasted with the smooth, silent, geometric – almost *peaceful* – drift of her body.

He thought he knew her.

He slammed his hand against the monitor screen, helpless. He yelled for help, into the air. 'There's a kid out there! Alive! Umm, portside, near the equator . . .'

More kicking, writhing.

There was no reply.

The young woman was still scratching at her throat, feebly. Jerking as if she was having some kind of fit. He thought he could see blood where she had ripped the skin, blood bubbling out into the vacuum.

Another kick of the legs.

Then she was still.

Maybe some last wisp of air had pushed her away. There were no rescue crews working out there, not in this area.

It occurred to him that this was likely to be one of the most compelling images in the news broadcasts on Earth in over an hour's time, carrying news of the crash, when the signals got there at lightspeed. And he hated himself for the thought, the calculation at such a moment.

Suddenly his throat spasmed. He threw himself across the cabin to the small bathroom, and threw up at the sink, a messy zero-gravity vomit.

Then he went back to his screens to watch some more. He felt, obscurely, that it was his duty to watch, even if he could do nothing to help.

He saw a grand piano drifting, stately, out into space.

24

Aboard the ferry, Emmanuel Caspar, staring out at a sky full of chaos, of spreading debris, was trying to prioritise. He felt frozen, though every second that ticked by felt like a minute, a minute like an hour.

He was commander of the elevator hub station. And, today, right now, of this ferry.

And father to Fabio, who was sitting right beside him. Caspar looked down. Fabio's eyes were wide open – his mother had always said he had beautiful eyes – open now and staring out at carnage, slowly scattering. But his mother had gone back to Earth.

And Fabio wasn't in any kind of pressure garment, unlike Caspar himself, unlike most of the ferry's passengers. He had come in late.

Act, asshole. Then think.

Caspar reached down under his own seat, pulled out a package, an emergency life-support bubble. A last resort. He handed the package to Fabio, who took it, looking bemused.

'We've practised with these things, Fab. Open it. Climb inside. Zip it closed if there are problems with the air. OK?'

He had never seen Fabio look so scared, not in his presence anyway. But Fabio started to open the pack.

'Dad? What's going on?'

'It's OK. It's OK.' Caspar could hear mutterings behind him in the ferry, more chaos unfolding in the fragmented scene out the window, a dazzle of messages on the console before him—

'Dad, I think it's stuck.'

No time for this.

Make time for him anyhow, dummy.

'Look, you just pull it out of its wrapper—'

'I'll help.' A woman passenger, in the row of seats just behind Caspar's position, leaned forward now, pushing at her own restraints which she started to unclip. A black pendant at her throat distracted him.

'Don't do that,' Caspar said, reflexively. 'Your own belt—'

But then he recognised her. Elizabeth Vasta, presidential science adviser. 'Oh . . . I'm – sorry.'

'It's OK.'

'Can you reach?'

'Pretty well.' She smiled at Fabio. 'Just pass the package up, honey. That's it. It's going to get crowded in here . . .'

Fabio smiled back and lifted up the bubble pack.

Caspar risked a glance back. All the other passengers were adults, he knew; all seemed to be sitting calmly, though they were mostly either staring into screens, or were just gazing out at the chaos visible through the mostly transparent upper hull.

Some tour guide I am, Caspar thought. *Keep your hands inside the car at all times . . .*

He flicked on the inboard announcement system, although most of the passengers could probably have heard him anyway. 'OK. Listen up, please. You can see there's been an incident of some kind.'

A murmuring at that bland cliché.

'There's evidently a breach of the pressure hull of the *Cronus*, along with a lot of debris. Up ahead . . .'

Stuff was spreading out in a slow cloud, like droplets of blood spraying from a wound. He leaned forward, peering harder. Yes, there were people in there.

Vasta touched his shoulder. She murmured, 'You can do this.'

He looked round, was brought back into the cabin. 'OK,' he said to her. 'Thanks. Sorry, folks. I need to keep remembering I'm station commander. You might also be reassured that my background is piloting, some of it military, so I do know my way around the controls of this thing.'

And he'd pulled rank to take this tub for a joy ride, with his little son in tow, on this extraordinary day – just because he could. And so he wasn't where he was supposed to be in this crisis – on the bridge, in charge. *Asshole*.

'So anyhow I need to keep an ear open for the comms on what's going on out there. But meantime let's make sure we can stay safe in here.'

He glanced around again. His passengers looked grim, scared, determined, or a mixture. A couple nodded back at him. Nobody panicking yet, at least. Good.

'Just close up your pressure suit if you're wearing one – if you haven't already – or else get hold of the survival bubble under your seat. Like the one my son is climbing into. Don't seal it until you need it.'

Vasta held up the fabric of the bubble she was working. 'Look for this,' she called back. 'Under your seat. It's simple enough.' She turned to Caspar with a rueful grin. 'So what now?'

Caspar tried to focus. *What now?*

Save more lives.

Prioritise, man.

He quickly set a course towards that spreading cloud of debris, seeking survivors. The engines pulsed, a soft roar, a kick in the back, and the ferry started to drift cautiously forward.

He had the chance now to glance down at Fabio in his bubble, Vasta still aiding him.

'Thank you for your help, Adviser. And I'm truly sorry you're in this situation, given you're about the most important personage ever to have visited the hub complex.'

'Then I'm glad you're at the controls, Commander Caspar.'

He felt like laughing, darkly. 'I only took this late ferry myself for a bit of adventure. Spectacle. Before we settle down for five years of spaceflight to Nine.'

'And I pulled a few strings to get aboard. All because I wanted one last ferry ride. We both lucked out.'

Caspar took another glance at his instrument panel and comms gear. All of which were blaring, messages on screen and in his ear.

He looked out of his window again.

The huge flank of the *Cronus*, around which the ferry had been crawling just before the incident, was now a wall to his right-hand side, close enough for proximity alarms to flash. The spilling-out of the ship's contents seemed to have slowed. Evidently nothing remained to be sucked easily from those breached under-the-hull compartments, after the initial plume of lost air had pushed stuff out into space. Now the *Cronus* was rolling on its own axis, so that the great wound left by the sideswipe of that dumb Lunar Consortium ship was lifting up and out of his sight.

And the ferry was now slowly nudging its way into the denser debris field.

Whatever had already spilled out of the ship was still here, all around them, a gruesome cloud slowly scattering. Some of this seemed structural: hull panels, even fragments of supporting beams, and slabs of the dense rock-like material – supplied from the Moon – that provided shielding for the passengers from cosmic radiation. Then there were what looked like internal fittings: panels of faux wood, even a table. Smaller pieces – dinnerware? Cutlery? Pillows, blankets. A picture of some kind, once fixed to a wall.

By now Vasta was sitting in Fabio's seat, with Fabio on her lap wrapped up in the survival bubble, open at the neck where his head and shoulders protruded.

'I suppose this could have been worse,' Vasta said. 'Could it? A more severe impact, or some failure within – the power plant blowing up—'

'Highly unlikely.'

Vasta smiled tiredly. 'Don't give me the PR line. I have got a science background. I can figure probabilities, and since the quasar I've more than once had to estimate existential risks on the spot in one presidential briefing or another. In short, you can't kid a kidder. And I know you must have planned in a range of catastrophic scenarios. Not you – I mean the designers of the *Cronus*.'

'To some extent. But you have to remember the *Cronus* has just been pretty hastily adapted, from an outer-planets-capable fission-engine cruiser to an Oort cloud explorer, running on fusion. There's a long-term goal to build much more smartness into our spacegoing structures—'

'So a strike like this would barely be noticeable.'

'I wouldn't say that. Much more survivable, though. One day.'

Vasta ruffled Fabio's hair. 'Less room for heroes.'

'I'll settle for more live cowards . . . Here comes more of the debris cloud.'

Much of it was petty stuff, but there was a lot of it. It swam around the ferry, like scattered fragments of a vanished world, Caspar thought now. Bits of cutlery. Books – real, old-fashioned, paper books carried into space, tokens of vanity, of luxury.

Towels, curtains even, stamped with the ship's monogram, an elaborate 'C'.

'Hubris,' Elizabeth Vasta murmured, looking out. 'That's what a lot of people will say about this incident. Especially the religious, I suspect. All this luxury, almost decadence, crammed into what in the end was a pretty fragile vessel. We have only been a few centuries in space. We dared go too far, and here's the result. It reminds me of the wreck of the *Titanic*. If you know about that.'

Caspar grunted. 'There were a lot of military sea crew in my family. One reason I got this job; that kind of family tradition can still impress. And this reminds *me* more of the *Lusitania* incident.'

Swathed in his unsealed survival bag, Fabio tried out that word. 'Lucy – Tony?'

Caspar ruffled his son's hair. 'She was a passenger liner, son – probably far more luxurious than anything the *Cronus* will ever aspire to. American ship. Crossed the Atlantic during the First World War, or tried to. Sunk by German torpedoes. I read about it. Before it went down it left a "dead wake", some called it, of bodies, life rafts, internal fittings – and bits of luxury, clothes, and menus for fancy meals . . .'

'I know about the *Lusitania*.'

A new voice breaking into Caspar's comms feed. There was no accompanying ID flag. A woman's voice.

He glanced at Vasta. She shrugged.

Caspar leaned forward. 'Identify yourself.'

'Well, I think you know who I am. Who we must be.'

'The crew of the *Aquila*?'

'Commander Caspar, I'm Doria Bohm of the Lunar Consortium.'

Vasta murmured to Caspar. 'Bohm. I know her, her rank. Can

you mute your conversation? So she's talking to us alone? On my authority, if you need it.'

He frowned, but tapped a button. 'Not even the ferry's passengers can hear us now.' Irritated, he scanned his data feeds. 'Consortium ship. I have your position but I can't see you.'

'I'll fire up the docking lights.'

And, casting around the sky, he saw a cluster of new stars shimmer into existence. Dimmer floods with wider beams revealed the ugly, blocky shape of the *Aquila*, familiar to Caspar from many briefings.

'You see us now?'

Vasta leaned into view and introduced herself. 'I am a special science adviser to the world presidency. I'm also witness to what amounts to a crime scene, here. As far as I'm concerned, everything we say here is on the record.'

A pause. 'Very well, Adviser Vasta. As I said, my name is Doria Bohm. I have a senior position in the Lunar Consortium. And my co-pilot—'

A man's voice. 'My name is Jeorg North. I'm actually, according to my passport and ID, an Earth resident, by law. Just to speed things up when they start issuing the arrest warrants.'

Vasta frowned. '*You?* So what are you doing out here, Jeorg North?'

'Following my husband, if you must know, Professor Vasta. He got a gig on the *Cronus* – his name is Bheki Molewa – unfairly. Long story—'

'And all of this damage, because of *that*?'

'I don't care what your motive is,' Caspar snapped. 'Your presence here is illegal, without the proper permissions, the licensing. You know that. And through your crass manoeuvrings you have caused physical damage to the *Cronus*, possibly to our installation here. Lives were lost. One of them could have been my son's. Or mine. Let alone Adviser Vasta's.'

Doria said, 'We only intended a gesture. The collision was a regrettable accident—'

'So you tell us.' Caspar's anger deepened. He looked down at Fabio, who, astonishingly, seemed to be falling asleep.

Vasta touched his arm. 'Commander Caspar. May I . . .'

He didn't want to yield the mic. He wanted to berate this reasonable-sounding woman, this Doria from the Moon. But knew he mustn't.

'Go ahead.'

Vasta leaned closer to the control deck. She said earnestly, 'You're conflicted, Pilot North. The incident is done, committed. The question is how we are all going to get past this, isn't it? If the *Cronus* mission is to survive. And so— No, wait. Let's do this all at once. Emmanuel, is there any way you could open up a channel to a particular passenger on the *Cronus*? There's a man called John Smith . . .'

Caspar checked screens. 'It depends. Things are going to be pretty screwed up in there. The emergency comms channel is most likely to be up, but it depends on whether the passenger you're looking for is still alive, bluntly.' He tapped a console pad. 'It's more than likely that he is, though. If not in his cabin, then at his emergency muster point—'

'Yes, yes,' Vasta said, a tad impatiently. 'We can review life-boat drills when we have time. Because for now, time is running out.'

He frowned at that. 'What do you mean by that? The rescue operation will take as long as it takes – and then the salvage and repair job will have to start, of course. It's going to take weeks now before the *Cronus* is ready to fly—'

'No. Not weeks. We have hours, at most.'

'Hours? Until what?'

'*Until the news of this incident reaches Earth, and Earth starts reacting.* Eighty minutes out at lightspeed, eighty minutes for any reply, right? Well, I want us to have stabilised this situation before any formal control can be imposed from Earth. We *still* have to get this ship, the *Cronus*, to Nine, as soon as possible. Because the *Cronus* and its expertise represent our best shot at responding to the crisis that seems to be pivoting out there. *We can't let the mission be cancelled.* The quasar alone is turning into an overwhelming, existential threat, and we have to deal with that. We have to *control* this situation – and that means we have to control perceptions.'

Caspar nodded cautiously. 'OK. But let's be clear. You are a senior adviser to the World President's cabinet.'

'I am.'

'But you are not actually the President,' Caspar said. 'You don't have her authority. You can't speak for her.'

'Noted. But she does listen to me, very closely. And I have you here, a senior figure at Saturn itself.'

Caspar felt deeply uncomfortable with this sudden turn. 'I don't feel I represent anybody except the agencies I report to—'

She ignored that. 'Meanwhile, we have two representatives of the Lunar Consortium on the line. Of which one, I happen to know, Doria Bohm, is pretty high ranking. I was briefed on this months ago. And – Emmanuel, have you found that passenger on the *Cronus*? That's why I asked. John Smith. If you can. You met him—'

Caspar tapped a comms pad. 'Of course.'

'Yes, we did meet,' came a cultured voice. 'This is what's left of John Smith, stuck in my cabin aboard what's left of the *Cronus*.'

Caspar nodded, smiled for the link. The smile was tight. He was aware that all this could well go public, and soon. 'This is Commander Caspar, John. We'll have you out of there, and the ship ready to resume its mission – well, whenever we can.'

'I'm sure you will. But for now . . . Ah, Professor Vasta. You have sent us some of your conversation, a few sentences. It sounds as if you have a proposition to make.'

'I think I do,' Vasta said. She glanced around, at Caspar, at his son apparently nodding off on her lap – at the ferry passengers behind them in their emergency gear, working their way through this strange, unwelcome adventure with apparent patience.

She said, 'John, you hear me? And Emmanuel, can you bring the lunar folk back in? *Aquila*?'

'We're here,' said Jeorg North.

'Me too,' Doria called.

Vasta sighed. 'Well, then. We're here. I suppose you're wondering why I asked you all here today.'

Leaden silence.

'OK,' Vasta said. 'Old Earth joke that doesn't translate so well any more.

'Let's look at the situation.

'In fact we are all here today because of Planet Nine, and the situation out there. Correct? You know we have a crew out there—'

'A crew of Conservers,' Doria said.

'It was a Conserver project from the start,' John Smith said mildly. 'A Conserver conception, Conserver funding, resources.'

'Very well, Doria, John. But whatever priority the Conservers may claim – whatever the creature they call Feathers really is, whatever the strange object Planet Nine has turned out to be – Earth is most concerned about the quasar-like eruption at the heart of the Galaxy. And, it seems, the only place we're going to get answers to questions about all that is out at Planet Nine. And, starting from this crash site, the only way we'll get *there*—'

'Is aboard the *Cronus*,' Caspar said. 'So what's your plan, Senior Adviser?'

She seemed to have to force a smile. 'Look. Here we are, representing the various branches into which humanity seems to be diverging. Ripping each other apart. Look at us in this battered ferry. Yet we have to work together, so that we can be saved together, if that's possible at all. Starting here and now.'

Doria said, boldly, Caspar thought, 'Well, then, that has to include the Consortium.'

But Caspar, with his son beside him, blazed at that. 'You come into a space I command and leave it littered with corpses. This was a criminal act. And now you demand representation. What political argument have you got to justify that? *You*, you personally—'

Vasta raised a hand, a calming gesture. 'Despite that we're going to give you, the Consortium, a presence on the Cronus. On my personal authority. As ratified, hopefully, by President Mason when she hears about this.'

Caspar had to protest again. 'There has been injury, death, material damage—'

'But we have to move forward together even so,' Vasta said. 'You can only make peace with your enemies.' She waved a hand. 'And whatever lies out there, at Nine and beyond, is bigger than all of us.'

John Smith said, 'And you're the genius who's going to handle all this, are you, Elizabeth?'

She smiled. 'Well, I'm on the spot. Anyhow that's the plan. All we have to do is to sign up to all this, and present Earth with – well, a fait accompli. I can hear you, Doria, John. Just giving you one last chance to object.'

John Smith was first to respond. 'That's a useful summary, Elizabeth. But I can't imagine the authorities on Earth or Moon condoning what you did, Jeorg North. And it's clear that the responsibility is yours. *You* won't be going any further – save back to Earth, probably.'

'Very well.' Doria sounded strained. 'I'll go with you. If you'll allow it, Commander Caspar. That's a wise judgement.'

And then Caspar sighed. 'I hope so. But all this after we have rescued the lost, tended the injured, and mourned the dead.'

Vasta nodded gravely. 'Of course.'

Fabio wriggled and stretched in his survival bubble, and looked up at his father. 'Are we there yet, Dad?'

25

Caspar, no diplomat himself, was never quite sure how Vasta pulled it off. But her recommendations stuck.

It took five days to gather the scattered dead, from within the stricken ship and outside it. To prepare the bodies to be dispatched across the Solar System, down the gravity gradients towards Earth and elsewhere. To repair the damage to the *Cronus* which, though lethal and dramatic, was ultimately superficial.

Five days' more preparation, and the rebuilt ship was launched at last – although with final repairs continuing inside and outside the wounded vessel.

And then, five *years* after the *Aquila* disaster, five years after departing from Saturn, and eleven years after Planet Nine's discovery by a Conserver crew, the Earth ship *Cronus* slid into orbit around the anomaly.

Year 11

AD 2266

26

On the arrival of the *Cronus* at Nine, its five-year journey from Saturn complete, by agreement with the *Shadow* crew the *Cronus* passengers and crew were held in orbit around Nine for a few more days while final details of quarantine requirements were thrashed out.

"Thrashed out" — as far as Caspar was concerned, it was a delay partly because of setting up of quarantine protocols and so forth, but also because of a good deal of antler-locking over control of the event between himself and Hild Kanigel, the evidently super-competent captain of the *Shadow*. Polite antler-locking, but antler-locking even so.

And on reflection, Caspar thought he would have been just as prickly over the arrival of strangers to his exploratory camp, if he had been in Hild's shoes. But at least it gave him time to sight-see.

On his last full day, having completed a last shipboard briefing with Elizabeth Vasta for download to Earth, Caspar stood with her at one of the ship's larger picture windows — a remnant feature of the days before Nine, when *Cronus* had still been a mixture of interplanetary freighter and luxury liner, before its refitting for this extraordinary venture out of the inner Solar System altogether.

And it was only by looking through one of these great portals that Caspar felt he could get the scale of all this. Even if all he could make out of Nine itself was a sharp-edged grey-dark circle, barely illuminated by the light of the distant Sun.

'Not much to see,' he muttered. 'For a quasi-planet three times the size of Earth.'

Vasta drifted over to his side, moving confidently and easily after so long in space, her surface pack in her hand, ready for the final descent.

'And ten times the mass, remember,' she said. 'Maybe not much to see. Unlike true planets, nothing to *sense*, except for its simple, huge presence. And I doubt very much it can be compared to a true planet, save for the mass, the size . . . A featureless ball – though not quite so featureless now, given the bits of human clutter the crew of the *Shadow* took down with them, the shelters they improvised . . .'

In response to her words, anticipating instructions, screens with close-up inserts, supporting the view through the big window, showed a scattering of interconnected bubble shelters, differing in size, set out irregularly on the surface. Most of the domes had lamps of some kind to make their presence stand out on the black surface. Looking like an improvised village, it was evidently a colony that had evolved rather than been planned.

'It looks – brave,' Vasta said. 'Doesn't it? Humans challenging the unknown. Umm, domesticating it.' And she touched the black pearl at her neck.

Caspar was distracted. Mildly irritated, as he often was, by her growing habit of touching the pendant, apparently unconsciously. He had no idea what the bit of jewellery meant to her. It wasn't even particularly attractive . . .

She said now, 'And *it* is evidently not a planet at all, whatever it is. But it's not a black hole either. Not any more. Something else.

Featureless save for that Hawking radiation, and the creature they called Feathers.' She glanced at him. 'I imagine you know what comes next? The planned experiment, which they've held off until we've arrived, is to reflect back more of the data the *Shadow* people detected in the Hawking radiation as they did before, but this time with a message from us constructed within. Something simple, I'm told – they're guessing that even dot-dash variations in intensity might be enough. Just evidence of structure, of intelligent modification – proof that it's not just a plain reflection. That might be message enough. Well, I've agreed it's the next obvious thing for us to try – once we've landed, and got the encounter stuff with the *Shadow* crew out of the way.'

He had to laugh at that. 'Now you sound like a true scientist. All the sense of wonder beaten out of you. "Encounter stuff", including Feathers, you mean? Meeting the alien?'

She smiled, self-deprecating. 'One must try to be objective. But, yes, the alien – and some believe she is the key to all this – or at least to our understanding of it— all this, as our world is being transformed through this contact. We walk in ancient dreams . . .'

A soft chime rang through the ship.

She smiled. 'Anyhow, I hope we won't be disappointed. Time to go?'

Caspar was back in ship's captain mode. 'Time to go. That's the call for preparation for the landing. So, as you know, we go down in groups. We don't want to overwhelm the *Shadow* crew, with them having been alone with all this for eleven years already. You're in the first party, of course.'

'Damn right I am. I can't wait – and I'm not alone in that. And not alone in being touched, already changed, by this event from afar . . .'

That was true, Caspar reflected, as he shut down screens with

275

touches, and led Vasta out of the lounge. Maybe this strange incursion at the edge of the Solar System was already changing mindsets. Even changing attitudes, revising alliances.

The Conservers, of course, had shared the news of their first cautious discovery from the beginning. Even the Lunar Consortium were cooperating now, once they had got over their tantrum at the launch from Saturn – and Earth itself, still a very divided society, increasingly battered by the quasar fall-out, was pulling together in the face of this strangeness. Yes, despite the destructive scramble that had accompanied the launch of this new fusion-powered version of *Cronus* from Saturn – and despite some disruption, such as among reviving religious groups – after five long years the various broad factions in human society, including those represented aboard *Cronus*, it seemed to him, were now working together to meet this strange challenge.

Vasta seemed to be thinking along the same lines.

'It's an old dream, you know. To meet the alien. Or nightmare. But one hope always buried in that dream was that maybe in the presence of some external entity, friendly or hostile, humans might finally recognise our own fundamental unity.' Her smile was dazzling. 'It's wonderful, really – all of it, isn't it? Save for what that damn quasar is doing to the Earth . . . And all happening in our lifetimes.'

Suddenly he saw why she did her job. Beyond the monster bureaucracies she must have to navigate, the sheer wondrous joy of discovery must still come breaking through. Even if all this was mostly someone else's discovery. And even if the responsibility that came with this particular job was huge.

He smiled back. 'Let's go see what's down there.'

27

Caspar, using his commander's prerogative, had selected and announced the members of the first landing crew some days before.

Just five of them for this first expedition, it had been decided, the names determined after consultation with Hild Kanigel, captain of the *Shadow* – as well as Elizabeth Vasta. Starting with Caspar himself, despite some grumbling from those left behind. He justified this, to himself and others, by the need for somebody in command to get acquainted with the situation as soon as possible.

And in terms of authority, he had to take Vasta herself down, as the most senior terrestrial on board, no less than the science adviser to Earth's global administration. And at the other end of the seniority scale, Doria Bohm was brought down to represent her lunar background – she was officially a vice coordinator of that community. And, you never knew, Caspar thought, it might even be healthy to have somebody along who was looking to *exploit* stuff, rather than treasure it, open-mouthed, as a gift from some kind of multidimensional god.

John Smith had to be there, as the most senior of the very few Conservers aboard the *Cronus* – and the *Shadow* had after all been a Conserver mission.

That was four. The fifth was Fabio, Caspar's son, now fifteen years old – and still playing chess with John Smith. Fabio who, in the end, after the *Aquila* crash, Caspar couldn't bear to leave behind.

Caspar knew he was accused of favouritism over this selection by, well, by just about everybody else of the *Cronus* crew and passengers who weren't going down this time. But they would get their chance. And what had inspired Caspar to bring Fabio down early genuinely wasn't favouritism – or anyhow, not that alone. It had been footage, shown to him by Hild Kanigel by way of preparation for the visit, of the creature called Feathers, and Salma – exotic alien and youngest member of the *Shadow* crew – playing some kind of netball-like game under their dome, and with Feathers apparently beating Salma hands-down.

Among the team down on Nine, and among analysts on Earth and elsewhere, there was a lot of debate about Feathers' actual age, let alone her equivalent in terms of human maturity. One thing everybody agreed on was that Feathers *liked to play*: she liked lively, physical games, running, chasing, throwing and catching, making stuff, and she needed companions of her own age, so to speak, or at least her apparent rough equivalent in human terms.

And while Salma, youngest of the *Shadow* crew, was doing a great job, eleven years on from the discovery of Nine by the *Shadow* crew, she was thirty-one years old. Hence, Fabio.

Well, Caspar had made his decision about the landing party for good or ill, and would brook no arguments.

And when the appointed hour arrived, the five squeezed aboard a space-to-surface shuttle: a craft that had once ferried passengers and materiel around the human colonies at Saturn, now, with Caspar himself at the controls, descending to Planet Nine.

28

In their years here the *Shadow* crew had set up a scatter of bubble-tent shelters, all grouped, Caspar learned, around the very first landing site. For safety's sake these were spread reasonably widely apart, but most had fabric tunnels interconnecting them. And there was an element of design that he could recognise immediately. The tunnel network had been designed, or evolved, to provide long stretches for the creature called Feathers to run, and lots of corners for her to escape to and assemble the heaps of junk she seemed to like to collect.

This was a habitat for humans, heavily improvised as a habitat for their guest alien. It looked like a heap of garbage. But he thought he could recognise at first glance the intelligence and patience that had gone into it all.

One of the larger, central tents had a brilliant red cross on its roof, its purpose unmistakable. And this was where Hild Kanigel, captain of the *Shadow*, had directed the *Cronus* ferry to land, near the medical centre.

Once down, the *Cronus* party, all suited up, scrambled out of their lander's airlock and made their way obediently to that red-cross tent. After a few steps Caspar was feeling his weight – and more, given that Nine's gravity was a little higher than Earth's. It was always the way after long-stay missions in zero gravity, including his time at the Saturn hub. No matter how much you hit the centrifuge and weight machines you always lost condition.

On their entry into the tent, through a fabric-walled airlock, Hild Kanigel herself was waiting. Masked. Wearing a nametag she probably hadn't had to wear for many years.

Wordlessly, she directed her guests through a tunnel of fabric, within which some sort of disinfectant, Caspar guessed, was sprayed over them, followed by a vigorous drying by blowers.

At the far side of the tunnel, they were free at last to break open their suits — but then had to submit to bot-administered injections, and to breathe into bot-held filters, all before they could be regarded as clean, inside and out.

Hild walked through all this with them. And, as soon as they had all finally got out of their helmets and gloves, Hild shook Caspar's hand.

And then John Smith's in turn, quite warmly. 'Advocate Smith. We never met before. But I'm so pleased a fellow Conserver has been able to make it out here.'

Smith looked frail and tired — he was seventy-six now, evidently a little overwhelmed, and not a natural space traveller, Caspar knew — but he rose to the occasion. 'And I'm honoured to be here. I can immediately see you've done remarkably well.'

'Seconded,' Caspar said to Hild. 'Both in terms of your survival and your handling of — well, whatever the hell this is.'

'We've done our best.' Hild, slim but tough-looking, grey-blonde hair cut short, looked neither pleased nor offended by the tributes. 'And I appreciate your not griping about our quarantine set-up, which is one way we've striven to survive. Come, walk with me.'

The shelter was crowded, Caspar saw, once inside, with a couple of the *Shadow* crew and various bots going about their tasks. There were bunk beds, supply heaps, what looked like medical technology, all obviously scavenged from the *Shadow*.

And as soon as they walked in, an evidently young woman – in a jumpsuit that looked a little too small for her – came running up, grabbed Fabio by the hand, and pulled him away. 'Fabio, right? Come on. We've been waiting for you . . .'

This must be Salma. Slim, dark – and a black pendant at her neck that caught Caspar's eye. A lens, it seemed, not a sphere like Vasta's, but still an odd similarity.

Fabio looked back at his father. Caspar made 'go ahead' gestures, and Fabio turned and ran off with Salma.

'So,' Caspar said to Hild, 'that's in fact why I brought down Fabio. I figured, as you have some equivalent of a kid down here, I should bring another kid . . .'

Hild smiled, warmly enough. 'Good thinking. Looks like it's going to work out, doesn't it? Come over, sit, talk. Get used to the place.' She led the way to a table with chairs, ship-issue fold-out furniture. 'And watch out for the slightly higher gravity – higher than Earth. It's deceptive; you don't notice it but it wears you down gradually.'

Caspar followed her lead, sat, and watched the rest of his crew. John Smith, who had barely said a word, had followed Hild and joined them at the table, apparently relieved to take the weight off his own elderly frame in the higher gravity.

But before Vasta and Doria could sit they were approached by a woman who Hild quietly introduced as Meriel Breen, apparently officially life-support specialist aboard the *Shadow*, but covering medical support also.

And Meriel, Doria and Vasta immediately seemed distracted by each other. Without a glance around, they stayed gathered in their own little huddle and made for another table. Apparently they were discussing something quite intensely. They even kept touching their own and each other's collar and neck.

Hild stared. 'What are those three up to, can you see?'

Caspar had good pilot's vision. 'I think they are . . . comparing pendants? Meriel looks like she has hers on a chain, dangling inside her coverall, right? She just pulled it out. Yes, a pendant. A black stone – it's like Salma's, which I just saw. Elizabeth has that black pearl. Oh, and Doria has something similar. I remember now; she's worn it all the time, but generally inside her top . . .'

'*Pendants?* Why that, of all topics of conversation in this situation? There's certainly no mystery about Salma's and Meriel's. They are lens-shaped – identical. Made of some kind of rare mineral. Black onyx, a kind of silicate, if I remember. Salma's mother had two of them – gifts from relatives on Earth. When she died, she willed one to Salma, and the other to Meriel. It was to make Salma feel like she had a bond with Meriel, I think. And with Earth being where the stone came from, maybe she'd feel less . . . less orphaned. But the others . . .'

'From this distance the others look pretty similar too.' He struggled to remember. 'I know Doria's is from the Moon; she has a kind of lens of lunar obsidian. Volcanic glass. And Elizabeth's is a black pearl. From Earth, obviously. Hm. Odd coincidence. They do look similar from a distance . . . Hild, why the hell are we talking about pendants?'

She shrugged. 'Because they are? Vasta has sent some virtual projections out here, as you know. I think maybe they noticed the pendant coincidence then. But what it might mean, given a feathered biped and a galaxy-core explosion . . .'

They shared a look. *Something funny going on.*

He suspected they were both too rational to want to pursue that line of thought any further. Not to mention too busy. Tacitly, they dropped the subject.

'So,' Hild said at length. 'Here we are. Sorry to have to put you through the quarantining. And sorry it's kind of slapdash. Everything about this operation has been improvised since we got here. But I think we've made it work. We are Conservers. We habitually live in small, isolated colonies and spacecraft – very isolated. We are hardened recyclers – were before we got here. And we know all about contamination and quarantine. Sorry about that.'

'No apology necessary. I'd have done the same – about the quarantine on the way in, I mean. Look, I commanded an out-post at Saturn. We didn't want to pick up any fresh bugs from visitors from Earth either, so we were always stern about such protocols. The *Cronus* passengers will tell you as much.'

Hild nodded. 'And in this case we needed to be additionally cautious—'

'Because of Feathers?'

'Yeah. When it comes to quarantine, Feathers is a wild card. We haven't taken any risks, given the basic exposure we've had, given that she's living with us and all. You'll know that she runs on protein-water chemistry as we do, but has an entirely dif-ferent amino acid base. The truth is we don't *know* whether we can infect Feathers with some human pathogen, or vice versa, or not. A reverse transmission could be disastrous, especially if it got through to Earth, given there are so many of us crowded in down there with, presumably, absolutely no immunity to such a thing—'

'And,' John Smith put in, 'transmission the other way would no doubt be just as disastrous, because there is only *one* of Feathers.'

'Exactly,' Hild said.

Smith said, 'But, if I may say so, I already see that you people have done a remarkable job in supporting this – fledgling, fallen from its multidimensional nest – this Feathers. You're to be commended on a human level, as well as the scientific.'

'Hear, hear,' Caspar said. 'Especially given the way you were just dropped into this extraordinary situation. I mean, you were one ship, here at the wrong end of the Solar System and sent out for quite different purposes entirely. You came out to explore Planet Nine, which was thought to *be* a planet of sorts.' He waved a hand. 'Only to find yourselves confronted by all this.'

Smith smiled. 'We Conservers applaud such triumphs of improvisation, by our fellows or otherwise.'

Caspar too had to smile at that. *Improvisation*. Yes, all of this little settlement felt like that. Why? Because it was so, of course. And had to be.

Before Nine, humanity's expansion off Earth, all the way back to the first brief stopover landings on the Moon, had to some extent been a venture into the *known*. You could *see* the first lunar landing sites from Earth. It wasn't like Columbus sailing over the horizon; it wasn't a trip into the unknown. Even Saturn – people had been watching ringed Saturn since Galileo; it was a wonder when you got there, but you *knew* what you were going to find – to a large extent at any rate.

Was this adventure spaceborne humankind's first trip into the true unknown? And, perhaps, with still more strangeness to come. What an experience. Not for the first time since the beginning of his exposure to the story of the Nine mission, Caspar found himself envying these people.

However, nothing stood still, there was no time for reflection. He saw that others were drifting towards them, seeing their discussion, evidently assuming an open invitation to join in.

Caspar had made an effort to memorise names and faces even before the *Cronus* had arrived here. So he recognised the oldest of the *Shadow* crew lumbered up now – Boyd Hart, that was the name. And Meriel, their de facto doctor and senior biologist, still talking quietly to Doria Bohm, sole representative of the Lunar Consortium, with Elizabeth Vasta trailing them, listening hard.

At a gesture from Hild, the newcomers pulled up chairs, sat with the rest, and the conversation flowed on seamlessly. Caspar found he was enjoying Hild's openness, the informal nature of her leadership.

But after letting the talk run on for a time, Vasta – carefully, tactfully, clearly not wishing to get into a leader-on-leader horn lock with Hild – raised a hand. 'Still, we do have some decisions to make. Don't we? What to do about Nine itself, going forward. And mainly, of course, in the short term, a decision about whether to reflect back the Hawking data a second time. With your constructed messages laid over the top.'

Hild nodded. 'Well, *we* think that's the obvious next step, but we've sat on that decision for eleven years now. I think I genuinely felt that we needed a wider group to consult – a group that represents to some degree the whole of mankind. Not just us, the Conservers, I mean—'

Boyd nodded back. 'Given that the first reflection seems to have woken up that quasar – or somehow woke it up twenty-five thousand years *before* any of us got here, to show up in our skies *now*—'

Hild said, 'That paradox, whatever it means, and its consequences, makes it all the more important that we consult, that we study the consequences before we act—'

Boyd snorted. 'Study? Guess, more like.'

Hild acknowledged that, and glanced around the group, looking for responses. Caspar, who aspired to be a good leader himself, saw that she was trying to keep the discussion focused while drawing in the rest of the group.

John Smith murmured now, 'Of course we can only guess at the consequences of a second echo. We would never have predicted the quasar paradox, would we? And why—'

Others tried to break in, but Smith held up a finger.

'And why just a *second* echo? Why not a third, or a fourth, or a fifth? Perhaps the – recipient – wants some kind of dialogue.'

Boyd nodded. 'That makes sense. But what "answers" have we got so far? You've got the unfolding of the black hole into this mocked-up world. And Feathers! *She's* not an answer to anything, just a whole bunch of different questions.'

'To which we do have some answers,' said Meriel. She glanced around at the group. 'So we believe. We transmitted all this back, shared all our thinking. How we eventually interpreted her presence, her nature, as evidence of her having come from a wider, older cosmos. Or cosmoses. If Nine really is some kind of wormhole-like bridge between universes . . .'

Vasta nodded. 'Your hypothesis has been well studied, and makes a lot of sense. You mean that Feathers' nature, her very existence, may be a message in itself. A message about the existence of these – higher cosmologies.'

'A message. Or a partial answer. Or a clue.'

'Or a lure,' growled Boyd.

Vasta nodded again. 'I wrote a couple of papers on this myself before we got here. Think-pieces, analysing your guesswork, and trying to go beyond.'

And Caspar, amused, noticed Hild frown at that 'guesswork'.

'Yes, it's a sensible hypothesis. But that is all we have right now – guesses.'

Caspar nodded. 'So, given what you know right now, what would you recommend to the authorities back on Earth?'

Vasta shrugged. 'Given my understanding as of this moment, that they authorise us to go ahead with the second Hawking message.' She bowed her head to Hild. 'I mean, to encourage you, the leader on the spot, to authorise *you*—'

'As representatives of the Conserver movement, which sponsored the original mission,' John Smith said mildly.

Caspar looked over to Doria Bohm. 'And what do you think? You stand for the lunar clan for now.'

An amused sneer. '"Clan"?'

'You of the Consortium, then,' Vasta said patiently. 'You are a power, with your own aspirations. You should have a say in this decision. That's why we brought you—'

'Damn right. Especially given the consequences – given that, as you say, the first reflection seems to have triggered a quasar event that might perturb half the Galaxy, never mind our pesky little Solar System.'

Hild nodded calmly. 'And so what would your recommendation be?'

'Oh, I guess I know what you expect me to say. We believe, above all, in opportunity. All non-terrestrial resources, and some terrestrial resources, should be seen as opportunities for human growth.' She eyed Hild as if goading her for an argument.

But Hild the Conserver, who might have rejected such arguments officially and viscerally, thought Caspar, stayed calm, expressionless. Not opposing. As did John Smith, just as calm.

Hild said mildly to Doria, 'So you believe that we should go ahead. State your case plainly, please. For the record.'

Doria shrugged. 'My recommendation is that we should go ahead with the Hawking echo procedure. Whatever all this is, given what we have seen so far – the exotic strangeness of the engineering – it must represent a chance to get much more data. Perhaps a huge opportunity for mankind.'

'Or a trap,' John Smith said calmly. 'We should consider that. All of this, the magical artefact, the strange nonhuman: all of it

287

baubles to dazzle the children, perhaps. Was it all a trap to lure us into triggering the Galaxy-centre eruption, somehow?'

Hild asked, 'Do you oppose further exploration, then, John?'

He seemed to think it over. Then he replied, cautiously, 'We are Conservers. We are not anti-intellectual. Indeed, it is only in the realm of the intellect that Conservers believe in growth. At least that is my interpretation of our philosophy. After all it was a Conserver ship that came all the way out here, *just to see what was here*, and we found all this. We have discovered wonders already – in this world-artefact, in Feathers – even if we don't fully understand them yet.

'Yes, I think we must go on. To see what's out there. While carefully studying risks along the way. Physical – the quasar – and even cultural.

'I have carefully studied the widening effects of the shock of this contact on wider mankind, of Earth – if only remotely. There has been a startling rise in religious sentiment, it seems, in response to this *miracle*, at the edge of the Solar System.'

Vasta nodded seriously. 'I should share more of my own briefings on such matters. But do you think such risks should put us off from exploring this phenomenon further?'

Smith shrugged. 'Given how much we have already done – and how little we understand, still – I would advocating going ahead with further studies, but cautiously.'

Vasta nodded again. 'My sentiments also. Given that all this isn't going to go away, it seems. We need to understand.'

Caspar waited a few more moments. 'Well,' he said at length. 'I suspect we have a consensus. We go ahead with the Hawking signal. There's no rush. We can draft a formal proposal – perhaps you and I can manage that, Hild, as the two commanders – but we'll need input from you all.' He glanced at Vasta. 'Especially you, of course, Elizabeth.'

Vasta nodded, as did Hild.

And then various monitors went off, pings from pockets in clothing, soft buzzings from gadgets on wrists or forearms.

Caspar checked his own feeds, linked to the *Cronus*, far above his head in its synchronous orbit. All silent. The alarm was local at least, down here.

Meriel got the details first. She seemed to try not to laugh. 'You recall we said that all we have uncovered so far, here at Nine, has been harmless? Well, not any more.

'That was Salma. Feathers just shot somebody.'

29

In Caspar's eyes, Hild Kanigel's leadership in this little crisis was exemplary, again. Decisive.

The incident had evidently happened in the largest of the bubble domes, and one of the oldest, it seemed, and the most used. That was where Salma and Feathers had taken Fabio, after the landing. Now, Caspar was told, Salma was hurrying Fabio out of there and through the connecting tunnel back to the medical tent.

Hild responded in a quick, orderly way. 'The rest of you stay here. We'll keep closed down until we can figure out what's going on. Meriel, you're with me. Suit up – we don't know what that dome's condition is, or the tunnels. We don't even know what "shot" means. And bring your medical bag.'

An unnecessary command; Meriel had the bag at her side, probably all the time. And as she pulled on her pressure suit, Caspar saw that she probably wore elements of the suit too, open, at all times, and evidently carried the rest. Always prepared.

Hild snapped, 'Boyd, you'd better come too.'

As the oldest, he looked to be the steadiest, Caspar thought. Another good pick.

But Caspar had a problem of his own.

He stood, briskly. 'Take me. Please. My son's in there.'

Hild hesitated for one second. 'Yes, Emmanuel, come. The rest of you, stay, please.'

Caspar scrambled to put on his pressure suit, those sections he had discarded. 'Also we have doctors on the *Cronus*, and facilities—'

'Later.' Hild glared at him. 'You three ready? Boyd, Emmanuel, Meriel? With me. The rest of you, be ready to assist, but not until I call.'

Vasta just nodded.

At a trot, Hild led the way to a zipper airlock – two panels to be passed through – and into a tunnel of fabric. There was no lighting here, and their suit lamps lit up automatically. The tunnel itself was pressurised, but, following Hild's example, they kept their pressure suits closed as they hurried through. Belt and braces, Caspar thought; good practice. But he felt heavy-legged; as Hild had warned, now he was moving fast, that extra ten per cent or so gravity here on Nine was heavier than he'd thought.

And all these shabby tents and fragile tunnels started to seem like each other.

'All this unprotected fabric,' Caspar said to Meriel. 'You don't get meteor punctures?'

Meriel shrugged. 'We're deep in the Oort cloud. It's a pretty sparse environment – all but interstellar space. Meteors, other debris, are few and far between.' She grinned through a flat faceplate. 'In fact if a meteor or comet fragment wandered by out here we'd wrap it, snag it, and build something with it. Or eat it.'

'We're there.' Hild had reached the end of the tunnel, a zippered flap. She glanced at a monitor. 'There's air, normal pressure inside. Good start.' She opened her faceplate. 'Whatever we see in there, just stay calm. We're the grown-ups, remember. Ready?'

And she pulled down the zippers, let the airlock flap fold back.

Caspar, Boyd and Meriel followed Hild through the airlock into the shelter beyond. Caspar found it was indeed much bigger than the medical facility where the *Cronus* crew had been gathered.

And it was full of junk, orderly piles of it.

Caspar quickly recognised what this particular dome was for, or how it had evolved at all events. After eleven years, it was full of *stuff*, new, old – evidently little in the colony was discarded, rather kept here, to be used and used again. This was a typical by-product of an isolated colony – a tradition dating back to bases at Earth's poles, for instance. Far from resupply chains, you never threw stuff away.

Caspar glanced at Boyd. 'Recycling?'

'Yeah,' he growled. 'And Feathers is always fiddling with this junk. I bet she made her "weapon" out of this stuff . . .'

Caspar saw that a group of people had gathered under the apex of the dome. Smart lamps hovered, their shifting light showing him their coveralls, mostly dingy, faded – save for one that must belong to Fabio.

And one other figure whose clothing – if it was clothing – *glistened*.

Caspar hadn't seen Feathers in the flesh yet. His heart beat a little faster. But—

Fabio. He was the priority.

Caspar and Boyd hurried after Meriel and Hild.

As he ran, reflexively, Caspar glanced around. The peripheral space had been roughly divided, by hanging curtains, into separate 'rooms' – a way to sort the junk. There was a big, open central area set out with chairs, tables, low cupboards, some of which looked like they had been scavenged from the *Shadow*, others adapted from other contents of the ship, packing material maybe. Another place to gather. This little colony was roomy, in its improvised way.

And, across the habitat, Fabio saw Caspar and started waving. 'Dad! Over here!'

Caspar and Meriel shared a glance, and then broke into a sprint. Again, Caspar felt that ten-per-cent-more gravity as his feet thumped over the floor. *The floor*: just scrap fabric, supporting junk heaps, stretched over the existential mystery that was Planet Nine.

When they reached the little group, Fabio came over to Caspar, and grabbed him in a hug as he had when a child.

Caspar stood back a little and checked his son over quickly. The boy was fifteen years old now, as tall as the rest – almost taller than his father already – but skinnier than most. And unharmed. Evidently, if anyone had got shot, it wasn't Fabio, to Caspar's guilty relief, and he briskly hugged his son again.

And now the victim did show up.

He was an older man – Joe Normand, as Caspar remembered from the introductions – shaven bald, heavy-set. The *comms guy*, he had called himself. And now he bent over a chair, to display a stick protruding from his right buttock.

Caspar found it hard not to laugh.

Meriel went straight to her patient.

And just to Normand's right . . .

The feathered woman.

Joe himself was still laughing, if wincing. 'Hey, Meriel. Hi, Commander Caspar! Look at me. Mankind discovers a new universe and I get shot in the butt.'

'Stay still, you idiot!' Meriel pressed down on Joe's upper

back so he stayed bent over the chair, and opened her bag. 'It's not terminal—'

'But it's in my terminus! Kind of poetic justice, don't you think?'

'If you don't shut up—'

'OK, OK. But look, it wasn't her fault. She *made* it, see. It was my fault for getting in the way—'

'Made what?'

'The bow and arrow.' That was Fabio. He went over to stand by the feathered woman.

Caspar tentatively followed, unsure how to behave.

But once he looked at Feathers up close, Caspar couldn't take his eyes off her.

She was taller than the rest of the crew – taller than Fabio. Her feathers – that really was what they were – were mostly sleek, shining, jet-black. On her back, they looked waterproof, fitting together like an exquisitely assembled tapestry. On her front and belly, though, the feathers looked softer – as if for warmth rather than protection. *Down* – the word floated into his mind. The body was very human-like, he thought, with the proportions, more or less, of a tall, graceful adult, but not muscular. At a glance he could not have distinguished the sex, male or female.

But the head was extraordinary, with a very human-looking rear skull, but a long, graceful face. A large forehead, huge black eyes, a small pale-blue *beak* for a mouth.

He had to go closer. He was fascinated. He took a step that way.

In response Feathers trilled, a deep-pitched song, and stepped back – and wings, stubby but authentic *wings*, unfolded from her back.

Fabio stepped towards his father. 'Take it easy, Dad. She's

already scared. She's sorry for what happened. I mean, she made the bow and arrow, but *she* didn't shoot it at Mister Normand.'

'No, that was me.' Another guy came forward, hand up. 'Zaimu. Propulsion tech and professional idiot. It was me shot Joe. Nice to meet you. We were just fooling around—'

Meriel hushed him. 'We'll deal with that later. Did you say *Feathers* made the bow and arrow?'

'I can tell you that.' Salma stepped out of the shadows.

'You are Salma. Born on the ship, right?'

'Yes, sir . . .'

But all Caspar saw of her, distracting him, was a black-disc pendant she wore at her neck, just like those worn by Meriel, Doria, Vasta . . . That weird convergence across the Solar System. Of *costume jewellery*. It had to mean something. But what?

Focus, Emmanuel.

Salma was watching him, looking confused. She seemed shy, reticent.

And Fabio stepped forward, concerned. 'Dad?'

'I'm fine. Sorry. I'm suffering from conceptual bombardment, I think.'

Fabio murmured in Caspar's ear, 'Go easy on Salma. Remember, before we showed up, the only people Salma ever saw were this crew. Plus an authentic space alien, to be fair. I think she's doing pretty well . . .'

'OK. Thanks. Go ahead, uh, Salma. So what about this weapon? Just tell us.'

At length Salma said, 'It's just another toy. We played, you know? Feathers and me, always, since we found her. And one game I found she likes to play is hunting. So I would heap cloth on top of a drone to make it look interesting, and let the drone run over the floor, or even fly up in the air. She used to just run around and chase it. But then she started making spears, just little sticks with points. I made sure it was all OK with Meriel and Hild. We all wanted to encourage her in what she enjoyed — what must be natural to her. Nobody was going to get hurt. And I knew the sticks she was throwing wouldn't pierce any of our tough habitat fabric, or . . . But I didn't know about the bow and arrow. Not until today.'

Hild said, 'OK, so who did show her how to make one?'

They exchanged glances, shrugs. 'I thought it was you,' Zaimu said.

'I thought it was you,' Salma replied.

'Huh. But if neither of us showed her—'

A voice boomed in the air, startling everybody. Including Feathers, who cowered back towards Salma.

'Then she invented it for herself. This is Elizabeth Vasta, in the med shelter. Sorry to startle you. You're sure? If that's the only conclusion. And that's pretty significant, if so. Look — I researched the theory of intelligence, human intelligence, before I came out here. Knowing I was meeting Feathers. And bows and arrows — that's a pretty important tech, and a widespread one. On Earth, I mean. The fossil record shows human groups — I mean, *Homo sapiens* — inventing the technology independently, in South Africa, Europe, Sri Lanka, at different times. An obvious thing to invent, I think, if you pass a certain threshold in cognition. But the pre-moderns, the Neanderthals for instance, never got it.'

Joe looked up towards the roof. 'So what are you telling us?'

'That bows and arrows are evidently a convergent technology. Given a brain and something like hands, something like eyes, something you can make the damn thing out of — and given something to shoot at, I guess — you're going to come up with a bow and arrow, or something very like it. Though Feathers may look different, and even if we haven't figured out her language yet, evidently she's as smart as any one of us. Smarter, maybe. Because she *invented* the bow and arrow, just as humans did, but all by herself.'

'OK,' said Hild. 'And what does that mean for us? I mean, we think Feathers was sent here to prove to us that in – some other place – wherever Planet Nine came from, there are people like us. A different universe, some of you say. People just as smart as us, even if they are different. And that other universe is so big, or so old maybe, that there has been room, or time, for people *very* like us to have evolved. And here's another example of that. With a similar body plan, you invent similar tools.'

Meriel nodded. 'We figured out that much before. We think we're being prepared.'

Caspar frowned. 'Prepared for what?'

Hild looked at him frankly. 'For whatever is trying to reach out to us. For whatever we encounter when we make the next step, reflect the black hole signal, the Hawking radiation, a second time . . .' She ran down.

There was a long silence. There wasn't even any radio chatter from the rest of the passengers of the *Cronus* that Caspar could detect.

'Well,' he said. 'What now? Professor Vasta, I guess it's your choice; you're the overall decision-maker now.'

'Agreed,' Hild said. 'So what next?'

A brief hesitation.

Then Vasta said, 'Thanks, Emmanuel, Hild. This is a fascinating development, in terms of anthropology. Which is *not* the right word. But I agree with the *Shadow* crew. I've looked over their discussions, their analyses. The insertion of this – person, Feathers, into our world, is surely meant as a kind of message. The questions are what that message is – a problem which I know you *Shadow* folk have studied intensively – and how we should respond. Or if we do at all. I think we need to consult Earth, one more time, and the other authorities, to make sure they're all on board. And then—'

'Yes?'

'Well, we only have one plausible next step at this point, I think. Paging Stephen Hawking. And get ready for whatever comes.'

Joe Normand grunted. 'Hey, is that all? What about my ass . . . ?'

They followed Vasta's lead in messaging Earth. But it turned out that the World President chose to participate in the next-step decision herself.

30

When she was summoned by Hild to attend what amounted to an intergovernmental conference, Salma thought she was probably going to be the most terrified person there.

'No, you won't be,' Hild assured her, as they hurried to the hastily assembled conference space set up at the heart of the largest habitat on Nine. 'I for one will be a pool of sweat.'

Conference space – a bunch of chairs cannibalised from the *Cronus* and the *Shadow*, set in a ring in this tent-like habitat, and all of it sitting on the fabric layers that lay over the faintly warm, unclassifiable surface of Nine, just centimetres beneath their feet. Salma did notice one odd gap in that ring of chairs, occupied by a heap of blankets and cushions.

'For Feathers,' she said to Hild.

'Obviously. We set it up for her the way we always do.'

'Will *she* be the most scared, do you think?'

'Well, she has to be here, but I think she'll be more bewildered than scared. Just more weird human stuff from her point of view. She'll be fine if you're at her side, as you have been from the start of all this madness . . .'

Hild herself looked tired, strained, aged.

Salma felt a twinge of sympathy. Salma knew that while she had spent the last few years 'running around with Feathers', as

Boyd put it, Hild had had to manage, not just the mission of the *Shadow* which was her nominal primary responsibility, not just an extraordinary pan-galactic incident, but now also the arrival of a liner full of experts and politicians – as well as an interface with Earth itself.

Hild was eighty-one, and had been commander of a long, long mission. It had shocked Salma when she'd worked out that Hild had been appointed captain of the *Shadow* when she was only a few years older than Salma was now.

'OK,' Salma said, 'so who *will* be more nervous than me?'

'Maybe Elizabeth Vasta, who has to report to the president of the world. Or maybe Melanie Mason herself. I mean, if *you* were world president – think of it. You sign up for your five-year term, then *three* more, expecting the usual issues: overpopulation here, a decade-long drought over there – oh, and this petty squabble with the Lunar Consortium. No, all that was manageable, you would think, on your inauguration day. And then, pow, out of nowhere, *this*. An existential threat to all of mankind – all wrapped up in a humanoid with feathers and some kind of relativity-busting eruption at the heart of the Galaxy . . .'

But Salma thought this was all evasion. Hild was on the spot, here and now. She wasn't talking about presidents. Hild was talking about herself. Years and years of this – mystery. This strange, calm, eerie, endless disruption.

She reached out for Hild's hand, squeezed it. Let her go as they reached the improvised conference set-up.

And Salma felt her own heart beat faster as she worked her way around the rough circle of chairs – ducking as an airborne camera drone flapped silently over her head, a reminder that this was going to be recorded, transmitted to all the human colonies, and probably preserved for ever.

She got to her seat, tucked between Emmanuel Caspar and

Feathers, already in their places. Feathers was trembling, averting those big bird-like eyes.

Salma immediately put her arm around Feathers. Once her feathers would have bristled when she was afraid, but she had learned that that tended to alarm the crew – she looked tremendously aggressive when she bristled, which was the evolutionary point, Meriel had said. So Feathers had gradually tamed that reflex out of her system. Still, Salma could sense her anxiety.

And so Salma held Feathers in a quick, tight hug, just as she had when they had first found Feathers alone and trembling in her coffin-like travel pod.

As people settled down, Feathers, calming, began looking around at the group – becoming more curious than afraid, Salma could see.

The group:

Hild, captain of the *Shadow*, and Emmanuel Caspar, of the *Cronus*: the local commanders, the two who would have the responsibility, Salma supposed, of implementing whatever decisions were made here today. She vaguely wondered where Fabio Caspar was. Possibly Feathers was missing the young man who had already become a close companion – the young attracted to the young.

The Conservers, of course, who had come out to Planet Nine in the first place, represented by Hild, Salma herself – and latecomer John Smith, the soft-spoken lawyer, short, neat, and looking impossibly old to Salma, even though, she had learned, he was some years younger than Hild. The Lunar Consortium had Doria Bohm, their sole ambassador, who had come out here on the *Cronus* – after having been involved in a crash between her own ship and the liner, at its launch from Saturn; Salma had never heard the full story about that, and was never likely to, it seemed.

And as for the Earth authorities, here was Elizabeth Vasta, science adviser to President Mason.

Whenever she saw Vasta, Salma's eyes were always drawn to the black pearl pendant she routinely wore – so like the pendants worn by herself, and Meriel and Doria Bohm.

The odd little mystery of the similar bits of costume jewellery intrigued Salma – indeed it nagged at her, vaguely troubled her.

She had confided in Hild, who had listened sympathetically, if sceptically. 'When we have a major cosmic mystery already, you're troubled by something like that?'

'You think it's just coincidence?'

'Well, it could be . . .'

'I'm being ridiculous?'

'No, no. Well, once I would have said – yes, it's just a silly coincidence. But – acausal quasars are ridiculous. Feathery humanoids are ridiculous. Planet Nine's flip-flopping is ridiculous. Who knows if this little puzzle fits in somewhere.' Hild had squeezed her hand, a gesture that went back to Salma's childhood. 'You'll figure it out. Just follow your instincts. That's served you well so far, and Feathers, and the rest of us . . .'

But Salma had to set that aside for now. The side conversations were quieting.

For, in a gap in the ring, the President of planet Earth had materialised, chair and all.

'Are you ready for me?'

Melanie Mason was grey-haired and smiling. *Grey-haired*: it was hard to tell her age, but Salma knew Mason had just started her fourth five-year term in office.

But she wasn't really there, Salma knew too.

'Take your time to get used to this – to me. All of you.' Mason's voice was gentle – and sounded, given the acoustics, just as if she were sitting in the habitat with them. 'I am not her, just a copy. An AI simulation of myself. *Her*self – I forget myself. But—'

'But with some legal validity,' said John Smith, the lawyer.

Mason now leaned forward, and smiled directly at Salma, who tried not to flinch.

'You're Salma? I've heard a lot about you – all of it good. Now, *you* understand I'm not actually here, don't you? I can respond to you, but—'

'Yes,' Salma said. 'You are a projection.' Hild patted her back.

John Smith said, 'An authorised avatar, in the jargon.'

Hild said, 'We Conservers don't use avatars, generally. They're seen as wasteful of resources. I can see the practical advantage, but there is generally enough time to arrange a genuine face to face.'

'But not this time,' Caspar said grimly.

'True enough,' Mason said. 'Well, if you aren't conversant with the technology, you should know that I was created, downloaded, about five days ago in fact – giving me time for various tests, including a face to face feedback session between me and my principal, before I was transmitted here – and it took the signal itself four of those five days to get here. When I get back, in four days' time I suppose, I'll go through the same process, a verbal debriefing with recordings of these events, and then a synchronisation back into the consciousness of my principal. The President herself.'

Salma frowned. 'So what will happen to *you*?'

Mason smiled at her. 'It's a kind thought to ask. To me? I'll always be there, for Melanie. As a memory, if a distanced one – as if you'd watched an event rather than participating in it.' She seemed to make a deliberate effort to smile at Feathers. 'I'll tell you this. I, she, President Mason, will never forget meeting *you* – whoever and whatever you are.'

Salma liked this woman, this not-person. And at the same time she felt overwhelmingly sorry for her.

John Smith said, 'Just to be clear, in legal terms, the simulated President here is empowered to negotiate, deliver instructions – even military orders – cut deals, just as if President Mason were here in person. The only caveat being that when the *real* President Mason hears about it all – in those few days' time, when the recordings of this session have got back to Earth at lightspeed – the real President has the power of veto. This is one way we've developed to manage human transactions in a Solar System that's just too big for us.' Comically, he raised a bony fist. 'Curse you, finite speed of light!'

Mason grinned. 'When I get back I may declare executive privilege and cut out jokes like that from the record, John.'

'Spoilsport.'

Salma glanced at Hild, who smiled. 'Well, I understand,' Salma said. 'I *think* Feathers could get the idea.'

Hild nodded. 'And I believe you.' She glanced around the group. 'You'd be amazed how much Salma has managed to get through to Feathers, with miming, practical demonstrations. And an awful lot of patience. Empathy.'

Salma felt herself blush.

'I know of this,' the President said. 'And I congratulate you. You have achieved remarkable things in a remarkable place. All of you. On the record, then. Where do we start? With the quasar?'

'I think we must start there,' said Emmanuel Caspar. 'Speaking as an ordinary citizen of Earth, which is currently suffering, so far as I can see.'

Hild said, 'I admit we are all still bemused by the timings. From our vantage point, out here in the galactic sticks, the quasar splash became visible in Sagittarius, at the Galaxy centre

– its light reached us – *just at the moment* that we first fed the so-called Hawking radiation signal back to the surface of Planet Nine, or the compact object it used to be. But the centre of the Galaxy is twenty-five thousand light-years away. The only way that timing could have been achieved is by having the quasar *ignite* twenty-five thousand years ago – so that the light had time to struggle all the way out here.'

Vasta nodded. 'I checked your original logs, looked at the timings. For the record, I can confirm it was all just as you reconstructed it later, and reported it.'

President Mason said, 'I've had a lot of time to think about this, had a lot of expert advice, and it still baffles me. As far as I can understand it, this means that whoever set off the quasar all those millennia ago must have been able to *see the future*. Or maybe they got a message coming *back in time*, from the future, their future, twenty-five thousand years ahead. Elizabeth, is any of this actually possible? Theoretically, practically?'

Presidential science adviser Vasta said carefully, 'I think I would say that while this is *theoretically* possible, depending on the advanced-physics theory you choose, *we* couldn't manage it. You're talking about extreme distortions of space and time. Black holes, wormholes – pieces of spacetime bent and stitched together in some higher dimension. It's not *impossible*, according to our theories. And we've seen a strange spacetime artefact in Planet Nine, right here.'

'We're sitting on it,' murmured John Smith.

'Indeed. But I . . . think I would not have declared such a paradoxical entity *possible*, for certain.'

'If you hadn't seen it change with your own eyes – or at least through the eyes of these witnesses.'

Vasta shrugged. 'Indeed. As John says, Planet Nine is a logical paradox you can actually walk around on.'

Mason looked at Feathers, beside Salma. 'And do you think this creature, Feathers, could make it possible? This . . . bridge across space and time.'

All eyes turned to Feathers. Salma gripped the tip of one bony wing-hand tight. Feathers stayed placid, amid all this strangeness.

'It's OK,' Hild said. 'She's used to scrutiny. Salma keeps her calm.'

President Mason nodded. 'You're doing a fine job, Salma. It won't be forgotten. I mean it. Somebody had to be the first human ever to befriend an alien, and it turned out to be you, and you did it very well. You'll go down in history.'

Salma had never thought of that. And she wasn't sure she liked it. She had the sudden sense of billions, trillions of people watching every move she made, now and in the future. She wished she could hide away, just her and Feathers . . .

Vasta coughed, an artificial sound. 'Madam President, perhaps we can hand out the medals later, when we've fixed the problem of the Earth being roasted by quasar fire?'

Mason smiled. 'Advise on, Science Adviser.'

'To answer your question, we don't believe Feathers has any, umm, control, over the mechanisms in which we seem to be enmeshed here. Or anything to do directly with the quasar, come to that. Our best guess – and here I endorse the preliminary conclusions of the *Shadow* crew, who have been here a lot longer than I have – is that she herself, her presence, is all *part* of the message. She's not a courier in that sense. She *embodies* information – or paradoxes. You see, the sheer unlikelihood of her nature – her likeness to a humanoid form – implies we are dealing with an origin in some other realm, another cosmos, which, compared to ours, must be either very old, or very large, or both . . . Large or old enough for such coincidences to occur.

She herself is a message transmitted without words.'

'So you theorise,' Mason said.

Vasta shrugged. 'So we theorise. It's all we can do without more data.'

'But we must prioritise. Back to the quasar. What *do* we know about the damn thing?'

Vasta and Hild shared a look, Salma saw.

Then Vasta, the senior figure, sat back. 'You've been on the spot, Hild, you and your crew . . .' She smiled. 'It's your quasar. You tell us about it.'

Hild nodded. 'OK. But, remember, Conservers don't *own* anything. Not even intellectual property. We share it all . . .'

'I wish you weren't sharing that damn thing,' Mason said.

Hild shrugged. 'Also we aren't specialists on stellar phenomena. We came out here thinking we were going to be exploring a rogue planet. We weren't properly equipped for this—'

'But you've been on the spot.'

'True. We did our best. And naturally, from the beginning we've observed, recorded, speculated. It's difficult to be definitive about any aspect of this phenomenon. Partly because what we see doesn't quite fit the theories we have developed from observing other quasars, features in other galaxies . . .

'We *think* that quasars are basically by-products of black holes – supermassive black holes, in the hearts of galaxies. We're talking millions of solar masses. Such things have strong gravitational fields, magnetic fields. And if such a hole spins, it drags a mass of galaxy-centre gas around with it. This is thrown outwards by centrifugal force, but the hole's magnetic field shapes the flow, so that you get plumes of material coming out of the rotation poles of the black hole – the north and south magnetic poles – along with immense lodes of electromagnetic energy.

And it is a hugely energetic event; typically you have the hole consuming the mass-energy of several stars per year to fuel it.'

'Hmm,' Mason said. 'And you think this is the mechanism we're seeing now at the heart of our galaxy?'

'Well—'

Mason pressed, 'Why should it start up *now*? And also, you said these . . . plumes . . . of energy get shot out from the hole's rotation poles, because that's how the magnetic field shapes the flow. But doesn't the central black hole spin in the same plane as the Galaxy itself? So shouldn't these beams be firing *perpendicular* to the plane of the Galaxy, up and out, not along a radius – not straight for us, *in* the Galaxy's plane? As this one is?'

Vasta said, 'All good points, Madam President. We can only describe a typical quasar. This evidently is something *like* a quasar, but isn't a *natural* quasar. We think this is a kind of – engine – a technology based on the manipulation of a quasar-like phenomenon. And because this instance doesn't fit any known pattern, it's difficult to make predictions about its future behaviour.'

Mason grunted. 'Try anyhow.'

Salma thought Mason was formidable. Totally in command of the room. And this was just a virtual copy of the real person, she reflected.

Vasta, a tough person herself, hesitated before replying.

Hild cut in, 'Well, what we do know is that its luminosity has grown, steadily – some believe exponentially – over the last eleven years, since its first detection.'

'Which was exactly when you opened the box on Planet Nine,' Mason said.

'Correct,' Vasta said. She consulted a handheld screen. 'And it's still growing. It's actually following the theoretical models we drew up in the beginning, pretty well. *How much luminosity* – right now it's delivering, across the Solar System, an extra half a per cent of the Sun's output, as it's received at Earth. So Earth is getting half a per cent more daily energy input than before. And the other planets are being hit also, of course.

'We learned all about the stability of Earth's natural systems, or the lack of it, during the climate collapse years, didn't we? The climate is a complex mess of flows of mass and energy and feedback effects . . . And so, just with that small nudge of that half of one per cent after a decade, the consequences – well, I guess we've all seen the news.'

Mason's expression was grim. 'As you implied, just as the climate is fragile, human society is still fragile. The memories are too fresh, the history too raw. Now people, nations, are reluctantly – but too readily in some cases – preparing for a return to the days of shortage and drought, famine, even war . . . As one example – Elizabeth will know this well – take the latest development in Africa: the Sahel is migrating south again, significantly.' She glanced at Salma. 'I imagine you know little of this. That's the boundary between the Sahara desert to the north and the savannah to the south, where the people and the animals are . . . Millions on the move, again. Just as our grand-parents witnessed.'

Doria Bohm spoke up forcefully.

'This isn't just about Earth, you know. The Moon too. Every planet, every asteroid and moon, every last rock floating around this Solar System will be affected by this heating. Including the Moon and its colonies.'

'Even the Sun, I suppose,' Vasta said, musing. 'If this goes on. The thermodynamic balance of the Sun could be disturbed.'

Mason frowned. 'What would be the consequences of that?'

'I'm sure somebody's modelled it. If the Sun's heat flow is

perturbed, I suppose you could be looking at mass eruptions, magnetic storms—'

'Saturn,' Caspar said, forcefully. 'Think about that. Where I used to work, where we rebuilt the *Cronus*. Ten times as far as the Earth is from the Sun, so it only receives one per cent of the luminosity per unit area that Earth gets in sunlight. So if you increase that—'

'Correct,' Hild said. 'The proportionate effects differ. For the Saturn system, that's a fifty per cent increase in Saturn's natural energy input already, right there.' She thought. 'The Saturn system is itself a big place. I can't imagine that such a small amount of energy in relative terms could do that much harm in the short term. The rings, though, are nothing but ice fragments. This quasar could make a mess of that, and soon.'

President Mason was frowning. 'A gruesome little spectacle in the sky, then, as we start to suffer down on Earth. *How long is this going to last?* That's the single most significant question I get asked. If it's short term, it's the climate crash again – ghastly, but finite in space and time, in resources, and we could put ourselves back together once again. More or less. If longer – what? We go the way of the dinosaurs?'

Vasta spread her hands. 'The truth is, we don't know. We can barely make a sensible guess—'

'Guess away.'

Vasta's smile was bleak. 'Is an avatar able to accept my resignation?'

'Sure, but my principal will just rescind it.'

'OK.' She glanced around at the others. 'Help me, here. We have enough data now to know that the quasar is increasing in intensity, in terms of energy delivered to the Solar System. As an extreme case, suppose the quasar illumination grew to *match* the luminosity of the Sun? At Earth's orbit, I mean. We might get *there* in a few thousand years. Or it might be faster. Most analysts think the growth is exponential, not linear. Perhaps fourteen hundred years—'

Mason cut in, 'And the consequences? Of a doubling of the sunlight?'

Vasta held up her hand. 'The warmth of the Sun you feel on your palm, your face – doubling that mightn't seem so much, but it would be enough to finish us off.

'We actually have a test case. Venus *already* gets about twice Earth's insolation, because it's that much closer to the Sun. That is, the solar energy that hits the cloud tops per square metre is twice what Earth gets. And look at the result. No water to speak of. Clouds of acid and cardon dioxide, covering a rocky landscape so arid and hot it glows in the dark . . .'

A brief silence.

'OK,' Mason said, abruptly. 'That sounds like a useful cue for a break.'

And Salma, for one, was relieved to be released.

31

People stood to get drinks and food, or just to stretch their legs. And there were side conversations. Vasta, Smith, Hild huddled over a console, murmuring about heat flows and 'illuminated interstellar sectors' . . .

Salma got some water for herself and Feathers – and seedcake for Feathers alone, one of Meriel's many minor biological miracles, created over the years.

Feathers herself wasn't scared, exactly, Salma knew, just wary. If something alarmed her she would sit still, preferably in the shadows or on the periphery of a group but not outside it, as if seeking not to be seen, and with somewhere to escape to if she needed it. Meriel said it was the typical behaviour of a creature in the middle of a food chain, adapted to being both predator and prey. Another small clue to Feathers' background.

The avatar of the President sat silent and still during the break. Salma wondered if she, it, were even activated. How strange, Salma thought, to have the most significant human being on all the planets represented this way, and *shut down*, an outsider to the conversations. But it was probably good for those present to be able to relax a little without that scrutiny.

At last, after about thirty minutes, the avatar leaned forward in her unreal chair, froze again.

*

That was evidently enough of a command to draw the group together again. People started to drift back into their places, some carrying drinks, others portable data consoles over which arguments continued.

Emmanuel Caspar came over to Salma with his drink. He asked softly, 'So what do you think of the President? I mean, I'm a mere captain of an interplanetary liner – and I ran a tiny colony at Saturn. That was tough enough. *This* is what I'd call command. And, listen, do you think Feathers is OK with all this talk-talk? I know she can't understand a word – can she? If she's distressed in any way, you don't have to leave; I could get Fabio to come take her away, look after her. They get on well, don't they?'

'Sure.' Salma thought it over. 'It's a kind offer. Thoughtful. Yes, I know Fabio is good with her. But—'

'What?'

She looked around at the group. 'This is such a big meeting. The President of Earth! Or her avatar anyhow. And it's about the strange situation that brought Feathers here in the first place. I have this feeling that she ought to be here – even if she doesn't follow any of it. In fact she could clearly never understand any of this.'

He nodded. Quite a situation, isn't it? But, yes, I guess you're right, she should be here if only for what she stands for . . .'

'I think we've come to believe that that's why she was sent here. Because she is a walking, living symbol of something else. She stands for something bigger. And what we have to do is to work out what that is . . .'

Hild coughed, politely.

They saw they were the last standing. They exchanged hasty smiles, joined the circle, and took their seats facing the virtual President.

Who suddenly seemed to spring to life again, as if a switch had been thrown.

'OK,' Mason began. 'I think we're nearly done for now.'

'Not a long meeting,' Salma whispered to Caspar.

'Presidents are busy people. Even their avatars are busy, I guess . . .'

Mason was saying, 'but I do still have some specific questions.

'I would like you to confirm something for me. Right at the beginning of all this, eleven years ago – when this quasar first lit up – the warming effects on the Earth were immediately apparent. But what about the question of how *long* we will be in the eye of this heat storm – how long before we might be free of it? I was shown some numbers back then, at the beginning. I'd like to know if the logic behind that prediction has changed, or not.'

Vasta took the lead. 'OK, Madam President. You want to know how long the Earth, and the wider Solar System, might be threatened by this phenomenon, this – custom quasar.'

Mason smiled. '*The Custom Quasar*. You can use that as the title of your book some day.'

'Let's hope there is such a day. But in the meantime – all we have is order of magnitude arguments, I'm afraid. Still.

'So, look, we can take the Earth's insolation, the sunlight energy it receives, as a starting point. A basis for scaling. And we know the quasar intensity is increasing, still. So suppose the ultimate purpose of the quasar is indeed to deliver an extra amount of energy to Earth equivalent to that solar energy density, per unit area. At least that's an order of magnitude to play with.'

Mason shrugged. 'Like Venus again? That seems a reasonable benchmark – and lethal enough, from what you say.'

'OK. But we know that the quasar beam doesn't just target Earth. That's probably impossible, given the smallness of the target, the distance. So we are passing through the spot, a wider beam.

'Now, the energy flow has been measured, by spacecraft across the Solar System – out to here, the most remote crewed station, and further by the robot probes. And it appears to have the same energy density right across the Solar System. No fall-off. Presumably the total *spot* is much wider still. *How* much wider is the question. And what does it take to produce that much energy, projected right out here, far from the Galaxy's centre?'

She looked down at her console. 'So, look – the most powerful quasar we know of – in nature that is, before the Milky Way quasar showed up – produces as much energy as you could get from extracting the mass-energy of the Moon, every *second*. Suppose the core quasar is as energetic as that.'

She got some gasps at that, but smiled and pushed on.

'Now, with all that energy output pouring out towards the Solar System – and if the, the *spotlight* beam spreads out so far that it's down to Earth-sunlight intensity across that whole range . . . well, you find that the area saturated with such energy, given such a source, is somewhere around seventy light-years in radius. Which is, what, nearly twenty times further than the nearest star? If we're somewhere near the centre of the beam, it should in fact be covering a few thousand other stars and stellar systems in our neighbourhood. That may sound a lot but it's actually a pretty tight beam, given that it crosses a galactic radius.'

Mason said, 'So many stars . . . I know this is all guesswork, but doesn't it seem kind of hubristic that all this energy, all those star systems, are being perturbed just because of *us*? . . . And how do we know it is us who's the target? Why *just* us?'

This time Salma spoke up, sitting with Feathers. 'But we do know it *is* just because of us. Don't we? We have Feathers. It started when *we* opened the box . . .'

Mason nodded. 'Fair enough.'

Vasta said, 'So, the question of *how long* we might have this quasar light inflicted on us? The Sun orbits the Galaxy core – the stars swim around the centre like shoals of fish, as I read once . . . So we are swimming through the quasar spot. That's a *big* spot, and, given the Sun's rate of motion, if we have to sail across the whole of the beam we won't get out for two hundred thousand years. Give or take.'

Mason nodded. 'The same estimates as a decade ago, when all this started. So you've only firmed up the case. I suppose there's a still worse possibility – that the beam might be redirected to follow the Sun as it moves across the background.'

Vasta shrugged. 'Perhaps. That could be. I suppose I'm conditioned to think in terms of natural phenomena, not a directed – *weapon*. But that's clearly not impossible. They would know the Sun's path . . . If so there's not necessarily any upper boundary on how long we might suffer this. But hundreds of thousands of years is bad enough.'

'All right. So that's far longer than is needed to reach the Venus state you described – twice the intensity in a thousand years or more, you said?

'Next question – what happens before that? Given it's a gradually increasing heat intensity, can you give me more milestones?'

Vasta consulted a screen. 'In fact we have some data, or at least projections, to build on from other studies. Most of you probably know about this – and you may well have seen this before, Madam President. We know that the Sun was gradually warming already – I mean, even before the quasar – through its own internal evolution, the depletion of its core fuel . . . If we wait long enough, the Earth will be scorched anyhow, quasar or not.

'But this increasing quasar input will do huge damage much

faster than that.' She looked again at the screen on her lap. 'Venus-Earth is perhaps thirteen centuries away. But, after just a *hundred* years, the total insolation hitting Earth – solar and quasar – will be up by five per cent on today's figure. In nature, because of the Sun's own slowly increasing heating – its natural heating – we'd have reached that threshold anyhow – but not until five hundred *million* years in the future. And we'll get consequences surely similar to the projections we have for that far date.

'It might not sound much, but much more of Earth's water, for example, will start evaporating, will linger in the air rather than fall back as rain – and we'll get even more heating from that, by the way; water in the air acts a greenhouse gas.

'Meanwhile the carbon dioxide cycle will start breaking down. The overheated, exposed rocks will weather, cracking, reacting with the carbon dioxide in the air, drawing it down . . . You might think less carbon dioxide is good, because less warming. Yes, but vegetation needs carbon dioxide to survive. The most advanced photosynthesising plants will wither first, without the cee oh two from which they extract carbon to build trunks and leaves. The herbaceous plants, deciduous trees, ever-green broad-leaf trees, even some conifers – most of our crop plants too – all gone.'

'All this after the *first* century?'

'All this after the first century. In the decades after that, ex-tinctions on a massive scale will follow – whole domains of life. Photosynthesis itself will eventually collapse. You might still get a few termites and such around the hydrothermal vents at the bottom of the oceans.

'But by two hundred years there will be a final "runaway greenhouse", as they call it, as *all* the water evaporates. The oceans gone. And life will dwindle further, until—'

'I think that's enough. Thank you. All this *if* we stay in that damn quasar beam, and *if* it keeps strengthening as it has so far . . .'

'That was a tough listen, Madam President. I suspect it's going to be a lot more complicated than that, in good and bad ways. Earth's systems have a lot of inertia, and a lot of complexity . . . But in essence, similar projections we made a decade ago haven't changed.'

Mason shrugged. 'But in a way the details don't matter. For sure it's going to be a tough tag-line when I run for re-election.'

If that was a joke, Salma thought, nobody was laughing.

Doria Bohm was exploring her own tablet. 'And don't forget the rest of us. Earth, with the richest biosphere, may be the most vulnerable and will suffer the most — but the other worlds will be damaged too. We on the Moon might survive in deep lunar caves with ultra-strict recycling. Any life on Mars we haven't yet managed to destroy will be lost when the deep, ancient aquifers finally burst and dry. The ice giants will melt. Oh, I just found an estimate: Ceres will be melting after about twelve thousand years—'

'The comets,' Hild said. 'In the Oort cloud. We will surely lose those quickly, given how disrupted each can be by the heat of a single passage past the Sun, lasting a few months of close approach . . .'

Salma had more or less followed these arguments, had heard some of it before over the years. But now, hearing it all set out so forcefully, so clearly, she felt overwhelmed. Was she going to live to see the end of the world — of all the solar worlds?

She curled over herself, knees tucked up against her chest, arms beside her head, a childish pose she should long have grown out of.

Hesitantly at first, Feathers put her long, fragile arms around her friend's shoulders, and hugged. Salma could smell her, the wood-burn tang of the feathers, heard their soft rustling.

Salma hugged back. 'I love you,' she murmured.

And Melanie Mason held up an unreal hand.

The chattering, the morbid speculation, stopped.

Everybody came to order.

'Thank you,' Mason said now. 'I've pushed you a long way here, into speculating about stuff you really don't know much about. I know scientists don't like to do that, and I appreciate it. This has been hugely useful – even if, I suspect, my principal will want to run it all through a dozen think-tanks to confirm it. But we are emphatic that none of this is in any sense *your fault*. You of the *Shadow*. There was a button to be pushed here; whoever got here first would have pushed the damn thing.

'But – I know the President is going to ask, because *I* would ask – what the hell are we going to do about this now? Or, more to the point, what are *you* going to do? Because you are the ones on the spot.'

'Nothing more without authorisation,' Hild said, looking around the group. 'I mean, from everybody. From all our – nations. Earth, Moon, Conservers. This is too big for our petty factionalism. Agreed?

'But as to what we could actually do now, given authorisation – the next step seems obvious. We try sending the new Hawking signal, to this world. On behalf of mankind. One step up from the simple echo we sent before. Maybe, if *they* know we're here, we'll be spared . . . Or not. Anyhow we deal with whatever follows. We, the crew.' She glanced around once again. 'If this audience is done let's start planning. And send that signal, since it's all we've got.'

Melanie Mason nodded. 'Wait for my authorisation – my

principal's, once she's absorbed all this . . . That's going to take days, of course. Lightspeed. And I should consult the Conserver councils, the Moon. But I think you could get on with your preparation for now. And then – well, we do what we can. Thank you again. Let's hope we can make sense of all this.'

Caspar grinned. 'And save the Solar System?'

'Ideally.' And the President of Earth winked out of existence.

32

Once the decision was made to perform the second Hawking experiment, Planet Nine was hastily evacuated.

The experiment was still under the control of the *Shadow* crew, but now the *Cronus* people were officially in charge of the situation. And Elizabeth Vasta's immediate recommendation decision was to evacuate Feathers from the faux planet. It would be the first time she'd been taken away from Nine since her first discovery and retrieval.

Salma, feeling somewhat excluded, tried to follow the logic of that. Vasta, with surprising patience for someone so high up in Earth's government, took Salma aside and talked her through it.

'I know you've lived here for eleven years, Salma. Much of your own life. You've done well to survive here, and to have explored the situation, all of you – and you, especially, Salma, have been crucial in supporting the asset.'

And that was a slip, Salma knew. *The asset.* A jargon term the Earth-based folk used for Feathers. Frowned on by all the *Shadow* crew.

'And I imagine it feels like home to you,' Vasta said.

'It *is* home. And it's certainly Feathers' home.'

'OK. But this is also a scientific experiment – probably of strategic, even existential importance for all of us. We have to control it scientifically, *and* have regard for safety.

'The last time the Hawking experiment was run, this whole object – artefact, natural phenomenon, Planet Nine – *unfolded*, didn't it? From a compact little ball to a planet-sized sphere. We don't know *how* that happened. We do know it's not some kind of miracle, as it followed scientific law, to some extent – the mass was conserved, gravity still worked as it should. But we have no way of predicting what might happen when we try again. Just as we never would have guessed what followed before – Feathers, and the quasar, a triggering that had to have happened in the deep past.

'But the best thing we can do is repeat the conditions we, or rather you, applied at that first experiment. You stood off from the black hole, in space, reflected the Hawking signal back – and then ran as the object expanded. So that's what we're going to try now. Use the same conditions, see what happens next. I mean, *nothing* might happen – nothing that's observable to us, anyhow. Or something as extraordinary as the last transformation. We just don't know. So we're being cautious, taking it step by step. As before we'll stand off while it all unfolds . . .'

Salma had no say, of course, in whether all this was to be done, and how. It was polite, and kind, of Vasta to try to explain the logic to her at all.

She still had the feeling that it was wrong to keep Feathers away from Nine, whatever they did.

She spoke to her friends from the *Shadow*, and they were sympathetic, but she got a lot of shrugged shoulders.

'We just don't know what's right or wrong to do here,' Meriel said. 'As we haven't from the start of this – adventure. We've always just had to feel our way in, step by step.'

'But now these people from Earth have ignored all that and are just taking over.'

'Well, that's government for you. And Elizabeth Vasta, for one, is much better qualified to make crucial decisions about this than you or me, kid.'

'But she hasn't *been* here. And she's not a cosmologist, or a biologist, or . . . She's a climatologist!'

Meriel had to smile. 'Like every planetary president's top adviser has had to be for a century. We'll just have to trust her to make the right decisions.'

Salma didn't, though. She didn't see how anybody, any person, could make the *right* decisions here, it was all so abstract, so huge. And certainly not a politician so remote she couldn't even speak to them in real time. She thought they should follow the crew's own instinct – the crew who had lived with all this for so long.

But she had no say in the matter. And nor, of course, did Feathers. And as crew from the *Cronus* helped the Conservers of *Shadow* collapse their big old collection of habitats and pack everything away, Salma could only stand by with Feathers, and watch, and try to stay calm.

Feathers was quiet, even sullen.

This is wrong, Salma thought. *Feathers knows it, somehow. I feel it.*

That feeling became stronger after the evacuation, and Nine had been left uninhabited.

Feathers didn't take to the strange environment of the *Cronus*. Once aboard, she had quickly found a corner in a disused hold where she could establish her nests of cloth and other junk – stuff donated from the *Cronus* crew and passengers under Meriel's guidance. Over the first twenty-four hours, Salma spent as much time as she could with her there.

And then a first attempt was made to 'light up Planet Nine

with more Hawking scribble', as Boyd Hart put it. To repeat the first run as closely as possible, the signal was to come from the *Shadow* as before, with the set-up assisted by crew from the *Cronus*, hand-picked by Caspar himself, and much more extensive science observation run from the larger ship. But Nine was evacuated of crew.

Salma for one was dubious. It seemed obvious to her that the first signal had evoked a human-friendly response – at least, the gravity had been acceptable for humans – and the presence of Feathers seemed nothing but a signal pointed straight at the human visitors. There was more debate about the evacuation. The idea of having humans down there now was pushed by Hild and Meriel, in the end vetoed by Elizabeth Vasta and Caspar.

So the Hawking signal was fired back just as in the first experiment . . .

But this time nothing came back from the signal itself, save faint reflections from the surface of the object. This time there were no changes in the basic configuration – the mass, the gravitational properties. No dramatic unfoldings of Planet 9 as before – or collapsing, come to that.

They let some time pass, in case of some delayed response.

When there was no response, they tried again. A second failure.

After that, Meriel spoke to Vasta, Caspar and the others.

With quiet insistence she said, 'Maybe we should follow Salma's instinct after all. And the rest of us from *Shadow*, frankly. Maybe Nine *needs* inhabitants, some of us, to make the next step work – in particular Feathers, whatever that step might be. After all, Feathers came safely through the first transition—'

'Barely alive,' Vasta pointed out. She shook her head. 'But what we're doing isn't working. We may as well try something else. A landing party, at least, though, like before. It doesn't seem right to send Feathers down alone . . . Even if your interpretation has always been that Feathers herself was essentially a message aimed *at* us . . .'

They left it for twenty-four hours before trying again – just in case there was some delayed reaction to their earlier attempt. Then, what Vasta called a 'landing party' was quickly assembled, briefed, and suited up.

The party of just two, as initially defined, was to consist of Elizabeth Vasta of Earth, and Doria Bohm, representative of the Lunar Consortium. Doria, a skilled pilot, could fly a shuttle down.

But none of the *Shadow* crew were to be sent down – and not Feathers.

Boyd Hart, the oldest crew member of the *Shadow*, claimed not to be surprised. 'It's all politics. Leaving behind the crew who have been here for years in favour of representatives of the two big power blocs, Earth and Moon, ha! What are they going to do, negotiate treaties?'

Salma, too, felt this was all wrong, but on a more visceral level. She was especially surprised at the exclusion of Hild, and she went and told her commander so.

Hild was philosophical. 'Well, that's a point. But I'm not going to protest. If *this* fails there will have to be other attempts. Things have a way of working out. You just have to be patient, Salma . . .'

Salma gave up. She did accept that, having grown up on the *Shadow* among its small crew, she knew too little about people en masse. She knew something about personal relationships, a little about feelings, but nothing much about politics. She didn't have the tools to argue the case.

And Hild was proved right, when the first signal attempt was made the following day.

*

Vasta and Bohm descended, crammed into a rattly *Cronus* shuttle. On landing they stood proud, side by side, in their pressure suits, with equipment sacks on their backs, and camera drones fixed to their helmets.

Salma thought they looked pretty silly when the Hawking signal splashed over them and Planet Nine remained stubbornly inert. And sillier still when they had to crawl back into the lander and scuttle home to *Cronus*.

It was on the day after that, in one of the grand lounges aboard the *Cronus*, that Hild called a meeting, and, in her soft, persuasive way, made a fresh case for a different landing party – finally including Feathers.

'Feathers came out of the first experiment, after all,' she told Vasta. 'You know we believe she is a kind of embodiment of whatever message we are being sent – part of it, at least. I know that you might think her presence would inject too much randomness into this, a lack of control. But maybe she is some kind of – key – to what follows now. Maybe we simply have to demonstrate we've been able to care for her – at least tolerate her. Who knows?'

A bit theatrically, Salma thought, Hild glanced around at the gathered group, especially the *Cronus* folk, as if daring them to contradict her.

But Vasta just shrugged, rather than argue back. 'On reflection I think you're right. And, further, we ought to have been listening to what you *Shadow* folk have been trying to tell us all along. You've been on the spot. You've made the right guesses, figured out the right logic, to get us this far at least. And yes, you've made such a good connection with Feathers.' She seemed to think about it for five more seconds. Then she said, 'So let's do it. We take Feathers down.'

Salma clenched a fist. '*Yes.*' It came out as a hiss – she'd used the exaggerated way she spoke the word, along with the gesture, that she used for Feathers. And, she saw, looking over, Feathers understood. A rustle of wing feathers.

In the discussion that followed, the rest of the new landing party quickly self-assembled, with some quick decisions by Vasta, Hild, Caspar.

'OK,' Vasta said at last, a monitor in her hand. 'So Doria Bohm is going to pilot the shuttle. As before. Otherwise, I will be going along. And, we agree, we must take the creature called Feathers.'

Just Feathers, Salma thought, seething inwardly. *The person called Feathers would do . . .*

'And if we take Feathers, we have to take Meriel, who's cared for her physical and medical needs since she was found.

'*And Salma*, who similarly has been a constant companion.'

And that was a shock to Salma.

Her first reaction was jubilation. Her second, a stab of terror. *Do I really want to walk through that doorway again? Even if I'll be part of a team. Myself, Doria, Vasta, Meriel . . .*

But Salma had an odd, unidentifiable feeling as she thought this through that this latest selection was the *right* one, regardless of discussions of skills and experience. It felt *right* to her, this particular group. A piece of the puzzle that slotted home, though she didn't understand how.

Half-consciously she fingered the pendant on her neck.

And the strange but familiar hand of Feathers slipped over hers, and squeezed.

It took six more hours for the revised preparations to be made.

Then another six hours for rest, mandated by Meriel for herself and the others, an injunction backed up by the medical team on *Cronus*.

Then they finally suited up. Feathers wore the clumsy environment suit, with its repairs and adjustments, that she had worn every time she had left the surface habitats since the *Shadow* crew had first discovered her.

And then, at last, the five of them crowded into that small shuttle, mated to the hull of the *Cronus*.

The passengers took their seats. From where she was sitting, Salma could see the back of Doria's head, sitting up in the pilot's position, hear her low voice as she swapped checkpoint markers with the *Cronus* crew.

At last the shuttle cast off from the liner.

Looking back, Salma could see the huge curved forward hull of the *Cronus*, that long spine, receding, slowly, slowly. The relative movements were silent, at first imperceptible – but acceleration smoothly mounted, pushing them back into their couches.

Doria, a little fussily, made the rounds of the passengers now, using handholds to brace against the acceleration, checking their seat harnesses.

And she repeated their planned itinerary. 'Remember the flight profile. We're decelerating from orbit around Nine. We'll get up to about a quarter Earth's gravity. That won't last long. Then we'll have a sterner bout of deceleration to lower us down to the surface – no air for aerobraking here, remember, you Earth folk. No gliding down. This will be more like landing on the airless Moon – my Moon. Earth's moon. Landing on rockets. We should be settling on the ground, at the site of the old habitat, in a couple of hours . . .'

As the shuttle drifted away from the *Cronus*, a drone, a floating tray, came sailing through the air past their heads, laden with food and drink packages.

Doria grinned. 'You can't fault the service. Or the automatics. Anybody want anything?'

But Salma was staring around, at the four of them — plus Feathers — gathered together for the first time.

Doria noticed, and approached Salma, feeling faintly concerned. 'Salma? Something wrong?'

Salma looked back at her, vaguely.

Meriel touched her arm. 'Are you OK?'

'Hmm?' Salma seemed to focus. 'Yes, yes . . . it's just — our pendants. She touched her own onyx pendant.

And the four exchanged glances, Salma, Meriel, Vasta, Doria.

Doria was the first, nervously, to speak. 'Look at the four of us. We come from across human space, gathered here like this, by chance . . .'

'Apparent chance,' Vasta murmured.

And yet, the coincidence of these pendants . . .' Doria shook her head. 'I was born and raised on the Moon. Elizabeth on Earth, you others — Salma was born half way to the Oort cloud. And yet *we all have these similar pendants.*'

Meriel touched her own pendant. 'The only non-coincidence is Salma and myself sharing gifts from her mother. Otherwise—'

Vasta smiled. 'Otherwise we're evidently dealing with forces we don't understand. From galaxy-centre explosions to costume jewellery. What next?'

Salma said, 'It must mean something.'

Vasta nodded. 'So it must. But that meaning will become clear in time, I'm sure. All we can do is explore it all, and that's exactly what we're doing.' She stroked Salma's arm. 'For now, just be glad we're underway. Time for a nap in these cosy surroundings, I think.' She settled back. 'Wake me if you need to.'

There was no need.

The flight seemed to pass quickly. Salma, holding Feathers in a light embrace, found she had dozed as well. And when she was woken, by Doria rousing them all with a noisy throat-clearing, she was surprised to find there was just a quarter of an hour before landing.

They settled in their couches quickly.

Doria called, 'Touchdown approaching. Check your straps . . .'

No air, no re-entry. No buffeting weather. No signals from the ground . . .

And so they landed.

After touchdown it didn't take long for the party to suit up, debark, and have the automatics disgorge their equipment. Crew and drones together dragged it all on trolleys a safe distance away from the shuttle.

Then the shuttle, self-piloting, lofted silently back to space.

So the party were left behind.

For a moment, they just stood in a circle around their heaps of gear, including a collapsed habitat module, tanks of air and water, heavy resource-recycling kits, a small fission-powered generator. After the brilliantly lit cabins of the *Cronus* it all seemed terribly dim to Salma. But under her feet the odd, dust-less, roughened surface of Nine was hugely familiar. *I'm back
. . .*

Meriel insisted that they got the shelter set up first, sealed and pressurised, with some of their gear stowed inside. 'Ready for a medical emergency,' she said.

The others weren't about to argue, and got to work.

'This heap of gear doesn't seem like much to take on an adventure like this, does it?' Vasta said as they worked, as if lightening the mood.

'It's enough,' Meriel said calmly. She glanced at checklists, then at Salma, Feathers. 'For us, after all this time, it's like coming home. *And* we didn't have such a nifty power unit before.' A gift from *Cronus*.

'Nothing but the best,' Doria said. 'And now . . .'

With the habitat hastily assembled, they stood together, distracted, looking around.

Doria was hesitating. 'You know the schedule says we ought to check out the rest of our kit. *Before* calling down the Hawking signal.'

Meriel nodded. 'But the kit's pretty smart. It would bleat if it was hurting. Also I can attest we are all fit and well. Somewhat accelerated heartbeats and breathing, in some cases. Oh, and Feathers is fine too, as far as I can tell . . .'

Doria glanced around at the group, standing in their pressure suits. 'You want to just get this done?'

Vasta, her face, like the others', illuminated by an interior helmet lamp, just smiled. 'I was thinking the same thing.'

'Then we do it.' Doria tilted her head. 'Bohm to *Cronus*, surface to *Cronus*. Joe, that you? I'm guessing you know what I'm about to say.'

Salma couldn't hear the reply from Joe the comms guy, but Doria laughed.

Then she turned back to the group. 'Done. He's counting me down to the switch-on of the Hawking echo pod. Eleven. Ten . . .'

Apparently on impulse, she held out her gloved hands, to either side. Salma took one, Meriel the other. They all joined in, standing in a ring – even Feathers, with a little encouragement from Salma, holding hands with Salma, Doria.

'. . . Three. Two. One.'

And—

Elsewhere,
Elsewhen

33

And brilliant light flooded over them all.

Feathers screeched.

Salma staggered, and reflexively raised her suited arm over her head. Her faceplate quickly cut down the intensity of light it allowed to pass, and her vision cleared, though she was left blinking.

The light was all around, dazzling.

Coming from a complex, shining sky—

Somebody ran into her, nearly pushing her over, then clung to her. It was Feathers. Her screeching yells nearly drowned out other voices.

But now Salma heard Vasta, calm, measured. 'Take it easy. Fix your faceplate filters . . . It's just starlight. I think. *Bright* starlight . . .'

Salma managed to get one hand free of Feathers, and with a finger stroked the side of her own smart faceplate. It darkened quickly – too quickly, and she had to dial the opacity back, to get a light level she could withstand.

Working partly by feel, she did the same for Feathers, who still clung to her in the glare, trembling.

Dazzling light. *Starlight?*

'Stand still,' Vasta said. 'Take your time. I think the gravity is a little different too. For now we just need to . . . observe.'

But her voice sounded choked-up, to Salma. As if she was trying to conceal awe.

Different gravity?

Still, Salma did as she was told. She gently pushed Feathers away, but kept hold of her hand. And stood there, and looked: looked at her companions, at the lander, their modest shelter, at their bits of equipment on the ground.

And, finally, looked into a sky that was dominated by a fist of light.

A fist clutching what looked like a kind of sword, a sword of swirling gases and more brilliant light . . . She was dazzled, it was hard to see anything clearly, but that was her first impression. Her head's first attempt to make sense of it all, she supposed. She touched her faceplate, stopping down the intensity further.

Now, looking again more comfortably, more carefully, she saw a knot of extraordinary brilliance, like a star – but not the diminished, distant Sun as seen from the Oort cloud, nor the more remote stars – a brilliant, blazing grain of light.

And around that vivid starlike point, a huge celestial light sculpture loomed, with billowing gases lit from within, by a frozen cascade of lesser stars – some showing blurred discs. A storm of light, it was like an explosion but so vast and slow it appeared motionless, like a still image in a monitor – a process, she supposed, working out on much vaster timescales than her own human span. That brilliant centre must be birthing those lesser stars, she thought. Stars like raindrops in a storm cloud.

And beyond *that* a curtain of still more stars, distant stars, bright themselves, all set against a wider background of swirls of light, trails of glowing gas. As if a galaxy had been dismembered by some predator, the scraps thrown around . . .

All of this was like a frozen explosion.

She was aware that Feathers was still clinging to her, tight, and yet not trembling now, not afraid.

Suddenly the light was blocked, and Salma flinched.

It was only Doria, standing in front of her, blocking the light. Salma, distracted by Feathers, hypnotised by the sky, hadn't seen her approach.

Doria peered into Salma's faceplate. 'I'm checking everybody. You OK?'

'Just.'

'Good. It's just a different place, is all.'

'A *very* different place—'

'A different sky, but nothing that can harm us – well, I don't think so. As Elizabeth said, gravity is different, though.'

Salma hadn't noticed. But then she hadn't moved from the spot.

When Doria moved out of her view, going on to Vasta, Salma tried a couple of steps herself. Yes, the gravity was subtly different, a fraction lighter than Nine had been. You could *feel* it, just with a few steps.

Feathers followed. She still held Salma's arm, but she was calming all the time, though looking around wildly, intermittently gabbling out some more of that strange speech. Absently, Salma stroked her back.

And she looked across at the others: Doria inspecting Vasta now, Meriel alone, standing staring at the new sky.

Feathers, evidently calming, at last let go of Salma. She began to walk, cautiously.

And then to run – slowly at first, faster and faster, until it became an almost joyous sprinting, jumping, kicking up the dust.

Dust?

Salma looked down at her own feet, her boots. She saw that

dust, dark grey, powdery, clung to the legs of her suit.

'Look down,' she called to the others.

Meriel was still gazing up at the sky. 'Look *down*? Are you kidding?'

But Vasta looked, and glanced over at Salma. 'Oh. No dust on Planet Nine, right? Dust here. And, yes, there's the different gravity.'

Salma said, 'Also there's Feathers.'

'What about her?'

'She seems different here. I mean, in her reactions. She seems excited – but more at home. Does that make sense?'

Meriel nodded. 'I trust your intuition.' She stole another glance up at the sky. 'What a firework display. Where the hell are we? Well, we've got the President's science adviser waiting to work on *that*. Come on. We've been inspected. Help me with the geology package.'

The geology kit was a compact little unit that stood on top of a slim pillar, about the width of Salma's bare arm. It wasn't hard for Salma and Meriel to haul this thing out of their heap of gear, walk it away from their arrival site, and set it up on an area not yet disturbed by their footsteps. Here, they let the kit's central smart pillar contact the ground – and, with a soft whir, it began to drill its way into the surface, sampling dust and rock, measuring such factors as humidity, heat flow, elemental composition as it went.

For Salma the simple, well-rehearsed chore of putting this together was oddly comforting, among all the strangeness.

Once the kit had started to work, Salma looked around at her companions.

Doria and Vasta were staring up at the sky, evidently talking on some private channel. Vasta was pointing at the biggest, brightest of the starlike objects, that knot of energy at the heart of the ragged galaxy — if it was a galaxy.

Feathers was still running around, Salma saw. She wasn't frightened, not if Salma read her body language correctly, and she was pretty confident of that after all this time. She really did seem at home in this gravity field, more so than on Nine.

But Feathers seemed to be looking for something — and yet 'looking' wasn't quite the right word. She peered at the ground, yes, but she seemed to be *feeling* it, somehow, perhaps through the soles of her feet, her boots. A sense of the ground itself, even — maybe she was responding to its deeper structure, perhaps a faint seismic trembling, sensing the tremors like the seismometers in the geology pack.

'I'll tell you one thing immediately,' Meriel said softly to Salma. 'This is a proper planet. Whatever it is, it's *not* some manifestation of Nine again. Well, I don't think so. But it isn't like Earth. Or any planet in the Solar System, past or present.'

That qualification puzzled Salma. 'How can you tell that?'

Meriel waved a hand at the geology pack, at preliminary readings and analyses scrolling across its face. 'It's amazing how much you can detect using a smart little pack like this, sitting on a planet's surface, and how quickly. Superficially this is like Earth. Similar size and mass. Composition, metals and carbon and silicon . . . Gravity gradients and seismic echoes are telling me that the planet has a dense core, probably iron, a mantle of rock over the top of that, and a solid crust on top of *that*. Like Earth in that way. Different densities at different depths. The surface rocks are rich in silicates — silicon compounds — with iron and other metals you find on Earth. Whereas the blown-up Planet Nine was uniform throughout, so the seismometers told us. More like a model of a planet, a mock-up, than a product of geology.'

Salma was impressed. 'You got all that so quickly?'

Meriel smiled. 'I told you. Smart kit. Vasta and Doria have feeds of the results; they're seeing what I'm seeing.' She gestured at the geology package. 'If you want to see for yourself—'

'I'd never understand it. Just tell me, please.'

'Well, you've had the headlines. This place is very Earthlike – oh, but very little surface water. None in the atmosphere. There may be caches underground, hydrated compounds in the mantle. Water chemically bonded with other stuff. But if there was any surface water, it's probably long sublimated away by now. As for life—' She glanced up at the gaudy sky. 'That big quasar thing – there must be a hell of a lot of ultra-violet in that light show—'

'True enough,' Vasta called over, evidently listening in. 'And any water would be long gone, dissociated into oxygen and hydrogen, the hydrogen lost to space. Just as once happened to Venus, and as will happen to the Earth in the future when the Sun heats up. If the quasar spares us, that is. However rich its past, this is an old, dead world.'

Salma frowned. 'Old? I don't see how you can say it's *old*. I mean, look at that sky. All those hot young stars—'

Vasta raised a finger. 'Well, they *look* young—'

'Maybe the planet's just been scorched bare.'

Meriel shook her head. 'It's nothing to do with the sky, or the surface. The intrinsic properties of the planet itself – the deep structure gives it away. I should have shown you before.' She tapped at the screen of the geology pack. 'You know that a planet like Earth has a lot of internal heat? Some of it a relic of its formation, when you had planetesimals – lumps of rock, even some partly formed planets themselves – slamming against each other and into the growing Earth. At least some of all that kinetic energy was retained, the heat of formation, still leaking out in human times, billions of years later. And *also* you would have radioactive products trapped in the mantle and core, fissioning away, dumping still more heat into the interior. In our time, there was still enough residual heat from all those sources to drive surface processes—'

'Volcanoes?'

'That, yes. Earthquakes. Also continental drift, rafts of granite floating on currents of liquid rock in the mantle. *But* all the time that heat was being lost to space, and there was only ever a finite amount of it.'

'The Earth was cooling, then.'

'Like every rocky planet. But still it has a liquid core, a liquid mantle. That's how hot it was, is. But *here*—' She pointed to a reading. 'Can you interpret that?'

A learning opportunity. She would always be the only kid on the *Shadow*.

She looked, gamely. If the gear had been from *Shadow* she might have had a chance, but this was *Cronus* tech. She stood back and shrugged.

'OK,' Meriel said. 'That little number, just *there*, is telling me that there is only the slightest dribble of heat flow coming from this little planet. It's almost down to ambient. I mean, the same temperature as the sky.'

Salma understood most of that. 'So what does that mean?'

'It can only mean that this is a very old planet – very, very old. Old enough to have lost almost all its heat of formation. So Earth's core and mantle are so hot they are still liquid, but those structures are solidified here. Our Earth is around four billion years old. I'd say that this world must be at least a *hundred* billion years old. Twenty, thirty times as old as Earth—'

'Wow,' Doria called over. 'But I've got an objection to that. A hundred billion years – that's, what, seven, eight times the age of the *universe*!'

Vasta came over now. 'I heard all that.' She tapped her helmet.

Doria said, 'Then I apologise for shooting my mouth off. Look, I'm just a bus driver here. Meriel is the local tour guide, while Elizabeth is Earth's top scientist—'

'No, I just have the awesome power to summon Earth's top scientists.'

'—but I'm getting increasingly confused. I mean, you're talking about this very ancient planet. Older than our universe, which is a big enough pill to swallow – even though we already thought that Feathers must come from a universe bigger and older than ours. But *look* at that.' She pointed at the sky.

Salma followed Doria's gesture, looked again at the complex light show in the sky: the torn gas clouds, the blazing stars.

'It doesn't get any less gaudy, does it?' Doria said. 'It's surely some kind of star creation event. And that is surely *not* the sky of an old universe.'

Vasta frowned. 'Well, that's one way of putting it. Gaudy – yes, I guess so. And if part of being gaudy is that you don't fit in, then that's gaudy all right. But – a *young* feature?' She was consulting a tablet on her wrist, squinting up at the formation in the sky.

'Is it a quasar, then?' Salma asked, impulsively. 'Like the one at the centre of the Galaxy?'

'Not quite,' Vasta said, still looking at her tablet. 'I guess we've all seen enough projections, reconstructions of quasars since that showed up.

'This is similar. You do have a central black hole – invisible to the naked eye from here – spinning, its magnetic field throwing around highly energetic, *hot* gases. Our instruments can see all that. Where the hot plumes hit the cooler, surrounding gas fields you get huge releases of energy, of radiation – visible light, in this case a *lot* of ultra-violet, and we need to be careful about that if we stay out here long.

'But, meanwhile, this is also a starburst event. It's producing a flood of new stars, something like a hundred solar masses' worth a year according to this clever gadget . . . But, if you take a closer look,' and she held up her tablet, 'if you do a quick census, you can see that there aren't so many stars as all that – which means what stars there are, are *huge*, most of them.'

Vasta hesitated now, chewing her lip.

She went on, 'Doria said this looks like a star creation event. So it does. But not like such an event in *our* time, the creation of stars in a mature galaxy like our own. What these look like, in fact,' she said slowly, 'are *the first stars* of all, born of the pure hydrogen and helium that came out of the Big Bang itself. You had immense clouds of hot raw stuff, mostly hydrogen, pummelled by the gravity wells of big primordial back holes, like *that* one. So these huge, hot, energetic clouds of hydrogen and helium would collapse to create enormous stars – say, twenty times the mass of the Sun – and fast-living. And they would gather around the big black holes, and that was the birth of the galaxies . . .

'Those first stars, though – they lived fast, died young. Once formed they'd fuse their hydrogen for ten million years or so, and then helium for a million years more, and then – pow. A supernova explosion would spread heavy elements around the place, products of the fusion processes, enriching the next populations of stars . . . It was the beginning of the overall mutual evolution of stars and galaxies in our cosmos. Orderly galaxies turning into efficient star-making machines, churning out sensible, long-lived, medium-sized stars like the Sun.'

Salma was getting confused. 'How can you know all this?'

'Because we – or rather the astronomers – have *seen* all this.' She looked at Salma uncertainly. 'You understand that – back home anyhow – we can see what happened in the past because of the finite speed of light? So light from stuff that happened *really long ago, really far away* can be seen *now* because that light took a *really, really long time* to get to Earth. OK? So we've *seen* early star factories like this in our own deep time, or at least inferred their presence . . .'

Salma looked up at the sky with awe, and a new understanding.

She wondered what Feathers was making of all this.

But Vasta was still speaking.

'Young, primordial stars. OK. That's how they look. But the immediate issue with *that* observation is that it's the opposite of your estimate of the *planet's* age, Meriel. If the star factory would fit neatly into the deep past of our universe – from about a third of a billion years after the Big Bang, in fact, I'd say – according to my tablet here, the planet we stand on would fit better in our far *future* . . . You see my problem?'

Salma thought she did. 'The planet looks like it's a hundred billion years old. The stars – what, a few million years? The planet and the stars don't fit together.'

Doria nodded. 'Exactly.'

'Damn it,' Vasta said. 'This makes no sense. If I wasn't the President's science adviser I'd stamp my foot.'

Doria grinned. 'Be my guest—'

And Salma heard a thin, caw-like wail. A sound she had only heard once in her life before, when Feathers had been badly injured.

She whirled around, guilt stabbing. She'd lost sight of Feathers, distracted by all the funny science. She'd only had one job here, after all – *there*.

Feathers was maybe fifty paces away. She was down on the gritty, grey ground, pawing at it.

Salma just ran.

*

When Salma got to her, Feathers didn't look up. She just kept digging, digging something out of that ground it seemed, throwing up plumes of the thin dust-like dirt.

Something that gleamed white. She was working quickly, around the space, hurling dirt in the air, exposing more of that white gleam.

Doria quickly caught up.

Salma gasped, 'You're too damn fit.'

Doria grinned. 'I used to command roughneck crews on the Moon. I had to set an example in the low-gravity gym . . . What *is* this?'

And they turned to look at Feathers.

Who now was dragging what looked like bones out of the ground. And she was moaning softly, as if in pain, as she built the bones she retrieved into disorderly heaps around her.

Bones?

When Meriel then Vasta got there, Feathers barely looked up.

'Damn it,' Meriel said, 'I got too used to that nice firm surface on Nine. Walking on all this dust just eats up your energy . . .' And then she peered into the pit, at the random, scratchy, agonised gestures of Feathers. *'Bones?'*

'Looks like it,' Salma said. She pointed. 'Those bones. You've studied her skeleton, its structure, the bones. I'm not sure. But the bones here—'

'Ah. I see what you mean.' Meriel tapped a button on her helmet which brought eyepieces down to the front of the faceplate. 'That's better, a little clearer. Yes, *they look like Feathers' own bones.* As we've studied with X-ray imaging. I'd need to gather specimens to be sure—'

'Like Feathers' bones,' said Vasta, walking up. 'That's the point, isn't it? Maybe that's why we've been brought here, to

345

this planet. *The bones of her people* . . . So was this a mass grave? Some kind of massacre?'

Meriel just frowned.

But Salma said, 'No, I don't think so. Look, now she's cleared so much ground – you can see patterns in the way the bones are arranged. Skulls at the centre, it looks like––'

'Yes, you're right,' Meriel said, leaning forward, evidently intrigued now. 'Breastbones, those big anchor bones for the wings, spread across that wider circle. And what look like limbs further out. I recognise some, most of these from the scans we've taken from Feathers herself over the years. But there's more than one body here. And, yes, look, as Salma says, this has been purposefully laid out.'

Doria nodded again. 'OK. So, not a battlefield – what do you think – some kind of ritual slaughter? A sacrifice?'

Salma, confused, not a little distressed, tried to think clearly. 'No. I don't think it's that. Feathers has made nests, displays of junk, back in the habitat on Nine. They can be big affairs, and they look a little like this. I mean, she doesn't use bones, but you have the same kind of concentric layout––'

'Yes,' Meriel said. 'I've seen the nests. I can see the resemblance. So you think this is more of a ritual place?'

'Like a cemetery,' Doria suggested.

Elizabeth Vasta nodded. 'It seems to fit. But with a different cultural logic. Not dust to dust. Nest to nest? You're born in a nest, you die in one, a ceremonial nest.'

'OK,' Doria said. 'So why is Feathers so unhappy?'

Salma looked at her, surprised by the question. 'Don't you see? Because this is Feathers' home world.

'Because these are the bones of her people.'

That stopped the conversation.

Salma wondered if they believed her. 'This must be *her* world. And it's a dead world, evidently.'

Vasta nodded. 'Long dead, given the heat signature. So she must have been taken from the deep past of this world, and was preserved somehow, to be delivered into our own time. Or some kind of match-up to time in our universe. And, here and now, she just found out her people are extinct.' She scraped at the ground with one dusty boot. 'I wonder how long these bones have been lying here, undisturbed . . .'

A long silence.

Vasta said at last, 'How could we not see that more quickly? Her world, of course it is. And she must have been scooped out of the past of this world, to be delivered here, its far future. There must be a – logic – behind all this. Deeper messages we're meant to absorb.'

Salma was distracted by the very fact of it. 'No wonder she seemed so comfortable moving around here. The gravity at least, even the texture of the dust—'

'Yes,' Meriel said, 'but – look around. We're so far in its future that the planet *itself* is dead, as cold as those bones, right to its heart. How would you feel if you were so lost in time that you found Earth in this state?'

Vasta nodded. 'OK. So, what next?'

As they talked on, Salma stood, brushed dust off her pressure suit, and made her way over to Feathers, who was still picking at the bones in the cemetery-nest. She seemed to have calmed – or maybe she was just too exhausted to be distressed any more.

Salma squatted down beside her, and embraced her. A hug, like the first hug she had ever given Feathers when she had been found, alone and terrified, in that strange casket on Planet Nine.

Feathers softened into the hug – but then pulled back, her eyes wide, peering over Salma's shoulder.

Salma turned.

And saw a sphere, perfect, dull black, maybe a metre across, maybe twenty paces away, hovering above the ground.

The others hadn't noticed.

And before they did, a voice spoke, either through Salma's suit's systems to her ears, or just in her head.

You will name me Terminus.

34

Everybody turned to see, evidently shocked.

Having made its statement – and Salma could see no speaker grille, could not see *how* it spoke – the floating sphere, Terminus, just waited. Floating at a little over head height, with no visible support against the planet's gravity, though that seemed a minor miracle by comparison.

What did seem extraordinary was that Salma felt no fear of this thing. Or awe. And neither, as far as she could tell, did the others.

'This feels *right*,' she blurted out. 'That we should meet this – thing. As if I knew we would see this, before we even arrived here. I mean, us – Feathers and the four of us.'

'Yes. This seems right,' Doria echoed. 'It feels right.' She seemed to have to tear her gaze away from the floating sphere, from Terminus, to the others. 'Right, *again*. Like when the group of us got selected as the landing party. That felt right too. Do you feel the same? I mean, the four of us with these damn pendants . . .' She touched her chest, and Salma wondered if she was feeling the pendant at her neck, under her pressure suit, that handsome disc of lunar obsidian.

Meriel glanced around, apparently shocked. 'Yes, the pendants . . . For me and Salma, gifts from her mother – tokens of Earth.'

Vasta nodded. 'And I always carry that heavy black pendant with me . . . A pearl, in fact. It's an heirloom. Seemed right to have it.' She looked at Feathers. 'Now I see these are all stones are deep black, like Feathers' own eyes.'

Salma was baffled. 'But we only met so recently. How could we all have these pendants *already*, like tags from the future? . . . It makes no sense.'

Doria grunted. 'A spooky kind of sense, maybe. But not the kind we're used to, I don't think. Not simple cause and effect. Like the quasar kicking off twenty-five thousand years before its light was supposed to reach Earth.'

Vasta said, 'Yes, maybe it was like a – a *forward memory*. We were given the pendants *because* we're wearing them now, together.' She laughed, uneasily. 'We were meant to be here, now. *Because* we are here, now. And it feels right, doesn't it? And here we are talking about pendants, while – *that* – is watching us.'

She turned to the featureless sphere, which hovered, still, silent, seemingly infinitely patient.

Vasta snapped, 'You. Terminus. You say that is the name we will give you. Or *have* given you. Cause and effect mixed up again . . . That is the only thing you have told us. Your name. Why that name?'

The voice in their heads sounded softly. *The name, Terminus, has deep roots in your cultures . . .*

Salma listened hard – concentrating more now that the initial shock of contact was past. To her the accent seemed a mix of the various brogues spoken aboard the *Shadow*, the few human voices to which she had been exposed all her life – aside from sporadic communications from the rest of the Solar System, and with strangers in the last few weeks since the arrival of the *Cronus*. Maybe the others had the same kind of subjective mix rattling in their heads – maybe that voice sounded subtly different to each of them. She ought to remember to ask . . .

She couldn't even tell the gender. It might have been more a male human voice than female, but it was hard to determine.

She tried to focus on what was being said.

'Deep roots in our cultures,' Elizabeth said. 'Well, that's true.

'Terminus was a god of the Romans. I know that much; I studied classics as part of my political education. I learned about the rise and fall of empires before ours . . . Also I wear a smart pressure suit, which is now reminding me that Terminus was a "liminal deity". A god of the edges, a protector of boundaries.' She glanced around, an uncertain smile behind her faceplate. 'I'm gabbling. Gabbling because I'm nervous. Does it show?'

Doria shook her head. 'You're making sense – as much sense as there is to be had in this bizarre situation—'

Meriel held up her hand. 'With respect – you're all talking too much. Let the damn thing speak.'

Vasta nodded. 'Quite right. Well, then – Terminus!' She faced the hovering sphere. 'Why that name? Why are you here? What do you want?'

I speak of change. I intend no threat. Change is inevitable but not necessarily a threat. I bring – hope. From across the boundary of your understanding, perhaps.

Vasta glared. 'So how do you know about Terminus, the name, the god?'

You just told me about it.

Doria frowned, shook her head sharply, as if trying to clear it. 'Wow. There you go again. Another closed causal loop. Like the pendants. It is because it is because it is because . . .'

Not quite. Your terminology is inexact. In fact, you have no exact terminology for these phenomena. I do not dwell in closed causal loops in any one universe. I inhabit many universes. I can cross many universes. Back and forth. I and my . . . cousins . . .

Salma was getting lost. We wear the pendants because we wear the pendants because we wear the pendants . . . But even so—

'Many universes . . . What does that even mean?' She glanced across at Feathers, who seemed to be listening intently. 'I don't understand.'

'You and me both, kid,' said Doria, evidently trying to keep Salma's spirits up. 'This is well above the pay grade of a lunar rock jockey.'

And Meriel reached out with one gloved hand to take Salma's. 'It's difficult for all of us.'

Vasta said wearily, 'Imagine trying to explain it to politicians. Which is what I'll have to do some day . . .

'Many universes. Look. Here's an analogy. Imagine a flat sheet – a blanket, a huge piece of paper. Going on for ever. That would be infinite, wouldn't it?'

'Yes . . .' Salma conceded cautiously.

'OK. And now imagine a whole lot more such sheets, but piled on top of the first one. Even though each one is infinite, there can be many of them. Many infinities. Just – stacked sideways, so they don't get in each other's way . . .' Vasta stared at Terminus even as she spoke about this.

'Nice metaphor,' said Doria. 'Even I can get it. That's how you get to be a presidential science adviser, I guess.'

'I guess,' Vasta said heavily, still watching Terminus. 'So, Salma, if you had all those sheets stacked up, and if you were some kind of worm that could crawl along inside one of the sheets – and then you chewed your way through to *go up or down*, where the sheets touched, you could cross from one universe to another. Why, there may be some regions of another universe that could be *closer*, in terms of accessibility, than regions of our own.

'Actually I think you could say that the idea of a multiverse is at the heart of our best theories of reality. We think that there is a sort of higher-dimensional substrate, a high-energy quantum foam, straddling all of reality. A foam which can spawn an infinite number of different universes — universes like our own. Or different. Like pages in an unending book. Or, bubbles in an infinite froth.

'Our universe was just one more bubble in that froth, which expanded into the big, fat, old, complicated, expanding universe we all grew up in. Just one more bubble.

'We even have some evidence for this. That our origin is a multiverse, I mean. There's a big cold spot in the constellation of Eridanus, as seen from Earth, a spot as wide as five full moons in the sky — eight times the usual temperature variation. That's one hell of an anomaly, isn't it? And our best theory is that our universe jostled against another in some higher-dimensional crowd as they grew—'

'Like rowdy teenagers,' Doria said. 'Always knocking lumps off each other.'

Terminus spoke now. *You have seen other evidence now. Evidence of the existence of the multiverse. You have seen evidence of contacts between universes . . .*

Meriel frowned. 'The multiverse? Contacts? Like Nine, which we thought was a black hole . . . ?'

Vasta said, 'At the fringe of our physics, there are ideas like this. I boned up on it all during the long *Cronus* flight — and picked some brains.' She smiled at Salma. 'You might like to know your mentor Stephen Hawking, he of the black hole radiation, developed ideas on these lines. He imagined an — ecology — of universes, several emerging from one, perhaps continually complexifying. And not just complexifying in its contents, its structure, but in the intricacy of its physical laws. Which could, possibly, retrospectively *adjust* the Big Bang the universe emerged from, so that those laws, in a sense, made themselves . . . Something like that. And then there were theories that some black holes could survive the death of one universe, to survive through another Big Bang – thus providing travel portals, perhaps . . .' She glared at Terminus. 'I think all this makes sense, in terms of our own fringe physics. But it's going to take generations of real physicists, not bluffers like me, to untangle it all.'

Terminus said, *You have been confronted with the existence of the creature you call Feathers.*

'Yes,' Meriel said. 'Yes! Which was some kind of proof of all that. So we were on the right track, weren't we? We talked about this, Salma. Your little friend . . . Remember how we speculated about how *unlikely* it was that two planets could produce humanoid-shaped species, as similar as, well, you and Feathers? How our universe isn't big enough, or old enough, to have done that with any reasonable probability? So she *had* to have come from someplace else. Some *universe* elsewhere. Bigger, or older, than ours – or both maybe.'

Vasta said, 'And now, standing here, you don't need an exercise in probabilistic mathematics to get the idea. *Look around you.* This planet, too old for our universe, remember?' She gestured at the sky. 'And that galaxy core up there – that's *too young*, right? There hasn't been a feature like that in our universe since it was half a billion years old. Compared to thirteen billion years today.'

You are correct. This place is artificial. It has been assembled as an intersection of three time zones: your own epoch, the very early days of your cosmos—

'This active galaxy core,' Vasta said.

And its very late days.

'Yes, yes. This ancient, dead planet, brought from the far

354

future.' She glared at Terminus. 'I don't know whether all this gaudy display is meant to uplift us, or crush us into some kind of submission.'

Neither, said Terminus calmly. *I have come here, I show you this, to save you.*

Vasta glared at it. 'To save us from what?'

From the inevitable extinction of your own universe, and all life within it.

35

There was a long pause.

'Well, that's a downer,' Elizabeth Vasta said. 'As the nearest to a government representative standing here, I officially have no idea how to respond to that.'

Meriel snorted. 'How about, *thanks*?'

Salma, thinking over all this, raised one hand – the other gripping Feathers' hand tightly. 'Terminus. I have a question.'

Ask it.

She flinched back at those words, coming as they did from a floating sphere. *It's just some dumb machine . . .* She lost her nerve. She looked around at the others. 'I don't know if I should say anything. I have no, umm, authority here. Is that the right word?'

Meriel, standing next to her, rubbed her back through her suit. 'You're the one who made first contact with the alien, kid. You have the authority.' She glanced over at Vasta, who nodded. 'Ask your question.'

Salma faced Terminus again. 'If you're so powerful – if you can cross universes – why are you even talking to us? Why don't you just – save us? Or destroy us? Or whatever it is you intend to do?'

Doria laughed softly. 'Good question, kid. And maybe one

the rest of us are too arrogant to have considered.' She faced Terminus. 'She has a point, doesn't she?'

Indeed. In a sense it has already been necessary for you to save yourselves. By getting this far.

That caused a pause. Salma was aware of glances from the others. But she had more questions.

'Have you saved others, before? Or helped them save themselves? Others like us?'

Yes.

'And are there others like *you*?'

Like me. Yes.

Vasta frowned. 'Like you?'

With similar origins.

Vasta frowned. 'What origins?'

Disparate. Isolated.

The multiverse is a very large place, growing continually and eternally, and it is almost totally devoid of life and mind. Almost, but not entirely. Life forms like yours — embedded in the physics of a given reality — can emerge from that reality. Spontaneously. It is rare, but it happens.

And, we concluded, we who owed our own lives to still more unlikely accidents, there is nothing more precious than life and mind. It is to be found, cherished, protected — encouraged to grow.

Vasta said, 'So what does that have to do with planting humanoids in our Solar System, and a quasar in our galaxy?'

Terminus replied bluntly.

You are alone in your universe. A potentially life-filled universe. Only you.

Your universe is young.

That there should be living things, arising from Earth, based on carbon and water, arising spontaneously − by chance, by random combinations, as it happened − is extremely unlikely. The probability that you exist at all, in such a young universe, is so nearly zero that it is all but inevitable you find yourselves alone.

In that, your birth was like my own. Highly unlikely.

Salma looked around, to see how the others were taking these extraordinary revelations.

Alone . . .

Meriel looked − disappointed. Doria bewildered, perhaps.

But Vasta seemed determined to pursue this logic. 'OK. Alone. Because either we *are* alone, the only sentients in the universe, or *isolated* − life and mind is so scarce we wouldn't have the time to find the alien before the stars went out. Or maybe not even the time for another instance of spontaneous life creation.'

Terminus seemed to hesitate. Then: *You are correct.*

'In that case,' Vasta went on grimly, 'we have a duty − well, not to go extinct, at least.' She smiled. 'Wow. You Conservers were right. We ought to survive as long as we can, if the universe is part of an infinite and eternal multiverse, much of it devoid of life . . . And I find myself in sympathy with a godlike being from a higher reality. Who'd have thought it?'

The others managed to laugh.

But Salma found she dared to speak again, to challenge.

'So, Terminus. How does this justify dumping a sentient being into another universe? Not to mention creating a quasar in our galaxy? And . . .' She lost her nerve.

The others glanced at her, and Vasta nodded. *Go ahead.*

She took a breath. 'Feathers here. Alone, terrified . . . You used her as a sort of teaching aid, didn't you? So we could figure out the context, the likelihood that she must have come from some other universe entirely. But if we hadn't found her, or if we hadn't been able to help her survive—'

It was a matter of means.

Of available tools, if you like.

The delivery of Feathers as, yes, an aid to understanding, was a by-product of the establishment of the bridge in the first place.

Vasta snapped, 'What bridge?'

You understand that a bridge must be made, built, between one universe and another. I needed such a bridge to reach you. But such a bridge cannot be built from one side only.

'OK,' Vasta said. 'If you want to build a bridge over a river, you have to start from both banks and meet in the middle.'

Doria murmured, 'Only somebody who grew up on Earth itself would get that metaphor.'

We could only reach out. We gave you Feathers. It was up to you to reach back. Or not.

'Ha!' Meriel's laugh was bitter. 'So it's our fault, even though we couldn't possibly have guessed the consequences of playing around with Planet Nine. But we went ahead anyhow. We can blame nobody but our own hubristic, meddling, impetuous selves. Without that we wouldn't be tangled up in all this, whatever it is—'

You would not have had the gift of eternity, Terminus said evenly. *Or the promise of it.*

Salma said, 'But it could only *be* us, because we are alone. We humans. He said so. We are the only ones he could – use. So how did you find us in the first place, then?'

The bridging technology is very old, and very smart.

That was all it would say.

'I doubt we could understand,' Vasta said, her voice colder still. 'Not yet, anyhow. Very well. And what of our galaxy? As Salma asked, has it been necessary to bathe planet Earth in quasar light in the process of creating your bridge?'

The disturbance is temporary. Yes, it was necessary to establish

*a high-energy link between your galaxy core and your home world.
Energy to enable the next steps in the process. We needed your help
to establish the bridge. It could only be humanity, for there is only
humanity in your beautiful but barren universe. But you need not
have chosen to participate.*

Vasta looked angry now. 'We didn't know what we were meddling with!'

Then, Terminus said, *you might have been wiser* not *to meddle
at all.*

Vasta glared, but evidently had to laugh. 'To be fair, that's
pretty much what I tell my students all the time. Good take-
home lesson—'

'But we did meddle,' Salma said. 'We did open your box. So
what now?'

Now, Terminus said, *we offer you eternity and infinity. We save
you from this.*

And the sky went pitch dark.

36

Salma felt Feathers cling closer, heard a low, caw-like moan.

After only a few seconds, their smart suit lamps lit up. They stood in their isolated splashes of light, hopelessly dim compared to the lost galaxy-birth glare.

Glancing around, Salma saw that nobody was moving, not at first. That was a drill she had learned during the long years on the *Shadow*: if the power failed, if the lights went out, you just stayed still, until you were sure you weren't going to collide with something, or suffer some other harm – or, worse, cause harm to the ship.

Terminus was just hanging in the not-air, its curves rendered visible, just, by the suit lights.

When the light didn't come back, Doria murmured, 'Come to me. All of you. Best we stay close.'

They moved in cautiously, avoiding any stray bits of kit on the ground. They came close enough to touch each other. As Salma hung on to a very quiet Feathers, Meriel rubbed Salma's own back. All of which Salma found hugely reassuring.

'So,' Vasta said, her voice admirably steady, 'did the stars just go out? The active galaxy you showed us—'

All the stars have gone out by now, Terminus said. *We are now in the very far future.*

'Nice display,' Doria said. 'Like a planetarium I once visited—'

This is the far future of the same cosmos. The active young galaxy I showed you has long since darkened, dispersed, even its dead stars evaporating from its gravity well. The planet you stand on was already old, as you know.

Vasta said, 'Feathers' planet.'

Now it is far older still. It still exists, in fact, only because it has been consciously preserved. For your convenience.

'Thanks,' Vasta said ironically.

You measure time in years. Very well. When you, these individuals, were born, your universe was thirteen billion years old. Your world was warm, active, illuminated by your star, and heated from within by its own store of residual formation heat, by radioactivity.

After ten billion more years your star will be a white dwarf, quietly fusing its remnant hydrogen and helium, yielding little heat. After a hundred *billion years, its Sun long exhausted, your Earth will be cold, inert, like this planet.*

After a thousand *billion years star formation will stop, across the universe, the raw material exhausted. A hundred times longer again, and the last stars will die. Soon even the star-corpse remnants will evaporate from the Galaxy – escape from its gravity well through chance collisions and encounters.*

Vasta grunted. 'Like gas molecules crowding out of an open jar.'

The universe will be populated only by supermassive black holes and stellar remnants, the cold corpses of the stars in evaporating galaxies – and cold, inert planets like this one. But in the still longer term matter itself breaks down—

'Proton decay,' Vasta said. 'Such a slow effect we aren't even sure it exists. Matter itself falling apart, after – what, a trillion trillion *trillion* years? And beyond that—'

Beyond that even the most massive black holes will evaporate.

'Hawking radiation,' Salma guessed.

Meriel rubbed her back again, through her pressure suit, a distant sensation.

There will then be nothing but a thin mist, the relic of the decay of matter itself, in an endlessly expanding spacetime.

Vasta said, 'They used to call it the heat death. From the Big Bang, through a few trillion years of light and life and hope, and then just endless expansion—'

You are not alone. We have contacted many others of your kind – I mean, the products of young universes. And we have found a way to save you.

Save you from the heat death of your universe.

Save you from an epoch like that of my own cold birth.

This is my promise to you . . .

Terminus fell silent. It just hung there, bathed in their suit lights.

And the sky exploded.

37

That was what it felt like.

Feathers squealed, and cowered away from the light.

Salma instinctively grabbed her, put her gloved hand at the back of Feathers' head, and pressed her face against her shoulder. And she jammed shut her own eyes.

Meriel called, 'Check that your visor filters are working. Resetting all of your suits remotely. Salma, check Feathers—'

'I'm on it.' Salma knew the drill; they had practised for such contingencies often enough. She tapped her own visor to ensure opacity, then opened her eyes cautiously. With the helmet closed, she saw only interior displays. She felt for the test panel on her own chest and tapped it. A display at the base of her field of view showed a mix of amber and green, the amber lights flicking over to green, one by one.

She was still holding Feathers, and when she touched Feathers' visor with one gloved finger she got a similar display, though the switch to green was a little slower. The human-intended suit, adapted to Feathers' physiology – hastily, and with much guesswork about the functions of Feathers' body in extreme conditions – was never going to be as finely tuned as it would be if there was a human inside. But it seemed OK for now, and she called that out.

'Good,' Meriel said. 'Everybody seems fine.'

Doria called, 'Umm, I'm following the light show with my own external monitors. I think it's safe to look out now. If you have any trouble seeing, any at all, or if there are any other radiation alarms in your suit—'

'Got it,' Vasta said.

Now Salma dared to allow her faceplate to clear to what seemed like transparency, but actually was, she knew, a heavily edited, reduced-intensity rendering of the reality.

The sky, another new sky, was a wash of light.

She saw an array of stars, shining brightly through a gas cloud, which itself was turbulent, frothy, multi-coloured, illuminated from within by yet more stars – as if boiling, but caught in a freeze-frame image. A barrage of stationary light, hanging over the ground of this dull grey, worn-out world, a turmoil on superhuman scales of time and space.

But there was a sense of depth. Some of those embedded stars seemed close, while others shone through layers of the cloud, through curtains of turbulent gas and debris. All frozen still.

And in among that stilled chaos, Salma thought she could see a tinge of *green*. Starlight, as if filtered through the green of the grasses and leafy plants in Meriel's hydroponic farm. How could that be . . . ?

It occurred to her to look around at her companions.

Doria, a few paces away, was looking down at the ground, in fact. Tapping her booted foot. 'Looks like the same unprepossessing planet. A constant in all this – transition. Even colder, if that's possible. And our heap of gear came with us, I'm glad to say.'

Vasta seemed to chuckle. 'That's a lunar for you,' she said. 'Always aware of what's under her feet rather than what's in the sky.'

Meriel snorted. 'And that's an Earther for you, is it? Always categorising, sneering—'

'Forget it,' Doria snapped. 'Offensive she may be, but she does have a point. We all need an anchor in this – unreality. But *I* have a point too, don't I? The ground underfoot hasn't changed so far as I can see. Somehow we've been riding this world as it has been brought to – to this place, this other universe, I guess. So at least we have some kind of stability amid all this chaos.' She seemed to have to force herself to stare up at the stars. 'Under a sky like a frozen explosion,' she said softly.

Terminus appeared to have witnessed their emergence calmly. It said, *Such transitions can be destabilising. In fact such young universes as yours are more amenable to interconnections through the higher dimensions. Engineering is more feasible—*

'Park it,' Vasta said.

She lifted her head, and Salma saw how the gaudy stars were reflected in her visor.

'All right,' Vasta said now. 'I've managed a quick survey of our latest new sky. And those are *young-universe* stars, are they not? Just as we saw when we first arrived on Feathers' world. Or rather, they're the kind of stars a young universe creates. Though this isn't my field. Have we gone back in time again?'

Terminus seemed to think that over.

Your thinking is limited.

Vasta frowned. 'Limited? I'm talking about time travel!'

Salma was still hugging Feathers close, though more gently. She tried to take all this in. 'So is this . . . place . . . very young? Compared to our universe. If those stars are like the early stars at home, Elizabeth . . . If that's true, *why all the green*?'

Vasta frowned, her expression visible through her faceplate. She looked up at the sky – and clearly picked out those huddles of stars Salma had noticed, with the greenish tinge.

Terminus hovered silently.

Salma pressed. 'Elizabeth, you said that these are very young stars, like the first stars in our universe. But the green – I thought it took billions of years for green life to evolve.'

'Photosynthesis, yes. On Earth.'

Salma waved a hand. 'So how come—'

'How come those morning-of-the-universe stars have their light filtered through the green? Shit. Damn good question, Salma. I don't *know*.' Vasta seemed to be growing agitated. She turned to Terminus. 'You are showing us these scenes. You want us to work this out for ourselves. Why, I don't yet understand.' She pointed accusingly at the sky, with one gloved hand. 'Am I wrong? Am I mistaken that those stars are like the first stars to form in our universe?'

You are not mistaken. Like those stars.

'*Like* them. Then it must follow that *this* universe is very young – probably not even a billion years old, compared to our universe of thirteen or fourteen billion years—'

You are mistaken.

'Then what—'

The stars are young.

This universe is not young.

It is infinitely old.

And infinite in extent.

And Vasta just stared. At the sky, at the floating intelligence, at her companions.

At the impossibly young stars in an impossibly ancient universe.

'Oh . . . I think . . .'

Then she crumpled, and fell back heavily on the ground.

*

Meriel hurried to Vasta. Doria followed, and got down on the ground beside her.

Feathers squealed with fear.

Salma held her tight. 'Hush. You stay with me. It's all right . . .'

Meriel snapped, 'Lift her head. Just a little.'

Doria got down further and cradled Vasta's head on her own outstretched arm.

Meriel tapped at a console on the chest panel of Vasta's suit and interrogated it with barked commands.

Then she sat back on her haunches. 'I think it's just a faint. She's overwrought. I think we all are.' She glanced back at the floating ball that was Terminus up at the strange, brilliant, green-littered sky. 'This has been too much. But I think she'll be OK if we get her into the shelter, out of her suit for a while. Salma—'

'On it.' Salma let go of Feathers, pointed to their heap of gear, and, in the mime-and-sign language they had worked out over the years, hastily told Feathers that they had to put the shelter up. They broke away from the group and made for the equipment pile.

Looking back, Salma saw Vasta move a little, lift a hand. Salma heard a whisper, indecipherable, in her own suit's system.

Meriel bent over Vasta and stared into Vasta's faceplate. 'What's that, Elizabeth? Your voice is very faint . . .'

Salma heard Vasta draw in a ragged breath and say, 'Infinitely old and infinite in extent my backside. What about Olbers' paradox? Answer me that . . .'

And she fell back, as if succumbing to unconsciousness again.

38

The shelter erected itself on a verbal command, unfolding into a squat cylinder a couple of metres tall, perhaps five metres across. Two bulbous airlock assemblies stuck out from the sides, at opposite ends of a diameter.

With Salma, Feathers threw herself into the task of fixing all this up. Something they could understand, Salma thought. Something they could *do*.

When it was finished, Feathers hung back, to give Meriel and Doria the chance to lift Vasta through one of the airlocks. After that Salma and Feathers were asked to wait outside, for perhaps ten minutes, so they could get Vasta settled.

Ten long minutes, under that weird, gaudy sky, under the silent scrutiny of the hovering Terminus.

Salma knew they were both relieved when they were, at last, allowed into the shelter.

The airlock was fabric-walled, closet-sized. Once inside, the two of them had to wait a couple of minutes in their suits as they were bathed by invisible but sterilising radiation. Even after they had discarded their suits they had to go through scanners, and potentially more cleansing procedures if necessary. It seemed impossible that any life forms could survive on the planet outside to make it into the shelter, let alone infect humans, or even Feathers, and Feathers herself evidently did not carry any pathogens harmful to humans. But Salma had grown up knowing that 'better safe than sorry' was the basic mantra for all humans in space.

Still, it was a relief to make it into the shelter proper – a low roof, but a roomy space.

By now things had calmed, Salma saw. Vasta was sitting up, leaning against inflatable cushions propped up against the shelter wall, with blankets over her lap, and even a hot drink. Doria sat with her. Meriel was pacing, and quietly dictating notes into the air.

Feathers ran straight over to Vasta and gave her a hug. Salma followed more sedately.

Vasta grinned, lifted her drink out of the way, and hugged back. 'I'm fine, I'm fine. I just got a little over-excited. System overload. Maybe I'm too old for this game – and all that zero gravity and cryosleep on the *Cronus* probably didn't help.' She stroked Feathers, curiously but tenderly. 'But I'm better now. Thank you for the hug.' She glanced at Salma. 'Does she understand?'

'She knows.'

And now Vasta called out more loudly, 'I know it wasn't your fault, Terminus. Can you hear me?'

I can.

A voice in the air, as if he – it? – were physically present in the shelter, Salma thought. A minor miracle that everybody reacted to with frowns and glances, then ignored – outwardly, at least.

Vasta went on, 'Terminus, I can see that you've been trying to protect us from all of this. The conceptual shocks. And you've done it well. Show, don't tell – that's your principle, yes? As employed by myself when addressing graduate students, politicians, and other forms of lower life. Oh, maybe I shouldn't make jokes like that before a godlike alien engine. But – hell, you're still wrong. An infinitely old universe? That's simply impossible.'

No reply.

'Huh. You want us to figure it out ourselves, do you?'

That is up to you. You say an infinitely old universe is impossible. I say it is not merely possible, but perfect.

Vasta frowned. 'OK, that's stumped me. Perfect?'

Meriel said cautiously, 'Take it easy. Thinking too hard just knocked you out, Elizabeth. So what was it you said just before you fainted?'

'What? I don't remember.'

'About some paradox—'

'Olbers' paradox?' Salma prompted.

'Yes! Right! Well done, Salma. Even when half-unconscious I was groping for the right argument. An *old* argument. From the eighteenth, nineteenth century? Olbers was an amateur astronomer – I think he was a physician by trade.'

Meriel grinned. 'All the deepest thinkers are physicians.'

'Yeah, yeah. Olbers criticised the then-popular theories that the universe must be infinite, on the basis that the sky doesn't *look* like it's infinitely deep. Think about it. Suppose space was full, *to infinity*, of a cloud of stars. The further away from you they are, the dimmer they will be. But every which way you look, *your eye would have to hit a ray of starlight*. And so the night sky would have to be as bright as the Sun, uniformly.'

'But we don't see that,' Salma said, cautiously.

'Right. We don't see it. So something's wrong with the assumptions. It makes no difference that the stars are gathered into galaxies; the galaxies would carpet the sky just as much. Dust clouds in the way? No, the starlight flood would just batter them with heat until they shone just as brightly as the stars.' She lifted her head, looked around, as if seeking Terminus. 'That's how we know our universe is finite, with a finite age. And the same applies here. So this universe *can't* be infinite, or infinitely old. Because the sky is dark. Are you listening to this?'

Of course. But your logic is faulty. This universe is infinitely old, and infinite in extent – but it is expanding.

Salma could see the puzzlement on Doria's face. And then what looked like a slow, reluctant realisation.

'Right,' Doria said. 'Of course. If the universe is expanding, any radiation, passing from far enough out, is going to be Doppler-shifted to invisibility, undetectability. Its wavelength would be stretched out until it became, eventually, nothing but a trace of heat. I can even see how the maths would work out.'

Meriel seemed to be thinking it through more slowly. Grudgingly she said, 'I think that's right—'

Salma broke in, 'I don't get it. Expanding into *what*? If the universe is infinite already, where else can it expand into?'

Vasta rubbed her arm. 'That's the trick with infinity. Remember the book with the never-ending pages? Infinity doesn't end, no matter how much stuff you push that way. Think of it as an unfillable garbage chute. Much like this conversation. Oh, hell, help me up, will you? I think I'm over my conceptual shock by now.'

Meriel helped Vasta up, but glared at her. 'I'll let you go. But I'll be slaving your suit systems to my suit from now on – just so you know.'

'Yes, Doc.'

Salma barely heard all this. She thought they were all missing the point about this supposedly infinite universe. As Meriel fiddled some more with Vasta's suit, Salma asked, 'So what about the life?'

They stared at her.

'The life in the sky . . .'

Then Meriel said, 'She's got a point. *The green stars*, remember? Not a lot of them, but—'

'Our instrument package agrees with her,' Vasta said. Now, ignoring Meriel's ministrations, she was scanning a readout display on her sleeve, near the pressure suit's cuff. 'We all saw the green starlight, right? My analysis here shows carbon compounds . . . I'm asking it a specific question. Yep, some of the chemistry up there is probably capable of a kind of photosynthesis, even if the chemistry's not the same as ours.

'Green stuff is up there, capturing a star's energy to make – well, more green stuff. Clouds of algae, maybe.' She looked vaguely at the opaque roof of the shelter. 'We'll need to do a lot more work before we can establish if all the green we see is natural – some kind of panspermia, life drifting from star to star – or if it's being given assistance from some kind of intelligence.'

Doria said, 'You're thinking Dyson clouds, or shells. Glass-walled habitats around a star, huge greenhouses grabbing the light, the green light leaking out through spaceborne forests . . .'

'Hmph. Just as you lunar folk dream of cloaking the Sun some day, don't you?'

Doria raised an eyebrow. 'Not really the time or place for a politically provocative discussion, Professor Vasta.'

Salma found she liked the idea. 'Stars turned green by growing things. Green from life. Life everywhere, then. In *this* universe.' And she hugged Feathers, who seemed baffled, but hugged her back.

'Yes,' Vasta said, pressing ahead, but evidently unsure of her ground. 'But it doesn't matter whether it's panspermia or some kind of conscious propagation. In our universe we see no evidence of life save on Earth, or life that's spread from Earth – into the ice moons, for instance. We think Earth life was perhaps a fluke: that some prebiotic evolutionary process happened to hit on just the right organic chemistry to support life, in a relatively short time, in a relatively small, young universe. Mere billions of years.'

Doria laughed. '*Mere*.'

'So just as our friend Terminus said, we are the product of a fluke. Alone.

'Whereas here,' Vasta pressed on stubbornly, 'here the universe is *so* big and *so* old that life has had time to spread all over the place. Maybe even to evolve independently several times. So we see green in the sky.

'And so, I suppose, it's quite possible for a being like Feathers to evolve, from an independent biosphere, *and* with similarities to the humanoid. Even though the unlikeliness is multiplied. There has been room, and time – probably a *lot* of time – for such unlikely occurrences to happen. If you want a lookalike, all you have to do is go search this place.'

Your argument is less wrong than before.

Elizabeth laughed hollowly. 'Thanks. Next time I need a job reference, I'll call you.' She looked around, as if trying to see Terminus beyond the walls once more. 'You're leading us to a conclusion, aren't you? *This* universe isn't just big and old. It's infinite. It's eternal.

'In fact—' She took a breath. 'This is almost heretical. This is what they used to call *continuous creation*. Am I right?'

A silence.

Then: *I believe I understand what you say. You must say it for yourself, however.*

Here, things are arranged differently.

Are you ready to come out and see?

39

The sky outside was utterly different now — though still brilliantly bright, Salma thought. Crowded with stars, some of them greened. But her suit visor turned nearly completely opaque, so that she saw only a dull-brownish version of the vivid reality.

The vivid reality: a galaxy, apparently a huge one, its edges ragged — and each dangling thread of that raggedness was a chain of stars, she knew — with a dazzling pinpoint of light at the Galaxy's very core.

And out of the heart of the monster fired two spears, both along the spin axis, above and below the disc — lines of light that looked to emulate in length the radius of that big galaxy, so spanning hundreds of thousands of light-years, and still coherent across that length. It could be a quasar, Salma knew now, maybe like the one emerging from the home galaxy in another reality.

Meriel, it seemed, more mundanely, had been checking the sensors mounted on her own suit. 'The environment isn't what we saw before the transition. All of you run a system check on your suits and visors. And keep on doing it until we're out of this intensity of light. The radiation levels are high too . . .' She thought. 'Very high. Ten minutes, then we're back out of here, into the shelter, come what may.'

And Vasta called, 'Terminus!'

I am here.

'Are we elsewhere in your eternal universe? What is this place?'

You will call it a creation node.

'We will, will we? Why?'

Because I just told you you would.

'These damn causal loops . . . OK. So what is this — an active galaxy?'

This would be one of the largest galaxies in your own cosmos. Were it in your cosmos. The key element is the central black hole.

'I thought it might be,' Vasta said. 'A quasar?'

Essentially. But an enormous one, and enormously powerful. Its mass is equivalent to the mass-energy of ten thousand trillion suns. Its mass usage and energy output—

'I get the idea. And what is it doing?'

Creating matter and energy from nothing.

Or rather, extracting it from the higher-dimensional substrate which underlies all our realities — as your theorists know. Your home universe exploded out of that substrate, in an instant. Here it is as if that substrate is slowly leaking material into this *universe.*

'Continuous creation,' Vasta breathed. She glanced around at the others. 'I know what this is. That's what it used to be called, as a theory. Continuous creation. It's a beautiful, but wrong — or so we thought — model of how the universe might work.'

Doria said, 'Imagine we don't know what the hell you're talking about.'

'OK. So the . . . place . . . he took us to before was another universe, but it was evidently *like* our own. With a Big Bang origin, and ages of expansion, and then a heat death termination. He *showed* us its birth and death . . . But *this* is another universe yet again — and fundamentally different.

'Suppose, instead of a Big Bang, where all the stuff of the

universe is created in a single flash, you start slowly, but just *keep on* creating stuff slowly. Just a dribble would be enough – just like here, if it lasted for ever. And as the universe expands that . . . new stuff . . . fills in the gaps.'

Salma tried to understand. 'Like a balloon. You could paint it, and blow it up further, and then the paint would crack and you'd have to fill in the gaps. But you'd need more paint to do that.'

Vasta said, 'That's the idea. Not a bad analogy. Except that *you would never run out of paint.*

'That seems paradoxical to us. But so, I suppose, should the idea of everything just bursting into existence all at once, in a Big Bang, and we accept that.' She tapped at her wrist console, peered at scrolling text. 'According to some of these old studies, you wouldn't need much new stuff to keep the expansion of our universe going. One model suggested you'd only need one new hydrogen atom – or the equivalent in energy, or some other form – one atom per kilometre-wide box of space, per year. Umm. That's, uh, one new *star* per year, or stellar mass, in a cube of side a million light-years – a box that could contain a galaxy cluster, like our own local cluster with the Milky Way and Andromeda. Which might contain two trillion stars.' She looked up and grinned. 'A formation just like the one we see up there. One extra star every year, or the material to make it . . . When you put it like that, it sounds almost plausible, doesn't it?'

She dug further into her information.

'I see that back on Earth the theory was popular for a while, and gave the Big Bang a run for its money – I mean, it tested that theory to its limits. But it was shot down in the end by observations – by the fact that the past of our universe, which we could *see* directly, thanks to the finiteness of the speed of light, was *different* from the present. On a large scale, I mean. And the future seemed likely to be different again, when all the stars go out . . . In a continuous creation universe, nothing would change, at least on the largest of scales . . .' She peered up at the 'quasar'. 'And this is a creation node. So, what material is being produced? New protons?'

Not directly, Terminus said. *The portal ejects what you might think of as super-protons, immensely heavy compared to the components of normal matter. Each masses a few hundred thousandths of a gram – or as much as a billion billion protons – and, once created, these particles each decay in the Planck time—*

'Which is fast. I get the idea. And then?'

That decay, and a rush of nucleosynthesis, yields a scattering of atomic nuclei – of simple elements: hydrogen, helium, lithium, boron—

'The elements created by our Big Bang.'

In theory. Here, you see, there is an ongoing process of little bangs, occurring all across this infinite universe – an infinite number, in space, and time.

And so this universe need never die.

Salma, listening to this, bewildered, dazzled – half-blinded by the light of creation – was overwhelmed.

Feathers was clinging to her in the face of this monstrous sight, and Salma clung back.

She looked around at her companions, at Vasta who stood bravely and alone in front of Terminus. But for now, none of them seemed to have anything to say.

The hovering black sphere was a sharp shadow against the turbulent sky.

At last Salma called, 'Terminus! Why are you showing us these things?'

To invite you to join us.

And live for ever.

And the stars began to rush by.

40

That was what it felt like to Salma.

Salma felt unbalanced, shocked – suddenly dizzy.

Feathers, never far from Salma in this place, clung still tighter to her, and buried her face in Salma's neck. Through the light fabric of their suits, Salma could feel the slight rasp of plumage. But Salma felt giddy herself, and was glad of the support, one living being to another, the feel of her, the weight. She looked around for their heaps of gear, all of which seemed unblemished. *We brought our stuff with us.* That was something.

Terminus hovered, silent, as if nailed in place beneath the streaming sky.

Meriel, the doctor, was the first to move, to take charge.

She went to Vasta first. The scientist was glaring up at the changing sky, as Salma had been. Meriel tapped the side of Vasta's helmet, and Salma recognised the protocol – checking that Vasta's life support was working as it should. Then she pushed her own faceplate close enough to touch Vasta's, and evidently spoke to her, the sound transmitted through the visors.

Then Meriel approached Doria, but the Consortium ambassador waved her away, and spoke for all to hear. 'Suit fine. I'm fine.'

'I doubt that very much,' Meriel said gently. 'These – jumps – are hugely disorienting. I have a feeling we might all need a little anchoring after this.' She looked around. At her companions. Up at the sky once more, where those stars were streaming, passing over her head. Ever faster.

Doria snorted. 'I just hope you aren't going to suggest we go inside the shelter and do a couple of hours of yoga.'

Vasta still gazed up at the sky. 'Well, I'd say we should keep that as an option. This is all − overwhelming − and is likely to get more so, not less. We are only human.' She grinned at Feathers. 'With an honourable exception.'

Meriel glanced around. 'OK, a compromise. Nobody wants to go indoors. But let's bring out stools, pallets. At least we can rest, rather than stand here like heroes defying the storm. Food, water . . .' She eyed Terminus. 'For your information, O godlike tourist guide, we also have sanitary facilities in our suits.'

Which Salma for one had used several times already during this excursion. She had to laugh.

Terminus did not respond. It just hung in the sky, patiently waiting.

Meriel grinned through her faceplate. 'Hasn't got much small talk, has he?' She moved towards Salma. 'Your turn for a check over, kid.'

Salma gently released Feathers − and she saw that Feathers went straight to Vasta. Elizabeth smiled widely, and tentatively stroked Feather's back with a gloved hand. Feathers stood closer, bowing her head.

Terminus hovered.

When Meriel was done with her brief inspections − including, in the end, Feathers − they set out fold-out chairs, and assembled a little heap of food and drink packets, brought out of the habitat, all accessible through ports in their suits. A blanket on the ground for Feathers, which Salma shared.

'Some picnic this is,' Doria said.

Vasta was staring hard at the sky. 'The stars rushing by . . . How close can they be? How realistic is this depiction? Terminus?'

The images you see are acceptable to your sensorium. Yet they show the essential truth—

Doria snorted. '*Acceptable.* Adjusted? Edited, for the low-browed apes?'

Vasta glanced at her. 'A message tailored for the audience. That's just good communication strategy.'

'If patronising.'

'Maybe it's no wonder you of the Consortium always lose the argument—'

Salma was growing exasperated. 'Oh, shut *up.*'

Meriel grinned. 'Seconded. Look – what is this now, Terminus? What are we meant to understand?'

What do you see?

Vasta stared up. 'Stars. Rushing by. Or, we are rushing by *them.* And – are they fading? I hope our systems are catching all this. Those are old stars now, I think – *very* old stars. And getting older as we – travel? If that's what we are doing.'

In the end, all stars die.

'Yes, yes . . . But – according to our theories, our models, we humans haven't *seen* any of the extreme ageing of the stars, because our universe is too young. We thought they might keep burning for ten, a hundred trillion years. Ten thousand times the age of the universe when we lived? But *these* stars . . .' She thought it over. 'Are the stars we are seeing now *older* than what we saw before?'

Correct. You are being brought to – a pit, if you like.

Salma didn't like that word. *Pit* . . .

This universe is one of continuous creation, as you have seen. Its fabric is continually renewed through the creation nodes — which are in turn fuelled by the energies of the quantum substrate — indeed, spacetime itself is rejuvenated. And so there are places in this universe which are younger than most others. But there are places—

'Which are older than most others,' Vasta said. 'Older than other parts. That's logical. And it's also logical that there must be places which are . . .' She seemed hesitant to say what came next. '*Infinitely old*. Terminus — is that where you're taking us?'

There was no immediate reply.

Her voice had been tinged with wonder, Salma thought. She had a stab of jealousy — and of fear. How might it be to know so much, to be able to grasp so much, so quickly?

And it grew dark, quite suddenly.

Salma saw that the last of the stars had faded out now. Was the sky black, utterly? No, not quite. She saw what looked like a quasar, far away, a galaxy disc with those characteristic plumes of shining gases. Another node?

That was the *only* feature in the sky.

Vasta said calmly, 'We spoke of the far future. We have analytical models of our own universe, at least. Projections.

'So we *think* that, beyond the age of star formation, the sky would be filled with stellar remnants — cooling husks of dead stars. The very last of them will decay to iron, the dead end of the fusion processes. Iron stars, and inert planets, and black holes. The galaxies will evaporate eventually, the stars and planets drifting out, or sling-shotting away . . . Each dead star, each cold planet, alone.

'But still there should be continuing processes. Matter itself decays. The planets will turn to atomic dust, and even the dust itself will crumble as the very atoms break up, the protons and neutrons of their nuclei evaporating away.

'And meanwhile the black holes will evaporate too. The bigger they are the longer they last. We thought the largest black holes, the biggest galaxy-centre monsters – a hundred billion solar masses or more – would be the last to go, after a trillion trillion trillion . . . six or seven times over . . . *trillion* years. After such a long time, even our numbering system becomes absurd. And after *that* . . .'

Terminus spoke at last. *You are approaching a part of this universe which is older still.*

Where all has decayed.

Where the only ongoing process is the flicker of quantum uncertainty. And yet—

'And yet information processing can continue,' Vasta said. 'Can it? We've modelled this too. At the rate of, what, a bit at a time every billion years—'

Slower than that. Yet thought can continue, slow, slow, even at such a rate—

'Minds can work, you're saying,' Vasta said. 'Actions can be taken, perhaps. Processes can continue . . . Oh. And agents like you – created?'

Salma could only stare.

I was not created.

Over still longer timescales, I – emerged. I and others.

'Yes,' Vasta said slowly. 'I think I understand. You are a mind created by, supported by an almost impossibly rare sequence of chance events. Like throwing a pack of cards up in the air: do it often enough and eventually they land in four perfect bridge hands. Do you play bridge? . . . No matter. Wait long enough, and anything can happen, no matter how unlikely. And even some kind of brain, supporting some kind of mind, of consciousness, could *spontaneously assemble*. Out of the drifting litter of dead stars and dried-out husks of planets.

'*A Boltzmann brain*. That's our name for it. You would just – wake up – in the middle of the darkness, alone.'

This idea seemed monstrous to Salma. She clung tighter to Feathers.

It is impressive that you understand the concept, Terminus said.

'And that is how you were born?' Meriel asked. 'And in this . . . place? Just spontaneously, out of all this darkness, this emptiness?'

Salma, struggling to follow this, asked, 'And were you alone?'

Alone, yes. In this emptiness, yes. Alone for almost as long as the lifespan of the originating universe that survived to birth me.

Alone, yes.

But then, not alone.

There are others. Some much older than me. Orders of magnitude more. And some of them found each other. At first just an awareness, at last a way to talk, slowly, slowly – and eventually a way to reach each other. To act.

And to form a common purpose.

Suddenly Salma felt overwhelmed. Standing on this barren planet, under an empty sky. All these words, from an entity whose nature she barely understood. She wondered if she was going insane.

But Vasta was still, doggedly, interrogating the floating sphere.

'So, this . . . league of Boltzmann brains. This pit in the sky is a place older than we can envisage. And yet – and yet, in a sense, it empowers. It creates these ghastly slow brains, like bizarre parentless offspring, these minds . . . Terminus. Is this place truly infinitely old? This location here?'

If it has a limit we have yet to discover it, to plumb it. Even we children of eternity. In there may be more hierarchies of minds, deeper yet. Even more unlikely creations of chance. Pursuing unimaginable projects. If so, even we cannot see them, contact them.

And perhaps there are ranks of entities older even than—

'Do you fear them?' Doria asked. 'These older ones?'

It is rational for the finite to fear the infinite. And even we are finite – even we quantum minds, born in the stillness.

Feathers was cringing closer to Salma now. Salma wondered how much she could understand. Or perhaps Terminus, this mundane monster, was talking to her too, relating all this in some language inside her head.

'Then be clear,' Elizabeth Vasta said boldly. 'What do these hierarchies of infinitely old entities want of us?'

Doria leaned over towards Salma and whispered, 'Now *that* is a woman who is used to browbeating governments.'

Terminus seemed to hesitate.

Then it said, *They want to give you what they have.*

They wish to give you eternity.

Salma immediately recoiled at that.

On impulse, she drew a little closer to Meriel, one of her faux parents from the *Shadow*. She muttered, 'To be like you? An eternity in a hole in the sky? Muttering and scheming—'

Meriel said, 'And one thought per trillion years, a twitch as some quantum continuum decays a little further. *How* will you give us eternity?'

Doria said, 'I think I've followed it that much. They want to give us a creation node. Or rather—'

'*They want us to help turn our galaxy into a creation node,*' Meriel said. 'Into a super-quasar. That's what this is all about. Finishing what they started, right?'

You are correct, Terminus said. *You have seen how the end result will be – the mature node you witnessed. You know now that your young cosmos can be manipulated, to host such a node. Young cosmoses are more suitable for modification—*

'So that's it,' Salma said, more sharply than she had intended. 'In fact even before you spoke to us you went ahead and *modified* our galaxy without consulting us, or anybody else who lives there. By building the quasar that's now threatening the Earth.'

Vasta sighed. 'But he knew that nobody else does live there, Salma. There's only us. In our *universe*. We know that now. I think we can trust him on that. Which is why we were . . . chosen.'

Meriel admitted, 'I'm not sure if I understand. Are these eternals not gods?'

'No,' Vasta snapped. 'Not gods. Hold on to that. We can't let ourselves become . . . worshippers. They needed us, *you* of the *Shadow*, to, umm, activate Planet Nine. The artefact. Remember – Terminus here has told us as much. What god needs *you* to turn a switch?'

That much is accurate. Conscious mind is needed to activate such a link. Even just one such mind. All of this project is about one consciousness reaching out to another, across abysses of reality.

'So it was a fishing expedition. And we swallowed the bait.'

You deliberately, consciously, operated the link. Some of those individuals here were involved in that moment of decision—

Meriel said, 'We could have had no idea of the consequences.'

Doria said gently, 'But you did it anyhow. And you are Conservers! We miner types are supposed to be the meddlers.'

Vasta said, 'Not to mention us home-loving types who are still getting the rap for wrecking the Earth.'

It is in the nature of consciousness to explore – of tool-making consciousness at least.

'Maybe,' Vasta said. 'And so you lured us in. And now you need us to do more, if this sky rebuild is to go ahead, correct? If you're to assemble a creation node in our universe? A node in the heart of our galaxy?'

To activate the link was your choice. You were free to ignore it. Now we need your help to bring you the gift of eternity, yes. To bring that gift to all your people, all your worlds – all of your universe for the eternity to come.

'Nice advertising pitch—'

Salma burst out, 'What about Feathers? Feathers comes from a tool-making, conscious species also, right? And you *used* her to – to make us understand, or at least give us hints about this multiverse we all have to believe we inhabit now. Did you *reach out* to her people? Did you promise them immortality? Or was she just a tool to you, a useful pet animal to bait and trap?'

There was a shocked silence among the humans.

Terminus seemed to hesitate.

'Good point,' Meriel whispered. 'And well made.'

More than a tool. But it is true that we did not reach out to her people. More than one intelligence inhabited her universe. The other was – dominant. And it had come to dominate the world, the ecosystem from which Feathers evolved.

Vasta said, 'Let me guess. And you negotiated with the other lot, the dominators, the slavers? You're attracted to strength, to power—'

To rebuild a universe is not a trivial task—

'Did you go ahead with these – others? The parasites, the slavers? Did you remake *their* sky?'

The experiment failed.

And that stopped the conversation. If briefly.

Vasta stamped over to the heap of supplies, found a flask of water, plugged it into her suit, took a sip through a tube. 'Well, we're learning a lot. *Why* did the experiment with these . . . others . . . fail?'

Terminus seemed to hesitate.

It said at last, *The failure was not unique, not unprecedented. In some cases the agents chosen for uplift have proved unsuitable. In other cases the target universes themselves have proved unsuitable—*

Vasta said, 'And what became of these other "agents"? You presumably completely disrupted whatever their own development would have been. Even their evolution? Did they *survive* contact with you? What about Feathers' people? *Are they extinct?* All of them?'

Terminus failed to reply.

There was a long, frozen moment.

Then Vasta said, 'I think we need another break from this. Some food. Sleep, even. This is getting too ugly for me.'

The rest stood, nodded.

Salma, holding Feathers tight, looked back. She saw Terminus hovering implacably against the black sky. She wondered what it was thinking. She wondered if it was communicating with still stranger entities in that pit of eternity in the sky.

She wondered *how* it thought. A creature born of randomness, born into this strange disorderly multiverse. A creature born without kin, without ancestry of any kind. And yet the fate of a world, of worlds – no, of a galaxy, perhaps even a universe – was hanging in the balance of its judgement.

She did not envy it.

Troubled, she followed the others to the shelter.

Once they had stripped off their surface suits, washed a little, eaten a little, and talked a lot, they all seemed drained of the last of their energy, Salma thought. And when Meriel suggested they should try to get some sleep, there was no objection.

But Elizabeth Vasta, angrier than the rest, asked for sleep medication.

41

Hours later, they stirred, woke one by one.

Salma, clinging to Feathers, was the last to wake save for Feathers herself.

Doria checked, looked around. Terminus still hovered outside the shelter, motionless.

They washed again, ate again. Vasta made them a kind of hot tea – a gift of the *Cronus*, Salma learned, packed for special occasions.

Huddled in the shelter, there was little talk.

Vasta seemed the most agitated, the most tense. It had been her idea to take the break, but Salma wondered if she had slept herself at all. Still, she seemed determined, if somewhat dishevelled.

When the various domestic routines were done, it was time to face it all again.

Salma felt oddly queasy. From the mundane to the existentially strange, in a few footsteps. A picnic breakfast to the destiny of the universe. She wondered if she would ever get used to this, despite all her years with the strangeness of Feathers.

Or maybe that was just how it was to be a human being.

Vasta said, 'Time to suit up again, I guess.'

Meriel and Doria shared a glance.

Meriel said, 'Elizabeth — I did think we'd take the time to talk this over before we went out there again. I mean it's a pretty weighty encounter we're going through, a big decision we need to make. And we're all exhausted. I think. Overwhelmed—'

'Maybe,' Vasta said. 'But there's only one question we need to ask.'

Doria frowned. 'What question?'

But Vasta, cool, determined, didn't reply to that. 'No more discussion. Let's get this finished.'

Meriel hesitated, then shrugged. 'OK. I hope you know what you're doing.'

Outside, Terminus was waiting, as far as Salma could tell hovering in the exact same place as before their break. Salma wondered what strange communications it might have shared with its own masters while the group had slept.

She wondered if it ever tired.

Or *he*, as she persistently found herself thinking of Terminus. If he didn't sleep, what must he be thinking, when alone?

Did he dream? If so, what of?

Her instinct at moments of doubt like this, through her life, had been to turn to Meriel, as a surrogate aunt if not a replacement for a parent. But Meriel was already marching, with Vasta and Doria, directly towards Terminus.

So Salma hugged Feathers, and followed the rest.

When they reached Terminus, Vasta took one step beyond the others and glared up.

'We have a response,' she said. 'But first we need answers from you. Or from those who control you.'

There is no direct control—

She spoke over it. 'Your objective, your first objective, in our universe is to transform our own galaxy into a creation node. A super-quasar. Correct?'

Your language is imprecise but not incorrect.

'And with time, once one node has been established – then you spread further?'

A single creation node is enough to ensure that at least part of a cosmos has become eternal. But, yes, the adaptation would be progressed, to other locations, other galaxies.

Vasta laughed at that, harshly. 'A pyramid scheme. You sound like the last app that tried to sell me life insurance. And this adaptation – just considering our own galaxy – it will no longer function *as* a galaxy, will it? As a star-making, naturally evolved machine?'

The normal functions of the Galaxy in that sense would be terminated for a better end.

'And Earth? Earth, that unique birthing place of life – unique in our universe, anyhow?'

The Galaxy's transition must necessarily impede the progress of life on Earth—

'Impede? Ha! There's a sales app's euphemistic language if ever I heard it. Earth is *already* being "impeded" by your clumsy toy quasar, my friend. And now we've *seen* a creation node. A planet like Earth could never survive on the fringe of a formation like that, could it? Even the radius of the Galaxy away.'

Before the node was initiated the planet would be – could be, if chosen by you – evacuated. The inhabitants made safe.

'As you've made Feathers' people "safe", have you? Where are they now? Oh, I'm sure there are a few samples safely locked inside some multiversal zoo, with other infant intelligences who have served the eternal ones' purposes – or might, some day. While you use samples of them, like poor Feathers here, for your ends.'

It would not be—

'Even if we survived your handling, it would be the end of us as a species, wouldn't it? In terms of our own development as a civilisation, even our future evolution. And *is that not your purpose*? To preserve, to sustain – but never allow to challenge?'

She paused, walked up and down before Terminus.

Doria muttered, 'That grandstanding might work in some government chamber on Earth, but I'm not sure it's going to work on Terminus and his puppet masters.'

Meriel smiled. 'But it's all she's got. And she's magnificent. It's a bluff, but what a bluff—'

'No!' Vasta cried now, waving a fist at Terminus. 'No, we will not cooperate with you! We will not help you set up your eternity machines in our reality. We reject an infinite future as pets of your masters. And we will not allow you to meddle with our own galaxy. If we're alone in our universe then it's ours to explore, or not. And to quicken. It would be an unconscionable crime if life were, after all, able to emerge elsewhere in that sea of stars, a possibility wiped out by you, because of our collusion.' She glared now. 'I know we don't have the power to defy you. And I know that I am speaking, without authority, for the whole of our species, past and future—'

'Not to mention the whole damn galaxy, past and future,' Doria muttered.

'You will spare us,' Vasta said. 'You will abandon your attempts to build the quasar, the node. You will allow Earth to recover. No. Hear me out. *You will also spare our world from twenty-five thousand years of emitted a Galaxy-core heat.* All the quasar radiation that's already crossing the Galaxy towards us. You will fix that too, as paradoxically as you like. And you will let mankind resume its course . . .'

'You tell him,' Doria called.

But now Vasta seemed to be becoming exhausted, running down. Salma, holding Feathers, thought she staggered a little.

Meriel hurried forward, put an arm around Vasta's waist. She tapped her own helmet. 'Enough. You made your point to Terminus. And all that's been recorded. When we get back home, and everybody figures out what you have done today, there'll be parades in the streets.' She led Vasta back to the hab, slowly.

'Huh. You really think so?'

'I really think so. But it's done now. Come now, sit . . .'

Outside the hab's fabric wall, Meriel helped Vasta settle on a stool. Vasta had her eyes closed.

But she seemed to shudder. Without opening her eyes she murmured, 'Oh, what have I done? Who am I to have negotiated away the future of the race – the world? I must go back – back to Earth. Explain all this, explain what I've done. Take the consequences.'

Doria knelt before her, held her hands. 'You were the person who was on the spot. You were the person who had to make a choice. Who else but you could have challenged Terminus? That's who you are. And what you did.'

Salma said, 'She's right.' Hesitantly, she hugged Vasta – but Vasta remained stiff, unresponsive, her head turned away.

'And,' Meriel said now, 'think about what you *didn't* do. Maybe you could have parlayed this confrontation into a throne for yourself. There are plenty who would have. Alexander of Macedon. Genghis Khan. Napoleon. Hitler. Lawson of the Appalachians . . . A throne of eternity.'

'Huh. I never thought of that,' Vasta said. 'I always figured ruling the world is an overrated ambition—'

You will be sent home, if you wish it.

That was Terminus.

They turned to see. That charcoal-coloured sphere still hung imperturbably in the sky.

Vasta seemed almost too tired to speak. 'Thank you,' she said.

Salma took a step forward. 'But what about Feathers? This is *her* home. Can she stay here?'

That was a sudden impulse on Salma's part, and the rest looked around at her, perhaps surprised.

If you wish it. If she wishes it.

'And I—' She took a breath. 'I will stay with her.'

Meriel sighed. 'I was fearing you might say that. Because that means I'll be staying too.'

'And me,' said Doria. 'Obviously.' She smiled. 'When you get back, Elizabeth, give my regards to Jeorg North. The bastard.'

Salma felt overwhelmed.

If you wish it. And.

Vasta looked up. 'And what?'

If you or your descendants change your minds.

We will be waiting.

42

They spent a few more days, thinking it through. Being sure.

They put their plans, again, to Terminus.

Again Terminus agreed to their wishes.

And then, it seemed suddenly, came the moment when Vasta, suited up, carrying a small pack of samples, data, records, walked away from the group and stood, as instructed, directly beneath the hovering Terminus.

In her last moments Vasta stared up at that charcoal-grey sphere, hanging in space without a tremble, as ever without visible support, a minor miracle in this arena of miracles.

The last couple of days had been one long hug, as Vasta suspected she would always remember it. She knew she would always miss these people terribly. She had become used to their way of pitching in and working things through, rather than having to figure it all out herself as a scientist working among hostile civilians back on Earth.

Now, whatever difficulties she faced, she would be effectively alone again – alone, among billions of humans, none of whom could possibly understand what she had been through. Alone for ever – as long as she lived.

She touched her throat, her pendant—

'No. I'm not ready—'

She thought she *felt* the folding of spacetime around her—

Year 54

AD 2309

43

And she found herself standing alone on a dark plain, under a crowded sky – but a familiar sky, star-scattered, with one brilliant stand-out pinpoint, and a clutter of engineering drifting above. Dark, drab ground beneath her feet.

This was Planet Nine, surely. That brightest star must be the Sun. She was a mere seven hundred astronomical units away from Earth, rather than universes adrift.

She saw no signs of a human presence down here, no habitats.

But there, yes, hanging in its stationary orbit like twin metallic moons, there was the battered old *Cronus*, its hulls multiply and visibly patched. When she inspected magnified images through her smart faceplate, the forward hull showed an odd yellowing to her eyes. The result of years of exposure to cosmic radiation around Nine, perhaps.

Years. She felt an odd tug of nostalgia – and a touch of fear. Had she been so long away? Had she jumped to the far future?

Still, there was nobody here. Nobody called.

She was the outsider here now. She had to be patient.

She set her suit comms system to relay a simple *I'm here!* message. Surely the *Cronus* would pick it up, if nobody closer.

She put her one small hand-package down on the ground beside her – the familiar charcoal-black ground of Nine, the near-Earth gravity just as she remembered it. And stood there.

She could do nothing but wait.

Belatedly she thought to look for the quasar spot in Sagittarius. She squinted, tried to make out the constellations—

'Identify yourself.'

The sharp words, loud in her earpieces, startled her.

Then light splashed around her.

Looking up, the glow was dazzling. Screening it with her gloved hand, she saw a small craft descending from the sky, coming down right on top of her – no, it was a little to the side.

'Nice ship. How does it work? I don't see any thruster exhaust—'

'Identify yourself.'

A gruff male voice. She sighed. 'You remind me of another disembodied floating head. We called him Terminus . . . he had no manners either. Oh, never mind.'

'Identify yourself.'

'I am Elizabeth Vasta. Science Adviser to the President. Umm, who's the President now?'

'Your identity is confirmed as Elizabeth Vasta.'

'How can you tell that? . . . Never mind.'

'You aren't the Science Adviser any more.'

'Well, that's typical. You'd think they'd have baked me a cake . . .' She was thinking slowly, she knew, despite the smart-ass quips. A way to cover when out of her depth, as she had felt many times when dealing with politicians and those who orbited them. As she felt now.

The craft descended further. The light splashing around her brightened further, and she raised a hand while her faceplate filters adjusted to shield her eyes.

'What date is it, by the way?'

'*Stay still. You will be taken on board for decontamination and interrogation.*'

'Charming. What date is it?'

'*Stay still—*'

'You can tell me that much.' She tried to keep the tension out of her voice.

'*The year is 2309. AD, that is.*'

'That late . . . ?'

So. Forty-three years since the arrival of the *Cronus* at Planet Nine. To her – what, a few weeks? Her own timeline and that of her universe were out of synch, it seemed, and maybe that was no surprise.

'Forty-three years. I wonder if the maintenance company is still looking after my apartment in New LA. I wonder if LA is still there—'

'*Stay still.*'

'Couldn't you tell me who you are? I'm a little disoriented down here.' She tried to keep the pleading, the weakness out of her voice.

There was a hesitation. '*I am coordinator of this facility. My name is Oliver Mason. I report to the colony supervisor, then to the government of Earth, then to the Solar System Council.*'

A Solar System Council, now. That was new. Or old, depending on the date; new to her. Sounded like a good idea. And . . . Mason? Any relative to the President – surely ex-President by now? *I knew she had a son . . .*

'Can't you tell me anything? What about the quasar? Uh, the Galaxy-centre heat source? Can't you tell me that much?'

Another hesitation.

'*The source was extinguished in the year 2266.*'

Just as *Cronus* had arrived, as her party had departed to . . . elsewhere. Terminus had kept his promise.

'I can imagine that much damage must have remained, even after the source was gone. You could tell me that much, surely.'

A hesitation. *'The world is . . . recovering. You will be briefed.'*

'Thank you. Thank you—'

'Stand still, please.'

The craft descended slowly, dazzling her with the arc lamps trained on her, so she could see nothing of it at all.

44

Two days after the return of Elizabeth Vasta to Planet Nine, Oliver Mason called what he termed a summit meeting.

And Tiff North's presence was summarily demanded.

The meeting was held on what had once been the bridge of the *Cronus*, before it had been decommissioned – the bridge of a ship Tiff's father, Jeorg, had once rammed with his own interplanetary vessel. Only to make his peace with the authorities, settle down, find gainful employment back on the Moon – he always was a gifted pilot – and become father to Tiff, a pilot herself, now forty years old. And Tiff, always attracted by the family legend, had travelled out to Nine on one of the many follow-up flights, and as a lunar ambassador had become a senior figure in the governance of the little colony that had developed around the old *Cronus* – with, thanks to her ancestry, a certain notoriety.

But despite such ambassadors – and even with the presence of the Conservers' antique *Shadow*, the first ship here – Earth was still in de facto control of what had become a strange little colony on the edge of the Solar System.

Tiff herself had been born some eight years after the collision incident at Saturn, born into an age still preoccupied with the mystery at the edge of the Solar System and beyond: the irruption of Planet Nine, Feathers, the Galaxy-centre quasar. She could just remember President Mason's fifth and final term. She remembered how those remaining of the *Shadow* crew had been lauded across the Solar System – some even going virtual for debriefings, even lecture tours of Earth, before receding back into the anonymity of their culture's deep-space habitats, and eventually back to Nine itself. All save Boyd Hart who had found the lecture circuit too much fun to abandon.

But that profound mystery had continued to loom over petty human disputes and issues – even as many of those issues, economic, cultural, even concerning the survival of the species, had intensified over the decades precisely because of the fall-out of that mystery.

And so, helped by the recognition, or notoriety, from her father's name, Tiff had put in for a placement here herself, in the rough-and-ready science colony that had grown up around Nine – this place whose existence had notoriously shaped her father's whole life, and, subsequently, hers.

Which was why Oliver Mason had now included Tiff in this meeting on the *Cronus* bridge. A meeting, she presumed, to decide how to handle the strange return of Elizabeth Vasta – once science adviser to Mason's own grandmother, during her terms as President of Earth.

Also in the meeting Mason had included John Smith, a now very elderly (said to be well over a hundred) and still unofficial ambassador of the group most outsiders still called the Conservers. Another passenger on that fateful flight of the *Cronus* to Saturn and then to Planet Nine, and another who had never gone home.

So, as Oliver Mason took the command chair once occupied by a long-retired Emmanuel Caspar, he felt that the main factions of spacegoing humanity could at least be said to be represented by the three of them: the Conservers, the Earth authorities, the lunar capitalists, working together in this age of tensions. Here they were, trying to handle something that had come from outside decades ago, and outside the human world altogether.

Something represented by Elizabeth Vasta.

And as they waited for her, they seemed to have nothing to say to each other.

At last the door opened. Vasta drifted in, made for the one empty chair.

'Sorry I've kept you waiting,' she said, a little breathless. 'The doctors nabbed me for one more round of inspections. You'd think they'd be confident by now, but I suppose they don't want me infecting such an illustrious group as this.' She forced a smile, looking around at them. 'John Smith. It's good to see you, even if our personal timelines are out of joint. It seems that space was good for your health.'

He just glared at her.

When she got no reaction, she sighed and dug a sleek tablet out of a loose shoulder bag. 'To business, then?'

Tiff just nodded.

Oliver, wordless, waved a hand at an empty seat.

Vasta settled, strapping loosely in.

Tiff had noticed that people seemed awkward around Vasta. But then she had just suddenly *reappeared*, more than forty years out of her time, and yet, evidently, so the doctors had said, only a few weeks older in terms of her own body's ageing. A fact which somewhat validated the fantastic account she had had to tell of her exploits beyond Planet Nine . . .

'Beyond' in some sense that Tiff thought she was never going to understand, not fully.

And John Smith, strapped tightly in his own orthopaedic chair, glared at Vasta.

'You're sorry for keeping us waiting? The waiting isn't the problem. The problem is the blasted truth of your existence here at all. And the strangeness of it. As you imply, why, when I knew you, we were about the same age. Now you've skipped forward, and – well, look at *me*.'

They all looked. Tucked inside his complex chair, he was a gnarled figure, short of stature, his face like crumpled leather. He wheezed, his voice was a scratch, and he seemed to be having trouble with his limbs when he moved, the gestures jerky, his hands trembling.

Tiff didn't mix with Smith socially, but knew something about him. He was an ardent Conserver, but Earthborn. Lawyer by training. A philosopher, not a pioneer, and a man of very strong views – if not of strong constitution. He had probably spent the first half of his life in Earth's gravity, and the second half in microgravity, Tiff quickly estimated, and he was evidently the type who would have avoided the mandatory exercising and diet supplements. And so he was bent over, probably in constant pain, swathed in thick clothing to mitigate the risk of bone fractures. Which might explain his disposition, Tiff thought.

Still, he had survived, and he had a right to be here as a *Cronus* survivor too. But his habitual scowl was like a fist.

Meanwhile Oliver Mason was forcing a smile, evidently trying to ease the tension. 'My grandmother used to say, as *she* got older, that the old envying the young is the worst waste of energy ever invented . . .'

Tiff suppressed a smile at that. Oliver Mason, grandson of the five-term President Melanie Mason, rarely missed a chance to drop that name.

'Wise words,' Vasta said, settling herself. 'But I am a special case. Out of time . . .'

As she watched, Tiff was distracted by the heavy pendant at

Vasta's neck, a black pearl on a silver chain. Part of her legend. Integral to the story she had brought home. The pearl drifted in the microgravity.

Vasta caught her looking – and she *winked*. Tiff looked away, embarrassed.

But Vasta spoke gently to her. 'You remind me of your father, if you don't mind my saying so. Flew out to Saturn with Doria Bohm, intent on mischief. But, you know, I spent the last few years, subjective years, travelling with Doria, and she was far from the . . . *radical* . . . I had taken her for. In terms of the politics of Earth versus the Consortium. All those endless arguments about nitrogen supply chains . . .'

'Oh, those arguments go on,' Tiff said. 'As you must have picked up by now. But the balance of power has shifted, as Earth recovers from the quasar heating. The lunar colonies, small as they were in comparison, were more self-reliant, more able to deflect or compensate for the quasar heating. And a quickly reviving lunar industrial base has been of great assistance to Earth's own recovery.'

Vasta raised her eyebrows at that. 'That's good news. Relatively. Well, the quasar is done with,' she said. 'Hopefully. You must have read my debriefs. We have – we *seem* to have extracted a promise from the entities we encountered out there that the process of transformation of our galaxy into a creation node has been terminated, permanently. "Been terminated" – I'm not sure if that's the right tense for the out-of-time being we encountered. It ceased, anyhow.'

'Leaving a huge amount of damage done even so,' Oliver Mason said.

'Oh, I know that. But I see that the recovery, or at least a strategy for survival, has been initiated . . .'

'Ha!' John Smith glared at her. 'What recovery? All we can do is flail helplessly, and wait until these meddling gods decide to turn their blowtorch back on again . . .'

Since Vasta's return, Tiff had spent some time working with her to bring her up to date – as one of this command group, she was one of the few allowed access to Vasta, and comparatively well informed.

It was now fifty-four years since the Galaxy-centre quasar had ignited, forty-three since it had ceased. But the effects of that decade of heating were still working their way through Earth's systems, a ghastly echo of the human-caused pulse of heat in the twenty-first century and after. And desperate solutions essayed then had been rerun now, most notably vast migration waves, millions of people on the move from the desiccating equatorial and tropical belts to the higher latitudes, especially in the northern hemisphere. In Russia, Asia, North America, scratch cities and camps briefly occupied during the peak climate-collapse years of the twenty-second century were hastily refurbished.

And all the while there had been whispers of wonders on the edge of the Solar System . . . As embodied by Vasta's own remarkable journey.

Well, the various authorities had had to deal with the quasar aftermath. And now it was time to deal with the rest of it.

But it seemed as though John Smith blamed Vasta personally. And perhaps others did too. Tiff wondered if Vasta herself was aware of this.

Vasta frowned back at John Smith, defiantly enough.

She said firmly, '*Flail helplessly*, John? I'm not minimising any of it. The suffering of the Earth, the other worlds. I'm not without understanding, not without imagination, or empathy.

I was a presidential science adviser, you know. Actually, for all I've been told, maybe I still am—'

'You're not,' said Oliver curtly.

'But you should not minimise the gravity of the decisions we had to make, off in the multiverse. We were offered eternity for mankind! But the price would have been the destruction of the Galaxy, perhaps of Earth . . . Even the destruction of the reality that made us what we are, and would have become in the future. Who were we to presume to make such a decision? But it was demanded of us anyhow.

'Since I got back, and before, I've been over and over this. I think we were drawn to the path of least harm, a path that might enable humankind to find its own destiny, eternal or not . . . And yes, we also extracted a promise that the quasar would be shut down . . .'

But then, apparently studying their reactions, John Smith's stony face, she hesitated.

Tiff saw that Vasta perceived suspicion here, if not hostility. A suspicion that she might be *bragging* about her encounters with these godlike aliens. And not understanding the plight of Earth, indeed all the human worlds. Minimising that plight. Not empathising. Grandstanding.

Still, Vasta seemed to choose her next words still more carefully.

'I am no ambassador for the eternals,' she said. 'You should understand that. Quite the opposite. I, we, negotiated. We did our best to persuade them not to continue what we saw as harm—'

John Smith glared. 'You negotiated with that feathered *thing* beside you.'

And Vasta recoiled at that. 'It wasn't like that. Oh, John – your language – we used to be friends, you've changed so much . . .

Look — Feathers was as much a victim of the eternals' meddling as we humans were. A symbol of it. More so, probably — and an inadvertent warning to us. Feathers had lost everything, her people, her world. All in order to serve as a kind of philosophical lesson for us, a race of strangers.'

Smith shook his head. 'I say again. You negotiated for the future of Earth *with an alien beside you*. And you claim you were not compromised? That you did not betray your own kind?'

Vasta glared back at Smith. Tiff had the feeling that Vasta had come here expecting to be interrogated — once more — about those strange negotiations off in the multiverse, but not with this much vigour. But, Tiff also knew, Vasta in her day had worked with high-ranking politicians, and she wasn't about to fold up now.

'I won't have this, John, this line of attack. We did our very best. We didn't ask for the damn job. Although it did seem . . .' She hesitated.

Tiff noticed she was again fingering the black pearl pendant at her neck.

'We did have the feeling that — well, we had been somehow *chosen* for the task. That we were in the right place.'

John Smith snorted his contempt.

'Well, *you weren't there*, John. If you had been chosen, perhaps you, we, would have made a different judgement . . . You can't know how it was. And if you won't listen to me, you can never understand. You may not understand even so . . . We tried our very best to find the optimal course for mankind.

'Ah, but maybe we were always going to be *blamed*, whatever we did. I think we knew that. Look — we didn't want such responsibility. Who would? Well, guess what? We had it anyhow, and we had to make our decisions, hoping we got it right. Oppenheimer and the atomic bomb.'

Tiff frowned. 'Who?'

'Ancient history,' John Smith said.

'Never mind.' Vasta looked around at their faces. 'Oh. Enough. I have a feeling this is a kind of hearing, not just a briefing. Well, that can wait. I have substantial work to do – a full report for the Earth government and the other polities, for one thing – maybe then we might have a properly convened hearing. Or they may choose to have me brought back to Earth – however long that might take. Or whatever they want. So, if you have no more to say—' She unclipped her harness, drifted out of her chair, made for the door.

But she hesitated, looked back. 'You see, *we* didn't know for sure if we'd got it right, then. How could we know? *You* don't know, here and now. But we had to choose, that's all. I guess we will all have to wait for the judgement of history. We did shut down the damn quasar. Just remember that.' She glared at Oliver. 'Now if you'll let me go, I still have some sleep to catch up on.'

Oliver gestured; the door at the back of the little cabin opened in response. And he called after her. 'Thank you, Adviser Vasta. I mean it – thank you. I for one do believe you did your best as you saw it.'

Vasta nodded generously enough at that ambiguous compliment, and drifted out of the bridge. Tiff watched her go.

The door swung shut behind her.

Oliver turned back to the other two. 'Well. Is that enough? Earth is pressing us for a resolution to this situation.'

A hesitation.

'Let's consult some more,' John Smith said darkly. 'Then we should make a decision.'

411

45

Elizabeth Vasta had been given a cabin of her own in the *Cronus*. The hulk's old passenger quarters were still cruiser-liner comfortable, even if *Cronus* was never going anywhere else again.

But all Vasta really needed was the zero-gravity sleeping cocoon she found hanging from one wall, and the zero-g lavatory, and what she thought of as room service.

That and a comms system, heavily filtered and censored, she was sure, but she was allowed to exchange messages with those she knew of the remaining crews of the *Cronus* and *Shadow*, still holding to their dismal posts all these decades later.

That, and a smart wall with news feeds from Earth.

Even if that news was still coming from seven hundred AU away, still delayed by at least ninety hours by lightspeed's crawl out to this remote location. Which ought not to be an irritation for a person who had once hopped on and off universes like escalators in a city-centre shopping mall, but was.

And again she explored the slow recovery of Earth, half a century after the lighting-up of the Galaxy-centre quasar – a lamp, she knew now, meant to gift immortality to this universe, in practice a torch scorching the living Earth.

But there was indeed hope of a better future, she saw. Over the decades she had been away, the Lunar Consortium, burying hatchets, had been manufacturing and orbiting vast solar mirrors to deflect the intensifying light from Earth. And now they were constructing a new generation of space habitats, built from lunar glass and filled with water from Ceres – specially licensed for the purpose by Earth, and Vasta smiled at the irony of that, remembering Jeorg North, first to Ceres and would-be protester at the launch of the *Cronus*. These transparent biomes were populated by blooms of blue-green algae, rapidly growing in the unfiltered sunlight. And, as Vasta knew from space-habitation studies from long ago, if you had enough blue-green algae, you could feed a world – even Earth, parched and disturbed as it was. She knew the Conservers wouldn't have liked it, and she sympathised with that, but she'd personally have made an exception for this case.

Across the mother planet, all you had to do was look up at the sky, to find hope.

She clung to that thought, trying to sleep.

Trying. Wondering what the next step would be for her.

No. *Knowing* what that next step must be.

She tried to reconcile herself to the inevitability of it. And she decided, on a whim, to see old friends. Even if only remotely. Even if it caused her still more trouble. The hell with it.

She did have a reasonable motive. Boyd Hart, of the *Shadow* crew, had recently died, at the magnificent age of a hundred and twenty-nine.

And she had been invited to send down a projection so she could take part in his funeral.

She jumped at the chance.

46

She remembered very well the virtual visit of President Mason to the little Nine colony. And she understood the process – that the avatar would act independently, speak independently, gather independent memories of the encounter. All this would be uploaded back to the original once the content was transferred back to Earth.

What she had not understood was how it would feel to have that content loaded back into her own mind, her cortex. How she would experience those memories for the first time – and only the first time.

It would be as if she was there.

When the projection link was established, it was as if she found herself sitting, once more, in the now-elderly hab that was still at the heart of the growing colony on Planet Nine.

Sitting in one of a ring of seats, just as when the assembled representatives had conferred with Melanie Mason, or *her* projection, at the height of the quasar crisis. But now Vasta was the projection.

And there was a coffin, set on trestles just outside the ring, covered with a flag of some shining material. Empty, she knew; Boyd had died on Earth, half-way through yet another lecture tour.

And the seats were occupied by people – friends – she'd thought she would never see again, even remotely like this. To be specific, three elderly men.

None of this was real, of course.

But she burst into tears. 'Oh, shit.' She buried her face in her hands.

The nearest of the old guys stood, and took a couple of paces towards her, before apparently remembering himself, and sitting back down.

'Sorry. I forgot. You're a hologram. And you can't hug a hologram . . .'

The voice was familiar, if kind of scratched.

Vasta made herself look up, control the tears, wipe her eyes. A smiling face. 'Fabio?'

He grinned now. 'Don't tell me I'm all grown up all of a sudden.'

'I wouldn't dream of it—'

'I'm fifty-eight years old, thanks. I'm still on the *Cronos*, still working on the mysteries of Nine. But I'm still a kid to this crew. I bet you don't recognise the others.'

She looked around. 'Well, I know the guy who should be in the box. Good old Boyd Hart. You know, I've learned he did so much media for Earth that he's probably the best known of all of you down there.'

'We know,' said Fabio's left-hand neighbour, sprightly, bald. Sour. 'In the beginning I had to set up the links for him.'

She smiled. 'Joe the comms guy. You've aged well. For . . .'

'You're fishing. Fishing is good. I know we're all out of joint timewise. I'm in my tenth decade by my body clock. And this fossil next to me is six years older; he was six years older when we were in our twenties, and is still six years older now. Say hello, grandpa.'

Vasta smiled again. 'Zaimu Oshima. Propulsion.'

'Right. Without an honest job since the *Shadow* reached Nine and we shut her propulsion down.'

'You're all looking good.'

Joe snorted. 'Except for Boyd. Always was a party pooper.'

'Look, enough of the how-are-you stuff. I want to hear every detail of how life has been for you guys since we all departed. Me and Meriel and Salma and Doria and Feathers. Every detail. And when I get folded back into my original on Earth, I'll cherish every word. Every smile.'

Joe hesitated. Then, 'You can stay as long as you like. Really.'

Zaimu said, 'We can keep you company in relays.'

Joe pressed on, 'You know, you don't have to – *leave*. Not permanently. We can take a backup copy of you as we go along. A copy that's independent of the original . . . You'll still be here. A part of you at least. Here for us, anyhow. And that's all that counts, isn't it . . . ?'

She nodded. 'Thank you. I'll think that over.'

'So, you first,' said Fabio. 'Spill the beans. Where the hell have you been?'

'Including all the stuff I didn't dare tell the authorities?'

Zaimu smiled, reached for her hand, pulled back a little clumsily. 'Especially that. You first . . .'

They talked for hours.

And when the recording was done, when she found herself back in her cell-cabin on the *Cronus*, she wept, alone.

47

A few weeks after that first showdown on the *Cronus* bridge – a few days after her projection's visit, and before Vasta had submitted her full report for Earth – John Smith called another meeting.

They returned to the bridge: Smith himself, Oliver Mason, Tiff North.

Without Vasta, this time.

'I've had more briefings from Earth,' Smith said, in his rasp of a voice. 'There are deeper currents here to consider, I think. Deeper than Vasta understands, at least.'

'Maybe more than we can understand too,' Oliver said.

Tiff nodded. A sensible enough remark. She had always found Oliver – once out of the majestic shadow of his grandmother – to be pragmatic. If one-dimensional, maybe. You couldn't spend almost all your life in an isolated place like this without missing a certain depth of experience. But he had run this stationary liner for decades now, without significant disasters. She could trust his judgement, as much as anybody's.

Meanwhile John Smith was a deeper thinker, still a Conserver, but an angry one now, Tiff realised, and – perhaps – a plotter.

Uneasily, Tiff wondered what might come out of this meeting.

John Smith began without preamble.

*

'It's the theological allegories that trouble me most.

'God like aliens promising us eternal life – literally? Scientifically? If we can only survive the ruin of the Earth in the process! . . . And the paradox is that it was we Conservers, with a mission to protect the worlds of the Sun, who gave humanity the opportunity to initiate the biggest cultural dislocation conceivable.

'We went out to take a look at Nine, just for the sake of it. And look at what has nearly followed. The ripping-up of the Galaxy, the universe! That's even if these godlike aliens in their black holes know what they're doing, and don't screw it all up. And given that they are god-*like* rather than gods, I very much doubt that they *do* know.'

'OK,' said Oliver carefully. 'So you're glad these eternals are willing to leave us alone, because you want humanity to find its own destiny – even if that means going back to Earth and leaving the universe untouched.'

'Yes, yes,' Tiff said. 'That's the standard Conserver creed. You know that we of the Moon have the opposite ambition – to spread humanity as far and as wide as we can, across the Solar System anyhow. What greater purpose is there than to bring to life a dead universe? And we believe the Eternals when they claim that's true of their thinking too. But if our corner of the universe is to be remodelled, we can do the damn job ourselves.'

Oliver held up a hand. 'While making unholy fortunes in the process. Look, let's stick to the point. Unlike my grandmother, I'm not empowered to speak for Earth, or even the government. But I am the moderator here. And it's Elizabeth Vasta who is *on trial* here. Correct?'

That seemed to quiet them for a moment.

Smith, the lawyer, shook his gaunt head. 'Not that. This isn't a trial. Not in any legal jurisdiction. But we do have to decide what to do with her. We three, at this moment, are in a position to influence future events, for all mankind, quite profoundly. *That* is the issue – what steps we must take, here and now. What is for the best.'

'OK,' Oliver said. 'But I *am* on the spot here in terms of the chain of command. That's been made clear to me.'

Made clear, Tiff knew, in several long, time-delayed briefings from the government of a still unstable world, a government scared of some kind of wild reaction to all this, the strange aftermath of the quasar crisis that had been the main challenge for Earth for decades. Tiff had a pang of pity for Oliver, who was surely too young, too inexperienced – despite his pedigree – for this.

Yet here he was, on the spot. Just as Vasta and her colleagues had been, Tiff supposed, when selected for their own extraordinary multiversal adventure.

Now John Smith scowled, Tiff thought – though his face was so lined it was hard to tell.

'Then bless us with your wisdom, O boy king,' he said.

'Yeah, yeah. Look – you Conservers are like the conscience of the race. You keep nagging us to do things efficiently, to *use* things lightly. While you of the Consortium are expansive, ambitious – you are interplanetary capitalists. And there's nothing wrong with that, intrinsically. And you want *that* system to keep working without disruption, as long as feasible.

'And Earth is – government.'

'The seat of empire,' Tiff said sourly.

Oliver didn't reject that, though it seemed to make him think.

'An empire? If you like. Actually I've been reading up on empires and other institutions of the past, thanks to John.'

Smith nodded stiffly.

'What does an empire *want*? Peace. Order. Commerce. Economic growth, in an orderly way. And whether you like it or not Earth still does control the Solar System, legally, economically. I suspect that most of its citizens still welcome that, and the order a central authority brings.'

'"Most",' John Smith said. 'Except the ones that might choose to worship the gods in the sky. And even an interplanetary empire might fall because of a prophet. Or a holy book.' He glared at them. 'There. I said it out loud. That's what you're thinking, especially you, Oliver. And that's what we need to discuss. Right?'

'Right,' Oliver said reluctantly. 'That is one reading of my briefing from the President and his advisers. Not to mention my grandmother's old team.'

'Well, then,' said John Smith. He dug into a pocket, and produced a Bible.

With bookmarks.

Oh shit, Tiff thought.

Smith opened the pages with a soft rustle.

A lawyer's rustle, Tiff reflected. Theatrical. Attention-drawing.

'You see,' Smith said softly, 'I for one do wonder if the implanting of such a figure as Feathers in our society was by chance. You'll know there have been religious interpretations of these events and discoveries from the beginning. The virgin birth! Matthew, one twenty-three. *Behold, a virgin shall be with child, and shall bring forth a son, and they shall call his name Emmanuel, which being interpreted is, God with us* . . . Not a virgin mother this time – no mother in our universe at all.'

Tiff frowned. 'That always seemed a stretch to me. That the Eternals would deliberately echo a human myth. How would they know? Why would they need to use it?'

Oliver said, 'We do have this testimony that the entity Vasta and the others encountered out there called itself after a Roman god. *Terminus* . . .'

Smith shrugged. 'So it knows us well enough to play that kind of card. And besides, a virgin birth might be a version of a universal myth, across any culture developed by a species with a form of procreation even vaguely similar to our own. You can imagine them repeating that kind of stunt over and over – the Eternals, I mean. The Madonna and Child, over and over, on world after world . . .

'But there's more warning to be dug out of our own experience, our own past. Listen to this . . . Ah, yes. Matthew, twenty-five, twenty-nine: *Immediately after the tribulation of those days the sun will be darkened, and the moon will not give its light; the stars will fall from heaven, and the powers of the heavens will be shaken. Then the sign of the Son of Man will appear in heaven, and then all the tribes of the earth will mourn, and they will see the Son of Man coming on the clouds of heaven with power and great glory. And He will send His angels with a great sound of a trumpet, and they will gather together His elect from the four winds, from one end of heaven to the other . . .'*

Oliver said, 'Wow.' His voice was small.

Smith closed the book. 'I could find such resonances in most major religions, even more. Again, maybe there are universals in all mythologies, even among non-humanoids, among any creatures with finite intelligences trying to understand the means and motives of apparently infinite entities above them. Gods of the Sun, the stars, gods of the weather. Gods of creation, of life and death.

'And I would wager that's what the Eternals play on. On world after world – in universe after universe.' He looked at them, each in turn. 'Now, you know why I've raised this. Here and now, while the situation is still . . . contained. Before some kind of messianic cult of the alien develops from the scraps of evidence that have already leaked into the public domain. A cult that might destabilise us for good – given that we now know that aliens with godlike powers *do* actually exist, and can cause such "tribulations" . . .'

Tiff frowned. 'Isn't it already contained? Feathers and her entourage are off in another universe. On her home world, if you want to believe what Vasta says. They won't be coming back here, so far as we know. Nine itself seems inert. In a few generations – if the quasar effects do fizzle out, if humanity survives – all this may be just a curiosity for astronomers and physicists to play with – and historians—'

'Except that there's one link left,' Oliver said.

John Smith turned to Tiff. 'He's right. One link. If it's all word of mouth, all these mysteries can be – debunked. But not if there's one person left in this whole damn universe who *knew* Feathers. One person who travelled to these other realms, or claimed they did. One witness who saw – what was it Matthew said? – *the powers of heaven*? Saw those powers exercised at first-hand. Who *touched* Feathers. Who spoke to her. Who heard the trumpet . . .'

Tiff felt she was missing something. 'You don't mean Vasta? You don't mean she's going to be this kind of witness to these events? *The Gospel According to Elizabeth*. Ha! . . .'

But, she saw, the others weren't laughing.

John Smith leaned forward, and Oliver copied him, almost unconsciously, Tiff thought.

Smith said, 'It must end here. It must end now. Or we will be saddled with these new gods for ever in our heads, even if the aliens do not return. And if they *were* to return, we would bow down before them rather than resist . . . It must end here. This – quasi-faith. Before it begins.'

Oliver's frown was ferocious, a scowl that lined his still-young face. 'Yes. You're right. The link must be broken, now.'

And they both turned to Tiff, waiting for her agreement.

She could not refuse – not that her refusal would have carried any weight.

When the discussion moved on to how it should be done, she left the room.

48

They came for Elizabeth in the dark.

She was in her sleeping pouch.

She was easily immobilised. Without words, they just pulled the pouch up around her body, trapping her limbs, so she would have had to cut her way out.

But she didn't struggle. 'It's all right,' she whispered. 'It's all right. I won't fight you. I – ah.'

She felt a needle press at a vein in her neck. Fumbles in the dark, a scratch.

'A little higher. You need to raise the needle a little higher . . . Whoever you are. It's all right. I forgive you. Remember I said so.'

She tried to raise her arm. Her exploring hand, inside the pouch, found her black pearl pendant, the chain already broken.

'It's all right. *I came here for this*. I came here for you, Feathers. So they would not go after you – so they could not *blame* you. It stops here. I – ah.'

A sharper jab in the neck. An instant of pain, and then a wash of a kind of warmth, spreading through her body. It was like falling asleep, softly.

'This is why I came home.

'To finish this.

'I came here for this . . . But . . . Joe . . .'

Joe the comms guy. What was it he had said to her avatar, on Nine?

'You know, you don't have to — leave. Not permanently. We can take a backup copy of you as we go along. A copy that's independent of the original . . . You'll still be here. A part of you at least. Or would have been part of you . . . Here for us, anyhow. And that's all that counts, isn't it . . . ?'

She smiled. *That's all that counts . . .*

And stars exploded behind her eyelids.

Elsewhere,
Elsewhen

49

After their first step without Elizabeth Vasta, they found themselves under a still astonishing, but familiar, sky. Still they were on Feathers' world, it seemed.

But now under the gaudy sky of the creation node once more.

Watching Feathers tentatively exploring, Salma smiled to herself.

And under it all, hanging halfway to the sky, the drab charcoal-black ball that was Terminus, as still and enigmatic as ever. Ancient world under brand new stars. Under the light of creation. Brought together by Terminus and the powers behind him, just to impress.

'Looks like Terminus delivered, huh?' That was Meriel, gamely lugging kit out of the lander within which they had made this final, pancosmic journey.

There was no reply.

The others were concentrating on the unloading. After all this was to be their final destination – their final encampment.

Away from the lander a heap of gear was building up on the ground already, Salma saw, thanks to Meriel and Doria working steadily together. Habitat wall, floor and roof panels, to be assembled in due course. Dried food packets. The components of a closed-loop life-support system to be put together, activated and tuned up, at which point they could put away the ration packs for emergencies. Water tanks, full, with recycling filters already attached.

Eventually, Salma knew, and though it might take years to finish the job, they were going to dismantle the lander itself. Oh, they might save a propulsion unit or two, maybe the smaller attitude thrusters, so they could go explore more of this ball of rust and dirt Feathers called home.

But, as far as travel went, this far and no further. When they were settled, when Terminus finally abandoned them — or at least when they finally told it goodbye — this little world was going to be their home. For good.

They'd talked it through, over and over. Even so, Salma suspected some of them still had doubts.

Now Meriel called again. 'So, Salma, did you get what you want? This dirt ball, that frozen firework display of a sky?'

'I got what I wanted. What *she* wanted. *Look* at her.'

She meant Feathers, who was tentatively exploring, one cautious footstep at a time. Right now she was slowly making her way away from the centre of their chosen landing site, their home, as if following tracks Salma couldn't see.

She seemed to thrill at the touch of the very dirt under her booted feet.

It is as you wished it.

Meriel looked up. 'So it is, Terminus, buddy. I guess you did your best. Thanks . . .'

They had all decided they had no greater purpose than enriching Feathers' life. At least the three humans had each other — even if in Doria's case they had met as strangers only a few weeks back.

And the ultimate dream, Salma knew, had been somehow to deliver Feathers to her home world. Ideally, not her world as it was *now* – whatever 'now' meant – not to this relic, a world several times older than any in Salma's home universe. Well, why *couldn't* Feathers be taken back through some fancy wormhole to her world's richer past? Just as Terminus and the entities behind him, on receiving the Hawking-radiation trigger that had activated Planet Nine, had evidently reached back into the deep past of humanity's own Galaxy to kick off the proto-creation-node quasar, an event twenty-five thousand years deep.

But Terminus had wheeled out an excuse it had used before. Universes were not all alike; not all could be manipulated in such a way. A young cosmos like mankind's, still awash with the fading glow of its Big Bang birth, was easily connected. But some universes – old, gnarly cosmoses like this one, apparently – resisted such violations. Somehow, in *this* universe, it had been possible to snatch Feathers out of her proper time and place, presumably in the deep past of this world, when it was young. But now it was impossible to return her – to her world, yes, but not her time.

None of them could see any point arguing. So the humans had decided to make the best of it.

After all, under the creation node, they had lost the past, but had gained an infinite future.

'We can fix this world,' Doria said now, walking up. Her face was obscured a little by a layer of grime on her faceplate, her gloves dark with it. 'To an extent.'

Salma said, 'You've been exploring.'

'And prospecting. Figuring stuff out. One good outcome, I guess, of the anal-retentive interplanetary politics of Earth governments has been that my people on the Moon have had to find new ways. Right from the beginning we have had to learn to extract what we need to survive from what's before us, from the most unpromising of sources – and to make a living out of it too. You might think Earth's Moon is just a ball of rusted iron and aluminium oxides. Well, yes, but you can use sunlight power to split those oxides to get usable metals for space industry, and oxygen for a variety of purposes including life support. Point is we can do the same *here*. Point is, this place is Nirvana compared to Luna. For a start, just like on the Moon, with enough power you can split all this rusty dirt back into iron and oxygen—'

'What power, though?' Meriel asked. 'Not geothermal. We know that this world is so old its very core is frozen solid.'

'Not that, no. Don't need it. We just use—' She waved a gloved hand at the glowing sky. '*That*.'

'The light of the creation node?'

Meriel smiled. 'Why not? Seems ironic, I know. Even disrespectful? But it would work. It's not as strong as sunlight on Earth, but we've got room to spread out some *big* solar panels.'

Meriel glanced at the imperturbable Terminus. 'That would seem – fitting, somehow. To use the energy of those young stars, being born in the sky, to bring this ancient world back to life.'

Salma frowned. 'I still don't see it. Won't we need a lot of heavy machinery to do all this? To shift ore and iron around, to build stuff – we don't even have the solar panels you talked about yet. We'll have to make *them*. Won't we?'

'We don't have it all yet,' Doria said. 'But we soon will, because we have what we need to get started.'

She went over to a heap of enigmatic engineering parts, and pulled out what looked like a toy to Salma, like a model tractor with a glistening solar panel on its back, and buckets on its sides, and small manipulator arms – some very small, very fine, almost insectile.

Doria lifted this to her eye level. 'Go forth and multiply, little buddy.' She put the tractor on the ground, and it rolled away contentedly.

Salma watched this. 'What's it doing?'

'It's looking for virgin ground,' Doria said.

'What for?'

'So it can gather in raw materials and make a copy of itself. And then those two will make two more copies, and the four will make four more copies. It's a replicator—'

'Ah. I've seen how these things work,' Meriel said. 'Before the mission of the *Shadow* – I imagine there have been many advances since. Salma, you just have to give these little guys power, and ground to chew up and extract useful materials like iron, aluminium, oxygen, a few grams at a time. Then these are all assembled into useful forms – to begin with, copies of themselves.'

Doria said, 'I made sure I packed a few of these before we were sent off into the void. Lunar tech. The final product, you see, comes when the replicators disassemble themselves again, leaving a heap of useful components to make – anything you want.'

Salma frowned. 'Won't that take a long time?'

'Not necessarily,' Meriel said. 'One becomes two, two becomes four . . . Just ten doublings gives you a thousand copies.'

'Anyway,' Doria said, 'that's the plan: to bring a dead world back to life.' She looked around and grinned. 'No matter how old and beat-up and worn down this place is, we can make it function again.'

Meriel nodded. 'And I don't think we Conservers need trouble our consciences about that. Without our intervention this world would remain – inert. Unchanging. After all, with its core frozen, all its tectonic processes ceased, there's nothing it can do to recover any function.'

But the earlier phrase Doria had used had stuck in Salma's mind. 'But you said, *back to life*.' She glanced over at Feathers, who was still exploring her world, one footstep at a time. 'Just processing iron and stuff won't really do that, will it? What about life?'

'Well, that's going to be harder,' Meriel admitted.

She was speaking softly, Salma thought, maybe so that Feathers couldn't overhear. Even though they were pretty sure that Feathers was still unable to understand human speech, beyond a few commands: *Run! Stop! Don't touch! Catch the ball!* The rest was all tactile, mime, though even that was not at the level of any human sign languages, just as rich linguistically as their spoken cousins.

Meriel said now, 'For one thing this desolate surface is pretty much barren of the basic ingredients for our kind of life – carbon, oxygen, nitrogen, hydrogen.' She glanced around again. '*But* – I'm pretty sure that if we drill deep enough we'll find organic-chemistry material. As far as I can tell, this world once had a tectonic cycle, like most big rocky worlds. You have a liquid iron core, a thick liquid mantle of some kind of silicate rock, and in that mantle you can have convection currents, great plumes thousands of kilometres deep. And *they* push at the solid crust, cracking and deforming it. So, as on Earth, continents drift around, and you get subduction, where surface material gets dragged down into the deep. And by surface material I mean water, dirt, soil, the remains of living things. The relics of ancient forests, to be dug out as coal or oil or methane gas.'

Salma thought she saw it. 'Carbon, oxygen, nitrogen, hydrogen. All down there, under the crust.'

Meriel glanced around at the grey stillness of this world, went to scratch her face, and seemed startled when her gloved hand hit her faceplate. 'We've never studied a world like this, either

434

inside the Solar System or outside, even in our remote studies of the exoplanets, planets of other stars. Because there was no world so *old* as this in our universe. But still – short of some huge impact that tore off the crust entirely, why shouldn't that good stuff be waiting down there, stranded when the tectonic flows failed?' She smiled. 'It's worth a try. But still, there's a heck of a journey to make between digging out billion-years-old lumps of coal, and restoring a biosphere.'

She glanced over at Feathers and spoke more softly, as if, Salma thought, she might fear that Feathers would overhear.

'For that we're going to have to rely on Feathers herself. We have identified her equivalent of DNA. As you know, her bio-chemistry is *like* ours, not identical in the chemistry, but we think we understand the functional workings of it.'

Doria nodded. 'What you mean is, you might be able to clone her.'

'Well, that would be a proving step – but not a particularly ethical one, unless we can restore some kind of biosphere for her and her – twins – to run around in. But I do think that's possible, the biosphere reconstruction, if, *if*, we can find some reasonably intact genetic material from some other organism. Bacterial or the equivalent will do. The bones she's already dug up might be a start.

'With the merest scrap of bacterial DNA, for instance, to compare with Feathers', I could extrapolate across the gap – the gap between big and small, complex and simple, old and new. In the longer term, I could make guesses as to what might have populated the various ecological niches on this world. Or at least classes of organisms. Maybe Feathers could tell us more, even if it's just at the level of instinct – what she recognises deep down, what she doesn't. And if we found more traces still, more clues, the more complete the reconstruction could become.'

Salma thought that over. 'We are all female here. We can never be mothers – unless we can find a way to make that possible for Feathers. If we can make *that* happen, we would be parents of a new world.' She thought again. 'An *eternal* world.'

'We can try,' Doria said. 'And – hey. Look up. He's gone . . .'

And when Salma turned again, she saw that Terminus had vanished.

It didn't seem to matter.

She looked over at Feathers, as she kicked at the inert dirt.

Under the light of the young stars, Feathers was building a nest.

Afterword

The idea that the enigmatic 'Planet 9', which may lurk unseen in the outer Solar System, is a black hole has been explored in a recent technical paper by Jakub Scholtz et al., 'What if Planet 9 is a Primordial Black Hole?' (arxiv:1909.11090v1, 2019). The Conservers' Planet Nine spacecraft mission is very loosely extrapolated from a 'Pragmatic Interstellar Probe' study run by Johns Hopkins University from 2020 (interstellarprobe.jhuapl. edu). The 'starship fusion drive' used for the flight of the *Cronus* to Planet Nine was based on the British Interplanetary Society's 'Project Daedalus' (see A. Martin (ed.), 'Project Daedalus – The Final Report on the BIS Starship Study', *JBIS* Supplement, 1978).

Sources on the (possible) industrial development of the Solar System include John S. Lewis's enduring *Mining the Sky* (Addison-Wesley, 1997), and Martin Elvis's *Asteroids* (Yale, 2021). A recent survey of lunar nuclear fuel sources is 'Nuclear Fuel Resources of the Moon: A Broad Analysis of Future Lunar Nuclear Fuel Utilization', by Gerrit Bruhaug and William Phillips, *NSS Space Settlement Journal*, June 2021. I have also drawn on my own work with the SPACE Project group of the British Interplanetary Society, with papers published in the Society's *Journal*, and its magazine *Spaceflight*.

Cosmology's Century by P. J. E. Peebles (Princeton, 2020) is an engaging if technical study, by one of the participants, of the development of modern ideas (that is, since Einstein) about the evolution of the universe – a development which has seen the generally accepted triumph of the 'Big Bang' model (the universe had a beginning) over the 'steady state' theories (the universe has always existed, more or less unchanging).

The best known champion of the steady-state ideas was Fred Hoyle (1915–2001), a brilliant figure who, among other things, unravelled the secrets of the manufacture of elements within the stars. The steady-state theories were finally abandoned after 1964, when the cosmic background radiation was discovered – a faint glow all around the sky, proof that once the universe was very hot, everywhere, a fact that did not fit the steady-state model. A late summary of Hoyle's arguments about the cosmos is given in his co-authored book *A Different Approach to Cosmology* (Cambridge, 2000). Hoyle also co-wrote an SF novel about our Galaxy's core becoming destabilised (*Inferno*, with Geoffrey Hoyle, Heinemann, 1973).

The implications for Olbers' Paradox if the universe were eternal were explored in 'The Dark Night Sky Riddle' by E. R. Harrison, published in *The Galactic and Extragalactic Background Radiation*, Kluwer Academic Publishers, Dordrecht, Boston, 1990.

Gravity's Fatal Attraction by Mitchell Begelman and Martin Rees (Cambridge University Press, 2021 (3rd edition)) is a fine recent survey of the science of black holes large and small. Stephen Hawking's later theories on black holes and the multiverse are explored in *On the Origin of Time* by his long-term collaborator Thomas Hertog (Torva, 2023). The idea that some black holes might be relics of an older universe than ours is described by Bernard Carr in *New Scientist* (1 April 2023, pp46–48).

An engaging recent study of the universe's first stars is Emma

Chapman's *First Light* (Bloomsbury, 2020). The 'cold spot' in Eridanus is discussed in, for example, Paul Davies, *What's Eating the Universe?* (Penguin, 2021) – as is the startling notion of Boltzmann brains.

Speculations on convergent evolution have been explored by (among others, and from different points of view) Simon Conway Morris (*Life's Solution*, Cambridge University Press, 2003, and *The Runes of Evolution*, Templeton Press, 2015) and Stephen Jay Gould (*Wonderful Life*, Norton, 1989). Other scholars have estimated the likely prevalence of intelligent life in the universe. A.E. Snyder-Beattie et al., in a paper titled "The timing of evolutionary transitions suggests intelligent life is rare", (*Astrobiology* vol. 21, pp265–278, 2021), suggest a probability of the emergence of intelligent life in our universe as one in a million trillion trillion (based on a need for twenty-four evolutionary steps), compared to my estimate of ten thousand times rarer yet. Time will tell. Bible quotations are taken from the Authorised King James version.

In the meantime, all errors and misapprehensions are of course my sole responsibility.

Stephen Baxter
Northumberland
May 2023

CREDITS

Stephen Baxter and Gollancz would like to thank everyone at Orion who worked on the publication of *Creation Node*.

Agent
Christopher Schelling

Editorial
Marcus Gipps
Claire Ormsby-Potter

Copy-editor
Elizabeth Dobson

Proofreader
Bruno Vincent

Editorial Management
Jane Hughes
Charlie Panayiotou
Tamara Morriss
Claire Boyle

Audio
Paul Stark
Jake Alderson
Georgina Cutler

Contracts
Anne Goddard
Ellie Bowker
Humayra Ahmed

Design
Nick Shah
Rachael Lancaster
Joanna Ridley
Helen Ewing

Finance
Nick Gibson
Jasdip Nandra

Elizabeth Beaumont

Ibukun Ademefun

Afeera Ahmed

Sue Baker

Tom Costello

Inventory

Jo Jacobs

Dan Stevens

Marketing

Javerya Iqbal

Production

Paul Hussey

Publicity

Jenna Petts

Sales

Jen Wilson

Victoria Laws

Esther Waters

Frances Doyle

Ben Goddard

Anna Egelstaff

Barbara Ronan

Andrew Hally

Dominic Smith

Deborah Deyong

Sinead White

Rachael Jones

Nigel Andrews

Ian Williamson

Julia Benson

Declan Kyle

Megan Smith

Charlotte Clay

Rebecca Cobbold

Operations

Sharon Willis

Rights

Tara Hiatt

Jessica Purdue

Ayesha Kinley

Marie Henckel